Personolly You

"Personolly Yours" Copyright © 2017 by Imelda Dickinson
All rights reserved. No part of this book may be reproduced, scanned, or distributed in any printed or electronic form without permission of the author.
First Edition: February 2017 www.ImeldaDickinson.com

Table of Contents

Dedication	Chapter 21, Imelda
Author's Note	Chapter 22, Margaret
Biography	Chapter 23, Margaret/Margaret
Acknowledgements	Chapter 24, Dolly
Chapter 1, Emily	Chapter 25, Julie
Chapter 2, Bessie	Chapter 26, Genie
Chapter 3, Dina Brigitta	Chapter 27, Liz/Meldie
Chapter 4, CC	Chapter 28, Keepin
Chapter 5, Laura	Chapter 29, Tai
Chapter 6, Deirdre	Chapter 30, Star
Chapter 7, Molly/Frances/Irene	Chapter 31, Rose
Chapter 8, Victoria	Chapter 32, Ruth
Chapter 9, Hanna	Chapter 33, Butterfly
Chapter 10, Rebekah	Chapter 34, Mary Beth
Chapter 11, Cara	Chapter 35, Nicole
Chapter 12, Joy/Faith/Heaven	Chapter 36, Sharin Carin
Chapter 13, Honey Girl/Annie	Chapter 37, Ginger
Chapter 14, Mary Lea	Chapter 38, Crystal
Chapter 15, Mimi Lea	Chapter 39, Janka
Chapter 16, Johdia	Chapter 40, Grace
Chapter 17, Jennie	Chapter 41, Dora/Issac
Chapter 18, Rainer	Chapter 42, Cookie
Chapter 19, Me/Hope	Chapter 43, Tanjuerie Tracy
Chapter 20, Holly Carol	Chapter 44, Karina/Meredith

Dedication

I dedicate these verses as purses not few
Individual tours, yours, mine too
Being you full grown woman or man
Or boys or girls this is my plan
To soar high to star studded sky
To believe in dreams, don't question why
Delve deep where human's sleep
Cling to Happy living in deep
Explore doors closed so tight
For dreams generated day or night
Or maybe at Dawn's blaze anew
Introduce me to dreaming you
Or midday words ponder, reflections
Expressions unique, fond affections
Afternoons surface meditations many
So dream your phrases if slight, any
Then write words of wild wonder
Alive from thoughts you often ponder
Shadows can flee for you and me
Capture then quickly if they flee
Write them down in your mind's glance
Till words upon your paper dance
Be it prose or poems look to see
Words gleeful together like you or me
Place then imaginary purses
Penned within creative verses
Imagine then a porcelain dolly
Who dreams frequently jolly
Be it outside worlds or indoors
Create your own... Personolly Yours
Imelda Dickinson, Writer and Poet
This book many times shows it!

Imelda Dickinson

Authors Note

In the stories told; most are true or some flecked with fantasy. It helps to explore behind a poet's door wonders of our mind. In all, my attempt in this publication was to create tapestries of truth, images of integrity, whims of wisdom, folds of faith, flowers of friendship, avenues of adventure, paths of patriotism, melodies of music, gems of genealogy, lifts of laughter, nuances of nature, scenes of science, triumphs in tragedy and depths of delight, caring creatures, patriotic portraits, wells of wellness, sights of science, co-mingled with fragrance of forgiveness.

Perhaps pieces of praise or slices of splendor erase bits of bitterness cast asunder. Parcels of praise will perhaps re-live as impossibilities make belief alive. Or, love's purest dimension will be limitless reaching out to the lonely, forgotten or unappreciated.

Now, my age retiring, words kindle more inspiring thoughts with new books in the process.

Biography

Imelda was born an eleventh child in Saint Cloud, Minnesota to Father Melvin Dickinson and Mother Margaret Wilwerding in a family of fourteen children. She graduated from Cathedral High in Saint Cloud. She was employed in fields of medicine, industry and later in natural health. She graduated with Honors from Clayton College in Birmingham with a Master's Degree in Natural Health. She helped plan a wellness department and conducted health seminars for many years and after retirement. Imelda has poems published with Sparrowgrass Poetry and World Poetry Anthology. Her website is www.imeldadickinson.com.

She enjoys three daughters, five grandchildren, and four great grandchildren and four great-great grandchildren. Imelda likes gardening, sewing, classical music, dancing, travel and old movies.

Acknowledgements

These affirmations are possible by creativity's intervention, inspired by readers and recipients' you and you and yours. I mention all recipients of my porcelain dolls, to my husband Doctor Bill, my six brothers and seven sisters, my three daughters, my grandchildren plus close friends. Also, my appreciation for their willingness to accept each doll, along with true stories written, or agreed to accept stories I chose to substitute.

I want to thank my daughter Molly who encouraged me to review my files and complete them for publication. Thanks to my daughter Julie for her artistic talent and editing skills for final publication. A sincere deep appreciation to my grandson Brad for his continued support. More gratitude mentioned to my daughter Marianne for her continued encouragement and support. In time, my gifts of porcelain dolls widely accepted are appreciated.

After much deliberation the decision has been made not to print pictures of the dolls. The publishing costs are prohibitive. It is easy to imagine their images in their individual descriptions. Now, my age retiring, words continue kindle inspiring thoughts continuing to write. Enjoy.

CHAPTER 1. EMILY

> "Dwell in possibilities."
> A quote from Emily Dickinson

Dearest Loni:

Thank you for accepting Miss Imelda's invitation for me to live in your home. She said she pondered about all of her nieces, which would be her first choice to have me, and it was you without much hesitation. Your art is beauty to behold. Part of your art portfolio sent to

Miss Imelda was shared with me and I delighted to see the wild animals you drew. I was told many of your family have been gifted with artistic skills, as well as poetry through Miss Emily Dickinson, so I will treasure this much, coming to stay with you. Don't be surprised, if I, your Doll Emily, seek out your Art portfolio. The one from when you learned to draw under the inspiration of wildlife Artist Walter Wilwerding of your grandmother's family! It will be a pleasure to page through and make acquaintances having conversations with the creatures within.

I am dressed to look like Emily Dickinson, your grandfather's far past family. For the most part, Miss Imelda's relative too, poet Emily Dickinson is pictured in her black dress. Attached to her shoulder represents her love for bluebirds.

In addition, Miss Imelda also hand created Emily's famous white dress for public affairs. I am wearing it of my own choosing since I enjoy being very sociable. For the daily mundane doings, like reading and writing poetry, the black dress is my choice, besides it has my tablet and pencil in my pocket available at all times. I tend to be very busy when I am left by myself, though I am never alone in my thoughts. Words and scenes and creatures and feelings, all live happily in my head!

If, in the future, you need to gift me to anyone in your family, Miss Imelda's next choice is your daughter Angie. These are the only requests she has for you, since…I am a gift special for you, another talented artist in the family. I will enjoy being close to you in your Art studio, with your animals that come alive as you draw them. Miss Emily and I enjoy the arts so much, quiet lives we both have! My favorite is wolves and I will introduce them all to her. I feel very pleased you have sketched them as a pair, since they are very devoted to their animal family and now I too, will have family. I have become very familiar with "Favorite Poems and "Selected Poems" of Emily's and I will recite them forever in my thoughts. I hope you like the poem about us; the three of us… Miss Emily and Miss Imelda, and me, doll Emily.

EMILY

My pen pensive to write, Emily
I'm unworthy to mention you
What phrase of praise for your poems
My inadequacy in full view.

My fingers tremble, anticipate
Ethereal visit to your Spirit high
Expressing doll gift to niece, Loni
Artistic, like you, does qualify.

You write words, paint pictures
Of beauty no matter choice kind
She takes pencil, draws pictures
Fame framed from artist's mind.

My heritage links us by Grandfather
Melvin Earl Dickinson, without falter

Loni's gifts from a Grandmother
Margaret Wilwerding's Cousin Walter.

Loni expressed Wilwerding gene
Proud to honor Walter's artistry
Learned from his instruction keen
As graduated art student degree.

Famous wild-life Artist pictures
"How to Draw Animals" on heavy paper
A whole chapter, "Cats in Action"
No line Loni's pen did escape her.

Loni painted color-filled pheasant
Your pen would flicker to flame
Its flight on studio's wet canvas
Claims "Pleasant" as its first name.

Across wide sea lurks a leopard
She draws in her studio space
Waiting for your Spirit's writing
Distinct, descript lines of his face.

Or dovetail fawn near mill stream
Playfully running downhill
Wink, puzzled you unnoticed
At twilight pause in night chill.

Thoughts surface, shadows mystery
Make-believes frequent to dwell
Lighthearted portraits joyful
Little children fun stories to tell.

Artists together commendable
Pictures drawn, penned words upon
Portfolio's wait long patiently
Unrecognized till after they're gone?

Or words to sing of Nature
Companion so steady for you
Friend always to inspire your
Writing word creations anew.

Loni's wood duck pairs swim pond
Distinct feathers swirl, curve line
Unconscious of precise beauty
Content in wet water world fine.

Loni's leopard's snarl ferocious

Face for battle, as your battles of war
Or do cat claws stalk Lonnie's buffalo
At grass graze or death's door.

Her drawing of field forests
Tall tree tips touch blue sky
Whispers to your gentle Spirit
Branches invite you two to rest by.

My dress, yours, as doll given
To Loni styled black to see
One bluebird on neck enclosure
Solitary, you chose much to be.

Bluebird on black, one is mourned
Among others a memory choice
Alone so close by my dolly ear
Sings songs for you in its voice.

Separate is your famous white dress
Elegant, unique, pleat design
Fashioned to meet guests of family
Graced socially as all of you dine.

Music tunes you knew so well
With family loved you did share
Then pen later in your room to tell
Your own kind of song a prayer.

House garden you tend your cathedral
Designed by Creator His way
Being woman as spiritual woman being
Adorn soul's blossom bouquet.

In your garden quiet thoughts carried
Known herbs or flowers for healing
Buds of beauty carefully tended
Relief's recommended in peeling.

The world you knew from books
Refresh repeats by ink well
Be it seas rage billows on page
Or meadows fragrance to smell.

Live flowers fold, or slant hillsides
Picture moments, your fingerprint
Or life lived as lived each instance
Traced love, cherish each imprint.

Your select poems as written
Only pieces published in your age
Were they just stuffed in your pocket?
Stacked or stored page by page?

You chose where, you chose when
Specific, adventures wide, varied
Curious, write words by poet's pen
Stacked, stored away or then buried.

Some say you were a recluse
Describes easy a misunderstand
To me, since, my best friends are
Words whimsical or wonderland.

Or, silence; blare rhymed mentions
Darkness; blast bright thoughts
Emptiness; fills dimensions
Loneliness; lost forget-me-nots.

Books now praise your writings
Were your words satisfied within?
Your Spirit content, your inner voice
Notoriety no need as shut-in.

Why did you shy from society?
Entertained by words, by phrases
Content, happy in what you did
Make alive poems on pages.

As Doll, Emily, I hold your butterfly
Warmed by bright sun on flower
First hides in chrysalis, hidden you were
Until beauty rises in power.

Ruby throat hummingbirds noticed
Busy wings pen's scroll painted
Sip petal nectar hours by day
Of so many you are acquainted.

Or golden bee flying its course
Never knows bee symmetry
Not designed to be a pilot
Back to queen, flies carefree.

I'll smell your garden flowers
Sprinkled in moist morning dew
Daisy eyes wide at dawn hours
Violets peek up, lower in view.

Buttercups blink, field news exciting
Daffodils listen not in high grass
Clover fields, dense, so inviting
Purple, red-pink colors surpass.

Sunsets you write touch my dark hair
Cast bronze or shades of red
Brief moments fill inspirations
Flame poem penciled ahead.

Your winds wave to me on display
So proud of kinship to review
Soft message breezes calmly say
Our dreams latent come true.

Or shadows show a lonely soul
Found in my own wonders land
All shapes move or stand still
Find fingers small in your hand.

Grief's you glean may linger
I'll provide calm, caring space
My little red heart inside my dress
Reflects empathy on my glass face.

My travels world over, ethereal
Journeys imagine, places abroad
Or next door close to family
Pathway beautiful, also applaud.

Death's ghost, your visitor, I favor
In realms humans don't understand
Beauty beyond death's fingers
In Universe perfectly planned.

Death's doorways open new portals
Entries too vast to understand
Supposed by human mortals
Portray us Paradise land.

Unresolved emptiness ferments
Relationships we sweeten, caring
Enduring tragedy's encounters
Understanding, deeply sharing.

Is energy released by human body?
Returned to Creator's dwelling?
Beyond even my imagination

I'll dream much longer for telling.

Seasons of snow and rainfall
Delight my musings some
Flakes of snow multi-shaped
Designs original, everyone.

Eastern birds colored in number
Could sing you daily a song
Your spirit would know appreciation
Of your words written yearlong.

Bluebirds, beckon more bluebirds
Robins, juncos, sparrows too
Chickadees, finches, meadowlarks
Circle gravesite named after you.

They flit, fly, warble goodbye
Sing in script concrete memory
Melody each their unique song for
Once human immortal Emily.
Perched on gravesite as you slumber
As we listen, we too can sigh
Perhaps sing our beloved music
Select songs for you while we cry.

Your hardships, severe suffering
I, as a doll, must learn to know
My heart ease playful or happy
Where doll dreams choose to go.

Raindrops, each their memory
Of caress once touched before
Or sadness changing images
Of happy before we once wore.

So sorrow can venture, visit me
We'll muse, ponder sharp pain
I'll call on Loni, my mistress
Knows pain severe, daily strain.

She'll soothe my first ache feeling
I'll tell her you knew it well
She hugs me, balms my hurting
Reads your poem "Amherst Belle."

Plant your heavenly gardens
Areas of amaryllis, aster, anemone
Borders of baby's breath, bleeding hearts

Columbine, clematis celestial grown.

Hills hyacinth's high, hollyhocks burst
Jasmine leaves or blossoms wind
Lilacs, lily-of-the-valley blooms
Tendered by your hands kind.

Paths of peonies, phlox, primrose
Roadsides boast roses in number
Sweet alyssum, sweet peas, trillium
I view forested garden in slumber

I dedicate then this history
To Loni, Artist, known best niece
Applaud Emily no longer a mystery
Poems published as past release.

Your poetry or letters continue
To touch living beings today
Tomorrow's literature lives on
Your books continuous convey.

You are a gift, I too smaller one
So privileged as appointee
Reminds all who see me or Loni
Describe famous Dickinson, Emily.

I'll wear your white dress elegant
As styled sophisticate to be
Pleased as a Doll to my niece, Loni
Proud as a Doll named Poet Emily.

P.S. That means Publicity Select.

Talked to a girl at the Emily Dickinson museum in Amherst, Massachusetts and she was elated about the doll Emily, but they do not have the means of accepting or taking care of the doll, but would like copies of the poem and pictures of the doll Emily and encouraged I continue to gift the doll to relative Loni. Framed poem sent priority mail.

CHAPTER 2. BESSIE

"Human Interest……quality of a story, as in a newspaper, newscast, that engages attention by enabling one to identify readily with the people, and situations described"

New NEWS for you by Dorothy Glovsky, Staff journalist,
Ashland Daily Press newspaper, Ashland WI.

"Mason woman is just a doll in her family's eyes" is involved in unique doll project. When completed will give away total of 44 dolls to family members and friends. Of the total number 42 adults and two children are doll recipients or sets of dolls.

Dickinson designs different clothing for each doll. She writes a letter of instruction that arrives first, and also a poem, which accompanies the doll. When finished she gives each doll a little red heart. Dickinson sends the doll unclothed, so the recipient can see the heart before dressing the doll. For Dickinson, who said she "loves doing this" each doll is special because the people who receive them as gifts are very dear to her. Imelda Dickinson is her maiden name, is writing a book about the doll project, entitled "Personolly Yours" which may have to have Personolly Yours, Too as second book. Each chapter brings an individual story of family and extended family she said. Human thoughts and emotions pass through the mind of a doll creating charm, mirth and gladness as the imagination gathers up the discovery of mortal beings forming human events. Mental images conceptualize into journeys, visions, fancies and wonderful adventures. In describing book content, she also said, "Shadows imitate injury and injustice as it twists through life and death." As a doll, tradition tells, is a figure representation of a human being.

She hopes the book, as written in prose and poetry with illustrations, will delight the eye and stimulate the senses for lightheartedness and entertainment for all ages when a doll is presented to primarily adult men and women to bring out the child they outgrew. She says 'They are stories to bring to your home with the home in focus and the family fused to include extended family dolls with distinct direction to "relive" human accomplishments. A quickening of the mind into fancied fancies; Illustrations of a moment of illusion with flashes of the twinkle and a minute of imaginary frolic.'

The project of work started soon after she remarried having been a widow for many years. Her new husband encourages her to keep her maiden name, having had some poetry already published. Four years ago she gave her granddaughter Bonny Karina an 18-inch porcelain doll. Bonny named the doll Imelda after her grandmother. Imelda husband Bill liked the doll so much he wanted one of his own. As a retired scientist the doll was made to match his interests. He named her Victoria after Queen Victoria. Part of her fanciful story relates, "Victoria climbed on a library table and discovered a microscope and slides where she discovered what people looked like inside." The project mushroomed into dolls for her six brothers and seven sisters plus extended family and friends. Sometimes the recipient knows about the gift in advance and Dickinson asks what name they want their dolly and why. If she agrees, she forms the story around the reason for the name. Otherwise she selects the name of the doll. She continues, "The minute I start writing about the doll thoughts rush through my mind. Sometimes I wake up in the night and jot down ideas or changes I want to make in the stories."

"For example, Imelda gets a new wedding dress and no one in the playroom knows who she will marry; Hanna waves to the Superior winds as she is stranded in a lighthouse and tells of the sea; Jennie represents a house wren killed by a sparrow that comes back to her garden keeper and tells her what heaven is like. Another doll Molly becomes an orphaned child who is adopted and finds her natural mother. Dickinson named the doll she gave her daughter Julie "Dolly" because that was her pet name from her first husband when she was a small child.

Karina is Dickinson's doll. She was broken in transit and "footicapped." Her daughter

Marianne, Bonny's mother, made special ballerina legs and feet for Karina to fulfill her dream of a ballerina dancing." When she has new legs and feet made, Meredith, a student in beginning ballet classes, teaches her to be a ballerina in the forested wilderness. Imelda gave her a little red heart. Miss Imelda is designing her ballerina dress to match her new pink shoes. Dickinson has special plans for Karina at the end of the stories Karina where a celebration is planned for a reunion of all dolls and Karina and Meredith dance for them in the moonlight. "

BESSIE

Our meeting by your request Dorothy
To Miss Imelda tells her on account
Of designs of porcelain give-away dolls
Now forty-four at last count.

You'll meet her at Washburn Lake
With Doll Imelda and Doll Karina
Granddaughter Bonny, friend Mandy
As swans swim in nearby marina.

42 adults and two children given
Introductions, photos, place sites
Little red hearts each doll entrusted
Daily Press staff Dorothy writes.

Designed dress describes doll's story
Miss Imelda pens event exciting
Human thoughts, emotions pass through
Mind of Doll dreams inviting.

Visions, fancies, wonders, ideals
Myth and joy models discovered
Mortal events, human literature
Describe journey of book covered.

Impressions intertwine stories
From life or ideal Doll's express
Human experience, heart eases
Reveal life's paths mixed access.

Drawn dress Miss Imelda sews
Costume fits doll's story to tell
As staff writer Dorothy soon knows
News article explains well.

Miss Imelda in appreciation
Of front page newspaper display
Lists "Mason woman is a doll

In her family's eyes" words say.

Miss Imelda gifts Dorothy a dolly
It's me, Bessie my name
Honors devotion to her mother
Intelligent, well-traveled proclaim.

Faithful wife, loving mother too
Dorothy's devotion remains the same
Respectful points of view
As memento her I exclaim.

My blue dress petals flowers
Borders lace twice on dress hem
Threads ribbon more lace on chest
Red satin ribbons accent all of them.

Match dress with lace trim
Slim strips fall down my dress
"I am too beautiful for words"
Dorothy, staff writer did confess.

Flat dark long hair like Dorothy's
My black shoes so sensible too
I'll roam to future appointments
As your Dolly Dorothy, helps you.

Seated pretty on wicker chair
My hat fabric alike my dress
Notes typed on my computer
As photos show I impress.

Newspaper staff drafts for you
Important as newspaper writer
Oh quaint stories we'll accrue!
Note my pink highlighter!

As Bessie, my little fingers
Press keys, I know each one
She tells me stories are happy
Human interest tales well done.

Dorothy's new cat, she names
Smudgie, black and gray hue blend
Sniffs at my face, at my hair
Plays with red ribbons descend.

Smudgie greets Dorothy downstairs
Waits for food promptly prepared

Ready for her after her long day
Avoids people unwanted or shared.

Once she had no place to live
Ran from dogs often her chase
Climbs tall trees; thanks for these
Fast ahead of dog and cat race.

Nights long in shelters chosen
Brick building, slab wood or old
Abandoned three seasons as feral
Rainy, bright sun or winter cold.

Once Dorothy saw her alone
Beneath her steps at backdoor
Says "Hello," she doesn't respond
Not used to humans anymore.

Back door reopens, Dorothy stands
Holds dish, smells cat food she can see
Placed under steps, closes back door
Knows cat is scared, cat is hungry.

Dorothy muses, cat may stay more days
If she feeds her, remain here she would
After work right away more cat food
Three days pass, cat must feel good.

She leaves back door open this time
Food dish inside past threshold
Careful cat enters home slowly
Strong interest in food bowled.

Dorothy looks at blurred marked fur
She eats warm food not so scared
Climbs up house stair steps for tour
Found a home, comfort shared.

Cat sees me prim on chair wicker
Glance turns to big wide bed
Jumps high, meows "It's quicker
Than old junk cars in a shed."

Dorothy loves cats, this one
Gray and black fur colors blurred
Named Smudgie at the same time
Well-chosen cat catchword.

Cat has me, doll friend in daytime

Dorothy, staff writer, work is at
Daily Press newspaper writing
I'm home; Smudgie safe, her cat.

I want her to write a story
How Smudgie came here to live
She is so busy with humans
So I'll make notes to her give.

She loves warm blanket provided
She naps on mornings when
Dorothy leaves for work early
Plays with a yellow ball then.

Or chose a black fly that happens
Find clear window to stand on
She chases fly away, not to stay
One paw slap then fly gone.

Fly gone? Smudgie ate it away!
Hardly a story dispatching
I may have to teach her manners
Or chase flies before catching.

As we remain room mates
Most times Smudgie ignores me
No interest in words I narrate
At bedtime sleeps with Dorothy.

Certain house cat will never leave
She pets glossy, silk, fine hair
I don't take time for sleeping
Cat content, this home no compare.

I pry through Dorothy's notes
Type more words on my computer
Attach Dorothy's clever quotes
No one will ever dispute her.

As my computer keeps clanking
My news to tell doll friends more
Dolls live first with Miss Imelda
I learned computers to explore.

Doll Karina has lots of time waiting
In her basket for new legs before
Meredith, ballerina, teaches steps
Karina dreams new legs and feet more.

Doll Emily's intent for an Artist
Known genealogy gifts varied
Brothers, sisters, husband, friends
Two children only dolls carried.

I miss Honey-Girl, Joy, also Nicole
So sensitive, love children so
Separated other states they go
New doll reports I must know.

Some day when doll gifts over
Miss Imelda doll celebration plans
Karina knows ballet steps for beginners
My reporting new news at newsstands!

Laura's dress texture exclusive
For little girl whose eyes cannot see
So she feels doll clothes all over
Treasured doll gift instantly.

Hanna sent to fond brother
As Captain of sea faring boat
On Great Lakes carrying ore
She learns quickly to stay afloat.

Victoria, proud, unsociable
Loves Bill, husband, no other
Molly's two dolls like words
Extremes said of life, each mother.

Miss Imelda tells me about dolls
When on the Internet we go
Devoted I am as her reporter
These stories I must always know.

Butterfly is mailed to California
Enjoys life, was sad before
Dina Briggita, CC stay close to me
Gifted adults live near next door.

Deirdre moves up Lake Superior
Where Irish wolf hounds play
I must contact her soon
What a story she will say!

Mimi Lea, Holly Carol on farm goes
New animals to learn every day
Imelda wears new wedding dress
Or new outfits to wear from display.

Small size Bonny dreams she'll wed
Someday that will be news
Toys question, no one has said
Who Bonny's doll Imelda will choose.

Keepin loves land America
Journey's across east and west
Knows all nations history
Instructs of land in U.S. best.

Julie, Margaret and Star miss me
Talk of gems grown to admire
Pearled music bring bands in unison
What a celestial choir!

Margaret-Margaret two names paired
Honor Grandmother's names same
Both honest, loving to two little girls
Share Ed Dickinson's name.

Rebekah still in school learning
To teach grades two and three
Rose isn't lonesome anymore
Visitor DJ fills her needs be.

Dora and Isaac teach healthy ways
Results successful amaze, share
Eight natural ways of health teaching
Lifestyle changes anywhere.

Merry Heart still merry
Paired contrast to skeleton Bones
Smocks colored by each health law
NEWSTART name published owns.

Tai went back to Taiwan
What a joy to know she is there
Lonely no more with new friends
Clown Beams and spotted loon share.

Gentle Genie notes now finished
Concludes sad and glad story told
Mary Lea's doll in Oregon State
Near ocean Dad loved to behold.

Crystal now Canadian, satisfies
Her health role important done
Part time visitors see her beauty

On bedroom quilt homespun.

Ginger sent off to west coast
To teacher of health and his wife
Who sings, teaches lessons on piano
Enriches each student's life.

Grace loves all her grandchildren
Young ones understand dreams
Why do humans have to grown up?
When children happier it seems.

Liz and Meldie dance together
In spite of time passed long
Friendships last with some humans
Preteens to seniors belong.

Janka's story could be many pages
Her tale not easy to write
A devoted Nanny's protection continues
From infancy to adult in their plight.

Me and Hope same dolly
Each story individual recite
Differ in stories, but happy
Some articles pensive to write.

Cookie is a bird many love
Her adjustment to places many
Enjoy her many travels
Don't miss one, promise not any!

I talk to Johdia and Grandma Doll
Their dreams surface easy
Live in deep woods with animals
Season's cold, warm or breezy.

Dolly keeps making jewelry
Ornate gifts for us dolls small
Jennie with Rainer still special
Two sisters close above all.

Muse with Cara what love is
Quotes for my notes noble
Tanjeurie still shines golden
Blazes sunset, regular global.

Ruth happy with Erica in Texas
Once poor weds wealthy man

Circumstance makes me dance
Read careful her Bible plan.

Sharin waits with Mary Beth
Dresses made, poems new read
Sure story's Miss Imelda chose
Message well thought of she said.

As news writer of human events
Man, woman, child read about
Each other, new tales, occasions
By Dorothy and Bessie do check out.

Won't miss stories with our pens
Doll friends transmit in my emails
Tales Dorothy, or me, Bessie sends
Story unusual or some folktales.

Smudgie meows about nine lives
Two lost, dogs annoy, now race ends
Purrfect now a cat, much to comfort her
Food bowl full or stair step ascends.

I read Dorothy's story to share
By Washburn Lake near marina
With close family and friends
Report new legs and feet for Karina!

Dorothy sure is excellent
Writing verse for humans to read
Fortunate am I to be here
Her influence just what I need.

I must think of ways to please her
She smiles at me when home
She pauses, examines my computer
Sometimes she reads my poem.

She laughs when Smudgie advances
Near me, plays with ribbons more
Sometimes on my lap she chances
to sleep. Comfort unknown before.

So three unconventional beings
Much different in personality
Content with each other
Good way relations should be.

If you have a story to report

To Dorothy at Daily Press call
She's excellent at penned support
I do stories for your child's doll.

I've found a home here like Smudgie
So pleased a reporter I became
I might avail myself at first email
Remember me, Bessie by name.

If you're lonely to Animal shelter go
Get cat like Smudgie caring be
Then read latest story to know
Front page updates from Doll Bessie.

CHAPTER 3. DINA BRIGITTA

"I must have flowers always and always."
A quote from Oscar Claude Monet

Dear Mabel:

Mabel, you chose my name, Dina Brigitta, because it is boasted by your Norwegian ancestry cherished by you embellished at a very early age. In your home outdoors, you have a perfect natural setting for your flower garden, fertile in floral design. My little friend Blooma is my miniature wooden Norwegian doll I keep close to me at all times. You will notice she has a water pail which is bordered in brass with painted enamel birds and smooth pink hearts. Stemmed in its center are a dozen decorative satin blue roses. She tightly grasps a small rope handle of her water pail holding my bouquet for you from Miss Imelda filled with baby breath arrangements brushing her small round face. Miss Imelda wrote my poem, which is placed carefully in her pail between blossoms. Little Blooma's floral tribute brought to you in her water pail makes us all bloom together in love with you.

My dress has ornate stems in the foreground of my native Norwegian black long skirt, over a bright red petticoat trimmed in black lace. My white blouse with fluffed sleeves hugs my wrist which has a bloom in it with my white apron hugging my small waist bordered with wide pinched lace. Small gold beads top shinier sequins sewed so carefully on my vest. You will like my felt hat; it keeps my brown hair away from my face since I plan on being a big part of your flower garden. Miss Imelda knows passersby who admire your garden, enjoying your foliage so much throughout the entire blooming season. She pulls my pantaloons firmly around my body. My tiny red heart clings close to my chest. Please notice my bell since you will dress me for the first time. I am decorated as a gift to you Mabel as a token of long friendship. For all Nature's seasons for all friendship's reasons, I am yours...Dina Brigitta

DINA BRIGITTA

Sixteen tulips, red ribbons wrapped

Gloss for close friend so dear
Sprouted for a springtime
In friendship's bud sincere.

Petals perfect to unfold
Perfumed blossomed choice
Expressing love's return
Bouquet's brimming voice.

My doll place prominent placed
High on carved stand
Compliments a wall painting
Of young girl, "Summer," I understand.

Gazes Dawn's breaking a bird
Perched in nearby tree
Sings to her "spring's song"
She turns her head to me.

"Welcome to this house, my dear
You'll find beyond your eyes
Blossoms burst for your water pail
Sure to hypnotize."

"Meet Blooma" I said proudly
"Small doll tends tiny flowers
Delightfully Norwegian she
Hard at work wee hours.

Hearts and flowers paint on wood
Multicolored bright
Wooden doll minute, oh, so cute
Costume colors blue and white."

"Says Summer, "Mabel's cultivated
Her garden; waters, plants seeds
Diligently demonstrated
Won't find many weeds.

She spends time with Mabel every day
"Proud you will be a part
Of this garden," Summer said
"Each bloom her work of art."

They turn to see Blooma bow
See blue roses in pail red
"I'll tend my blossoms too
In my bucket" Blooma said.

"This early morn, we'll adorn
Mabel's perfumed pathway
Moonlight hours, or early Dawn
We three every day.

Summer's stories tell our tale
Blooma's bouquet whimsical
Crowded in wee wooden pail
Readied journey magical!

Her bouquets show many ways
Bloom color artistic hue
Excited, Summer bursts
"Let me show you quite a few."

They slip out open window
Hands clasp, all withdrew
Past windows, barricades and walls
Greet dawn's air-moistened dew.

Mabel's garden shows bouquets
While friendships new profess,
Names describe their type quaint
Unique each a floral dress.

SNOWDROPS once slept
Is first to bloom
CORIOPSIC MOONBEAMS apply
Palatial perfume.

LADY SLIPPERS polish pink
Near JACK IN PULPIT'S throne,
LARKSPUR stems wave at us
Warm breezes on loan.

SNAPDRAGONS hug high walls
DAY LILIES dazzle high,
VIRGINIA BLUEBELLS twinkle
Behind SWEET WILLIAM'S sigh.

GLADIOLAS glorious flash
BUTTERFLY BUSHES gleam
BLEEDING HEARTS broadcast
PEONY petals preen.

JASMINE PERFUME'S incense
ANGELICA, IMMORTELLE
Flower full essence,
In Mabel's gardens dwell.

Roses, flushed, florid
Felicitous full bloom at noon
Regal display, salute our stay
Charming the sweet perfume.

FIRST EDITION, QUEEN ELIZABETH near
HARRISONS, DANA and OLYMPIAD
CURLY PINKS, GIVENCHY
Such splendor never had!

GOLD MEDAL, full of promise
Cheers POLO CLUB right on
As lavender VIOLETS faces
Blush MARIANA'S echelon.

CHRISTIAN DIOR fashionable
Flush GUY LORACHE so red,
As BEVERLEY HILLS rolls up
ICEBERG petals outspread.

Smelling ROSE'S fragrances
MON CHERI, red as flame
SHEER BLISS, FIRST LOVE and HONOR
SUMMER SHINE yellow came.

EVENING STAR'S light
ROYAL HIGHNESS, all waxed PRISTINE
GRAND MASTERPIECE'S grandeur
In EUROPENA, what a scene!

DOUBLE DELIGHT, next DUET
Add a TOUCH OF CLASS
As FAIRY PINK clusters
Brings AMERICA's top brass.

MR LINCOLN'S GARDEN PARTY
CHICAGO'S PEACE, color three
Yellow, pink, ruby red
Met mist-white JOHN KENNEDY.

Kiss MISS ALL AMERICAN BEAUTY
With BRANDY, SONJA'S style
Gala rise before our eyes
Near border brick laid aisle.

RED MASTERPIECE parades
DAINTY BESS, FIRST PRIZE
Crowning accolades

Floral fantasize.

SEVEN SISTERS, PILLOW TALK,
PRINCESS OF MONACO all aglow
Crowns ROYAL HIGHNESS
At formal garden show.

BELLE STORY in POLYANNA
And EMPRESS JOSEPHINE
Meet COUNTRYMAN near a lake
CELESTIAL, serene.

Pearl SWAN shimmer shadows
On water silver bright
BALLERINA pink and LITTLE WHITE PET
Electrify this night!

RODEO DRIVE, OLE, LANVIN
Prance near proud too
This parade, no charade
You agree, won't you?

Cardinals, red-plumed twitter
Near MORNING GLORY vine
PEONIES puff perfumed swells
Around Mabel's flower shrine.

HYACINTH high esteemed
Hug HIBISCUS in summer's breeze
VERONIA brush MOSS ROSES
With tenderness, with ease.

CHRYSANTHEMUM whiffs
DELPHINIUMS sway a bit
Peek at orioles on tree branches
Songs, Mabel's favorite.

Robin's bob among green grass
Of enameled chlorophyll
Sunlit spangles floodlit rock
Where beams a DAFFODIL.

On Day's new flashlight
Ahead of dawns first kiss
Brushing Night's gray whispers
Mabel's garden you can't miss.

Dina Brigitta and Summer saw
Blooma add bouquets first kiss

Baby breath blooms daintily
Blooms tiny human's often miss.

Winding spirals, each unique
Wink, blink, nodding "Hi's"
In this summer's day of holidays
Summer closes not her eyes.

Back in place in Mabel's home
Stationed regal place unique
Summer, Dina Brigitta, Blooma
Each display a boutique.

Then, season's sun changes course
When blossomed petals fall
Closing Mabel's garden blooms
Flowered bouquets magical.

Perfume autumn's dress crisp
Preclude winter wind weaves
Textured pictures too complete
Clear crystal make-believes.

When spring's song wakes summer
Stirs, waken familiar tunes
Choice seeds new grow anew
Beamed by midnight moons.

We'll clasp again hands to see
Grandeur blossoming
From Mabel's garden gardening's
Buds grand beginnings.

Out of gardens growing
Friendships flower rare
Bouquets today again say
Friends are blooming there.

As doll I stand by Blooma's side
Summer's painting close to us seen
Recall flowers flowery petals
At summer's flowers scene.

Nature opens its bounty
Mabel's gardening traces
Planting, faithful tending
From seeds of small faces.

Grow beauteous in stature

Like us, one and all
Different shapes, being contrasts
Such excitement for a doll!

Feel unique, impressions rare
Stemmed by glory's wonder
Loved by Creator's care
Digging deep down under.

Original sweet bouquets
Creation's image flowers
Prime perfumed sachets
Enjoyed so many hours.

In life's garden of verses
Prompted by Master's praise
Blaze in phrase to amaze
Bouquets bloomed raise.

Enjoy us, dolls and painting
Develop stories, not so few
Decorate to view, adorn
For Mabel, we all thank you!

Dear Miss Imelda:

My words don't express the joy I feel when you came over and gifted me with Dina Brigitta and her little doll Blooma. The flower perfume from my garden slips through my front room window as I carefully dress her so perfectly. What a dear demonstration of our friendship these many years working at the college, as well as a personal friendship that blossomed over time. My other friends come and go and always admire both of them. I make it very clear the painting of Summer's "Spring Song" is all part of their gift to me. Dina Brigitta is more than perfect; such carefulness you did in completing my Norwegian ancestry is so appreciated. She is alive to me and I enjoy her every day as I pass her near the Dining Room wall for all to see. Thank you so very much for your generous gift of friendship that blooms every day in my special way. Love Mabel

CHAPTER 4. CC

"Love has no desire but to fulfill itself. To melt and be like a running brook that sings its Melody to the night. To wake at dawn with a winged heart and have thanks for another day of loving."
A quote by Khalil Gibran

Dear Clara:

As you can see, I am meant for thee! In memory of your dear husband, Ig, who thought the most of you. Miss Imelda knows you miss him so much she designed me to keep you company in his memory. Life here is not eternal, but surely in our dreams it is and when we pass to the other realm, our dreams become realities. I will be with you so share his memory in keeping your dreams alive.

SEE, SEE CUTE CLARA "CC"

Friends of friends meeting friends
On occasion surprises
Ready to burst stuffed inside
As a Doll magnetizes.

Leafy branches flowered too
Alike etch my blue dress
Lots of lace netting mesh
My bosom buds caress.

Hat laced chase beads of blue
Dressed unique, for I speak
Of a special couple Ig and you
Chase memories unique.

Husband thoughtful for his bride
Bursts love deep in warm heart
Like mine, shiny red and bright
Reminder of Clara, his sweetheart.

Mild mannered, Ig, now memory
My presence sure to tell
Of gentleness, unselfishness
Of Ig looking back so well.

In my basket wee to view
Is squirrel, feathered bird
He loved much, their lives touch
Soft spoken he was heard.
Ig, so big in caring
Treasured his only bride
Calling her "Cute Clara"
Expression silk inside.

Strong moral fiber, compassionate
Temper sweet, polite, courteous
Ig loved Clara, so complete
Fine character to discuss.

Years yielded more years
To grace their time alone

Accepting her maternity
To children not his own.

For better than worse wedded
For rich love, ample means
Till sickness claims her husband
When death comes between.

A wife lost her husband dear
To sleep in deep dark pit
But I stand to ease suffering
To bring back love a bit.

Clara's gifts of crystal animals
Shine beams on sunlit days
Twinkles flare his presence when
Loved animals trace bright rays.

Mouse chews Ig's driftwood
Birds live in his house's nest
Owl perches on high branch
His woodshed's early guest.

Butterflies fly flower-like
Float near crystal swan
Turtle goes by lazily past
Ig's birdhouse on front lawn.

A dear heart painted red
Flash flickers most of all
Steady manifestation
Deep love once magical.

Remember he only loved you
Those tender many years
You were his "Cute Clara"
By name you're souvenirs.

My brown eyes ever watchful
Memories drift my way
Catching them as blossoms
In small basket, your bouquet.

Should tears fall down your face?
Oft humans cry, I know
My hanky white of flowers blue
Will catch painful flow.

Pleasant thoughts fill your mind

Your husband's place long ago
His spirit remains remembered
To rest your heart upon, so.

Catch my smile upon my lips
Always there to rely upon
Feel my little red heart
Love for you to sigh on.

Whisper Ig's gentle word
"I love you, wife, my "CC"
Tenderness you heard
Cute Clara, come see, see.

Bird houses built, gifted then
Small, quaint, sturdy style
Right for petite wee wren
Bird dainty so fragile.

Friend farmer moved to town
Has replica of his barn
To house his plenty birds
View birdies newborn.

An oarsman off duty winters
Has facsimile boat to store
Sunflowers on house mid-deck
Bird eater's galore.

Ig's martin house many rooms
Shelter extended family
Aristocratic birds like housing
Calculated so carefully.

Small measured log cabin
Logs horizontal in place
Gifted to Clara's friend
So happy was her face.

A church house for a pastor
Includes steeple high
Bird songs chorus choir
Heard clear when you stop by.

A veteran disabled from war
Gift given bird house unique
Waves miniature 50 star flag
Secure placed at its peak.

Ig enjoys gifts so plentiful
Bird houses to gift when
He knows he builds happiness
To receiver's over again.

My dear Miss Imelda:
It seemed so casual when you called and said you were coming over after work at the library and we would have a cup of coffee! You were not here only five minutes and in visits my daughter Jennie, all the way from Minneapolis! When you went out to your car and brought in a big box I was really bewildered. I knew then our meeting was special. Well special is hardly the word. When I opened the box and saw my beautiful doll I was not sure I could read the poem with both of you here. She is so lovely. She is in all the style and colors I would have ordered if I had the chance to order something so very beautiful. Yes, I loved Ig very much and he is still a big part of my dreams and respect. Your design of CC is perfect, even to the hanky I already need! Since you saw I was highly emotional, I appreciated your request to leave and come another day to take pictures of glass animals. I promised I would read the poem when I was more relaxed. Thanks for hugging both of us when you left. Jennie will stay with me this weekend. There are no words in the dictionary to express how I feel, but thanks so very much. I will keep her close to me always where I can see her every day. I love you. Clara

Jennie called me when she left her Mother after the weekend was over. She was right, Clara was highly emotional. She could not finish reading the poem, so Jennie finished for her. Jennie said she cried with her. She even had to wash CC's little hanky because it was so wet. Jennie loved the doll and knows her Mother loves it so much, as she says; there are no words in the dictionary to describe how she feels. Thanks so much Miss Imelda. You must really enjoy giving these gifts because they are more than special. Thanks for making my mother so happy.

Dear Miss Imelda:

My doll CC is so happy there with me and my memories of my husband Ig. Anyone who visits me admires her so much there is no one like her they say. Every day I pick her up and find something else beautiful about her and I can read the poem now without crying. Thank you for having my daughter Jennie here, it helped me get through the weekend. Please come over for dinner after work on Thursday evening. CC and I have a lovely dinner planned for you. See you then, and thanks again so much. Love Clara and CC.

CHAPTER 5. LAURA

"The best and most beautiful things in the world cannot be seen
or even touched, they must be felt within the heart."
A quote from Helen Keller

Dear Kristen:

I am so excited to be your new friend. My designer Miss Imelda knows your Grandfather who has asked me to make you a special doll. I told him I would make your doll with textures you could touch and recognize what they are since you have sight impairment. He has also arranged to have a reporter at our luncheon meeting next week. I will have to wait, but am so excited. You will know why when you read the poem Miss Imelda wrote for me to you. Se you soon…Laura

LAURA's LAUREL

Positioned on a table high
Displayed in prominence
My heart, brand new, quivering
Expectancy intense!

My Designer fluffs my fluffy dress
Last moment touches gentle
"You're a beautiful doll" she said
"Eye-catching ornamental!"

I say farewell to doll friends
Dina Brigitta wants to pose
Photo with me remembering
Our thoughts of "Suppose."

Silver glasses now in place
Focus dining table quaint
For Lady Kristen, age at six
Our meeting first acquaints.

She'll excite within her little heart
Beyond eyes that cannot see
For blindness causes clouded veil
Today gets gift, that's me!

My glasses round, just like hers
Are windows for her mind?
Delights she'll know with me in tow
Sensational, I'll remind.

Her "Papa" walks her to my side
As Grandfather so surprised
To find me in this restaurant
For a luncheon advertised!

Newsman arrives on time
Introductions polite made
Surprise before our eyes
Our appointment top grade.

Have you been a celebrity?
Flash cameras blaze white hot
It's new to me, for you see
It frightens me somewhat!

Reporter standing, pen in hand
To write about a tale
When a lady of importancy
Learns of me and Braille.

I hear our news will travel
Across page printed news
Of a County Journal
To share with you our views.

Family will see our photographs
We'll giggle (as girls do)
Meeting meetings at a lunch
Together me and you.

"She's yours," Miss Imelda said, "To keep"
Child eyes dimmed to see
Reach to feel me as her gift
Love blossoms instantly!

Your social manners finely taught
You find quick time to say
"Thank you, Papa, to bring me here
This busy holiday."

"She's dressed in green" I heard her say
"My favorite color green!"
Her eyes faintly shadowing
Sight so dimly seen.

Soft hands stroke my seed-pearled hat
Trimmed in lace around
Top stylish ostrich feather
Whitest to be found.

She touched my golden braids
Jeweled by my glass face
Nestled in a collared fur
Of elegant white grace.

She felt my velvet cape brocade
Embossed figures welled
Fingers tremble anxiously
Fond feelings instant held.

Raised rose in my dress perfumes
She probes my under slip
Satin gloss, shimmered net
Frost crystal-laced tip.

My poem in green satin-lined
Matched muff to clearly tell
I belong to this Lady small
Our meeting going well!

Then, her hands careful claim
My small waist to hold
Me to her face moist with tears
Eyes sightless closed.

My hand slips out of ermine muff
To touch her cheek of skin
Warm, silken, soft she is
Completely feminine.

"Laura" she says, (she chose my name)
"I feel you are my friend
We'll learn all wonders of
Worlds of Let's Pretend."

She held me to her shaped ear
I whispered voices low
I said to my new confidante
"New visions you will know!

I'll view vast continents
Know lands far and wide
We'll climb highest mountain peaks
We'll cross the Great Divide.

We'll soar above blue heavens
Where only eagles fly
Swoop some more past Braille's door
See What, When, Where and Why.

We'll cross river currents
You'll see wide oceans deep
We'll explore Star's gated door
That opens eyes from sleep.

Word windows we'll unlock ajar
Worlds we never knew
Touching grand experiences

Learning Braille with you.

Round glasses, mine, see beyond
Windows of your mind
Delights I'll show for you to know
New pictures will unwind.

We'll ride rims of excitement
From your desk at school
Stories stormy or perhaps
Beside a mirrored pool.

I'll see for you, so you can see
We'll touch, we'll smell, we'll taste
We'll learn learning other ways
As fingers dot in haste.

You'll feel how feelings can begin
You'll touch the varied dot
You'll taste Life's sweetness
You'll search and learn a lot.

You'll reach others blind to know
With eyes that see with eyes
That teaching is for everyone
No matter what their size.

We'll look in human hearts
Love's learning site not new
Light from an Eternal Source
More gifts for me and you.

When twilight closes shadowed lens
Bright light, images vast
Will slip between dim lit vaults
Blaze new ways past.

We'll explore together as we learn
Laurels will claim first prize
You'll see, Kristen dear, you'll see
You'll see without your eyes!

P.S. That means Pleasantly Special.

I received your "Thank You" card
"Want to Know a Secret" print
Signed by Me and You
I really had to squint!

Been reading about Braille for us
By Louis Braille in France
"Six-dot cell" working well
As our fingers work, advance.

We learn Louis himself was blind
From accident at age three
Played with tools in Dad's harness shop
Yet advanced, learns marvelously.

Excellent organist cellist he became
Gets scholarships to attend
National Institute for Blind Children
Continues teaching, to recommend.

We learn together, you and me
You may grow up to teach Braille
Get an Educator's degree
You'll graduate without fail.

Grandfather will be so proud
To hear your name as he holds me
Whispers "Kristen and Laura" out loud!
You'll see Kristen, dear, you'll see.

Laurel's claim first prize
Together always we remained
You've seen without your eyes
With doll Laura you named.

CHAPTER 6. DEIRDRE

"There are no strangers here; only friends you haven't yet met."
A quote from William Butler Yeats

Dear Mary:

Fairfax, your calico-colored library cat advances, supposedly secretly, up to me propped against the floor where I and my tote bag rest against the Circulation Desk of the Northland College library. He brushes his long fur against my Irish colored green dress with white eyelet pinafore enough to wrinkle soft cotton folds. He sniffs my dark brown hair, and knocks off my wide-brimmed hat with lining of more green fabric to match my dress. His paw strokes playfully my green satin ribbons that fall from my hat simultaneously with the ones that drop from my waistline. He nudges my book bag out of my hand from my white porcelain basket they are stored in. He sees my name on the other side of my book bag.

He meows, "Dear, Deirdre, don't be afraid," he purrs softly; "I live here in the library day and night. My favorite places are high shelves where I can paw through my feline history of lions and tigers in faraway places. So I know I am very famous and important. So glad to meet your acquaintance!" I tell him I am a gift from Miss Imelda, who works for you, Doctor Mary, in the library. I am so glad Fairfax is near me by now, the library doors have closed and lights are out and it is getting dark but for slants of windows on the north side. Fairfax tells me to hold on to his strong, long tail because he sees very well in the dark, or I would be lost and you would never find me soon enough to go home with you before the long weekend. I so look forward to meeting your big Irish wolfhound dogs. They are much preferred over this sneaky conceited cat! My dress rustles between tall and small books and I am glad my hat is on the floor next to my book bag I left at the Circulation Desk, it could be forever lost in here. The outside air is now foggy which makes it darker in the library. It reminds me of a quote Miss Imelda had on her desk:

"The fog comes on little cat feet, it sits looking over the harbor and city on silent haunches and then moves on." A quote by Carl Sandburg

Fairfax takes me to a large book named "How to draw cats" by Walter J. Wilwerding. I took the opportunity to tell him I have a doll friend named Emily who was a poet relative, and also a niece Loni, who is an Artist, and she draws cats like Walter. Fairfax did not seem interested in anyone but himself so he decided to fall asleep in my lap. His purring calms me I as I look around for a book title of interest. I do not venture far from Fairfax's tail or I would be lost.

I feel something pulling on my skirt, only to find that Squint, my little boy leprechaun had found me after crawling out of my book bag basket. Because he likes the dark so much he is not afraid, and wants to see what mischief he can get into. He said he found a shoe by the door of the library that needed mending, and after he got it fixed he dragged it to the floor space of the library showcase that is decorated each month with information about objects pictured there. He said there were many photos of other leprechaun's, fairies, and mythical creatures to celebrate Saint Patrick's Day. His shoes were shined and the gold buckles glistened in the moonlight. Squint says, "Perhaps, Deirdre, Miss Imelda says I am about important little people in an Irish world far away. " He pinched Fairfax's ear, only to find a quick claw response that caused his pointed hat to slip off his head. I asked him to go back to my white basket and read my books I brought with me. He did not want to because they were not Irish enough. Besides, Squint remarked, your name means sorrow, and your story is sad. I like meanness and mischief and playing pranks on people and things. I will go back to the book bag because I don't want to know that a cat lives here.

While Fairfax is sleeping I hear a tiny noise in the next section of books called Reference. Then, all of a sudden a small wee elf fell off the shelf on the floor. I asked him to come to me, walk up my sleeve and stay away from the cat sleeping on my lap. He followed my instructions perfectly and just fit in the nape of my neck. He whispered to me he used to be in a history book writing about elves in Ireland. When the student picked up the book paging through it so quickly, and pages already worn from use, he fell out on the floor. Now the book is overdue he heard students say at the Circulation Desk, and he has no place to go. I asked him his name, reminding him, everyone must have a name. He said he did not know his name; it was in the book somewhere. Deirdre said she would call him "Self." She told him she was a gift to the Head Librarian and she will be going home with her. "Self" asked her to take him with her, maybe elves and fairies live up there in the wilderness.

Deirdre pondered the thought. She explained to "Self" she would check her pantaloons to see if there was enough comfortable room for him to be stored. If so she would take him with, plus it would protect him from Fairfax who would be waking up soon. She lifted her leg and the pantaloon had enough space. She told "Self" to "ease down her neck and crawl in the hole she would hold open. He must never make any noise until she gets to Mary and Jim's house because he is a stowaway, plus Fairfax would be sniffing her and that may make Mary wonder what I am up to before she takes me home. "

I thought morning would never come; Fairfax protected me all night and brought me back to the Circulation Desk. Squint was there and I told him to be quiet the rest of the day. We did not need to give Mary any reason not to take us home with her today. I heard the back door open, and she came directly to me and my book bag and my basket and brought me to her office. "Self" made no noise and I was proud of my clever thinking.

After work Doctor Mary brought me to their car where Jim was waiting for us. It was a long journey along Lake Superior, then up to the northern hills, down a long dirt road and then they drove into a quaint home overlooking Lake Superior. I could hear two dogs barking their welcome to them home. She called to them, Maeve and Ben. Of course, both of them full bred Irish wolfhounds. Entering the house, she places me on a table by two large dining room windows. Her husband looks at me carefully examining my basket treasures. He likes my dress he said. Mary lets the dogs out through a dog door where they can come and go when they are home or into the night. Mistress Mary sits down and writes Miss Imelda a letter.

"Dear Imelda Marguerite:

Thank you so very much for the lovely doll. You must have put in many hours in the design and making of Deirdre. Thank you for your thoughtfulness, artistic talent and patient needlework. I look forward to reading Deirdre's story. Sincerely yours, Mary."

DEIRDRE

My stowaway "Self" pinches my leg
Ever so softly his reminder
Obedient he's been, my instructions
To find fairies, find elf home finder.

I stroke "Self's" body so small
Assure him it will be soon
Nightfall fast approaching
Already I see full moon.

Dogs in back yard near dog door
Maeve happens to glance at me
I beckon her "come," work to be done
To Superior lakeshore I must be.

Mary and Jim bed early tonight
Maeve slides in house dog door

Jowls dripping wet, but I can't fret
Think of little "Self's" needs more.

Maeve runs to lake, no concern I might break
Sets me by Big Rock carelessly
Leaves me alone running with Ben
I stroke "Self's" head tenderly.

I picked up a stick, knock on Big Rock
From side crack hear loud yawn
Voice garish, "For crying out loud
What is near me going on?"

I explain as a rock he doesn't move
He must know stories told near
Where do fairies or wee elves live?
In this remote country up here."

Rock yawns, goes back to sleep
Thinks he dreams commotion.
Beside rock wiggles wee fairy
Deirdre excited, such emotion!

Asks fairy "Wait just a moment"
She has small responsibility
Eases out "Self," a patient elf
"Where do elves live here, Fairy?

What is your name, why are you here?"
"I'm on my way home, my name is Mari
From secret dimensions, continuous sphere,
Away from people, so legendary.

Our Counselor Fairy is so very wise
'Very Fairy' in her head has 'knows.'
I'll take elf "Self" with me
She'll tell where elf home goes."

Deidre holds "Self" gently again
Asks him not to be afraid
"Fairy wings strong soar safe as she flies"
So proud to help in this crusade.

Fairy "Mari" flies toward moonrise
Above pampas grass, high weeds tall
"Self" wrapped around her slim body
Little elf no trouble at all.

Deirdre waves to "Self "once her cargo

Just in time, Maeve comes to fetch her
By Big Rock makes noise like a snore
Appreciates help Rock gave for sure.

Protecting "Mari" fairy more
She pats Rock's head though thankfully
Maeve gallops Deirdre to dog door
Her jowls wet again as can be.

Moonlight shadows on house wall
Relieved "Self" will find family
Shaped Mary's desk notes of a doll
Curious to see, I read it's about me.

Impressive beauty child named Deirdre
Forced living in forest with nurse mother
Quietly 'til grown betrothed to become
King Conor of Ulster's bride, none other.

Deidre has plans as bride to marry
Has raven hair, skin snow white, lips red
Mother knows of one courtier male
Deirdre asks, make acquaintance instead.

Meets him at dawn in forest hunting
Man of dreams one of three brothers
Ardan, Ainnie, it is her lover Naoise
She wants to marry, none others.

Young lovers in Irish love stories
Elope at once, oppose King's decree
Spies report to King Deirdre married Naoise
Enraged, orders expel out of Ireland country.

Exiled with two brothers to Scotland
They live a year safe in tower
In harmony four of them happy
Far away from evil King's power.

Jealous King invites them back
To Ireland to feast with his court
Jealously coveting Deirdre for his bride
Plans with spies murder in transport.

Deirdre dreams dreadful flashback
King first chance will kill them all
Brothers her caution don't heed
Plans return to Ireland, King's call.

King's spies hunt, plan to kill begun
Journey betrayal expertly their plan
Naoise and Deirdre travel together
With brothers Ainnie and Ardan.

Naoise shot first by spy's spear
Dies in arms of Deirdre, beloved bride
His brothers were killed next to him
Her dream now real verified.

Deirdre forced return to King's castle
Her grief continues in sorrow
Does not speak, does not smile
Inwardly carefully plans for tomorrow.

Adorns herself regal colors of royalty
To prepare court wedding in style
King's bride-to-be rides in chariot as
Sovereign queen-to-be profile.

Crowds cheer pompous procession
Her beauty unsurpassed in the land
King success at last claims her glamour
Will submit to his love on command.

Deirdre waves to citizens in submission
Kings subjects applaud her presence
Unaware of her devious intentions
In public, pre-nuptial pretense.

She asks coach driver "Drive faster"
Protrudes her head out chariot space
Flying rock strikes her beautiful head
Battered bruises over her face.

Deidre slumps in chariot, dies instantly
Jealousy of King destroys beauty found
She is buried near lover and brothers
A yew tree grows from the ground.

Joins branches together all of them
If cut, grows more profound
In death two lovers, two brothers
Together. Their story spellbound.

Doll Deirdre grieves lovers sorrow
Can she a happy reunion dream?
Can love be restored though broken?
After such a murderous scheme?

She'll devise plans tomorrow
Wretched tale ends tragically
For Naoise and Deirdre feels sorry
Their love stopped pathetically.

Dogs Maeve and Ben come in house
Maeve picks me up, mouth at my waist
Runs fast out dog door, dangling
To Lake Superior in haste.

She puts me down by red bush then
Runs with Ben to lake streak
I see firefly beetles everywhere
Mesmerized by each light unique.

Am told light is nerve controlled
Lightning bugs close as my cheek
Say, "We use light in defense, find mates"
Deirdre enjoys light mystique.

Delightful display in full moonlight
Sits there for Maeve's return, waits
Moonlight beams glowing shadows
Full moon shadowed portraits.

Hears whisper beside soft ground
Close to her feet she looks down
Below four leaf clover green leaf
Is tiny fairy dressed in face frown?

Wee fairy says she danced too far
From friends in meadow over there
Deirdre asks if she could hold her
As moon's beams shine in her hair.

Smooth hands tiny, small body frail
Fingers slim delicate in form
Bright eyes like stars fallen
Deirdre dreams a transform.

"My history is sad, wee fairy"
Tells wee fairy long story told
Of Naoise loving Deirdre
Of evil King's carnage bold.

Can fairies where she lives love them?
In meadow, love's memory survive
To dance, play among moonbeams

Enjoy each other again live?

Learn to dance as fairies do
Protected on sparse meadow floor?"
Deirdre pleads; wee fairy
Asks her to not tell anymore?

Little fairy cries tiniest tears
Sad story strain on wee heart string
"Maybe fairies that lived in Ireland
Were destroyed by evil king.

Love's memories can live anywhere
You could make her real in a poem
Their love so tender and precious
Live in hearts, Deirdre, like your own."

"Take me to meadow where fairies dance
If Deirdre and Naoise spirit appears
I must ask dog Maeve transportation"
First, wipes Fairy's tiny tears.

"If Maeve brings her to meadow this night
I must first tell him, wee fairy, you are real
You know how dogs like to fight
She must understand you're not a meal!"

Maeve returns, jumps close to Deirdre
Her legs so long and so high
Perfect to run toward a meadow
Whispers in Maeve's ear trip to go by.

Maeve kneels down close to listen
Who shows up unannounced...dog Ben?
He almost crushed wee fairy's feet!
Deirdre commands him to "stop" then.

Whispers to Maeve again dream plan
Unsure she can find Fairy Street
Wee fairy flies to Maeve's ear
Points coarse to east past field wheat.

Moonlit night tonight helpful
To locate her fairy friends nest
Fairy wiggles in space of Maeve's ear
Perfect space for a rest.

Maeve picks up Deirdre, fairy holds on
Long legs flee across plain

Her nose pokes wide grasses tall
Wee fairy slides out ear again.

They hear beautiful faint music
Found wee fairy's hometown
Wee Fairy waves to her fairy friends
Asks them to listen, sit down.

All wonder where she has been
She explains Maeve, Deirdre a dolly
Another dog not here, named Ben
Deirdre repeats her name allegory.

"Of two lovers who wed but now dead
Evil betrayal of King Conor's spies
Destroys lovers beauty once wed
Dreadful, tragic tale full size.

Can we carry perfume in Irish Country?
Here in your dance hall charade
Hold fond memory to me precious
Renew their Spirit's waylaid?"

"Very Fairy" checks her "knows" file
We wait patient for her to convey
She states "she knew Irish benefactor
On a Time Once Far Away

We'll consult energy wave transports
Come back Deirdre, another day"
So Deirdre thanks wee fairies
For myths, Irish legends today.

Happy we believe in fairies wee
Blows kisses, leaves fairy throng
Friends made to a doll and a dog
As Irish as Irish can belong.

Proceeds fast in Maeve's mouth
To find wolfhound pal Ben
Away from fairies secret meadows
Maeve drops her near Big Rock then.

Deirdre walks past flowers in forest
Near tree trunk strong with spaces
Sees two winged creatures, one "Self"
She stands by tree trunk she traces.

He peeks, brings his companion

His friend elf as pretty as can be
Introduces "Herself" to Deirdre
"Happy together in their tall tree.

"Very Fairy" knew only of one elf
Left in meadow, others gone away
When "Self" meets "Herself" instantly
They become new elf family.

Don't feel loneliness ever
"Self" showers "Herself" flowers any day
Never debate not being together
Wee fairies greet them every day.

One day they will have little elves
Form small clan in forest again
Pick wee fairy flower bouquets
Come, visit us, Deirdre again."

Deirdre says goodbye to sweet couple
Love is sweet wondrous thing
She was small part to small "Self"
"Herself's" love to him bring.

Deirdre walks back to lakeshore
Where Ben splashes Superior Lake
Certain he has found unusual fish
Half human, half fish, a mistake.

Deirdre shouts, "Ben, be careful
Mermaids need swim to shore
Be gentle, they're harmless, so tired
Need move toward less water, or

Mermaids will be captured by humans
Exposed to dangerous circumstance
Unsheltered by seas moisture
On high waves mermaids dance."

Ben stops attention, finds stray cat
Maeve joins Ben long legs pursue
Cat climbs tree, so dogs, that's that!
Dogs prowl more things to do.

Deirdre walks toward creatures
See mermaids swim close to shore
Invites them to rest upon beach
Watch fireflies light night sky more.

Mermaids six in number crawl
Up on sand, stretch out body fin
Weary from long lake swimming
Dodge boats, skis, ferry's coming in.

Mermaids share stories to Deirdre
She tells them her Irish lore
Wonders if humans convey
Concern for creatures, or

Myths and ballads written
Some true undocumented
Mermaids or mermen smitten
By humans discontented.

Lakeshore ablaze with fireflies
Court dark lighting this night's stay
Time to go home, almost sunrise
She's been enlightened all the way.

In distance, what is Maeve bringing?
Maeve picks her up jowls dripping
Drops Squint, her Leprechaun!
His mischief must be slipping!

Wounded slight Squint moves toward
Big Rock, safe, who sleeps night and dawn
Maeve follows Ben quick pursuit
Another adventure to pounce upon.

Deirdre's pantaloons slip lower
These trips her only travel feat
Maybe Mistress Mary sew them?
In home on shelf watches dawn greet.

Deirdre a new day out glass pane near
While Mary and Jim breakfast eat
Grateful couple brought her here
Many friends new to meet.

Dogs Maeve and Ben locked in hall
Stories to tell humans won't know
New tales to know come nightfall
Where did her leprechaun go?

As dogs frolic in woods or by lake
Tag along is Deirdre glass doll
Experiences more exotic wait
Possibly hear wee fairies small.

Deirdre and Naoise's reunion plan
Alive meet again across upper skies
Above Ireland's skies span?
Away from ugly plans, lies.

Day passes quickly, dogs sleep
Wake; slurp prepared food in a pan
Mary and Jim come home a moment
Open dog door fast as they can.

Drive off to who knows where?
Already Maeve has escape plan
Picks me up by waist closer
My pantaloons don't slip again.

Off we go doll partner with Maeve
Swift Irish wolfhound Ben
I'm dropped by Big Rock hurried
I straighten myself, near crack again.

Polite inquire if Rock saw Squint?
Leprechaun hurt last night, stopped by
Rock complains, "Leave me alone
I used to not be bothered." Sigh.

"You and those dogs making noises
No longer snore at the moon
Last night a little fairy asks me
When you will visit her soon?

Told her to come back in a month
I can see her better full moon?"
Deidre sits calm quiet beside
Big Rock, contemplates fairy soon.

Glances to smooth beach sands
Reads words written carefully
"Thanks for rest," mermaid's hands
Maeve comes by walks slowly.

So unlike her leaps and bound
In dripping jowls holds Mari Fairy
Drops her in my lap, this hound
Runs without stopping contrary.

I wipe Mari's face with my dress
She rubs off remaining saliva flow
"Deirdre, I have so much to express

Get Maeve to take us to our meadow.

"Very Fairy" has news for us all
Naoise's spirit near Deirdre's found
His brothers she can't recall
Looked carefully auras around.

Maeve comes back holds Squint again
Not wounded, "Put him down there
Under four leaf clover near Big Rock
We have long journey to take care"

Deirdre puts Mari Fairy near her ears
Tucks safely legs collar of dress
Off they go Maeve's leaps and bounds
Their taxi an Irish express!

To field meadow filled with fairies
Maeve drops us on meadow floor
To find Ben out there somewhere
Barks, be back again some more.

"Very Fairy" so happy to see Deirdre
Has spirits of lovers in her file
Knocked safely for their releases
Explains the must wait awhile.

Deirdre sees fine formed figures
Resemble lovers once told
"Very Fairy" opens file door gently
Transparent's transplant new from old.

Lift upward, lovers together
Arms tight as original they were
Toward moonlit sky lifting
White cloud lifts him and her.

Wave goodbye to new friends below
Fairies whisper softly "adieu's shown"
Preserved love of Naoise, of Deirdre
Love alive, fairies now known.

Maeve stands beside her unnoticed
Maeve says she misses a lot
Running too fast leaps and bounds
Thanks her for coming to this spot.

To see fairies bring happiness
To earth when happiness was lost

Long ago in his Irish country
Lovers alive high, star-crossed.

Maeve takes her back to Big Rock
Squint actually waited this time
She puts Squint in her pantaloon
Toward home hills to climb.

Home near her basket puts Squint
She will counsel his wanderings far
He pouts near her silly books
Recalls next town has a bazaar.

Deirdre reminisces her namesake
Her husband in meadow she saw
Happy faces again deeply in love
Miss Imelda will yell "Hurrah."

She looks in her basket for Squint
Not a sign of wise leprechaun
He ran away, did not want to stay
More adventure or mischief on lawn.

Perhaps he will meet wee fairy
Who can teach him fancy things?
Soon forget naughtiness or pranks
Fix fairy shoes or shoe strings.

They'll teach dancing in his shoes
With buckles of shiny gold
He can show his pot of gold stored
At foot of rainbows circle fold.

Deirdre is content in wilderness
Each night finds something new
Maeve develops more manners
Doll's important tasks to do.

Mistress Mary will like my poem
From Miss Imelda who gives her me
To remember she too was a child
Filled with dream's memory.

Dances of Life angle Mother Earth
Glide, slide, swinging new birth
People of Secret scurry to seed
Sow malice, misspent in greed.

Polluted air, seas, trees and land

How long can Nature withstand?
Spin speeches spiral to send
Suffering sprawls Earth to mend.

In her adventures she must find
Dreams cast aside Beauty's bend
Impress humans who visit us
Mystic real stories to send.

If humans take time to listen
Stored stories in prayer
Deep within us, uniquely styled
Remain responses to share.

Mislaid Ancient Irish Children
Deirdre's dreams gave light
Fulfilled fairies intervention
Lover's loves in spirit unite.

Namesakes for sake of a name
Once sorrow once now after all
Name remembers a love restored
Deirdre with Naoise, with Deirdre a Doll.

CHAPTER 7. MOLLY/FRANCES ANN/MARY IRENE

"I hold my daughter in my arms and thank God for bringing her to me.
If the standard route for creating a family had worked for me, I wouldn't have met this child.
I needed to know her. I needed to be her mother. I know now why all those events happened.
Or didn't happen. So I could meet this little girl. She is, in every way, my daughter.
I am carrying my Funny Gift from God and all is good."
A quote from: Nia Vardlalos. (her name means Instant Mother).

Dear Molly...
The long train ride from Minnesota to New York was frightening, for me still a mere child teen. I had never been out of town far enough to know how big the world was. I was seventeen when engaged to a student at the local University, I found out I was with child. When I told him, he said he was already married, and I would have to wait until he could work things out. When I told my Mother, she said she would send me away to a Foundling Home in New York that also had a school to study nursing. I was to study, and when the baby was born, leave the child for adoption, come home and start over. No one else knew I was pregnant at that time, being the 1940's it was best to remain quiet on the matter. I left during early term, and showed no signs of weight. I boarded the passenger train, and recalled my father was so proud of me having been accepted in the nursing class. I cried on the way, especially when the train whistled at certain track changes. When I arrived at the Chicago station the terminal was so large I had to learn how to get directions to the train I

needed; again I heard the whining, screaming whistles that sounded as frightened as I was. Miles increased farther away from the home I knew, my loneliness was so deep I wished I could drown in it, but then I knew I was carrying an innocent child, I was the one illegitimate.

I was met at my final destination by a Catholic Nun who greeted me kindly, ushered me into a car and we drove out of the city to the Foundling hospital. When I settled in, I didn't have time to be lonely, with my nursing lessons and writing reports and of course, my continuous nausea from pregnancy. The time for my baby to be born seemed to progress nicely. My brother Frank was in the U.S. Navy, stationed in New York at the time, so he came to see me on occasion so I could leave the home chaperoned. It meant so much to me. My Mother had contacted him, so he knew about my stay there. My nursing class lessons were sent home with excellent grades. Finally the baby's delivery time came, which was long and painful. At birth I was not given anesthesia, with the Nuns statement I must suffer for my 'sins.'

Yet, inside I did not feel any need to suffer, as my child was being born and given away, and that would make someone who could not have children very happy. That was my only suffering; I could not bring my baby girl home. After two weeks of convalescence, my brother Frank was getting leave to take me home. As we left the hospital, he asked me to stop by the nursery window to see my baby. I looked at babies in their cribs and told myself there was no one there that was mine. When I assured him I knew which child was mine we left and I closed the trip to New York with finality firmly fixed in my mind. I would never see her, ever. She was a healthy eight pound baby girl.

Many years later, I wrote this poem to the Foundling Hospital where my little girl was born. I was already married and had grown daughters of my own, who knew they had a mystery sister somewhere. It was the rule at the Foundling Home only the child born there had the right to search out the origin of their natural mother. My child had written to them a year prior, so my poem was sent to her in response. This, as you know, was my poem!

CHILDLESS MOTHER

Father God that I may know a girl babe born to me
Unwed teen year long ago misty eyes did not see
From birth beyond days I kept arms empty void of her
Vow given for her life someplace else more secure

Foundling doors close at last, lonely months in halls to stay
I passed once cradle small, brief glance, then on my way.
Black, curls frame her little head, were eyes closed brown or blue?
Would she be safe as my own as whole bodies split in two?

Her name was false; mine was too for select measured time
Act out pregnant pace to neither wait nor claim child mine
In reflection, perhaps, a smile appears on an infant face
"Goodbye my child, I wish you well in someone else's place."

> Father God you know all things of humans great to very small
> Remember my newborn baby girl whose birthday I recall
> You know desires deep in her heart, her dreams you can uncover
> Should she want to know me too a girl her natural mother.

On May 12... my own Mother's Birthday

My office phone rang, "Special Student Programs" I replied, my usual response on the first ring. The person the phone said it was long distance from New York... a flash reflective thought could not place any reason of business to contact me from New York. A lady asked for me and I responded, "This is she." She said, "This is an Infant Home in New York!" Suddenly my thoughts drifted back over 30 years ago. I became no longer a professional business woman answering my phone, but a human being full of anticipation and wonder. I heard her say she was Asst Director and had received a response to my inquiry to make known, the birth records of a little girl born to me. My daughter had responded to my request and would like to exchange names! Peacefulness engulfed me that was calm and gentle and I knew my prayers of last year when I wrote a poem to this very little girl so etched into my memory were answered. I was afraid and unafraid. Dark shadows crossed my mind from the past! This was all so confusing. I told myself those days I could not see my child. I could not hold her if I was to never see my family again. I remember when I left the home my brother Frank held me so close. I told him I named her after him, Frances Ann. He took my arm and said "Find her and look at her, this only time." I thought I saw her, her hair was black and curly like her father; she was beautiful. My brother says "Let's go." My thoughts came back to today's phone call. She said I was a grandmother! I looked at the calendar on my office wall. It was my Mother's birthday. I thanked the God I knew for this gifted phone call, thanking him for her protection, which I reflected he already protected her all these years.

Ten days later the phone rings again at my office, it is the Foundling Home again. Documents are complete and she tells me my girl's name is Molly. I thought what a beautiful name. It is musical and it belongs to my little girl. The music of her name rings in my heart and rests there in the new sense of belonging
Molly called me when I got home she phoned. I was asked a battery of personal questions, about her father, about the circumstances involved, in my final signature to agree to make the adoption final. It was emotionally draining to re-live this life that I had tucked away in my memory. She asked me about my life and I told her whatever she wanted to know. I wanted her comfortable to know she could call me at any time.

A few weeks later she called and asked me if I would meet her Science Professor, who had relatives in Duluth, not far from me. She had a very high regard for him. I suspected she had the right to ask someone to meet me, so he could evaluate my character and report back to her. Her Professor, Doctor Bill called and set up time to eat over dinner. He said he was six feet 4 inches tall and the ugliest man in the world, so I would have no problem picking him out of strangers! I found that amusing. As I waited for him, a tall man came up to me and said, "There could have been 300 women coming thru that door and I would have known which one was Molly's Mother." That began a visit lasting six hours! Bill's wife had died years ago and so too did my children's father, when they were very young. He was soon to retire as a Cancer Research Scientist. His first love he said was when he looked under the microscope and saw all the wonders of the human body!

He knew Molly's adoptive Mother and Father. They were good people he said! Molly also has an adopted brother. She was married with an infant son. Bill and I visited and met many times later and became close, with Molly as our special connection! I had written several poems to him, it seemed to be the best way I could communicate my fond feelings forming so solidly. He was the first person I ever introduced to my childhood recluse diversion, when under stress, called "The Meadow."

Back to my meeting my dear Molly in person....I met Bill at the same lobby I met him for the first time. He was on his way back to New York and was to take me with him to meet Molly and her family. I was very grateful. On our way, going through Michigan, I was having panic reactions about meeting Molly. I wanted to return home. He rented separate joining hotel rooms. He came in, comforted me that he would be with me every moment I was with her that I need not be afraid. He assured me she was a special person and she would not see me in any critical way. The next morning we were again on our way, I was comforted and unafraid.

Arriving in New York, after a rest, on a Sunday, he escorted me to meet Molly. I did not know how I would react. We got out of the car, and there she was standing at her front door with her husband Vinny and she was holding her baby son, Bartholomew. We walked toward them, and I did not know what to do, Bill was holding my hand. As Bill let go of my hand, although we did not hug at first, she reached out and gave me her son. My heart nearly exploded with joy, to touch her offspring and also my own blood. It was so special to link the two together to put balance into my life. I stayed with her family during the day and took care of little Bartholomew and met Bill's family evenings and weekends.

Molly and me now have much history and we are as close as any family...NO SO MUCH MORE...as we were once lost and now we are found! So my story goes on, not only in my heart, but now in real life... How blessed can one person be...to have found my little girl Frances Ann.

FRANCES ANN

Once, on a time period Former
A baby in August was born
Her mother, young, unmarried
Product of lost lovelorn.

Not once, as an infant, she held her
Sad girl, burdened with care
As mother, chose to leave her child
For someone else to be there.

Silence passed between them
Thirty plus muted years
One Mother's Day she found her
Erasing where-about fears.

Never, as a child, she knew her

Never, as a young woman grown
Until she too became a mother
Searching for kinship known.

Words now of mother to daughter
Shared many moons hence
Greetings, meetings, feelings
Emotions mounted immense.

No shadows cloud now her visits
Knows once choice then was true
Love was enough to let her go
Full grown, gifts doll, me, to you.

"Frances Ann" name given your dolly
Name given you her infant new
Left alone at Foundling Home
Thinks she saw but never held you.

My dress lavender in shadings
Lace hems fluff here and there
Light purple, your color, flounces
Fair flowers bloom everywhere!

Lace apron skirt netting
Surrounds me, just like a queen
Purple buds cinch my small waist
My cap holds flowers between.

I want to claim sitting unique
One special place in place
One of my own from a mother
Never touched your baby face.

Nor, do my views bring staining
To blot your own Mother's care
Or your Father who adored you
Through your life they were there.

Grateful I am to be with you
Thankful your parent's loving care
Cherished Child Chosen from another
Mother conditional as fair.

My name, Frances Ann, is chosen
After dear Brother Frank who came
Visits in New York where stationed
In United States Navy time frame.

Both far from home of our childhood
Companionship important increased
Until time came for his transfer
Both ride home bus released.

Ann's name of my dear friend
In school together to share
NEWS, views our life together
Orphaned, lived in home there.

Reminds me I am sewing
Frank's doll Hanna her dress
Fabric of lines, sew waves waving
Must sew slow, follow pin press.

Some dolls are special, I am
Reminder to you once a child
When dollies are important to talk to
Your colors favorite styled.

Love comes different in seasons
Measured in balance by Truth
Blessed am I to now know you
As souvenir of your youth.

Your natural mother has told me
Two sons born by husband and you
When they see me as your Dolly
Introduce me, please, to them too.

Bartholomew, close to five years
Could boast to friends, he could
Of His Mummy who loves a dolly
Can grown up's be understood?

Or William, curious and charming
Can captivate easy a heart
That glistens, as my doll heart glistens
Where child imaginings start!

I could pass Sleep's beginnings
Into child's bedrooms to chase
Mechanical toys, special for boys
Entering a marathon race!

Even though dolls, like glass ones
Should sit quietly on site
I would enjoy them watching
Active in a pillow fight!

Gladsome, cheerful, fun-loving
As "Frances Ann", merry I'll be
Adopted for a Mother's keepsake
Pretend-tious am I by degree.

This gift, of me is tender
From one, not melancholy
Loving you now more than then
Happy Birthday Molly, your Dolly.

When I was first visiting with Molly in her home I found out her adoptive mother's name was Mary Frances, so when naming Molly as an infant…Frances Ann…it has to be a 'synchronicitious' thing, so naturally I had to write a poem about it. Seems I can show my feelings best that way! My husband, Bill told me about Molly's parents, so I made a doll for her mother, Mary Frances! I was fortunate to find a miniature baby doll, without clothes in a quaint boutique shop. So I dressed her in a baptismal outfit, know her parents would have had Molly baptized!

Molly invited Bill and I for dinner and invites her mother Frances Ann and her father William as well. When we all meet, Molly graciously brings her Mother in the room and says, "Mother, I would like you to meet my Mother! She leaves me alone with her to chat. I sat in a chair next to Mary Frances, a moment passes, and then she puts her hand on my arm and says, "Thank you for Molly!" "And my new dolly!"

MARY IRENE

I sit in black leather chair mute
Nonplussed, muse, moments pass
Frances places her hand on my forearm
"Thank you for Molly" first-class.

Protective parent obviously
Answered prayer immediately
First day Frances and husband William
Cradled child their adoptee.

My silence unresponsive
Opportune to gift her her doll
No name, but baby doll dolly holds
A memory miniature recall.

She examines fabric, her colors
Doll baby's baptismal dress
Exact pattern of Molly's, says
"So thoughtful of you to express."

We relax, casual visiting

Invites me to her home next door
Would like to show photographs
Expresses gratitude to me more.

Explains she prayed for me daily
First year Molly was new
I could have claimed her then
Assured her decision I wouldn't do.

Molly announces dinner is ready
I could see she was happy to see
Two mothers adopted and natural
Visit together splendidly.

Molly introduces me to her father
As my Doctor Bill's wife
Close acquaintances they are
In Molly and Vinny's life.

I could see he adored Molly
As his own daughter, none other
Boasts they also have a son
After Molly adopts her brother.

Bill and I leave soon after dinner
Polite messages were exchanged
We walk out the door of happiness
Unnecessary words rearranged.

Next day takes me back to Molly's
She takes me to her mother next door
Her dolly with baby stands on piano
She sits on stool, sweet as before.

Asks if she can play a song for us
Molly returns to lab, goes out the door
Frances plays "Blackhawk Waltz"
My smile appreciation more.

Tell her my beautiful Mother
Was accomplished musician long ago
Husband William seated in next room
Waves "Hi" listening to radio.

Frances brings album of photographs
Pictures of daughter Molly's life
Filling spaces in my own thoughts
My decision larger than life.

So small as when I left her
Growing to toddler then older
Each photo a happy girl
Happy parents' shareholder.

I ask her if she named her dolly
Entreats me if she can select one
Agree, her decision appropriate
Doll holds her baby Molly redone.

Selects her own Mother Mary Irene
Dolls represented in this family
Adopt each other serene
Mothers mothering mothers see.

Grateful I came with my Bill
Involved, contributing interludes
Contentment, fate filled
I am repaired damaged goods.

Bill's knock on Molly's parents'
House located next door
We leave together, me thanking
Her parents love to her more.

I only gave her life, they're love
Took over; I closed the door
Then Creator of all life reopens it
I learn to love her once more.

Happiness gifted in miniature
Greatness grown in between
Displayed gifts fragile strengthened
With Baby dolly and doll Mary Irene.

On the way back to the cabin I thank my dear husband for his perception; his protection, his love. He smiles, holds my hands, says he loves me. We listen to raindrops falling on the roof of the car, another "experience" he loves.

When we returned back to Wisconsin I received the following letter from Frances….

"Dear Imelda:

" A special thank you message intended to express a thank you for your lovely gift and for your thoughtfulness. Thank you for the lovely doll. Your delicate handwork is certainly an expression of your love for your hobby. I have sewed all my life and so have an appreciation of the time and patience you offer when you give this gift. Thank you for our kindness.

You ask me for some insight into her name Mary Irene. She is my gentle, quiet Mother. I love her very much. She and my wonderful father were both very Irish, they had seven fine children two boys and five girls. We loved each one, by their example with their good hearts. She was quietly strong with lifelong endurance, patience and perseverance that kept her family strong, God loving serving people. Inside, she had a light spirit and would sit down spontaneously and play the piano and "The Blackhawk Waltz," my Dad's favorite. She and Daddy loved their family. They lived to be 86 and 92 respectively and I am sure they are serving God in Paradise and praying for all of us. I hope your Christmas was a happy reunion with your family and that the trip home with your precious Bill was a pleasant change of pace in this world. God send you his choicest blessings. Love... Frances"

CHAPTER 8. VICTORIA

"We know what we are, but not what we may be."
A quote from William Shakespeare

VICTORIA, Bill's dolly

On her toes she measured just less than two feet tall; yet, because of her regal appearance she dominated everyone. At the moment, she was sitting on the top of an entertainment center unit in a small efficiency apartment next to Doctor Bill's laboratory. He was her only master. Master indeed! Didn't they know she was royalty? Her legs and feet rested on the smooth top and she could see pictures of the world on the map around her where there were pins stuck in areas Doctor Bill had visited and lectured about science. This is where Victoria sat day after day. Next to the laboratory and lecture hall she could listen and watch curious events take place in this more curious room. As her friend Francis Ann said, "It was more and more curious each day!

Victoria wore a beautiful red dress that was trimmed in white lace. The skirt was long and billowed. It rustled when she walked. Oh, yes, she could walk, but only when no one was around to see her. Victoria wore black shiny patent shoes over white cotton stockings. She had a regal face with hard, blue eyes that fitted the queen image she was. Her dark flaxen hair was brushed back and tied in a knot, a delicate lace covered hat rested daintily on her jaunty positioned head, a small white fan rested on her lap. She really needed that fan as at times the fumes and odors in the strange laboratory were more than she could bear! She loved her mistress, Miss Imelda, but not compared to the love of her Master Doctor Bill.

Doctor Bill was a tall, ordinary looking man, middle-aged, whatever that was, since time was not of much importance to her. He wore glasses, many times on top of his head, which made Victoria laugh inside, because she knew he didn't have eyes on top of his head! His hair was thin and unruly, except when he greased it for some special occasion. Usually, he wore a white coat that had his full name in red letters stitched just at the top of his breast pocket. In front of his name were the letters Dr. whatever that means, for Victoria didn't know, because he never treated sick people and she thought that was what a Doctor was. Instead, he always seemed to have his head in a book, punching keys on an odd-looking instrument, cooking up messes and bad smells, or looking into a tube that was pointed at a glass slide. Victoria was not dull; she wanted to learn, so she watched every move Doctor Bill made. Some people called him a research scientist. In time, Victoria knew she would be able to tell in advance what he was going to do, so she became a scientist too. She took notes like he did.

Unknown to Victoria's Master Bill, she prowled around his laboratory at night, as this curious room was called. No one knew of these adventures except Anony who was a small, white mouse with small pink ears and a long pink tail. He lived beneath the tabled counter with his family. Anony was also curious as to what was going on. He had learned, after dreadful trial and error, not to eat everything he found on the floor of this laboratory. Some things made him very sick. If it smelled good, he thought it would be good to eat. If it had no smell or was very stinky, he had to be suspiciously careful. He found crumbs in the lunch room, aside from the laboratory, and found enough food there for him and his small family.

Anony had anxiously watched Victoria carefully climb down the entertainment center unit on her way to the laboratory. Then she managed to get up onto the adjacent stone top table which extended all around the room, a strange sort of bench with a water trough running its length. It was located against the wall; there were all kinds of plumbing pipes and outlets that provided air, gas, electricity, water and even vacuums. The space beneath the bench was filled with drawers. Walking down a bench surface could be hazardous, since it was covered with instruments whose red or green lights blinked on and off. One also found strange shaped glass flasks and tubes. Some of the glassware was connected together to form peculiar shapes, all tied together on a tubular support system, standing 3 or 4 feet above the desk surface. Under some of the flasks was a four-inch rube connected by a rubber tubing to the gas outlet. These units produced an intense flame when lighted by a match. They were called Bunson Burners. There were a number of them on each bench. It was no easy task for Victoria to find her way around this laboratory without tripping. She surely needed to be quiet snooping around late at night!

Victoria's Doctor Bill's microscope: A Tube-like machine. That one looks through to magnify things as placed on the slide by 10 to 500 times or more. (The microscope magnifies or makes things look larger than they are. It lets man explore the universe of microbes, cells, etc. It was invented by a Dutch dry good merchant and Janitor. He ground over 500 lenses before he finally perfected his first microscope.) Of all the instruments the one Victoria was most interested in was the tube with a light at one end. When any object, even a drop of water, was placed on a glass slide and inserted between the end of the special tube and the light, one could see things that were far too small to be seen by a human naked eye. Things such as; bacteria, blood cells, skin, and whatever notes on the tabletop said. This instrument was like a telescope in reverse and it was called a microscope-used for small viewing. It had to be focused by moving the tube up and down by means of a small knob located on the side. She watched Doctor Bill, and it looked easier than it was to do by herself. It was at the microscope that Victoria first met Anony.

She had been trying for nights to push the switch that turned on the light. Unknown to her Anony was watching, his whiskers moving nervously from the edge of the water trough. Cautiously he edged himself into sight. Victoria did not scream but calmly asked, "I don't suppose you could help me, and I can't seem to turn on the light." First, Anony could see better than she could and thus he introduced himself as Anony Mous and offered to help Victoria with her explorations. With that Anony climbed up on the cord and when they both pushed the switch at the same time the light clicked on. Victoria was so elated that she hugged Anony and thanked him. They had formed a partnership instantly. Often she hung on to his tail for safety.

Victoria's Doctor Bill had taken a sample of blood, mixed it with some chemical to prevent it from clotting, and let it stand on the Laboratory bench. When Victoria saw it that night it had slowly
separated into three layers. The first thing that they did was to take a glass slide from a little wooden box marked 'human blood'. After quite a struggle, they finally got the blood side on the microscope stage that was located just beneath the tube and above the light; the other end of the tube had an eye piece so that one could look down the tube. Inside the tube were small pieces of glass carefully ground so that they magnified whatever she looked at. No way could Victoria or Anony adjust the end of the tube to fit with their eyes so they settled it by taking turns looking in the eye piece and Anony rested on her shoulder. You see he was just as curious about all this stuff as she was. No matter how hard they looked they could see nothing but the gray circular light at the opening of the tube. "Of course" Victoria said, "He turns this knob. He is always focusing with it while he looks in the tube." Together they take turns moving the knob back and forth. As they did, the tube moved up and down, finally shapes of hundreds of round objects came into view! She had heard her Master call these objects "cells". They were like small balloons of different sizes floating in the blood. She remembered that Doctor Bill had told a group of students that the body was made up of billions of cells of different sizes, shapes and duties to perform.

He had told his students that they were little chambers containing life's treasures. Originally, they had been called cells because they reminded one of the first men to see them through a microscope...of "the cells of little rooms that the monks lived at in the monasteries." Students would interrupt him and asked him why he had a doll on his entertainment center in his apartment they often visit by invitation. He said "Because Victoria listens to everything I teach her, that's more than what you students do." Doctor Bill's comments made her even more proud of herself than she usually was already.

Anony said, "Look, there is hundreds of little round globules that look like red balloons or more like saucers." Victoria now appeared to pause, and then said confidently that these must be the cells Doctor Bill called red blood cells. Now, she remembered that he had said that the average man had 25 million of these cells and that humans needed all of them. They were so small that one could line up thousands of them in one inch! She told Anony that she had heard Doctor Bill say that they carry the oxygen from the air that we breathe all the way to the big toe and back again! One day she would be as smart as Doctor Bill was and she told Anony she would teach him then.

Anony was curious about the fewer but much larger, white appearing cells that had dark centers of different shapes. Victoria couldn't help but feeling superior cause she could answer that question, even though she had never seen them before. You see, Victoria had been a good listener while she sat on top of the entertainment center unit during Doctor Bill's lectures. She explained, "those are the white cells; without these marvelous white blood cells to fight and try to kill any germs that get into the human body, it would be hard for humans to stay well. Remember now, when human's scratches get infected, a white, smelly substance called pus, forms and comes out of the wound. That pus is mostly an army of white cells that have mobilized to fight the war against the infecting germs. Often they eat the germs. Many of these white soldiers are lost in the battle and found in the pus. You couldn't live long either, Anony, without these marvelous white blood cells. I don't need them Anony, I don't get infected." Victoria also told him that the blood cells were floating in what was called plasma.

Doctor Bill had illustrated the Red Blood Cells, the small layer of White Blood Cells floating on the surface of the Red Blood Cells and the liquid that all the cells float in are called The Plasma. Anony got so excited that he asked "Victoria, but that's human blood. I wonder what mine looks like. " They both wanted to find out. They spent a long time trying to figure if they had the courage to cut his skin so they could collect a drop of blood. Finally, Victoria was brave enough to stick him in his foot with a pointed needle. Sure enough, a drop of blood promptly appeared, just as promptly as Anony said "Ouch!" Together they managed to spread the drop of blood on a glass slide. This was not easy because it took all the strength they had, then, to place the slide on the platform between the tube and the light. Now they knew how to adjust it or focus to see the cells. Yes, there they were! They looked just like human cells...exactly!

Anony cried out in joy "I am just like a human!" "Well, yes and no," retorted Victoria, "Seems as if your cells in the blood are the same, although I am sure mine will be even more scientific." With that response, Anony grabbed the little needle and cried 'Let's see, Victoria." Victoria bravely held out finger, Anony jabbed it; she had no pain at all, no blood appeared, and in fact the needle did not even make a hole in her finger! Anony did not realize she was made of porcelain clay, neither did she! They tried her arm, and only a small, twisted mass of thread-like material appeared. "I told you mine was different, no doubt more elegant" snapped Victoria. Together they placed the small wad of Victoria's thread on the slide and looked at it through the microscope. No cells were seen, only strands of string-like material all twisted and matted together in a hap hazard manner. This was the cotton stuffing that filled Victoria's body! "Oh dear, Oh dear, I appear to be quite a mess inside" she lamented. "No, No" Anony comforted her, "You are the most beautiful unmessy lady I have ever seen, let's look at some more slides. We'll get to you later."

Doctor Bill had an illustration of human skin as examined under the microscope. Note that, again the tissue is composed of organized cells of different types. Alas! Alas! Victoria's blood turns out to be strands of thread. After much effort, they located a slide marked "human skin" in the rear of Doctor Bill's slide box. Victoria, from listening to Doctor Bill, knew that a small piece of skin had been treated with chemicals and embedded in paraffin wax to form a solid block. This block, she knew, had been cut on a special instrument to give very thin slices of the skin. These slices were mounted then on the glass slide so that one could look at the skin under high magnification through means of the microscope. This time when she and Anony finally got the tube into focus they saw a beautiful array of cells of different types all attached to one another! "Oh how beautiful," Victoria cried! The cut section they were looking at was straight down, vertical through the skin. Anony noticed first that there were differences in the type of cells or layers. Victoria quickly explained one moved deeper into the body, the outer layer, or epidermis, as Doctor Bill called it, seemed to be granular-like, sand particles glued together. Now and then the cells formed a canal to the skin surface. The canals contained a piece of rope in each one.

Victoria said in her haughty mannerism, "That has to be a strand of hair!" Sure enough, she was right, as usual. She further explained, "Oh, see those little clusters of cells and those that form rings and tubes? They have to be sweat glands and little fat glands humans have." Deeper into the skin they saw large bodies of cells with oil-like droplets within the cells. Anony, always hungry, guessed correctly, they were fat cells. Finally they noticed a series of large cells that could branch and get smaller and smaller. Some were filled with a red fluid and some with a milky-like fluid. It didn't take him long to observe that the red one were the blood canals and Victoria then guessed that the clear ones were the separate circulatory system. She tried to remember, "Oh yes, the lymph system." It had something to do with the defense against the germs. Humans were always around germs it seemed.

Victoria then wanted to cut a small piece of Anony's skin to see how much like humans he was. When they had talked this over, they guessed it would be like a man's and they were correct! Under no condition was Anony about to let Victoria cut a piece of his skin. The needle prick was enough for him. Since Victoria felt no pain before, and perhaps they should use a sliver of her own covering. Of course, Victoria did not favor this idea, since, curiosity always won with her; she agreed to let Anony try to cut a small piece of skin from her forearm. Of course, he had instructions to stop immediately if it hurt too much. He was delighted, and with the scissors and with all feet balanced managed to snip off a piece of Victoria's skin. Surprisingly it cut easily, and again she felt no pain and there was no sign of blood, the portion was thin like paper or cloth and it folded easily. "Hum", Victoria said, "That's strange indeed!" Finally, after much effort, they got Victoria's skin sample under the microscope. "Now, Anony, you will see how regal I am. You are just a pink-eyed, white mouse with pink ears and tail," To their surprise, and to Victoria's shock, she didn't look at all like a human. Alas: Poor Victoria: Her skin, when magnified, turns out to be strands of thread woven to form cloth.

What they saw when they looked through the tube at the smear of Anony's blood: millions of these cells could easily fit on the head of a pin, Note: Many red blood cells, the much fewer and larger White blood cells. Also note that each White blood cell has a dark nucleus or central control system.

She said, "I feel like a human, I look like a human, I think like one she felt; I learn like one I know." But, all the slide showed were threads crossing side by side and up and down. Anony jumped with glee. "Your skin is like cloth people buy in a department store! You see. You are no better, if as good as I am". Victoria began to cry big sobs. Anony felt sorry for her. "Don't cry Victoria, "Remember you are as good as the best, but no better than the rest. " Victoria had learned an important lesson tonight, during her other important discoveries. Victoria dried her tears and thought she would see Doctor Bill when he got up in the morning. He would know how she could feel better. After all Anony was only a mouse. Even though she spent the entire night with him learning how to use the microscope doesn't mean he knew how to understand it. After all his name was Anony Mous and no one knows who these people are.

She returned to the entertainment center unit table where she stands so regal like and became the queen Doctor Bill said she was. She was going to make a real effort to be nicer to the dolls Miss Imelda makes and writes stories about and sends then to different places. She asked Miss Imelda to take a picture of her with Honey Girl, Mimi Lea and Johdia. She won't call them Asian immigrants anymore, except Miss Emily. She was not an immigrant;

she was an important poet, and Victoria liked to be with famous people. Emily was not very sociable but neither was Victoria, so they got along very well. She noticed on Miss Imelda's sewing table there were pieces of a white laboratory coat she must be making for her. She felt so much better about Miss Imelda now and not jealous of her attention to Doctor Bill. Victoria is so glad she never sleeps, so she does not ever forget things she learned.

It seemed morning would never come so she could see Doctor Bill. He walked toward her, and just seemed to know how perplexed she was. He picked her up and brought her into the bedroom where he sleeps. He said, "At times, Victoria, I tend to get melancholy, and when I first got to know Miss Imelda she told me of an old oak tree she used to climb up to the high branch and look out to view an expanse called a meadow. She would make believe she was a ballerina and would dance for hours. Sometimes she would talk to the animals she would meet and tell them her dreams. I go to this meadow she introduced me to now in my mind with her now and watch her dance. Then he read to her the poem "The Meadow."

THE MEADOW

When I go to The Meadow of my childhood
Momentous memories there to see
Known to me since early my years
Perhaps age seven, plus three.

Maybe former years unremembered
No matter; this place is my own
Sitting alone, awesome in wonder
Of marvelous creation shown.

Then, years add two, maybe five then
Each time frequent visits there
Special to ponder delightfully
Myself with My Self dreams share.

Wheat field golden, swaying
Light breeze lifts my gossamer dress
Once heavy cotton, homespun
Is full-circled, loose without press.

Dancing is easy in The Meadow
First a skip, frisk flutter; glide known
My world spins away, my feet seem to say
The Meadow is a place of my own.

Steps glean over cowslips or buttercups
Forget-me-nots delicately small
Alfalfa fragrant in mixed clover
Barley blends oat stems grown tall.

Wild purple violets bloom brightly

Kiss night air fragrance sweet
Red Clover mix with golden dandelions
I avoid crushing them with my feet.

No one knew me if I go to The Meadow
Childish dreams left there to rest
Full grown now I walk on tree threshold
Dreams return, yesteryears best.

One dream was always a tall Stranger
Approaching from distance so far
Sometimes I'd look for giant figure
Come closer at Meadow gate ajar.

Never no one there in The Meadow
Just fantasy, wonders full, my pretense
Only friendly fields, fine flora
Plain paradise found in a sense.

Years pass, The Meadow views dimmer
Possible dreams broken or lost
Aesthetic views change patterns
Life's blessings or blows claim their cost.

One spring, in middle of my years then
The Meadow vision returns happily
When my husband Bill and I married
He walks in The Meadow with me.

We share our fancies, or real things
"Life has been bittersweet" I said
He says, "Rest Love, peace is with you"
Strong arms around me firm spread.

Bill walks, we talk in The Meadow
What a friend, I've found at last
At times he's close I can touch him
He laughs when I dance too fast.

One autumn golden leaves in The Meadow
Fell, scatter in carrousel confusion
Bill lectures away, my Meadow different
Strange excitement, unruffled illusion.

In the distance my view sees a figure
Tall, yet steps now much closer
Walks steady with firm purpose
Real now, near meadow gate poster.

My Bill returns, steps in The Meadow
Says, "I watch you dance and careen
Alone, at times reckless abandon
Many times you are my dream.

One time young in innocence budded
Not much beyond toddler in stance
Then, taller, but smaller than woman
As little ballerina would dance.

Butterflies flit flutter past shoulder
Curious of capricious graced girl
Arms lift, graceful, just floating
First parquet; a twist, then a twirl.

Then curtsey and bow to rest then"
At my feet, tall stranger no more
"I miss you when away, so grateful
Together we sit at The Meadow's door."

Hands meet, eyes acquaint then
His big hands gentle, firm, tender
Their touch soft, protective again
Eyes clothe me in love's remember.

He respects Creator in life's stages
Man of integrity, truth is his banner
Unafraid of fierce conflict or decisions
Yet socially graceful in manner.

Our love unique close united
Talk or listen in private world wide
Of Once upon Time measured seasons
In The Meadow hands side by side.

Creator of life blest our commitment
Of union launched by Divine Hand
Near us to cheer us, to guide us
In The Meadow together planned.

If you need a hiding space special
Pick up life, gather your Love then
To windows of your mind refreshing
Bask in The Meadow's pleasure again.

Doctor Bill continues to hold Victoria close to him as he reads the last of Miss Imelda's poem. There is a knock on his bedroom door. It is Miss Imelda; she hands him a small, white laboratory coat. On the left side of the pocket is an inscription in red colors, which reads: 'Victoria' and underneath the words 'Research Student'. Doctor Bill takes it from her, slips it loosely around Victoria's shoulder carrying her gently. He puts her on top of the entertainment center. He smiles as usual at her and turns away. This is all Victoria needed for encouragement on the day she was so disheartened. She has much to learn, much to do.

Maybe someday Miss Imelda will take her to her meadow sometime too. She vowed to be much nicer to her. She discussed it with Miss Emily and she agreed it was a splendid idea. Miss Emily will be leaving soon and Victoria will miss her. Emily encouraged her and told her to "dwell in possibilities" in her research. She has Mary Irene and little Frances Ann to visit with for a little while between her studies. So many dolls have left for new homes. She will be nicer to them now, should any return or new ones brought home. She looked forward to seeing Anony after nightfall, with much to discuss and research with him. She fondled her white laboratory coat; it was so white, just like Doctor Bill's, with pockets for her notes. It has her name tag designed by Miss Imelda's grandson Bradley with a scientific logo beside her name Victoria, Research Student. Her leather briefcase, so effectively designed by her daughter Julie, holds all of Doctor Bill's illustrations he made just for her. She will enjoy her scientific research so much, and everyone will notice her new laboratory coat and briefcase that looks like no other. She must remember to thank Miss Imelda, Julie and Brad. She figures, if Master Bill loves her so much, there has to be a good reason. So, she will love her more now too!

Seek Well (Sequel) Victoria
          "What we have deeply loved, we never lose,
          all that we deeply love becomes a part of us."
          A quote from Helen Keller

Bill and I were going on our seventh year of marriage. His health was declining and his physician in New York required him to spend winters near him in Buffalo, New York since winters at the cabin where we lived may not have driveways plowed soon enough in the event he had to get medical treatment. I needed to continue employment at the library since if Bill died before I did; I needed income to support myself and my needs. We agreed to this arrangement. We talked regularly and I continued to write poetry to him. I was scheduled to visit my beloved husband right after New Years, since this last Christmas his children agreed to have the family together. I did not want to interfere with this family reunion. It was not because we were married, he just did not know.

The Saturday before Christmas Day, Bill called me throughout the day wanting to be with me. I encouraged him he just had a couple days to wait and I would be with him for New Years for three weeks vacation, and spring would soon come thereafter and he would be back home again at the cabin. I read to him a poem I had just drafted. I filed it in his poem portfolio and read again his favorite, "The Meadow."

        Years pass with Doctor Bill and
        Miss Imelda must part for winter season
        His health not as good as once was
        His Doctor advises recluse life a reason.

        For three years he goes back to New York
        Miss Imelda works in Wisconsin to wait

For return of her beloved husband
Drive up roadway to cabin's gate.

Each time he travels with Victoria
Back and forth across states constant
Along too her research companion
Anony Mous, pink mouse assistant.

Saturday eve, pre-Christmas he phoned her
"Guess where I am, beloved wife, friend
I'm in bed for the night, out my window
Soft raindrops fall off gable-end.

"Are you in the meadow?" she asks him tender
"Where we are together, though apart?"
"I'm in the Meadow" he said, "I'm there
In The Meadow of each other's heart."

They talk of this season of seasons
Of a Babe born one holy night
To bring peace to a world in darkness
Bring goodwill by His holy light.

They talk about a Christ called Jesus
Perfect, a Model for all
Talk of His love protecting
Our family's individual.

Converse of families, their children
Each unique, their own special way
Being together soon again
After this New Year's Day.

"Remember last fall" he said
Laughed and hallowed our time
Together like lover's years ago
These meetings their paradigm.

"Remember sweet spring of years
New fresh air soft breezes flow
Many laughs, a few misty tears"
Love follows wherever they go.

"Summer's alive with picnics
Lakeshores, sunsets each best"
His writings to reach out to mankind
Her poetry written by request."

"Walks in deep forest or city"

Their rapture softly caress care
As winters arrive blanketing
Diamond-stud snow here and there.

"Drives on dark forest roadways
Singing songs of old in the air"
Seven years of seasons known now
"I love you" again they share.

She tells him "I'll hug your pillow left here
When with me lay your head
Stay in "The Meadow" there without me
We'll be together soon" she said.

"We'll listen to soft raindrops
In our forest wilderness room
Coyotes howl messages clear
Busy bats fly pass your tool room.

Come home soon, darling, dearest"
Couples talk together hours at ease
Christmas will be in one more day
Today share love's best memories.

Confirm benefit of raindrop showers
Bill esteemed simple joys of life
Experienced at forest cabin all hours
Since married husband and wife.

No desire to be elsewhere, not any
"I love you" again they share
Dancing together in the meadow
In their dreams together there.

This night in Bill's apartment, Victoria
Could not go to Bill's laboratory
Bill missed Miss Imelda so much
He takes Victoria to bed, tells story.

Desire for Miss Imelda increases
Each year greater than last
They have so much fun together
With her is less downcast.

He tells Victoria he is grateful
To tell her how he can feel
She is his queen always to seem
His confidante daily, like real.

Tonight her Doctor is drowsy
Closes eyes, tells her his love
Well beyond any friend in this city
Rain drops outside gable above.

Recalls in cabin they enjoy raindrops
Whisper soft on their love best
Victoria remains on his pillow
Doctor Bill's hand on her chest.

She never was in his bed before
Being near her Doctor Bill at best
At dawn can't feel wrist pulse beat
In morning early, Victoria depressed.

Her red heart feels pain's heat
His arm moves not, nor his chest
Victoria stays as Doctor Bill placed her
Bewildered, thoughts show new interest.

Strangers come in Doctor Bill's bedroom
Take him away, leaves her on pillow, unsure
Anony runs to her in Bill's bedroom
She sits up holds him in her lap, obscure.

Pair puzzled on Doctor Bill's pillow
Misunderstand mishap so weird
This storm within, winds billow
Is it Bill's Scottish fellow "Misleard?"

Molly telephones Miss Imelda her husband Bill was found dead in his apartment on December 24, Sunday morning. A nurse in residence there knew Bill; wondered why he hadn't picked up his Sunday paper nor answer his phone. Miss Imelda told her she had talked to Bill many times the Saturday before Christmas having had several beautiful phone conversations and said "goodnight." Bill's sons had him cremated; he would be buried next to their mother. The death certificate showed Bill never remarried. Miss Imelda was numb with grief and confusion. Molly said if she came to Buffalo she and husband Vinny who would attend the funeral with me. I discussed it with my children here in Wisconsin and we agreed Bill was already cremated. They would help me have a memorial here in Wisconsin. I thought that was wise counsel and had memorial services in my own church.

Molly asked Bill's son Jeff for Miss Imelda's possessions and she was given his doll Victoria. Imelda wrote a poem for his Doll Victoria. She made Victoria another laboratory coat and sent it to Molly to replace the one that was missing. She also sent her a new Anony Mous restored and painted by daughter Julie, with pink eyes, ears and long pink tail.

Victoria now lives with Molly and next to her dolls Frances Ann and Mary Irene. For the most part, she is in Molly's laboratory with Anony and his family. She wears her new lab coat inscribed in red and green, "Victoria: Research Student." Daughter Julie designed her leather briefcase with a smaller name tag. It holds Doctor Bill's original drawings and descriptions of a microscope, skin, blood and plasma.

In apartment door walks Molly
Miss Imelda's daughter dear
Picks up Victoria his doll gently
In Doctor Bill's N.Y. bedroom here.

She takes Victoria and gently
Says, "Doctor Bill has gone away
Where people go no longer living
He talked to Miss Imelda last Saturday.

Come home with me, Victoria
Dolls Frances Ann and Mary Irene
Will comfort loss of Doctor Bill
Grief will be less then between.

Dreams in you will return, if you will
I work in research laboratory new
A microscope resembles Doctor Bill's
To continue research with Anony too.

I invite Miss Imelda out to visit
For weeks as long as she can
We can start for you more family
As life with Doctor Bill began.

Memories can resurface
Love given you unusual, tender
No one loved you as he did
His dreams filed in your 'Remember."

Miss Imelda's words penned poetry
Calms your absence of Doctor Bill
His Spirit surrounds your Spirit
Rejoins happily as you will.
...
Sometime in the night raindrops
Became snow when he was asleep
Blankets his mortal body
Silent as mute Sister of Sleep.

At cabin field coyotes howling
As they did many times before
Seems his last word to Imelda sighs
'Darling I won't see you anymore.'

God's hand closed his eyes in a bedroom

Gently shuts "The Meadow's" doors
...Rest well beloved husband
Devoted friend to Victoria, yours.

The Prince of Peace, the Good Shepherd
Say's Earth's life is not the end
One day in "The Meadow of Meadows"
On golden streets of heaven's bend.

Smell fragrance of a Rose of Sharon
God's beauteous gardens behold
Perched on moon flower's wide petals
Sits Research Student Victoria bold!

That day we'll rise to be chosen
By the King of Kings, God's son
To live for eternity in heaven
Where new lives really begun.

You'll counsel Scientist of the City
In chambers of knowledge unknown
Your questions unanswered answered
Body temples, immortal then grown.

Your ache for the lone and afflicted
Soothed by Great Physician of time
Weary no more, forevermore
Where to heaven's hills you climb.

View valleys, rippled rivers, dense forest
Embrace loved ones among flora
In "Many Meadows" voices singing
Ethereal, eternal bright aura.

I'll join you in Golden Meadows
When called from earth, "it's time"
To meet you again as I did long ago
Toward you my spirit will climb.

Where loved ones forever will see
No tears, fears, suffer no more
In Meadow of Paradise we'll be
Research new worlds to soar.

For now apart, my beloved Bill
With our dolls choice each one apart
Dream dreams of us together where
Our love is buried in our heart.

CHAPTER 9. HANNA

"Be not the slave of your own past plunge into the sublime seas, dive deep and swim far,
so you shall come back with self-respect, with new power
with an advanced experience that shall explain and overlook the old."
A quote from Ralph Waldo Emerson

Dearest Frank:

I look like a doll, I act like a doll, but more than that I am a replica reminder of the Great Lakes and Long Ships passing...ore cargo barge freighters. Through open water I sail with fear and fortune. I anchor in deep fathoms seas, frenzied waters, beneath a magic and mysterious sky. My blue and white-channeled dress reminds you of chiseled features of white wave drifts and wild, gusty winds. My frosted lace could be wind-whipped sea spray. My cheeks resemble the gentle smell of waves lapping the immense freighters on the "inland seas" of the Great Lakes you sailed. Perhaps when you return to your home, the moonlight may shine in my face to look like the solid seal of a moon seen on great waters. When you see my apron, over my gathered dress, you will be reminded of tons of waters plunging over cascades of waterfalls along craggy cliffs jutting out of the shorelines. My red lips purse like wild roses hugging lakeshore bushes rambling through meadow marsh field grasses waving to sunny marigold borders. Since the only boat she can remember you piloted is the S.S .Hanna, I am named after this ship. I hope you will like having me around.

Miss Imelda designed me just for you, as your travels all across the sea took you to places foreign; many of no doubt were Asian by descent. Surely you met some with dark hair and white skin, pretty Geisha girls, like me! Maybe that is why my face, hands and feet are called China glass, because they made my body parts. I have many sister 'dolls' that Miss Imelda has dressed and found homes for.

So, my design is almost finished. Miss Imelda just sewed the pearl droplet on my apron. She hopes it will remind you of droplets of dew forming on the boat railings, or oval moon drifts across the sheer night sky, or pellets of cargo stored in the belly of ore ships. Or, perhaps ornaments of achievement you won on your climb as a pilot seafarer Captain in your chosen carrier directing on-hands sailors on deck, dock, helm, hatch and mast. Of to the seas, Captain Frank, the clouds or waters wait for us. The clawing winds do not make us hesitate, we hold steadfast and resolve our differences I the gold minds of thoughtful patterns that bind us.

Before we take to the sea, I found this verse telling of the friendship between you and Miss Imelda. So, our readers understand how close you two have been through the years.

BROTHER FRANK....AND ME

Big brother Frank when I was small
Age apart not much one year past
We grew close together knit

Personalities contrast
Much to learn, much to see
Brother Frank and me.

Years pass too quickly, though we think
Growing time is slow to pass
Teen years our worlds ours then
Frank to Wild West by railway fast
Much to learn, much to see
Brother Frank left me.

Into a cowboy's life he rode
Lived on prairies lone and wide
Learning from Life, good and bad
I missed him deep inside
Much to learn, much to see
Brother Frank, remember me.

My life not gifted so carefree
As his in style for men
Unbound by convention, tradition
I stumble again and then
Much to learn, much to see
I long for Brother Frank and me.

War tore family's limb from limb
Frank answers America's call
Served her well, joined sea ranks
Sailed oceans nautical
Much to learn, much to see
Brother Frank, proud by me.

Sadness crept into my life
Voyage from home I carried
An unborn child, bitter born
Afraid, alone, unmarried
Much to learn, much to see
Brother Frank, there for me.

Wars pass, personal or otherwise
Love of sea in Frank claimed
Him Captain Pilot on Great Lakes
New family for him claimed
Much to learn, much to see
Brother Frank, separate we.

Careers and children older now
Land claims my brother's trade
He married, me too, more family

Good fruit, as parents made
Much to learn, much to see
Brother Frank and me.

Wilderness you loved, now I know
Deep forest voices wild
These you knew years ago
When we parted, me a child
Much to learn, much to see
Brother Frank, think tenderly.

Should your years tinged with care
Long for wild coyotes wail
Or miss meadow's buttercups
Silver moon, star studded trail
Much to learn, much to see
Brother Frank, visit me.

We'll walk the railroad ties again
We'll climb tall old oak tree
We'll picnic along wild riverbank
We'll talk, we'll disagree
Much to learn, much to see
Brother Frank and me.

If life on earth holds promise
If our life here bittersweet
What life for us beyond beyond?
At Eternity entrance meet
Much to learn, much to see
Brother Frank, be with me.

He said, wise Master said, He did
In a Book written divine
Full of Wisdom we can know
Unanswered answers combine.
Much to learn, much to see
Brother Frank, read with me.

When my life is over, when
My Spirit goes to meet
My God, my prayer will lift up high
For loved ones there, complete
Much to learn, much to see
Is Brother Frank and me.

HANNA

I'm aboard!
Nautical am I to navigate
Ride white bouncing main
Sail imaginary winds
Swelled by hurricane!

Dress white, blue and white
Remind of water not motionless
Or ice chisels, crystallite
Or lighthouse lights access.

Or mist bound under skies dim
I recall sweet sigh inland sea
Of whiteness ever winding
Clear, full sight of me!

My apron streaks lavender
Glitter splash of sunset blaze
Deep blue forms bridge fast asleep
Fog hushed, in peeping haze.

Or ziggy-zaggy coastlines
Carved cliffs break new ice
Dunes like powder snowdrifts
Stained rocks paint caves Paradise.

My green hearts pass blue ones
Seek to join earth and sea
Pine, birch and maple trees
White-capped waves filigree.

My sleeves, like clouds, billow
Over awkward, huge, ore boats
Submerged in Great Lakes depths
Calls Superior Sea promotes.

Demanding competitor doll, am I
As sea dogs camp huge ships
Mysterious union of Soul secrets
At mercy of harsh wave, wind whips.

My cap balloons curled patterns
Of waves curl huge or wide
Upon "Seas of Sweet Water"
Captain Frank controls wave-guide.

These long and latitudes we travel
Vessel on seas unforgiving
Ghosts of ships not done well

Some crew no longer living.

Sailing winds insufferable
Story of fleets vanished told
Galaxies shiver, lights winking
Lighthouse warns blink bold.

Ore boats float forward, onward
Officer, mates, ore-boat crews
Drive ore wealth on water's implant
Company orders start sail, refuse.

Ore freighters pierce Nature
On gateway to oceans vast
To portages old, little me, bold
Become's Neptune's enthusiast!

My presence to you floods legions?
Of memories long, long past
Of ships undulate dote on wide sea
In deep blue kingdoms vast.

My tresses silken, shiny
Like sandy beaches we view
Don't overlook me tiny
I sail with my Captain too.

We view clear on shoreline
Tangled with driftwood adrift
Plunged by angry sea strew
Curious tourist may lift.

My blue eyes shine beams bright
Like lighthouse unveiled in mist
Fogged by gauze-winged angels
Dodge whistle blinks missed.

Pearl bisque I am in whiteness
Fragile strength holding on calm
Fast snow and sleet hurtle ore boat
A sailor ponders wonders wherefrom.

Will I bring cadence of movement?
Flow smooth, as boats often do
Midst gulls of wet sea viewing
Long ships in Great Lakes blue.

Can I barge, carrying kindness?
Dispatch love to a brother?

Transmit tenderness to convey
Once friendship like no other.

Set sail with me believing
A Cutter, as I, can agree
To smack a packet of memories
On Superior Sea, You and Me.

Ketch glimpse of delightful pictures
When guests visit port-of-call
Not a mirage me a mapmaker
Contained in your porcelain doll.

Later…

Captain Frank boards a taxi boat
Visit friends at lighthouse living
Across long bay the only way
Friendship choice in giving.

He takes me boxed, his gift
Carefully, thoughtfully made
No place safe to store me
Sail past ice caves melted cascade.

Land lakeshore of lighthouse
Takes me, boxed on house stair
Visits his friends with family
Husband and wife, a little girl there.

Afternoon past time upon us
He leaves lighthouse visit then
Forgets me inside a box, on steps
I lay still, quiet again, when.

A big noise I hear against lighthouse
Wind gusts fearful speeds rise
As Great Lakes Big Storm notorious
Poor me alone, glass, small size!

Sprays hurl over tall tower
Sea waves hit rocks aground
What if I am washed by the sea?
What if I never will be found!

Swift shoreline waves hold secrets
Deep loss perish in harsh blow
Did my Captain arrive shore safely?
Will I see him again to know?

More waves plummet in sequence
Three billows after each other
Shake me near my old box
Down one step, down another!

I land, propped by small window
View swells so high and wide
My little red heart frightens
I know to be scared inside.

Is land traffic paralyzed, I wonder
Unsafe for Captain's friends to come
To lighthouse steps, to interior
Find me frazzled, undone?

Stories of Sea Lake, said My Captain
Records anxiety, misery and loss
Damage caused by Big Storms
Names list in legends across.

No survivors tells story of horror
Newspapers write pages of boats
Hit by gales, vessels all lost
Driven ashore, sunk; record notes.

Ore carriers of Hanna fleet mentioned
Desperate battle to keep afloat
Lost entire crew, bow above water
I muse, story as this, with no lifeboat.

Handicaps these hard to handle
Gone my Captain's warm embrace
Not his strong hands to hold me
Absent kind looks on his face.

Night passed again, darkness darker
My view propped on cold stair
Of lighthouse, who lost her light?
No human knows how to care.

Dawn peeks through my window
Dry now from once waves so high
I hear faint steps near lighthouse door
It opens, I hear a little girl sigh.

She picks me up to hold me
My fears gone an instant for sure
Her parents come in to get her

Tell her "put me on stair secure."

Averse, hugs tight to loose me
Little girl's little tears fall fast
She does not have her own doll
To love, to talk too, is downcast.

My arm caught in her sleeve then
I could not bear her to go
She places me careful back on stair
I feel lost, again, do they know?

Days pass two, and one more
Waves no longer reach high
I hear steps near lighthouse
In my loneliness, again, I sigh.

Door swings wide, and wider
My Captain stands there so tall!
He did not forget me, "He missed me!"
His Hanna, his porcelain doll.

His arms hold a Dolly different
With curls around her sweet face
He carries us out of the lighthouse
I see the little girl closer in place.

My Captain reaches for her hand
To place there for her, her new doll
In gratitude for taking care of me
So down lighthouse steps didn't fall.

Little girl's eyes bright and happy
To think this new Dolly will be
Hers forever, I know I could not be
It's only Captain Frank for me!

Back to boat taxi from lighthouse
Not in a gift box no more to lie
But in the arms of my own Captain
Happiness waves cover me high.

Together we approach land shore
"I am so happy" is all I can say
Beyond me waves wave the same
Winter break soon over causeway.

Glassy sea blueness again to claim
Inland waters for us will wait

Captain Frank and Hanna by name!
He walks me to crow's nest gate!

CHAPTER 10. REBEKAH

"It takes a strong person to say "I'm sorry,
and an even stronger person to forgive."
A quote unknown

Dearest Miss Imelda:
I am hoping you consider me a "select" friend when you complete your Doll book, 'Personolly Yours," as I would love to have one to add to my Doll Library. I have over 1,000 dolls, range in size from one inch to 38" and from 1800's to the character dolls of today such as John Wayne, WC Fields, Groucho Marx, Marilyn Monroe, Mae West, and Louie Armstrong. My collection started as a result of my daughter who had at least one doll. She always had many dolls and when people returned from far off places she got at least one doll which started a collection of my own. I will be looking forward to hearing from you; I don't say that to anyone!   Love Bonnie

My Dear Bonnie:
"My, but I am excited, Miss Imelda is packing me up, ready to go, and she is packing herself too! She is going to see New York, New York with Bill, and I am going with her! All this time I was sure I was going to live with you in Michigan. You have waited so long, just a little while longer, please. She will be going to New York City with her husband while he attends cancer research lectures. She will also have the opportunity to meet with her brother Frank who is at the Navy base not far from there. What will this ever do with me? I don't know I will have to wait to find out! Miss Imelda will tell you about it in her poem. I am really excited about is coming to live with you and all the very important dolls you have in your collection. I know will become one of the many. I hope they will like me. I know you will like me because Miss Imelda says you will love me. I can hardly wait. My name is Rebekah.
One-day
Bill and I arrive at the Bentley Upper East Side Hotel which is only a ten minute walk to the Memorial Sloan Kettering Cancer Center. He will be meeting with scientists most of the day and I told him I would be contacting my brother Frank at the nearby military Navy base in Saratoga Springs, New York. Frank has good and bad news he said. I did not tell Bill about bringing my doll Rebekah; she is wrapped in my terrycloth housecoat unseen.
Twos-day
My brother Frank contacts me by phone at the lobby hotel; with an appointment at 2:00 pm for only one hour.   He tells me he has located our sister Rebekah and he wants us to meet her together. She does not know I am in New York City. He will arrange it and call me. Don't forget the doll, he says.
Mends-day
Frank calls; he will bring Rebekah to Central Park tomorrow at 2:00 pm. at the tulip beds in Shakespeare's Garden. Rebekah is very fond of tulips and likes to read Shakespeare. He says, "Tomorrow put the doll on the park bench and hide behind the tree behind the park bench. Don't let anyone take the doll."
Hers-day

I tell Bill I will take a cab to Central Park and meet my brother Frank and my sister Rebekah at Shakespeare's Garden. He will be in lectures again all day so wished me a good time. I am dropped off at the Central Park Conservatory Information Desk and transportation is provided to me to arrive at Shakespeare Garden. I am early at 1:30. I see the park bench and put Rebekah next to me. At 1:45 pm I am to leave the doll alone. I see Frank approach the Garden. Rebekah is as beautiful as ever. She strides over to the park bench and picks up Rebekah. It is amazing Rebekah looks just like her. She holds her tight and starts to cry. Frank sits with her and then beckons to me behind her back to come to the park bench. She is shocked to see me and wants to walk away. Frank brings her back, still holding the doll, and says he has something to tell both of us. Our Father, Melvin is dying and he asks Frank to find his lost daughter Rebekah. She has been gone a long time. With much searching and private contacts Frank finds out she is being supported by a wealthy business man in Brooklyn who does not allow her to go anywhere or do anything socially with anyone except with him privately. She would like to leave, but does not have the funds. I asked her why she was attracted to the doll Rebekah and she said she had a doll at home as a child; this doll looked like herself. She wanted to return home and start over; go to school or something. She would talk to the doll about her feelings years ago and when she ran away she gave the doll to Miss Imelda. This was a total surprise to Miss Imelda. She could only surmise Rebekah, in her long absence from home, imagined it in a dream and believed it. I did not tell her the doll was promised to my friend in Michigan. I promised Rebekah I would try to get the funds for her from my husband. Frank told her he would help her with some of his stipend from the Navy. She must not tell her companion but did not want to be supported by him anymore. I told her she can justify her leaving because of another man and that was close to the truth. Of course, the other man was our Father, very ill asking for her. She agreed to meet us at Shakespeare's Garden on Sunday at 2:00 pm while her suitor was still at work. I told her she could hold the doll all the way back home.
My-day
I arrive back at the hotel just at the time Bill comes from his lectures. He asked me out to dinner and I was elated since it would be easier to discuss my situation with Frank and Rebekah in a public place. During dinner I explained the situation with Rebekah. Bill was reluctant to get involved since it was dangerous in weird situations of intimate involvements. I asked him to think it over since he was very wise in solving problems.
Satters-day
Bill does not have any more lectures to give or attend and we are preparing to leave New York. I asked him if we could stay one more night since Rebekah was to meet Frank and me again at the Shakespeare Garden in Central Park. Since we were driving back to Wisconsin he agreed to stay one more day. He said if Rebekah returns to Minnesota he will contribute to her education as long as she remains in school. I was so elated; eager to assure Frank that Bill offered to help support her to go to school. He is such a darling.
Suns-day
Sunday morning we are packed and ready to go. Frank has called and Rebekah will be at Central Park. I was reluctant to leave Bill at the Information Desk alone but he decided to wait to see if Rebekah would be coming alone with Frank and me. I took the doll Rebekah and got a ride to the Shakespeare Garden and Rebekah and Frank were waiting for me. I gave her the dolly which she hugged so hard and would not let her go. She had no luggage but for a small handbag. I was proud of her; she had made her first attempt to leave her life here behind. Frank rode with us back to the Information Desk, shook hands with Bill and said he had to get back to the base. He had only a short leave time from the base since he was asking personal emergency leave to go to Minnesota to be with Dad since he was

getting worse. Bill assured him he would be taking the girls to Minnesota as soon as possible. I gave Rebekah a tablet of loose leaf paper and asked her to write something to our Dad in case we didn't make it in time.

Two days later Bill and I and Rebekah arrive at our log cabin in the woods, only to refresh ourselves overnight and ready ourselves for the four hour trip to Minnesota to see my Dad now in the hospital. Frank is there and has told him he has found Rebekah and Miss Imelda and her husband Bill will be bringing her to see him. He seemed to feel better, even sat up in bed and smiled. Frank stayed with him all night, when he woke up on occasion he could still see Frank.

Rebekah and Miss Imelda arrived that afternoon. Frank and Miss Imelda left her alone with our Dad. She was there three hours. When we knocked on his hospital room she was holding Dad in her arms. He was at peace as she held him in her arms; both asleep. Frank said we had both arrived in time.

Later, Rebekah had the notebook I had given her on our trip back to the Midwest. She said she was writing my Doll Rebekah's story. After our Father's funeral she would finish the story. She asked not to return my Doll Rebekah; she wanted to keep her until registration at the University this fall. I agreed. I assured hear my sweet husband Bill had already made his quarterly payment at the University. She said she also made application for grants suggested by the Registrar. She signed up for a teaching career for children grade two and three. Frank hugged her and said he was so proud of her. We all are. By the time fall came Rebekah had the Doll wrapped very carefully for me to ship to my friend Bonnie in Michigan. She was looking forward to her classes with a full schedule she thinks she can handle. After she gave me the doll I handed her a book on the "Complete Works of Shakespeare" which she liked.   Rebekah's poem is below.

REBEKAH'S PORTALS

The hospice hall near Papa's room seat siblings all thirteen,
Accomplished now by the last somehow, one wayward libertine
Singled out by last request, assembled by Father's plead
His last bid, proud invalid, to fill his dying need.

She sat upon the cold, hard chair, her scarlet dress hem fell
Its flashy line in bold design, revealed Rebekah well
Erotic idols courted she, unmoved in dearth desire
An unholy flame, she became sin's ragged robes on fire.

Slim form forms heathen goddess, loved woe-begone to site
Profits pay priced decay as lady of the night
Rebekah ponders Papa sent petitions of fervent plea
To help regain her noble name from wrongs in ashes be.

Brother signals her entry to ailing Father's bed
Her rightful space in eleventh place, she walks with fear ahead
The door closed behind her. Papa's drowsy body wakes
Rebekah's gait, from hurried wait, dead silence overtakes.

His frail hands fragile now she clasps to her bosom's fold
Her lips caress his feebleness in gentleness to hold

"Oh Papa! I'm here now, Papa! I should have come before
What can I say to repay years I did ignore?"

Illness curbs his voice so still, eyes glad her closeness nigh
Lures light to rise in Rebekah eyes, her greeting a goodbye
"Oh dearest Papa, I yearned for you when I was wrong
Pain filled years, crying tears longing to belong.

I loved you when so very small when frail my form was seen
I loved you, Papa, to and through our bitterness between
Not once to me, dear Papa, your love did you express"
She kisses now his ashen brow, "Do you love me Papa, yes?"

"My sordid life so weary, your mercy now I plead
For all my shame on your good name for all my own misdeed"
Rebekah's Papa visions her, figures seemed to show
Silk dress pearl-white like stars so bright, fair face, soft cameo.

Brown eyes unfallen innocence, long hair spun gold again
His little girl, without a curl, runs to him from the glen
Thin arms entwine around his neck, full lips feel cheeks of tan
Her timid voice his special choice, gifted a countryman.

Rebekah's Papa's eyes opaque search his daughter's face
Resembling faint beneath the paint a classic Mother's trace
In strength's last effort Papa breathed garbled broken cries
"Condemn me not, no matter what" words muffled agonize.

His shallow breath, in feinted smile her forgiveness he needs so
His love inside spills outside beyond his vertigo
Her gentle arms lift circled now, waste frame so weak
Breast laced in red holds Papa's head, time short in which to speak.

"I'm sorry, Papa, Papa, my bitter life has cast
Tarnished stain to remain love's prodigal outcast"
Mercy fills a sickened room, pardoned floods convene
Papa's words unsaid to a girl in red healing Grace has seen.

Papa grips her crimson dress to draw her closer still
As if to lease joy's inner peace, forgiveness does fulfill
Rebekah's guilty burden lifts wrapped in Heaven's care
Sin's release God's masterpiece softened in repair.

Rebekah's healing Spirit joins sheer radiance in her face
"Oh Papa, dear, she whispers near, "You're going to a hallowed place
Where Mama greets your coming, more beautiful than before
When her you meet, my love entreat, take to the Golden Shore.

Then, Papa, listen, Papa, a message you must bear

Gethsemane our legacy remembered by her prayer
Once more, I love you, Papa; don't wait this journey's glow"
Richly proud she prays out loud "I'll love you where you go."

Papa's body quiet breathes last upon the chest
Of a daughter come, once burdensome, last at his final rest
In repose, she placed his sleeping on winter's solstice season
Time to go through the portico of life renewed in reason.

Rebekah, evening's lady, reborn from sin's grave tomb
This tale to tell means all is well consumed by her heirloom
Out of door of death hears chorus music angels knew
No crimson dress, no adulteress, hearing Papa's "I love you."

My dear, dear Miss Imelda:

How lovely "Rebekah" is---what a pleasant surprise to come home to! I had been to the flea market at Shipshewana all day and came home hot and tired to be greeted by your parcel which I opened and was greeted by Rebekah's sweet smile and dressed so beautiful, like she was about to attend a "Cotillion." I did see her shiny little heart and could tell it was pulsating with love. What a poignant poem!! I could feel, actually feel, what was being felt in the poem! You have such a way with words. If and when you have your book published I'd love to buy one so please, let me know.

I really do love Rebekah. And I say Thank You, Thank You, Thank You, from my heart. I have over 1,000 dolls, but I or Richard bought them all, with the exception of a couple sent me by a friend in Australia and ones sent from friends in South Africa and Zimbabwe and have very few of anything given to me. When I do receive something I truly treasure it, and when someone has taken the time to sew it or sew on something for it that makes it more special, and you have done it all with Rebekah. She was welcomed by all of the dolls, none were jealous for they know that in my eyes they are all very special for their own individual reasons It was a joyous reaction and all telling her what beautiful curls she had. They and the bears decided to throw her a "welcome party" and she was so pleased to be welcomed as warmly as she was a bit nervous and tired after her trip. Richard took a large Grandfather clock case, which lacked a movement and made me a very nice showcase for some dolls. Rebekah will be one of them standing in the clock renovation. Love and Hugs.Bonnie

CHAPTER 11. CARA

"Love conquers all things; let us too surrender to love."
A quote by Virgil

Dearest Jean:
I have so much love for you, as you can see it spills over on my dress! I love you...I love you...all over. Then, in my basket is the real story of love, as it is written in a book both you and Miss Imelda know so much...The Holy bible. My poem makes it easy to say and feel since I am Cara, your little girl. Since you and your husband Robin have three sons, I will be

special as the only girl in your immediate family. So I will get lots of attention, and when and if they marry their children will grow to love me very much since I love little children. We think the same way and image lovely thoughts. We live close to belief.

When I become a part of your family, we will remember the extended family I came from and all my doll sisters I have grown to love through the months of waiting to come and live with you. There is Emily, Rebekah, Honey Girl, Mimi Lea, Hanna, Dolly, Honey Carol, Nicole, Laura, Hanna, Jennie, Imelda and of course, Karina, who patiently lays in her basket with no legs for months already. She was broken in transit here. Miss Imelda's daughter Marianne is very skilled in molding new ballerina legs and feet for her since she makes rag dolls commercially. So Karina's leg and feet dreams will soon come true.   That is a very big dream when you don't have any legs.   When I am gifted to you, there will be other dolls I won't have the privilege to know, but someday I will. I have grown to love them like sisters, extended sisters, like you and Miss Imelda are. I love you very much, will you love me too?
Cara

CARA

My dress all red with words
"I love you" in every thread
"Red and white, I'm a delight
For all, children too," I said.

My dress white lace borders
Hems, sleeves, straw hat too
Why I'm sewn with love above
For your family and you.

My basket holds red hearts painted
Words that love should mean
My poem below will show
Description explained between.

What is love? Holy Bible, verse four
1st Corinthians, Chapter thirteen old
Will satisfy man's needs more
In this book the Bible told.

Stories written very old
Of people big and small
Bible story too has told
Live Golden Rule for all.

"Love is patient, enduring, calm
Composed tranquil, serene
Tolerant, don't complain between
Not jealous, filled with envy mean.

Not boastful, proud, not haughty

Love demands not our own way
Not selfish, rude, that's naughty
Love irritates not any day.

If holds grudges stored away
When others wrong, use zeal
Learn forgiveness each day
Be lovers of truth, honest, real.

Oppose unjust action in court
Think truth always wise
Lies damage, wound, harm families
Tear reputations down hard to rise.

Burdens innocently accused
False witness harbor truth lost
Be loyal to loved ones
Doesn't measure value cost?

Those who left never return
May not be forever astray
Encourage them if needed
Defend, help them today.

Practice kindness in all things
Is part of Creator's plan?
What if Holy Bible was never read?
By Buddhist or Muslim clan?

Will you love them as God said?
Created as man kind of man
Or if an Atheist living
Was harmed by fellow man.

In their lives by Christians
Where is Love's sanctity?
Or if a woman homeless
No place to dwell, no job to see.

How will Love find them?
Their tale miserable long view
What if man is falsely accused?
Of wrong he did not do.

False witnesses go free
Prison walls unjustly knew
Judgments made in unison
Shameful actions added too.

Brand those in ragged clothes
Find those desperate breed
Show them love by Christian
Muslim or Atheist's creed.

Can love cover these in need?
At nightfall, stars at night
Glisten, shine, glow beams
Creator of Universe is right.

Loves unconditional it seems
Searches hearts of those on Earth
Records thoughts, memories
All lives, since their birth.

Secrets unknown by these
Who judges false their plight?
Knows not God of Universe
May claim them this very night.

So love all those you know
Follow Truth, Life and the Way
Church doors closed to some
Their self righteousness convey.

Dominate thinking supposed
Of another's opinion profess
Life on earth may be measured
By Holy Spirit's valued assess.

I ponder different wonder
Opinions consider disclosed
Research of quotes varied penned
Some listed below disposed.

Concepts of love's beauty cast
Individual quotes of love flow
May remain in hearts steadfast
Even a Dolly does know!

What is love in conclusion?
Is all what Holy Bible writes
Summed in other quotes saying
Written individual foresights.

"Love has no conditions. when we put conditions,
when we put barriers and boundaries, then we lose love.
Love is condition-less, love is barrier-less.
Look at the moon, stars, trees;

Just on for everyone.
When our love also flows for
Everyone, you become very natural"
Puja Swamiji,

"The one who loves all intensely begins perceiving
in all living beings a part of himself.
He becomes a lover of all,
a part and parcel of the Universal Joy.
He flows with the stream of happiness,
and is enriched by each soul. "
(Yajur Veda) Hindu

"Islam and Sufism are one. Teaching that
to understand Islam one must be a lover,
how can one understand Islam?
when the heart is empty of love."
— Zarina Bibi

"Hatred does not cease by hatred, but only by love;
this is the eternal rule. If you truly loved yourself,
you could never hurt another. Peace comes from within.
Do not seek it without."

"Resolve to be tender with the young,
Compassionate with the aged,
Sympathetic with the striving
and tolerant with the weak and wrong.
Sometime in your life, you will have been all of these."

"Love and compassion are necessities, not luxuries.
Without them humanity cannot survive.
. Love is the absence of judgment.Give the ones you love wings to fly,
roots to come back and reasons to stay.
Love and Compassion are the true religions to me.
But to develop this, we do not need
to believe in any religion."

"This is my simple religion. No need for temples.
No need for complicated philosophy. Your own mind,
your own heart is the temple. Your philosophy is simple kindness.
"All major religion teaches us traditions carry basically;
the same message that is love, compassion and forgiveness. .
. the important thing is they should be part of our daily lives."

"The whole purpose of religion is to facilitate love
and compassion, patience, tolerance, humility, and forgiveness.
The greatest obstacles to inner peace are disturbing emotions
such as anger, attachment, fear and suspicion, while love and compassion

and a sense of universal responsibility is the sources of peace and happiness."

All above quotes from the Dali Lama

Even Helen Keller, who was born blind and deaf,
could see God. No doubt, in her silent darkness,
every fragrant flower, every ray of the warm sun,
every taste that touched her tongue told her that
there was a God who created all things. Jodie Foster
shouldn't therefore be surprised that people
are surprised that she's an atheist.
Ray Comfort

As an atheist, I am angry that we live in a society in which
the plain truth cannot be spoken
without offending 90% of the population.
Sam Harris

Mr. Speaker, the fact of the matter is that the Ten Commandments
are a historical document that contains moral, ethical,
and legal truisms that any person of any religion
or even an atheist can recognize and appreciate.
Cliff Stearns

In America, now, let us - Christian, Jew, Muslim, agnostic, atheist,
Wiccan, whatever - fight nativism with the same strength and conviction
that we fight terrorism. My faith calls on its followers to love one's enemies.
A tall order, that - perhaps the tallest of all.
Jon Meacham

if you look within the United States,
religion seems to make you a better person.
Yet atheist societies do very well –
better, in many ways, than devout ones.
Paul Bloom

"With or without religion, you would have good people
doing good things and evil people doing evil things.
But for good people to do evil things,
that takes religion."
Steven Weinberg

You don't have to be brave or a saint, a martyr,
or even very smart to be an atheist
All you have to be able to say is
"I don't know"."
Penn Jillette

Surprise of being loved.

It is God's finger on man's shoulder.
~Charles Morgan

"Love has no desire but to fulfill itself.
To melt and be like a running brook
that sings its melody to the night.
To wake at dawn with a winged heart
and give thanks for another day of loving."
Khalil Gibran

"Let your love be like
the misty rains, coming softly,
but flooding the river."
Malagasy Proverb

"Love is an act of endless forgiveness
Love must be as much a light, as it is a flame."
Henry David Thoreau

"Love is a tender look which becomes a habit".
Peter Ustinov

"Love makes your soul crawl
out from its hiding place"
"Smile at each other, smile at your wife,
smile at your husband, smile at your children,
smile at each other -- it doesn't matter who it is –
- and that will help you to grow up
in greater love for each other."
Mother Teresa, Catholic Nun

"That best portion of a good man's life;
his little, nameless, unremembered
acts of kindness and love."
William Wordsworth, English Poet

"You cannot do a kindness too soon because you
never know how soon it will be too late."
Ralph Waldo Emerson

"I've learned that people will forget what you said,
people will forget what you did,
but people will never forget how you made them feel.
The thing to do, it seems to me, is to prepare yourself so you
or you can be a rainbow in somebody else's cloud.
Somebody who may not look like you.
May not call God the same name you call God –
if they call God at all. I may not dance your dances
or speak your language.

But be a blessing to somebody.
That's what I think."

"A bird doesn't sing
because it has an answer,
it sings because it has a song."

"My great hope is to laugh as much as I cry; to get my work done
and try to love somebody and have the courage
to accept the love in return. You can't forgive without loving.
And I don't mean sentimentality.
I don't mean mush.
I mean having enough courage
to stand up and say, 'I forgive. I
I'm finished with it.'
Maya Angelo

"The truth is rarely pure and never simple"
Oscar Wilde

...

What is love in conclusion?
Is all what Holy Bible writes
Summed in other quotes saying
Written individual foresights.

Seek within love's treasures
Display tokens best you recall
Scaled by Creator's measures
Suggests Cara, your loving doll.

CHAPTER 12. JOY / FAITH / HEAVEN

"Sometimes your joy is the source of your smile,
But sometimes your smile can be the source of your joy."
A quote from Thích nhất Hạnh

Dearest Julianne:

Twilight is just beginning to place shades of shadows on the woods. Small, night lights for wee ones, like me, who like to wish very hard. Then, I heard the telephone ring, it sounds like bells. I love bells, as you will see by my necklace and my hat pin. Miss Imelda put her sewing down and answers the phone. I hear her voice. She is happy, she is talking to you!

My, such happiness bells can bring. Miss Imelda returns to her sewing and picks me up out of the basket. She looks into my face and tells me YOU will come to the log cabin to stay a full week. You will come here to pick me up personally. She says, "No tight boxes with plastic peanut packing for you, my dear!" I was so excited I almost did not hear her say, "You will fly on an airplane and live in the state of Washington. She said you will name me when you meet me on your visit here. I did not feel like a Nobody anymore.

It is getting later in the day for all of us. The moon brings light shadows as shapes dance on log beams of cabin loft or against the tall burl supporting them. It is as if they dance for me, because they will miss my appreciation of their movements during the night time hours. Their silent messages inspire my whispering and murmuring outside into inside. The forest shadows will be with me wherever I go. The woodland bent branches ever ready to hold birds of the air after their fluttering. The ruffled grouse will not Shirrr again for me when I leave this place. I will remember blue jays swoop greedily to the bird feeder. The horned owl will still hoot in the maple tree winking at the ceramic owl perched on the Manzanita tree twigs hanging on a rustic shelf on the east wall of the log cabin. The wood duck continues to dodge swiftly between trees, then glide and swim the smooth, glass-like surface of the pond just outside the cabin southward. The pond is chilling as their rising whistle lifts, so distinctive from other birds! The opossum will come in the spring to hang from the maple tree, sleeping and yet does not fall. Darkness covers the forest. My days will now be numbered here. . I hear the coyote howl in the far meadow, the Canada geese honk in protest. It is now I realize I will miss this forest. I will miss watching Miss Imelda's comings and goings, her dolly businesses in the loft. She spends many hours in the loft writing and sewing, making doll dresses and stories to sow seeds of happiness to those she loves.

I look at Honey-Girl, Mimi Lea and Star. They have become my sisters in my long waiting period being here. Distance will soon come between us. I know how Miss Imelda feels when she gets lonesome for her sisters. Honey-Girl's honey-colored dress is a sharp contrast to Mimi Lea's blue and white and Star's royal blue royal dress. I have no more to say, because I am not even named yet, but I am loved by a sister's memory.

Through November to remember...Today is not just any day. It is my birthday with you and your birthday, later than it once was. I hear the cabin door open and close. The place where my heart will be skips and I do not even have my heart on! I have no heart, no dress, no under things, no name. How can I be a sister with so many things missing? Then, I hear double footsteps on the gnarled stairway to the loft. Then, I see you, Julianne, both of you together, you and Miss Imelda. Sisters coming to greet me! Then, you picked me up and said, "Hello!" I thought that was my name and then remembered it was a greeting. I felt the same warmth between sisters that I felt for Honey-Girl, Mimi-Lea and Star. It seemed I had my heart already. Both of you looked so happy together. Like sisters who love each other. I heard you and Miss Imelda talk of sharing, when you were younger and now again a little older. I felt a part of this and know why it was so necessary to wait for desires of the heart!

Then, Miss Imelda put my factory clothes in the recycle basket, and measured me for a new dress. She wanted you to remember this, Julianne. Like childhood times. You looked through books to find a name you liked, while she sewed my under things. As if Miss Imelda knew my love of the forest, she chose fabric with golden leaves, to remember the massive oak, maple and aspen trees with a warm brown sprinkled in to let us know summer is gone and the fall season is upon us. My sunny, yellow dress seemed to take shape. My dress fabric has fine lines treaded as if sunbeams, so familiar to me, blended brightness of all good things. Delicate, screened yellow and white, square lace enhanced yellow even more as it edged my dress so delicately. My sleeves puff full, as I recall the winds winging through the branches. The matching circle of my hat, with more lace and careened squares, is dabbed with yellow bows seeded with golden dots and a tiny bell. A bell to remind me of the twinkle-like stars I have learned to love so. Miss Imelda says I will also be able to see stars where I am going! I have a hard time understanding that! Stars in the same place when you travel so far apart? My dress is finished. My bell necklace will be placed on me by you, Julianne. Months, or is it years, of waiting are over. Evening moves on as you and Miss Imelda talk of sisterly things. My under things hug my body keeping my new red heart close to the place it is supposed to be! I can hear it, I can feel it, and I saw it when Miss Imelda placed it to my chest! I have had enough joy and happiness this day. It won't be difficult to wait for my new name tomorrow. For now I am a sis, a miss, a lady, a cutie, a doll.

Night falls silent in the loft again. Two sisters sleep. Happy faces. Julianne places me next to Mimi Lea, Honey Girl and Star. It was so very thoughtful of her to place me between them. Sisters would be that considerate. My sister Mimi Lea thinks I am beautiful. She will be shipped away tomorrow to a sister who lives on a farm and will get to know animals, like I have, or maybe not so wild. Star's usual bright smile widens, tells me she will live with Miss Imelda's brother and his wife. Star has helped me understand some of the many lamps in dark sky that flicker while some humans sleep. We laugh and giggle as the field mice scurry across the front lawn looking for something to eat. She says she will miss me when I go. We are most grateful they have not found us, since we are rags and cotton fluff inside and we would make great nests for little ones. What an unpleasant thought! We tell each other to remember these happy times when we are as far away from each other. Honey Girl said she will get a new sister, after she is sent away. New exciting, comings and goings to remember for making dreams, memories left behind, or better yet, to take with us.

It was such a delight being held by Miss Imelda, twisted this way and that getting my final stitches on my new clothes. It was fun to hear you both laugh together while she sewed. Do you remember when you looked through her books? You liked the one you had never seen before called a "Dictionary of Thoughts" put together by Tryon Edwards. I like him very much because I finally get to try on clothes with my thoughts. My snaps are being put on my dress so it does not fall off, I heard you reading sayings from famous people like...

South said, "The very society of joy redoubles it; so that while it lights upon my friend it rebounds upon myself, and the brighter the candle burns the more easily it will light mine."

Both of you like this one you say, the warmth that shines from the flame of love between two sisters makes me light and warm inside.

Remember when you read what Spurgeon wrote? 'There is a sweet joy that comes to us through sorrow." Why did you both like this one? Perhaps, because you have both tasted sorrow. Sorrow is when Miss Imelda misses you so far away. But, she says the pleasantness of your thoughts bring you close to her.

Of course, you remember when you read what Fielding penned. "Great joy, especially after a sudden change of circumstances, is apt to be silent and dwells in the heart rather than on the tongue." That sounds like me! I dwell in the heart, and someone has to write my thoughts! What a sudden change of circumstances for me to be late for a birthday and then ready for a long journey. I am excited about us flying together in an air plane, in the air she says, in a wind so like the wind that whistles and whispers to me in the loft of the cabin!

Then I remember when you said, Richter said, "Joys are our wings, sorrows our spurs."' Certainly, I am no sorrow. Wings it will be, for both of us you said. Joy! That's it! You said, Joy! That's me! It was when you were convinced for sure that is my name! My name is JOY!

I am complete now for the journey to Minnesota where Julianne and I will spend more time with sisters and family. Julianne keeps me very close to her all the time. Honey-Girl has already arrived at sister Mardelle's. We will all go to visit Marie where Mimi Lea lives. Star is left behind at the cabin until her story is completed. It is a good thing I do not get tired; I am too busy learning about humans.

Julianne, I want to remind to you all things about joy when I come to live with you. When you see the little bell necklace about my neck it will bring all these mental keepsakes to your mind. Of quiet reflections, together as sisters, thinking back and ahead. Deep expressions of love, bringing with it joy. Little treasures through me, more now, with your visit, so beautiful, back in Wisconsin, in a small log cabin in the wilderness. Then, new joy as we travel to a state far away in Washington. My heart is full. I am where I imagined I could be.

On the waves of twilight, night shadows across the lofty ledge, deep in the woods of Wisconsin, where Miss Imelda dreams, with joy, when I was on an airplane ride...I muse....

"Julianne was most careful to place me in the book bag Miss Imelda gave her with the dove on it. Little did you know when she gifted you this carry all, that I would actually have a dove on it to remind me of a heavenly Spirit as a dove of peace? The book bag gave me a chance to stand upright as I fit on the ledge of the airplane window armrest. I kept watching Julianne's face; she seemed so calm, sitting in the air plane on the ground! I do not see Miss Imelda's face among the many faces seen from the big window in the airport lobby. I only see a touch of loneliness and now I know distance between those that I love, and yet being with someone I already love. The airplane windows are small, unlike the large, clear, tall panes of the log cabin. I hear engines roar, and my new little red heart looses a bit, but Julianne's gentle, readjustment of my book bag stays me as she readjusts herself in her seat, and I feel glued again. I can see trucks with suitcases moving away from me and I am glad I am not in them.

The airplane rises into the sky. I see tall trees, very much like the trees in the dense forest I knew. We move faster and faster, as I quickly say goodbye to the lands of my sisterly beginnings. Forest farewells. Then in a flash, they seem to be under me again, mostly naked trees of their leaves. I see a view I have never seen before. I see bird nests, large and small, filled with memories of a former spring nesting season. I see branches broken by strong winds, some supporting each other. Like sisters do. I saw others lying on the earth they once came from, bent and broken, ready to become earth again and I wondered if that was what sorrow was. Then the trees were gone and I saw parcels of land as if they were stitched together, as Miss Imelda's quilts were. I saw gray-brown blankets of land with patches of snow, sparkling like diamonds fallen from the sky. An occasional small black and white cow seemed to be appliquéd in contrast to the beginnings of the winter season. Golden prairies seemed to roll away, dotted by houses where people lived. The air was so clear and I wondered why Julianne was sleeping.

I remembered joys are to be our wings. I was not afraid. I was happy to belong to Julianne, also happy to be with Miss Imelda. I wish I would have enjoyed her more and not complained so much. I am glad I did not forget to tell Honey-Girl, Mimi Lea and Star important friendship things and dreams. The plane jerks, and for a moment I forgot where my wings were, but the passenger next to Julianne tells her something about air pockets. Since I was standing in a book pocket I felt safe. The pilot announced the weather would get stormy and cloudy. We were crossing Minnesota and entering the Dakotas and a few hours would be in Montana. That must be what Miss Imelda means when she talked about mountains of high country. Then, we will fly over Idaho and Washington State. The map on the seat in front of me tells me the route we are taking; telling me the distance is long. No wonder sisters miss each other.

We fly out of the storm. The bumps were plenty and they woke Julianne up! She puts her fingers on my face to let me know she loves me. Fluffy, white clouds seem to float past my window. Once, I used to sit on them in my wishing hours, while they shaped pleasant animal forms for me. Now we pass through them. They seem to drift, then sail without direction. They move gracefully past my window again to greet me briefly as they slip off the silver airplane.

Now we are flying 30,000 feet up. Since I am only 28 inches tall it is hard for me to imagine that many feet to count. The sky is blue between patches of dancing or floating clouds. The gold of my dress matches the gold of the sun. I see a round rainbow, brilliant in all the colors directly in my view. I know why on earth it just rests on the earth and is not fully round. How marvelous is the world we live in. My favorite twilight entering night is about to begin. Just before the sun's brightness filters on between clouds, I see the sky painted the most beautiful colors before Today sleeps. There are bursts of orange, crimson, pink, with lavender like little, colored arrows darting in perfect pattern. They seem to scramble for a last moment's notice before the veil of twilight wraps them in her gentle embrace. The last curve of sun slips between the horizon in a burst of red, and blinks farewell at me. Purple shadows cover the earth in semi-darkness. Julianne is asleep again. Her hand circles around the handle of my Dove book bag as I feel her tenderness in my little red heart that seems to be growing bigger.

The plane is flying lower. I am still awake and so excited. It seems the stars are upside down and the earth below shines lights and colors of all kinds, telling me a season of Joy has come to earth to remind mankind of the Christmas season. House tops glisten with lights of every rainbow color as the festivity approaches. I see majestic, spires, evergreen trees pointing skyward, decorated in full view in a dress of glory for the season. I remember then, Miss Imelda says I was late for Julianne's the birthday because I will see the Christmas season begin high in an airplane. I see brightly lit homes that house family. I am family. I am filled with joy. There is lots of family behind me and ahead of me.

It has been wonderful to have wings. The stars in the sky blink and glitter a natural shine unthreatened by man's colorful competition below. The Big and Little Dipper, my friend Star told me about, and I once knew in the forest, recognized me in my smallness peering out a small airplane window. I thought hard enough, so hopefully, the Little Dipper will tell the other stars I will still see them as I did in Wisconsin, when I live in Washington, so far away from each other. The universe is so wise to know where they always are. I thought to myself, will Man find peace? Will Man find it in the noise of the world? Will it filter down between the tree tops and roofed houses to settle dream dusts where it lands? We are preparing to land. The airport landing is in clear view. I am home Miss Imelda. Julianne is with me. So are you. Let me tell you more in my verse, tucked in my hat, now what do you think of that! Joy"

JOY

White dove on my shoulder
Perched rest, (as Spirits do)
Tranquil as we repeat
So much love to you.

In noiseless contentment
My stay near you is blest
Reminds you of a sister
Gave joy to you as Guest.

Content to be excited
Good natured bringing cheer
To your days across the miles
Her laughter will endear.

Lift spirits high on sunshine
Thrilling through and through
Be overjoyed, ecstatic!
Joy belongs to you!

Little hands reach out
Open palms to pray
Always, your safekeeping
Tomorrow and every day.

Once, sisters walk wooded paths
Deep thoughts of tenderness
Of years young, close beside
Child's homestead's address.

Fields of grain, meadows ripe
Harvests gold in view
Fruit of the soil, of summer's toil

In country sisters grew.

Summer leaves were painted
Green shades warm in season
Crisp autumn golden, red leaves
Change another reason.

We must die to self and gain
Seeds of greater rapture
Watered by Spirit of God
His fullness we capture.

Practice Great Beatitudes
Exalt those heavy laden
Downcast, heart sore, lonely
Child, man or maiden.

Oft times will is wistful
Mournful, tears appear
Sprinkle then, Joy's sparkle
On sadness interfere.

Charge gladsome tidings "enter"
Merry content to see
Quickly lightness covers
Darkness cannot be.

Skip, dance, shout about
Clasp hands open with glee
Be happy in a good mood
Celebrate with me!

Be cheerful, be excited
Thrill by a small thing
Rejoice in our birthdays
Later remembering.

Sisters share small dreams
Where wishes come to be
Hope forms larger ones
Contained for you and me.

My wish for you a holiday
Days throughout the year
Sorrows less, forgetfulness
To sadness when near.

Peace Divine promises
Celestial Love came

Bring joy to mankind
His message we proclaim.

Bear another's burdens
Carry good news where
A gentle voice soothing on
Whispered wings of prayer.

Swiftly lift your spirit
Soar exalted lofty skies
Sheltered by a Master's care
Watched by heaven's eyes.

Grasp happiness elusive
Life's measure please enjoy
Think of sister's love for you
Giving me to you...JOY.

Months pass; I am becoming acquainted with Julianne's daughters Michelle and Janelle. We all live in a large home on Myrtle Street. They have a big dog named Buffy. He lives on the south porch of the house. When he talks he just says "BarkBarkBark." I guess he will never know new words. Julianne says he does not need them. Julianne talks to Miss Imelda a lot and I am glad she tells her I am happy here in Washington. Julianne invited Miss Imelda to come and visit her and she will bring two new dolls for her daughters, named Heaven and Faith. Funny, I thought we have thoughts of heaven and faith with us anywhere we live. Julianne says Miss Imelda will be here in two weeks! I don't know how short or how long a time that is, since I don't concern myself with Time much. I am all over life, behind, beyond, yesterday, today, and tomorrow.

Every week Julianne takes me in my book bag to work with her at the nursing home. Every time I go, I am placed in the lap of one of her patients and I learn so much about memories from ladies and gentlemen who do not get too many visitors. If they do, I am introduced to children of all ages who come to visit, which I really enjoy. One time, a lady held me like an infant and would rock me back and forth. She sang to me like I was her own child; I almost felt like a child! Another day, lady covered me with her lap quilt that had beautiful flowers one it and I thought I was in a garden. She stroked me on the quilt where the daffodils were woven in the fabric. I was glad she noticed my pretty yellow dress Julianne likes so well too. Another time a lady had a visitor with a little girl, and the little girl held me and did not want to let me go. That sure made me feel good. Julianne always comes to check on who has me so I won't be afraid she would forget me. One lady got a comb out of her pocket and started combing my hair; she herself didn't have any hair, so I suppose she liked to comb mine. A man stopped by and told her she was as beautiful as I was. That was so nice of him, don't you think? He comes to see her after she gets some kind of treatment. So you see, just because I am a doll doesn't mean I just stand around not paying attention to things, or sit and do nothing! Some days a man brings a big St. Bernard sheep dog, bigger than Buffy is at home. Everyone likes him. I don't hear anyone call him a name so I call him "Bernie." He came over to me sitting on a man's lap who was watching football on the television. His nose was cold and wet and licked my leg for too long a time. I was glad he didn't visit long. Sometimes Julianne has to work the night shift and I am glad she brings me along, that is the best time for me to make-believe. One time she left me with a man who cannot walk and needs a wheelchair. I was sitting in his wheelchair with a big stuffed rabbit he got as a present. The rabbit was holding a Green Bay Packers banner, but he wasn't sure why he was moved here, he was happier living in Wisconsin. I told him so many things about Washington State that were just as beautiful as Wisconsin, and maybe when his owner would watch television he could see the Green Bay Packers play football and he would not be so grumpy. He promised he would do that, his owner, Andy, sometimes took him with him in the wheelchair when he was driving around the nursing home. He would hope it was the same day the Green Bay Packers were playing. It will be, Joy says, "you have to have faith. " I live with Faith, who is another doll, and she says if you believe something long enough it will happen. Besides, I hear rabbits hop around a lot so you should pay attention to what you may see during the night hours when patients are sleeping. I am here almost every day and I see some wonderful gifts people get from their families." Patients really love Julianne; she is so kind, attentive and gentle and she really likes working in the nursing home where humans have lived a very long time on earth. Days and nights pass following each other and I love it here in Washington State in the city of Spokane. Dawn is in full bloom out the exit window, and Julianne has me tucked under her arm, safe in the Dove book bag Miss Imelda gave her a long time ago called Once. Miss Imelda arrived while we were at the nursing home!

One day, Julianne and Miss Imelda and my new sisters Heaven and Faith go to the Riverfront Park where there is 100 acres of lush, rolling hills along the beautiful Spokane River and falls. We are on our way to the original 1900's Looff Carrousel. As we approach the Carrousel we see prancing horses, carved from solid blocks of Chinese Elm wood by a German woodcarver, Charles Looff, in a far off place called Germany. This magical merry-go-round was erected in about 1908 at the old Natatorium Park along the Spokane River. It was restored for the Spokane Parks Department; it is now housed in Riverfront Park. It has 180 lights, 331 mirrors and is 50 feet in diameter. I read about all of this when we were in the Gift Shop and there was a post card by Tim Dunahee who writes about the Carrousel. At first, Julianne and Miss Imelda placed the three of us on a red bench, all seated together while they sit across from us. It is so good to see Miss Imelda again, and she held may hand so tight before I was seated next to Faith and Heaven.

Miss Imelda placed Joy on a fierce looking tiger looking not too joyful so she was placed back on the small bench where people stopped by to comment on how beautiful we are. There are children who want to ride the horses nearest to where we sit. We are feeling pretty important! We go round and round. The third round and music stops   Julianne picks up Faith and places her on a white horse with jeweled bridle that has a round ornament that looks like a bright sun. The harness is all across the body with gold saddle trim. His horse head is high, ready for fast moving, and Faith sits so pretty on the saddle, holding on to the gold post with only one hand! She winks at me to whisper she calls him Sig, for Siegfried. Sig's mane is full and long on his neck and looks like it moves with the slightest wind. His legs are formed for prancing. The music starts! We all watch as they go by once, twice and three times. I am distracted by the green dragon with his red tongue hanging out. I wonder what Faith is saying to Sig.

Faith leans forward and introduces herself to Sig and tells him the name she calls him, since she did not know he had a name. She tells him her name is Faith and he wanted to know what faith was. She says it was believing in something you have not seen, like heaven, where she will go someday. It is much higher than we are, and we can't go there on our own. She said she has a sister named Heaven and that it is found inside of us where dreams and good thoughts are made of. Her other sister is Joy and she is happy all the time because her mistress is a nurse and being happy is healthy. He tells her he is glad she talks to him; he is very lonesome for His German woodcarver, Charles Looff, who designed him to run and prance so well many years ago. He misses the warm hands and gentle touch he had, and the conversations of what Charles would do next to make him so strong looking and attractive. All of a sudden, Sig is running so fast he breaks loose of the Carrousel gold post base and heads for the sky with Faith holding on with both hands now!

<u>The mechanical crew at the Riverfront Park is at their wit's end, they called the local ambulance helicopter service to report the missing horse and no one wants to believe them, it is a prank, and they hang up!</u>

Heaven and Joy continue sitting on the Carrousel bench and they hear the other horses neigh and snicker, softly, so no one can hear them. They whisper they were surprised with the prancing horse running off like he did because they remember Charles Looff, the woodcarver telling them it was their responsibility to make children and humans happy; their beauty will be sufficient for their services. Heaven was concerned that Faith would fall off, so high in the air, but Joy reminded her, her name was Faith and she is used to believing she was safe even in the air now with Sig.

Faith encourages Sig to bend his head to look below, where he lives and find something beautiful about his home in Washington State. She tells him she just moved here too and is finding her home and companions just as lovable as the ones she left behind in Wisconsin. "Look, Sig," she says, " there is part of green meadows where you live, and go through that big cloud below you and you can see clearly the cascading waterfalls of the Spokane River, and look, Sig, there are cable cars sailing over the Falls just as we are, only we are higher! Now, slow down, Sig, there is the Park Tour Train that humans take to see all of Riverfront Park, and we can see it all from up here! See the big black spider below as it moves around and moves its legs? All in one place! Oh what fun! Be careful, we are sort of close to the big Ferris wheel! Look at the children wave to us, Sig! Oh, look below at the Red Baron and all those children happy with their parents and friends. See over there, Sig, there are real ponies, they are shaped like you, Sig, but not as beautiful, but children are riding them around the park. Oh Sig, you live in a marvelous place. You are a legacy from the past, Sig you are so famous! You must like it here. I do. Over there is the Enchanted Forest with mini-golf players with all those creative pathways to go through! Listen to the screeching monkeys, they must have lived somewhere else, and they are having fun here. Oh, Sig don't prance so fast, we can't miss seeing the Clock Tower over there, but don't bump into it. You are only used to going certain directions. The Clock Tower is very old, built about the time you were and everyone comes to see it. You are history, Sig. You must want to stay here. Look at the Rotary Fountain, everyone wants to see that where they can make wishes, and we can make our own up here! Look at the big Red Wagon. My friend Miss Imelda has a small one just like it, but this one takes 300 people. I had a ride on her small red wagon and it would only take three of us dolls! "Sig begins to turn around; his prance is to get off the sky. He sees the Carrousel becoming clearer and clearer. His gait gets slower as he heads for the Looff Carrousel just below.

Heaven could still see Faith on the carrousel horse in the far distant sky. Twilight is soon upon us. She peers into the sky again, and look! Joy, Faith is coming back! At first, it looked as she could not see Faith, but she believes she was there and was sure she would return, as Joy said. Before, it seemed hours that she kept looking at Faith in the sky but now it looked as if they were headed back this way! The horse was prancing closer and Faith was still holding on with both hands. Did she raise one for an instant to say Hi and she would be back soon? I hoped so.

Sig's approach is much closer now, he is so careful to fly evenly with such a treasure on his back as Faith was. He could feel her near his shoulders and also inside where she said faith begins. Maybe she will come and visit again and he can find out more about Faith and her sister Heaven can tell him about heaven where Charles is. Sig misses his other horse friends and will be glad to be home. The Carrousel horses had their heads turned toward the sky, so happy their co-worker missed them enough to return. Charles, creative as he was, built a special mechanism in their necks in the event such an occasion arose, so now they can use it. No one seemed to notice, but them, of course. His approach is just perfect and as the next customers are waiting to mount the carrousel horses, he slips gracefully into his empty golden post. He is so grateful for his woodcarver for making him perfect. And, now Sig knows Charles is in heaven watching all of the Carrousel horses he carved to perform so well. The merry-go-round mechanics just changed shifts; they check his position, and as Sig knew, it was perfect. But the mechanics were so busy they didn't even notice. Humans miss so much!

Faith's friends were waiting on the same velvet bench. Faith whispers into Sig's flying mane, "Sig, I'll see you in my dreams, be sure to be there! I'll bring Heaven with me and she can tell you more what heaven is like, but we were so close to heaven when you were flying so high. Charles is up there."

Faith is lifted off the Carrousel horse by Miss Imelda and Julianne carry Heaven and Joy to the car parked not too far away. Faith looks back at Sig; he winks at her, and she knows he is happier. She hoped he saw her bright right eye wink back at him; having faith as she is she was sure of it. She has so much to tell Heaven and Joy tonight now that she is taken away from the Carrousel. I guess the little Bible, which is still in her pocket, reads about heaven being up in the sky! Faith will be so glad to know she was closer to it than Heaven just reading about it when she would let her borrow the little book. It will be just like Faith to agree. Of course, Joy will hear it all, and be joyful as she always is.

CHAPTER 13. HONEY GIRL / ANNIE

"Life is a flower of which love is the honey."
A quote from Victor Hugo

Dearest Mardelle:

Happy Birthday We! Yes, you and me! My name is Honey Girl. Do you know why? Because my dress designer, Miss Imelda, says when you were a little girl your Mother and Father called you Honey Girl. I look like a honeyed girl, sweet, soft and easy to love. Mardelle, my heart glistens just like yours, only yours is on the inside and mine is on the outside. But that doesn't matter to me, love can be either, Miss Imelda says.

I am coming to live with you, but Miss Imelda has to make me a new dress. When I came to her log cabin in the northern woods of Wisconsin I was in a very slim, dark box, and I thought I would never see light again. That was not bad enough, someone I don't even know threw my box I was in to another dark place and broke my foot! I could hear the glass fall around my leg making noise all the way to Miss Imelda's house! I did not think she would keep me because I was partly broken, but she said Mardelle would love me just as much, maybe even more, because I was broken in places. It is a good thing I did not get my head broken since I am told you take care of older people, and I would like you to take me where you are so I can see them and maybe they will take their hands into my little hands and we can love like you do. So it was Miss Imelda's daughter Julie who fixed my foot in not much time at all and even polished my shoes black! Now that I have a new foot and it matches my other one just fine, so I will leave here soon. I hope to bring you fond memories of your Father and Mother as their Honey Girl. I never had a Father or a Mother so you and your husband will be those things to me. Our birthdays will be the same, only I will be much younger, like you were when you first became Honey Girl.
I will arrive on your Birthday Honey Girl. When you dress me, please be careful of my heart. We will need it. I love you already... Honey Girl

Honey Girl

Once there was a Honey Girl
Youngest of them all
Sister small for all her years
To our parents devotional.

Music to one's ears is she
Honeybunch, so sweet
Darling child who brought delight
To whomever she would meet.

Mother's special sweetheart
In days bygone these years
Now it's time a Honey Girl
Again reappears.

Gowned in yellow hearts
Or red, stripped coloring
Ribbons satin here and there
Such flattery I am offering!

A Sweetie laced in flowers fine
Filigreed in style
Bright-eyed face looking at
Another Honey smile.

My heart outside glistens
Like yours does yours within

Though this way we are different
We both are feminine.

My ruffles decorate me up
Web filigree flounces fall
My scarf could have been yours
As remember you recall.

My Designer designs are for
Delightfulness to you
She tells me you have baskets full
Of things for me to do.

Windows wide to peep afar
Such sunsets crimson scenes
Moonlight bright into the night
Mystery of Might-Have-Been's.

Sounds of crickets, frogs or such
Dwell in nearby stream
Silver waters trickling through
My dollish wildest dream.

Love me, please, Fine Lady
Polished, porcelain me
Well behaved, considerate
Gracious as you are we.

Polite, I am well-spoken
Beloved as still you are
Precious to one's fancy
Your Lady popular.

Your sister Miss Imelda
Thinks you will love me so
Since I tend to have my fears
I really need to know.

Will you find me lovable?
Endearing to your heart
Winsome or charming
Instant quickly start?

Memories, she says
Like those long ago
When sisters close as two
Shared thoughts secrets know.

As closer both you grew

Friendship two sisters small
Yearning to express by
A miniature small doll.

Mailed to your address
I'll learn love deeper yet
From trials not of your doing
You will never forget.

I claim some for my own
Because our hearts console
Reaching out to those in need
Make broken pieces whole.

Though mine is so much smaller
Reflecting little schemes
My nature likens yours for sure
In your girlish dreams.

Honey Girl I love you
Happy Birthday You and We
Gladness and lightheartedness
Is sent to you, from me.

'To my dearest Miss Imelda:

I arrived all in one piece, thanks to you! It was a long ride. I was glad when I was dropped off at my new home. Thank you for giving me my Birthday and new family.

I could not be loved any more than I am already. I love to be out in the country here with the meadowlarks singing and the whole beautiful countryside. Honey Girl is teaching me about many colorful birds coming to eat at her south window. My favorites are the colored finches that have colors like me. They like the daylight, but I like the night the most. She has glass bird statues on shelves which I will visit in the moonlight hours to learn about what they do and why they have feathers instead of dresses like me.

Thanks for my beautiful dress. Mardelle's guests come over and they admire me and even look at my pantaloons, but I don't mind. Her husband, Marvin, likes me very much and takes me for rides on the tractor with lots of children including her daughter Annie who comes to visit. She loves me very much. She has a dolly friend who will come and live with us, so I will have someone to share my secrets with. I still love you too and always will.

Say Hi to my Dolly Sisters Mimi, Joy and Johdia who I miss but I may see them sometime when they come here to visit. We have lots of company here.   Love...Honey Girl

P.S. That means Passionately Selected

ANNIE

Yesterday Mardelle and Miss Imelda
Drove to a garage sale in town
Found a glass doll who looks like me
But had a soiled gown!

Her hair needed combing
Her eyes downcast to see
Mardelle said she would buy her
To give daughter Annie.

We drove back home, they forgot
We would visit Mimi Lea's place
Unnoticed my disappointment
My ungrateful look on my face.

They looked for fabric for a dress
Mardelle washed doll face and hair
Found material of sheer sky blue
They sew in front of me there!

Dress became a full round skirt
Pearled lace bodice and sleeves
A waist of pale pink ribbon tied
Matched hat Miss Imelda weaves.

What a transformation
From the garage a ragged mess
Into a lovely doll, like me
Living at the same address!

I introduced myself to her
I'm polite, words not too many
Said to her, "I am Honey Girl"
She said, "I am Annie."

I am Annie here to tell you
Of a daughter Mardelle had
Born without enough oxygen
Her brain damaged bad.

Mardelle and Marvin nursed her
Days beyond two years
She did not talk, did not walk
Causing family tears.

They exercise her legs to move
Often throughout each day

Search ways to improve
Her life lived in harm's way.

Joyously later two years
Annie walks ready and straight
Into the arms of Mom and Dad
As families celebrate!

Doctor visits made often
Cerebral Palsy is diagnosis
Mental retardation severe
Bleak permanent prognosis.

New doctors know how to treat
New research, new drugs appear
Consultations endless
Discoveries disappear.

Annie lives home sixteen years
Occasional words breakthrough
She loves her bedroom pleasant
Sleeps late she likes to do.

Shelves decorate by Disney toys
Mickey and Minnie Mouse
Even 'Indian' and cowboys
Stuffed animals stuff the house.

She likes fingernails polished
Hues different color or design
Admires rings on her fingers
Hands soft, taper, smooth line.

Enjoys hamburger with French fries
Or root beer floats to share
Her transfer to a Group Home
For special extensive care.

Family visits her frequently
Continues love to her nearby
We sleep alone when she's home
She walks in bedroom, says "hi."

No thoughts what she missed in life?
She never learned to cry
She laughs when stories funny
Remembers those who stop by.

I watch her peaceful sleeping

Parents love fills her smallest place
One day her visit home empty
Of Dad Marvin's loved face.

Her mother tried to tell her
He died, gone to heaven's doorway
She did not cry, looked puzzled
Mardelle took her to where he lay.

She stroked his hair in tenderness
Her Dad sleeps, her voice not hears
Mardelle took her home again
Her look puzzled again appears.

She holds Mom's hand, asks for Dad
Mom says "Dad's gone" interim
Annie says "I am so sorry to him"
Stated, becomes personal seraphim.

Such peace, empathy for her years
Still eyes can't cry tears
Her brain was clothed by love
Parents blessed by God her years.

What she could have learned to grow
Stunted illness she misunderstood
Misfortune lived but didn't know
No growth from first childhood.

Each year she grew but never knew
What is normal for me, for you?
She does not know hatred, envy or
Jealousy, deceit, bitterness too.

She suffers silently when in pain
Does not know how to complain
What lessons can she learn from us?
Examine ourselves, our own brain.

What can we learn from her?
With an injured part of brain
Annie's angelic nature obvious
Her gentleness admired remains.

Once I was stored in garage cold
Forgotten, no one to belong
Mardelle came, with Annie's name
New emotions brave and strong.

We don't know how to handle life
Until strength from somewhere
Develops what can be strengthened
Improved by offered prayer.

As a doll collection, Honey Girl
Our gifts or stories convey
Tenderness and love of family
To broken spirit Annie's way.

Where her brain is less limited
To work, understand, to learn
Did not know pain her parents felt
Her birth medical false discern.

Courage, trust and steadfast love
Covered Annie all these years
When she dies Mardelle says
Angel voices chorus cheers.

When Mardelle joins her husband
A new daughter they will know
To love again for eternity
Watch daily new Annie grow.

We don't know how strong we are
Until strong the only choice
Be aware of victims of Cerebral Palsy
Listen to their Spirit's voice.

In verse of treasured things
Words remain near Angel wings
Past new birth season springs
Invite strengths in bad beginnings.

I'll remain on Annie's dresser still
With Honey Girl mischief late
Count raindrops on windowsill
When Annie visits we'll celebrate.

We'll watch birds, squirrels chase
But my love best of any to be
So grateful, so dear, not many
Near Annie always, I am her Annie.

CHAPTER 14. MARY LEA

"When someone you love becomes a memory, that memory becomes a wonderful treasure

to always hold in your heart, miss you forever and always."
A quote from Author unknown

Dearest Mary Lea:
Isn't it exciting? Aren't surprises wonderful? I am your porcelain doll to remind you of a father and mother you and your sister and brothers loved so very much. My dress with its purple background has aqua blue flowers to remind me of the ocean your father sailed. The pale formed leaves beneath remind us of them wherever we are on the west, the Midwest, the East and the Southern part of our wonderful United States to include Alaska and Hawaii. Miss Imelda has travelled in her employment and journeys to see family in many of these different states. Now you, their namesake Mary Lea, be sure to read Aunt Marie's stories of the two of them together.

Your Dad was only 17 years old when he joined the Navy. His ship was lost in the Pacific theatre as a result of a Kamikaze pilot aircraft hitting the ship, sinking it and killing most of his shipmates. Lea was found missing in action. He was also a Gunner on a merchant ship, the U.S. Hope. After the service he became a master plumber where he settled in California as well as a lifetime county Sheriff's deputy. He loved your Mother Mary Ann very much and they were married when he went off to sea. Miss Imelda wrote this poem for them.

TO SEE THE SEA

Lee and Mary Ann's wedding
Choice Bride knows guarantee
Four weeks before military
Mission sails Groom out to sea.

Assembled crew on ship's ocean
Couples stroll thru garden shored
Walk slowly to plank for boarding
A sailor's love for wife implored.

War uncertain for lovers
Promises faithful exchange
Marriage vows pledge fidelity
Before shipped to sea long range.

Mary Ann holds Lee closely
Past garden's path design
For separation approach easier
Their hands closer entwine.

Deep seas flirt with sailor's life
Its beckon now watchword
Four footsteps pace flowered path
Goodbye farewells often heard.

Ox-eyed daisies petals white
Yellow discs gleam in centers

Purple spike fireweed flutes
As ocean boat harbor enters.

Shamrock fanned leaves of
Clover forage fixings grow
Dog roses arch branch shrub
Married lovers paused to show.

Lavender fragrant spills sea air
Full blossoms flower scent
Slight trace space too soon bare
Near coupled loves absent.

Golden buttercups intense
Brilliant in bright sun
Reflect past dream memories
Newlywed love as done.

War ship swings lazy to and fro
Waves lick warm afternoon
Prepared in summer's radiance
Of seasons' flowers bloom.

Thoughts drift from Sailor's stay
Flushed new marriage days
Her small hand, slim ring band
Seals vow complete bouquets.

"I pick daisies days we spent
Nights purple passion plays over
Smell sweet rose aroma, dear
Comfort surrounds red clover.

Breathe lavender's fragrance
Bold buttercups have sighed
Recall summers bouquets here
Dear husband," sighs his bride.

"The blossom vaults follow my love
Illusion past ocean's sea vast
Petals sail, beg journey's safe
My loving arms wait tenderly" passed.

Hands unclasp, he leaves today
Beloved Sailor to sail ocean blue
Wraps vision petals bouquet
Live hearts read, "I love you."

Miss Imelda, my designer, has loved you and your family a very long time even though she lives many states away. Often lives become distant, but not so with us, we will become closer together. Your father, though long gone, is still very dear to Miss Imelda's immediate family. She has a genealogy book that shows pictures of Lea and a copy of his poem he wrote just for their parents on their Golden Wedding Anniversary. Enjoy. Miss Imelda knew him very well and he meant every word written.

" GOLDEN MEMORIES"

Just can't seem to write any more
The words don't seem right, Mom
So I thought a little verse or poem
Might help out matters some
You see, like this, I've time to think
Of what I'd like to say
And make the little words mean a lot
In a different sort of way
Sitting here, so far away
Kind of makes you lift a sigh
Just to think of all the memories
That money just can't buy
Why, when I was born some years ago
I heard Pop moan and fret
Margaret, for goodness sake
He's the ugliest you brought me yet!
At the age of one, I know for sure
You really had a time
Feeding me, keeping me dry
So that I wouldn't whine
Or older kept asking why?
At the age of five, I don't recall
If I was good or bad
But I know darn well
I wasn't the best you had
From five to twelve, that childish age
You know, when kids learn a lot
I know I tried my darndest
To do things and not get caught
The next few years, I was really big
I wanted to be just like Dad
Well, Mom you really know the reason why
He's the best Pop I ever had
When Service came and Navy bound
This little lad from home
To go out and roam this great big world
And doing it all alone
That's when I was bad, so long ago
Out sailing on the seas
The things I will cherish all my life

My golden memories
Like when we'd gather round and sing
At the end of our working day
Someone would always sing off key
And you all would look my way
And Dad, just sitting around close by
Just gazing into space
For hours he'd just sit right there
Not moving from his place
Then there are times I have to admit
I was really bad
But I was always rewarded by
The faithful hand of Dad
There's lots of things I could put down
Things I won't forget
Why, when I get old and gray
I'll remember them yet
Things I remember all seem so good
Cause there was much more good than bad
So Mom and Dad you must believe
It's the best life I ever had
It's not so much the big things in life
That seems to stick with me
It seems much more the little ones
That makes my memories
You know, Mom, I wouldn't want
To live my life again
Cause all those little memories
Would all be different then
Now, what am I trying to tell you?
In this little poem
Well, Mom and Pop, I'm telling you
There just was no place like home
I know sometimes I hurt you
With things I've said and done
But find a little place in your hearts
To forgive me, Pop and Mom
It's important, this little thing I ask
For my body and mind to be free
For this little something to add
To my Golden Memories"

Poem by son Leander Dickinson
For Golden Wedding Anniversary of
Mom and Dad October 1955

Dear Mary Lea:

Years passed between our beloved brother Lea and his family. On frequent occasions he visited us in Minnesota, welcomed by all, especially my Mother and Dad. When he became ill all the sisters went to visit him in 1982 and I wrote him this poem...

AS I SEE LEA

As you walked upon Life's pathway
Trails' paths with valleys low
Or mountain peaks, verdant hills
Each passage made you grow
Some led to dreams afar where sun
Shines bright on a western coast
Where brother Lea's travel rested
His roots deep as deeper most
His family became one of his own
His career well chosen, sure
In time he found homestead roots
Visits frequently as voyager
His door always opened wide
To mankind fowl or beast
Lea took time, in his own time
From great to least of least
Some steps along Life's pathway
Were labored, tired and long
Times he found a listening ear
For conversation or a song
His days measured joyfully
Sadness visits but not to stay
Because dreams do come true
Somehow he found the way
Now illness claims a cold attack
To discourage, to claim it's due
Brother Lea meets it head on
What Life's paths expect him to
He has byways to the wilderness
Routes chartered channeled far
Each day of yesteryear refined
him to days formed particular
This pen pursues this tribute
To brother Lea, especially fine
He crossed my pathway many times
As treasured kinship mine
Our springtime years behind us
Summer's season too is past
Approaching autumn beckons now
View its brilliant colors fast
Many miles behind our footsteps
More distance ahead I see
Look up my brother, see the sun

Beside your Spirit your family
Swim again refreshing rivers
Watch sunsets burn orange-gold
Laugh again at life, as before
'Cause you're Papa's special mold
Reach for faith, not sight
Believe impossible again real
Clasp hands loving you most
Love warms you where you feel
Roads of life wind on shorter
But steps of foot don't fade
Sit down awhile, rest another time
Beside loved ones in soft shade
Remember life at its filled fullest
With fierceness in its prime
Can be strong with gentleness
On pathways measured time
My love sears you this message
Written with my love of God
Touching you now, my brother Lea
From sister you love called Mod
Penned with love and affection
Encouragement wide as your sea
I love you now and always
This is how I see brother Lea.

CHAPTER 15. MIMI LEA

"In the sweetness of friendship let there be laughter
and in the sharing of little things the heart finds its morning and is refreshed."
A quote from Kahil Kibran

Dearest Marie:

This is a very Happy greeting for your birthday from "Someone" you don't even know yet...me! I'm an 18 inch, glass porcelain doll, in a long, slim box. I am thin and beautiful I am told. Since you will "adopt" me, I will become your very own "confidante!" My dress designer Miss Imelda wants you to choose a name for me. It should be a girl's name you would have named one of your own girls, if you would have one extra! I will call you Grandmother; Miss Imelda says you are one.

Isn't it nice to have someone to adopt and then be able to name them after you get them? Already I have adopted sisters; Emily, Honey-Girl, Johdia, Imelda, Karina, and Victoria. And do you know what? There will be more! Birthday gifts for birthday girls. Isn't it exciting? All my sisters look like me, but Miss Imelda changes them with new clothes and new stories. I overheard my friends in the factory, where I am made, that all of us have the same dress and hat! Isn't that dreadful? Can you, dear Grandmother, imagine a fate as awful for a girl?

I can't. I will arrive at your house with a red hart, new underwear, a new dress and a new hat. I do hope I will have a name before then. There I go fretting, and with my new heart!

Happy Birthday, dear Grandmother, for you and for me. Don't forget to write Miss Imelda my name. It would make me sad to arrive so lovely at your home and not have a name. That would also mean no poem for me! I would not even know who I was; much less expect you would recognize me! We could never stand for that! Oh, dear, there I go fretting again! I don't like changes unless I make them myself, so I can fret quite easily. Oh excitement, the telephone rings and it is "Marie!" There is a very long wait, seems you can't shut them up, I mean, I am waiting here! Miss Imelda finally hangs up. She comes back to me, says, "Well, Mimi Lea, guess we better get you dressed." I have a name, I can't believe it, and it seems just right for me! "Miss Imelda will get my attire all fixed up pretty...then set to work on my poem. All done soon and I will be shipped to you ASAP. No need to fret at all, what I was thinking...I have the best sisters to love me.

COME AND SEE, "MIMI LEA"

When you open up this box
From New York to you sent
Read what Miss Imelda
Has for her comment!

"Mimi Lea, my little one,
"I'll miss you so, but wait
Listen to the wonders
Prepared for an immigrant!

Your name, my glass-eyed damsel
Is found in family lore
Of love between a sister
And brother long before.

When miles were great between
She tells of playful banter
Mischief to get into, so
Old stories told, enchanter.

Not often seen with a sister
Or brother in between
Close in companionship
Together not often seen."

Mimi wrote stories about Lea and she together:

"As children on the Homestead farm
We and neighbors play baseball
In summer on large green meadow
You hear "Play ball!" from the hall.

Mom's harvest crates of peaches
We saw. Lea made my dolly bed
Had to have some for his airplanes
Wood tapered wings widespread.

We thought of ways to make our play
Fun, creative, enjoying too
After our chores were done
Pals together. Plans new to do.

Our dog, Barry's mate, had puppies
We dress them in dolly clothes
Pull around yard in red wagon
To sales market? Who knows?

A day crews came to burn deep ditch
Near our Homestead home
We decide to make a campfire too
From ditch blaze take "on loan."

Lea chose to be wild cowboy
Then, I, an Indian became
Hoopin' and hollerin' around campfire
What fun to play this game!

Mother saw black smoke rising
Not safe, close to chicken coop
She puts campfire out at once
March us to house; no supper soup.

To bed to ponder our naughty ways
Missing more our campfire blaze!
What fun to watch flames soar high
Together, those were the days!

Age nine/ten went to Grandpa's place
Freeport Farm, walk pasture for pigs
Near straw pile, pigs housing space
Climb down and up our digs.

Steps repeat, more steps retrace
Laughed together, yell a lot
Until pigs came back to see
What we do in pasture pigs got.

Our mess, their catastrophe!
Built by Lea and Mimi sure
Mischief made their parade
Comrades misbehave him and her.

All this commotion quickly heard
Dad and Grandpa came to free
Us from pig dangers attention
To naughty Mimi and brother Lea.

Another fall season we visit again
Play Hide 'n Seek upstairs alone
I can't find Lea anywhere I look
He forgot our game well-known!

I hear noises under Grandpa's bed
He's hiding, a big box he found
Of homemade, summer sausage
Beckons me don't make a wound.

Cuts chunks with his jack-knife
We munch-lunch a misbehave
Forget Hide 'n Seek, too full to play
Must hide what box gave.

Full satisfied, put back in space
Return downstairs to family
No suspect; guilt not on our face
Stand Mimi and Lea innocently.

Our farewell lunch smoked sausage!
Ice cream, cookies, homemade cake!
No one understands why we don't eat
We are so full, we can't partake!

Because Sister Mimi's mischief
Naughty Prankster Brother Lea
Hiding under Grandpa's bed
Disobedient together eat finders free.

We grow older, Lea U.S. Navy joins
He loved his country so
Serves loyally in white uniform
Where ever he would go.

I wrote him letters regular
So my love for him he'd know
He'd write me too travel news
Of places on ocean travels go.

His ship U.S. Navy Liberty
So proud I am of my brother
So I name my Dolly, 'Mimi Lea'

Sibling love like no other.

Past Navy term he chose to move
Out West to California state
Married with his own family
Near San Francisco's Golden Gate.

I married too, with my own life
More loving letters always sent
One time my husband and I
Took vacation, off we went.

To visit Lea and his family
Stayed at his home many days
Played music tunes of yesteryear
Reminisce our childhood ways.

He takes us to a marina where
He parks his spacious yacht
We stroll beside it casually
To its' name he chose the spot.

He points to caption "Mimi"
Bold, black letters in script
A testimony of brotherly love
Minute marvel manuscript!

Name not of wife or children
He is proud of his selection
Tears in my eyes, no disguise
Perfect mutual affection.

We get in, he pilots cruise
Of bay, surrounding sea
Toward vast Pacific Ocean
My hubby, Lea and me.

Air breezes most pleasing
Close boats popular greet him
Cruise waves high, lands few then
Scenes Lea knows each rim.

We sail for fun filled hours
Such beauty for us to see
Toward ocean wide and vast
What a journey jubilee!

Back home, Lea says "I'm tired"
Asks me play piano tune

Tells us his illness is leukemia
Treatment will begin soon.

Sad, I play 'Whispering Hope' he likes
Many waltzes we used to share
When he plays his accordion
At family visits anywhere.

He dozed, I play for hours
He is peaceful where he lays
My precious brother many years
Covered in Love's bouquets!

His sickness goes in remission
Visits us in Midwest over again
His birthday same as our Dad's
"Golden memories" his, shares then.

We celebrate parent's years 50 wed
Thirteen children meet together all
Each with families outspread
All write stories gifted at hall.

To parents lovingly remember
There guidance strong and steady
Each writes letter fond mentions
Their discipline always ready.

Few more years pass, his illness
Returns now full blown
His life expectancy shortens
Time for last family visits shown.

All sisters' travel to see Lea
Time left on earth to live
I stay night and day, I cook
Chicken noodle soup him give.

Each day a new container froze
Just in freezer, Lea, just look!
Each meal made, lots of love
Mix with music from songbook.

Last visit of sisters and brothers
To one living life full blast
Helped others when he could
His flag always half-mast.

His children call him 'Courage'

'Industrious, 'Lovable', 'Kind,' 'True'
'Generous,' 'Helpful,' 'Adventurous'
A Dad to always come to.

To me he'll be more than friend
A brother dear when we were small
Always together, good or bad
Reflect in gift 'Mimi Lea', my doll."

Now illness parts these two
Stories she did you tell
Of comrades sealed as soul-mates
Each loved each other well.

You'll hear music's memories
Echo's soft in night air
As Mimi and Lea play old songs
So easy did they share.

She'll place you near her piano
Where Brother Lea did stand
Playing tunes of yesteryear
On his accordion grand.

She'll whisper notes sung softly
Verse grasps tender years
Or sing Western songs he liked
By Sons of the Pioneers!

Pure country air refreshes you
New animals, new birds
Not in your factory's wildest dreams
Voiced in dollish words!

Hear field cows, chicken noises
Co-mingled with winged bat
Defy dogs racing chase pasture hogs
Who chase the barnyard cat?

Tell tales you hear of crafty bear
Who stalk spring fields to roam?
Oh, "Mimi Lea", adventure waits
Full in your new home!

Red roosters crow quite early
Most humans sleeping then
Ardent lovers of their voice
Show-off's in chicken pen.

Hen's speckle eggs lay in nest where
Retrieved pheasant eggs placed
Hatch, born, grown, mom hen runs off
Follows adopted chicks she raised.

One time Mimi puts duck eggs
Under mother brooder hen
Full-grown, swim in puddle ponds
Confusion returns each rain then.

Will she see her chicks as ducks?
When her 'chicks' go off to swim
In puddles not chose by Mama Hen
They go far out on a whim.

Graced deer will come at midnight
Munch new meadow hay
Goat "Forty" near, new danger
Hopefully you stay away.

In the house from all things
That doesn't know how to play
Dream awake in moon's light
Until dawn brings new day.

May your presence delightful
To all who see you sit or stand
Where a Grandmother chooses
Close by Brother Lea's photo grand.

Enjoy lots of children visits
Sizes gentle, often ones wee
That's how loving starts and lasts
Like once Mimi and Brother Lea.

Brings affection to fill your heart
To bursting, I suppose
Watch fond family around you
Live and love how it goes.

One last wrapping, carefully
Before journey to far farm
Across country miles so wide
Unique in their own charm.

Such fun she'll have to dress you
To my Sister, now you go
She'll show so much love to you
Beyond what you now know.

> Your dress so white, colored hearts
> Trimmed in wide blue lace
> Crisp crinoline flounces full
> Lace pantaloons encase.
>
> Soon your travel time is done
> You'll live in a special place
> Sit and stand for all to see
> Your painted porcelain face.
>
> Remember your first birthday
> Gift to sister from me
> Welcomes you as family
> Doll name chosen, "Mimi Lea."

Later PS... That means Personolly Superb!

Dearest Miss Imelda and Doctor Bill:

"Thank you ever so much! "Mimi Lea" arrived last week and we just love her so much already! She is beautiful and her poem is so precious. We'll treasure them always! I really loved her outfit. You did a superb job. Thanks so much for your thoughtfulness about stories I could remember about our Brother Lea. You were so much younger, and our brothers closer to my age, so I became close to them, both Frank and Lea. Again, thanks so much. It is such a pleasure to be loved and treasured. "Mimi Lea" wants to say a few words....she talks a lot!" Love, Mimi.

Dearest Miss Imelda and Doctor Bill:

Glory and Hallelujah! New words I learned yesterday! Made my safe trip to my Grand Parents. I just knew this would be my final destination when I was handed to someone so gentle. Then, as you said, I hear so many funny noises, and then Light! Then, a man picked me up and gave me to a lady, and I saw gray curly hair, big brown eyes (moist already), behind a pair of glasses. I could feel love already. Then, I heard a small, miniature voice that said, "Oh, Gramma, she is so pretty." I was then formally introduced to Angie. She is pretty too! Then I met her husband, Jerome, who teases everyone a lot. Tomorrow I will meet more of my kin in this family. You were right, this family never lacks for love and friendship. I hear birdies all day, and outside lots of farm noises I am becoming familiar with. I sit on the stereo, near a picture of brother Lea, as he stands near an old car. Mimi is next to it in a rocking chair where she sits and reads a lot. She wants to enjoy my presence near her all the time. She delights in showing me off to everyone who comes in the house! Thank you for making my lovely clothes and sending me here. I will always love you as well as my new family. God bless and keep you both! My heart will always beat with love for you both! Love always, Mimi Lea.

CHAPTER 16. JOHDIA

"Success is knowing your purpose in life,

growing to reach your maximum potential
and sowing seeds that benefit others."
A quote from John C. Maxwell

Dearest Adeline:

This year, for your birthday you will receive me! That is who I am since I don't have a name yet! Everyone has a name, not only in the make-believe world, like mine, but in the mortal world as well. Guess what? My dress designer, Miss Imelda decided you will give me a name of a girl who is very special to you. She told me you love your daughter, Diane, so it isn't that. Your son John is a man, and I am not that! I will be your extra, and you will receive me in your home. What's more, she says there is a doll that sits on your davenport all day. I wonder if she will like me even though I am different. I have sisters, just like you. My companion all the way from the state of Minnesota is Mimi Lea. I will miss her since she is ready to leave here next week. Honey-Girl will be leaving soon too, she lives near you somewhere. I cannot leave until you call Miss Imelda my name, so I know who I am.

Miss Imelda says where I am going your family believes in instruction and education and I will learn all the time. Miss Imelda says she loves me so much it will be very hard for her to let me go. I have sat on the floor of her cabin for so long, waiting for a new home and a name, she has got used to me smiling at her all the time.

My birthday will be the same as yours, and we can celebrate together! Perhaps you will write a letter to Miss Imelda because she has been very good to me. I arrived at her house and my dress was a mess. My hat was crooked and my body was coming apart mostly on my right side. I don't look shabby anymore. Miss Imelda made me new underwear, and I got my new red heart right away, not like the other dolls.

I sat close to the sewing contraption Miss Imelda makes doll clothes on. She calls it a Singer sewing machine and I landed right on the table part, hoping Miss Imelda would see me, so she would not forget I only had underwear on. It worked. Now I have the most beautiful dress and hat to match! She says I must travel, (oh dear, not again) in my underwear, but when I come to you, you will dress me. That is so you will like me more, and know that my beautiful heart is for me, and you.

Miss Imelda opened a letter from you dear Adeline, and reads to me "Her name shall be…Miss Johdia..the combo of my 'other' children's names." I thought and thought and realized, this name being so special, I will never be just an ordinary doll, but will be family! You said I will be very special, your Johdia. More you told…"You see when I was only five or six years old, (and that is longer than your pretty porcelain head can imagine) our home burned down and my only doll of a lifetime was gone. So I know her doll spirit has come back thru you, joined now you will be like royalty to me and my make-believe world with all the stories I read to my second graders will be with you to share. So glad to have you coming 'home!' " So thrilled was I to hear your story, explained dreams I had that made no sense, but now prove why I have become your present. Miss Imelda packs me hurriedly and off I go to be with my beloved past childhood friend and also my new unmother.

JOHDIA

Johdia's dress of flowers small
Creamed satin, apron laced
Brown straw hat, jewels here or there
On upright chair is placed.

A message comes into the room
From mail slot in midday
Miss Imelda smiles, letter post notes
"Little Miss Johdia" "Oh Hooray."

"For me," she says, "Come and see
My first letter sent by mail
Miss Imelda please read to me
Each word in fine detail."

Little Miss Johdia, you are blest
As heir to my Sister wise
Is elated to receive you to her home
Your heart your dollish size.

Visions you, because of two
Children she loves so
As sunshine on rainbows gold
To this house you'll go.

Un-mother, wants you to join
Her household in affection
Replaces her once only doll
Unique, small child collection.

Prepare for many stories
Heard by students who
Lavish rich imagination
Delightful through and through.

Of far off places, distant lands
People unique, different so
Children can learn of others
Together as studies grow.

You'll hear birds told in kind
Both free and caged wings
Find treasured make-believes
Exciting wanderings.

Even shadows close on Night
Your search may change a bit
Explore a hand collection
Your own will favor it.

Un-Mother tells your fears
Will vanish when you see
Old, wise Grandmother Doll
A friend, you will agree.

Be sure to keep your dress prim
Be proper when you sit
Recall manners graciously
To our guests exquisite.

Listen well, attentively
Observe choice many things
You'll find new dwelling place
Past human's uttering's.

One day you'll meet children
Grown past child once wee
Formed your name Johdia
Un-Mother's name for thee!

Be serious, yet, be impish
Though prankish you do tend
She says for you to counsel
Grandmother Doll, depend.

Be half full of mischief
Filled up of elfish glee
Be everywhere, but nowhere
And sad, Oh, never be.

Perhaps in many rooms
Treasures you will know
May you replace her little doll
Burned in fire long ago.

When Un-Mother too was child
Talked often to her Dolly too
Told her dreams, far extremes
Came true as fast she grew.

Never replaced her dollish face
Missed her every day
Can't tell her "I love you"
Privately her own way.

Bring back happy memories
Restore to once child living
Sister, Johdia says to you

"Birthdays, unmother, are for giving.

Days when born we were
Life full for living free
Celebrate, years happy
Enjoy large family.

Introduce family to me
Young and grown to know
To love a special way
Now off to you I go!"

I hear noise of my wrapping
Darkness soon gone to uncover
Large home, husband and children
Look, there's my Un-Mother!

Lifts me gently, takes my clothes
Examines my little red heart
Gives me her first light kiss
Begins to dress me, a work of art.

Snaps close, dress neat in place
On my head my straw hat
Sees my pleasant porcelain face
What do you think of that!

She talks to me softly clear
Now grown, dolly to own
"I love you, Johdia, dear"
Her eyes moist, we're together alone.

Lifts me tenderly to next room
Says children away at school
We walk by cages side by side
Introductions now house rule.

'Holly' a green parrot, she says
'Maxwell,' companion, Blue gray
Live, caged, each separately
Words different they convey.

Outdoors feeders invite feather friends
Size, color, unknown to me
Quiet and peaceful at Woodlawn
Diverse sights to see.

I'm placed in their front room
Near Old Grandmother Doll

She's plump, small smile, friendly
Wears no 'thinking cap' at all.

unmother takes her to rocking chair
Where old dreams are left behind
Windows near, wide and clear
Perfect for curious mind.

Her apron note "Sit on Grandma's lap"
Where unmother places me
Room for both of us, perhaps
She's cuddly, warm embraces be.

I sense bits of emptiness as
Children grow much older
I am sure in this household
"Jewels of Joy we'll fill," I told her.

The front door room closes
Unmother reviews teacher review
For young children, educated special
English and mathematics too.

I asked Old Grandmother Doll
If I could go with her to school
Her reply, I start happy cry
"Yes, as exception to her rule!

She took me once as visitor
Children had no Grandmother
Each child sat still upon my lap
Tell secrets untold to no other.

She has a special collection
Of glass hands, what they do
Folded hands, fingers lift, point
Of visions high to view.

Hands store rings for fingers
Or ears to pass on through
Open hands, hand held flowers
Closed hands; numbers 102!

Poet hands poised in place
Stories for any season
Hands clasp, pray, lift prayers
If any concern or reason.

I'll bring you to the display

We'll visit hands some night
Before donation they will be
To local County Museum site.

Husband, John, builds things
Days in workshop yonder
Past window to extreme right
His tools are called "wonder."

Builds cedar rocking chairs
For children up to age five
Rock back in Time or Future
When dreams appear alive.

Cedar airplane with rockers too
Wings wide front back, small tail
Gifts for children's fantasy
Flights fan fairytale.

Little children forget, hurry so
Make-believe storehouse leaves
Dreams come back once more
Stories new child weaves.

He designed biplane rocker
With wheels to ride outside
If child imagines long enough
Over his workshop door can ride.

He loves to fly in azure sky
As we do on stimulation
His first solo flight, age sixteen
Pilot, U.S. Air Force formation.

He taught four hundred students
At local State University
How to fly, charged no fee
At city airport nearby.

Excited, I say, "Grandmother Doll
Come to workshop late
We could go, I could show
My flight brigade so great.

Airy-fairies fly silver wings
As pilots form flight stories
Patterns perfect, taught below
On ground flight laboratories!"

We muse together this very night
Moonbeams slide on window pane
Shadows tall, some shapes small
Land on ceiling John's airplane.

Horned owl perched on oak tree
Grandma says, "His eyes so keen.
He can view your curiosity
Times even what you dream.

Tomorrow you'll meet children
Let me tell you stories now
These children active, inventive
Search often to know how.

Once chased dangerous mink
Thought he could be nice pet
Beast ran faster than they
Not realized danger threat.

Swim in lake near brick house
With otter, frolic and play
Wood ducks, mallards and often
Blue Heron visits summer's day.

Watch beavers gnaw tree popple
His under stream store home
John and Diane visit them
Uninvited. Want to be alone.

Quick to swim away from them
A presence not to look upon
Lots to learn in tender years
Found in home at Woodlawn.

Quiet peacefulness wakes up
Each year, the 4th of July
They climb 60 foot ladder tree
Isn't tree guessed too high?

Rockets boom, burst, explode
Dazzled flares cascade.
Ruptured skies shine or blink
Pour flame brilliant made.

Deafened blasts continue
Seems they sit for hours
Until grand finale shoots
Continued varied showers.

Excitement gone down they climb
Old 60 foot ladder tree.
Proud to be an American
Enchantment naturally.

Below live creatures small and great
To discover, homes uncover
Be beetle, wasp or worm or bug
Brought each seen by Mother.

Grandmother Doll rocks old chair
Where dreams are made to last
A new night waits in this household
Johdia's home at last.

CHAPTER 17. JENNIE

"The poet judges not as judge judges, but
as the sun falling around a helpless thing."
A quote from Walt Whitman

Dearest Catherine:

By now the word is out you will receive a doll on your birthday! A double birthday, mine too! My dress designer, Miss Imelda tells me in your whole family of fourteen you are the first girl! So, that makes me a guest to the First Lady! My premiere is not only genetic by you being the eldest, but topnotch. Being of such crowning glory, you will find my chapeaux to celebrate the occasion in high fashion.

Miss Imelda tells me you have three girls in your family and one son. Fun. Also that your granddaughter's name is Emily too, named after your father Melvin Dickinson's family poetess. I have the same doll friend Emily who is very important to me. Poet Emily wrote many poems to tell how she felt, but they were not found till much later after she left this earthly plane. But that is all right, isn't it? I leave this earth many times and return whenever I want to, my mind creative that way. My dress finery is almost finished. My little satin purse will hold my poem message to you. So, my blue ribbon of triumph will be my name from you.

I am a very good listener. I am told you like music. Already I have heard some of the music on Miss Imelda's radio. Lovely classical music is artistic, similar like you and me. I am told that you know how to sew too. For this reason, special care has been taken in the design of my outfit. I am covered with hearts of blue and green to remind you of the earth and the sky that surrounds the beautiful flower gardens you have. Flowers of so many kinds you are familiar. I am told that you sew quilts with flowers printed on the fabric that looks like the gardens you have. It will be exciting to live at your house.

I love you already! I have a very winning personality; in fact, I can be anything you want me to be. I can imagine happiness already in my new red heart I got just a few days ago. This means that we dolls are ready to be adopted when we get our red hearts. They become the seed of happiness for daydreams and night adventures. This means we dolls are ready to be adopted when we get our red hearts. They become the seed of happiness for daydreams and night adventures that border on the ridiculous to the extravagant! With my fine clothes I am advised that you have a collection of shoes of all shapes and sizes! I will delight in using them during my midnight shopping. Shoes to become whatever I want to be in! I look forward to living with you, my First Lady! Being the very gentle woman you are, a noble doll such as I am, can be your royal princess. I am yours.

PS. That means pretty special.

Miss Imelda said you called her on the phone and my name is "Jennie" and I will learn about it when you read the poem she is sending to you. Love...Jennie

JENNIE...WHEN AS A WREN

One day in the beginning
Of spring, alive with new birth
Aloft old apple tree branch
Housed wren busied on earth.

Old wren house many years hanging
Seems vacant, as often they are
Until time for nesting
Spring's song on calendar!

Unknown her nest a-viewing
Each day from paned window to see
Was Catherine, a family's First Lady
Happy wren tenant to see.

'Jennie' she named house wren
Plain, common, gray-brown in plume
Sang songs gloriously pleasant
Filling Catherine's piano room.

Wren family near family human
Each song singular because
One sits on a branch as a songster
Another plays piano applause!

One day, a sparrow killed Jennie!
Catherine saw Tragedy fall
Outside, lifts Jennie's last breathing
First touch, last devotional.

Jennie dies in human hands holding
A house wren, happy that spring
My doll represents her memory
Wee wren's remembering.

My dress paints green hearts tiny
Like apple buds leaf when new
Fragrance Jennie flew through
Blue hearts chase blue hearts too.

Blue as sky Jennie sailed
Wings short carry plump body
Tail cocked upward she scaled
Lines jag white, zigzag oddly.

Like vocal repertoire for a bird
Short season her songs singing
Perhaps a duet you heard
Clouds cotton fluff azure sky bringing.

Backdrop fashioned divine
For birds, like Jennie, house wren
Croons notes clearly fine
Ate seeds of happiness then.

Dwelling in house tiny then
Warbled trills to your household
Jennie, wee house, wee wren
Awakened new day for her bold.

Across midnight sky blue
Voices of Jennie may bring out
Chirrups she used to do
Fragments of joy fall out.

My doll eyes open watching
For shadows just inches long
Haunting wee wren house
Soft chords vocal in song!

I tell her, once in a spring time
Glee filled her wren heart
She lived near her First Lady
First loved human counterpart.

When you play your piano
Ebony, ivory pearled keys
Tunes of Jennie may tune out
Balanced on spring's breeze.

Songs stripped wave ribbons
Like my dress across clear air
Look out windows for Jennie
Another wren may be there!

Remember joy she gave you
Reminisce happy her song
Admired wren for a Lady
A season her little lifelong.

Reflections of this little bird
Enlarged mental impressions
By me, a doll, named from a wren
Fills her common expressions.

I sit upon ornate quilt
Kaleidoscope design you made
Colors vivid everywhere
Catherine, as seamstress, first grade.

My hat smooth satin
My small purse matches too
Soft contrast to fabric grand
So sitting prim is what I do.

Memories make more memories
Some fancy, some plain, so many
They flit from me to you then?
From wee wren I'm named Jennie.

Letter from Catherine:

Dear Imelda:

First, I want to thank you for my doll Jennie. She is so pretty and lovable. I cried when I read her story. I am sure my grandchildren will love her because when they come over they play with my older children's dolls. Thank you again for Jennie. She will always be in the family. My husband and I will be celebrating our golden wedding anniversary. I hope you can come. Love, Sister Catherine
My dear Sister Catherine and Jennie:

Thank you for an invitation to your 50th wedding anniversary! Knowing Jennie as I do before she came to live with you, the words came easy for your anniversary poem from her, as below. Enjoy. Love to you all, your sister Miss Imelda

GOLD RETOLD

A golden, glittering censor

Was hanging over me
Burning bright it would seem
Around your family.

Flights of Time fluttered
From its Wonderings
When dreams become Realities
From Memory reckonings.

Then, Jennie's golden wren house
Flashed into my view
Wondrous remembering
When she lived near you.

Horizons golden fused to flow
Beneath burnt sky ablaze
As Jennie's fine feathers
Brush image of Earth days.

As I saw this vaulted vision
Fifty wrens, just like she
Soar above lace treetops
Brilliant for even me!

Gleaming, golden wings
Wave to wedded years
Lift your vows said aloft
Then Jennie disappears!

Paths golden streak upward
Stroke on Glory's sight
When Jennie came to visit us
This her golden flight.

Many more happy years
Winged wish for you all
Make more earth memories
From me Jennie, your doll.

CHAPTER 18. RAINER

"Emerald slopes became so tall they touched the clouds, and showers painted diamond waterfalls that sluiced down cliff sides."
A quote from Victoria Kahler

Dearest Meecy:

Showers and showers of love to you this very day! My name is Rainer. As you open this package, very carefully, you will see why. Your mother, Lorraine, was called Rainer by those who loved her. She was fresh as the spring rain, cleansing, and saturated her love to all who knew her. May I remind you of her beauty?

My umbrella covers a "rain tub" which Rainer always had ready in her small country farm yard. If you turn it carefully, it will play the song "Raindrops falling on my head." On it are colorful flowers of strawberries, tucked along the pathways is a mother hen and her chicks. If you look you will find a baby kitty, white and snowy looking, just waiting for you to notice.

My poem tells you about rain and the sweetness it brings to all growing things. Then, after a rain, perhaps a rainbow will appear and strips of ribbon shooting out from my tub tell you of the colors a rainbow can bring. Did you notice the blue of my dress...like the sky after a rain? Or the brilliant red of my hat and apron...like the sunset after a rain. Do you like the blue satin roses pinching my waistline? Rare they are, like your mother was. Gentle like soft rain she was. She loved you very much. I hope you will love me very much. Even though Rainer has long since been called back to the earth, where also the rain goes, it is hoped my freshness will remind you of her. I hope I will bring to you some measure of happiness her memory brings. It's just you and me now. We can dream a lot together. I know Rainer would have loved me. So we have a place of our own together... Doll Rainer

RAINER

Last preparations made ready
Blue in my dress as drops of rain
My red pinafore borders
Red ribbon lace over again.

My hat matches my pinafore
Music box and umbrella too
Perfectly packaged I am dressed
Bring Mother's memory to you.

My song of falling raindrops
On my head makes you smile
Mother hen and her baby chicks
Safe with small white kitty, while

Covered by matching umbrella
Mom's rain tub important for all
Grows things she touches with care
Her success sensational!

We greet you like memories
Mother brings night and day
Loved animals, dense woodlands
Separate her special way.

Familiar with walks about farm
Talks to green leaf, new bud flower
Knew their names every sprout
Walks among them in light rain shower.

Stormed woods naked in view
Abandoned bird nests all sizes
Wait spring's return birds she knew
Often new ones, her surprises.

Black bear stretch muscles asleep
Tends newborns growing well
Long training bear needs to keep
Her den a ne'er-do-well.

Tumbleweeds leftover tumble
Late winter forest wakes up more
Catch them if you can as
Field mice scurry on forest floor.

Castoff feathers, twig, scrap discard
Nest supply for new mates unmet
Perfect place in Rainer's backyard
Safe, secure dawn, dusk or sunset.

Deer tracks break rank turn new
Footsteps on deep winter snows
Newborn fawn helpless is safe
Space hidden mother Doe knows.

Canada geese soar cloud lofty trail
Seek to find each a place
Mate for life their new families
Unafraid in Rainer's space.

White trilliums, gold daffodils floral
Crocus, small purple petals peek
A goddess within each laurel
Care tended by Rainer to keep.

Coyotes howl social voices
Dance flirtatious mates roam
Desire afire in springtime
Find dens, make a new home.

Inside basket, fine flowers
Rests poem's dispatch to you
Months I waited this moment
When doll friends of mine too

Are packaged separate goings
Excite each entre nous!
I sit still where you put me
In chair, or rocker with view.

I listen for you in your bedroom
For whisper of Rainer's voice
She made mini-books of calendars
Artistic finger monthly choice.

January; white, cold winter
Blizzard dreadful, ice storms drear
Snowflakes like diamonds fall
Wink at Rainer then paste here.

February; red, view valentines
Hearts spread love everywhere
Rainer was expert doing that
Home whispering a prayer.

March; bright green, new birth
Animals, fields, grains, flowers
As rain drips her "rain tub" full
Water for tending long hours.

April; blue, more rain to Rainer
Helps new things grow better
She walks to her silver mailbox
From Mother, pictures and letter.

May; yellow, smiles brightness
Color rainbow's interpretation
Seven vivid shades stripe blue sky
Rainer chose all in cessation.

June; bright golden, full blossoms
Delight fragrance she knew well
Plants in her garden for eating
Vegetables nutritious to tell.

July; bring harvests more golden
Canned she preserves foods fast
Care cleaned, carefully storing
For winter's eating to last.

August; tan, extend late harvest
Of field grains for animals tend
Prepare for barn safe storage

Morsels for mice even lend.

September; school books for learning
White pages bring stories to know
Places near or far to visit to
Rainer's rocker with Meecy they go.

October; orange, cuts spooky eyes
Of Halloween, scary at best
Diverts daughter how to bake
Pumpkin pie, tasty for guest.

November; brown, usher thanksgiving
For happenings all yearlong
Grateful for all twelve seasons
Rainer enjoyed her lifelong.

December; red, Christmas holidays
Teaches Meecy holiday's song
They hear on their radio
Most times join a sing along.

Her art work on each booklet
Misplaced by years moving spaces
Remains in my bygone memories
Delightful as Rainer's face was.

Praise to a Sister continues
Years gone, fragrance lingers
Raindrops fall on your head blending
Colors painted by her fingers.

Blends sketch mother's memory
Though years an absentee
Magnificent colors shine to see
<u>Rainer's gentleness a guarantee.</u>

Red; for deep love freely given
To husband, child, close family
Plenty time showered unselfishly
Considerate, noble was she.

Orange; colors Rainer happy
Warmth her countenance sings
Joy to every girl and boy
Nature's gift of living brings.

Yellow; like sunshine, beams brightly
Helps others in hardship toils need

Lifts burden bleak, she does speak
Encouragement, comforts indeed.

Green; like leaves in springtime
Her touch alive, springs new birth
Refreshment follows her being
Exceptional, always her worth.

Blue; calm nature obvious
Within suffers silent health cares
Unknown, forces anxiety
Salves private by her own prayers.

Indigo; symbol her trust, her truth
Quality Rainer had all seasons
Began as youth to maturity
A friend to cherish all reasons.

Violet; colors image regal
Royalty her canopy, though poor
Spirituality idealistic, sincere
Praise Rainer in this memoir.

Her name, like rain cleansing
Wipes dark sadness she knew away
Lifts spirits higher than blue sky
Creates new birth, another new day.

So color pathways, bridge gap
Rainer created by her passing
As first sun's rays ancient or rich
Around colors none surpassing.

From fire, water, air, earth
Paint portrait of Rainer devotee
Since newborn in families' birth
Can you qualify better than she?

As you know her personality
As diamonds sparkle dawn's dew
Rainer a gem to know any day
Everyone agrees, you too.

Flowers bloom, grace her garden
Foods grew healthy by her hand
Animals greet her gentle summons
Their needs she did understand.

See her form in fire of rainbow

Ablaze with purpose to send
Warms to all who knew her
Heartaches easy to mend.

She walks in rain for cleansing
Felt darkness shed bleak cover
Dries off depression, if visited
Loneliness did daily discover.

Water fallen, flows freshness
In air fragrances alive, like new
Brings heaven to earth visited
Her Spirit's presence to you.

Bridges span spirits special
Presence pure Rainer can give
Enjoy pathways knowing her once
One earth this Angel did live.

Enjoy her raindrops falling
On your head when they fall
Dropping fond reflections
Of Sister Rainer, choice of all.

Fine qualities her life long
So humane to explain her
Represented by a doll after all
Privileged to be called Rainer

CHAPTER 19. ME / HOPE

"Music is the universal language of mankind."
A quote from Henry Wadsworth Longfellow

Dear Gretchen:

Miss Imelda, your very close friend, says I am the first little girl in your life! Your children are sons. So, I know I am to be very special. Even more so, Miss Imelda says when you called her on the telephone many, many miles away you had already selected a name for me, before I ever became ME. So, I must always be true to myself and you in all that we do. She tells me your favorite color is red. Like red strawberries you and your father would pick together, or apples, juicy and red from the orchards in the fall, or red lipstick you wore when you went out in public. Your mother's tulips blooming in the spring, along with her red poppies. Lots of red is in my dress to remind you of these happy things.

Being girls as we are we can choose red ball gowns, red hats, red shoes, red purses, red dresses, red cars, and the list can include all we want, as that I hear is a gals prerogative! Friendships can be in colors too and for some as close as you and Miss Imelda are, the glow will also be red, because friendships should be like the glow like a warm fire, inviting, and calm. I will love to share my life, sitting in your lap, in front of our friendship fire. Love... ME

ASPIRE TO INSPIRE

God's gifts to man plenteous
Gifts you are doubly favored
Singing from deep soul, blest bequest
Play on keys tuned savored.

Music is song of creation
Divine Echo by God's hand
Fair gift, music, for God's glory
Peaceful poetry, playful a command.

Beckons mankind back to Creator
Magnificent in meaning to blend
Vocal or instrumental arrangements
Soothe species to enjoy till life's end.

Will your music, mellowed medicine
Salve hearts breaking so now?
Will your song sounds from your throat?
Bind broken minds, mends to allow.

Will pipes piping from church organ
Pierce air glad tidings to rise
Soft medleys rest to those weary
If loved ones lost in cruel cries.

Will your voice sing solos in the beginning?
When couples join wedded days new
Will you play at dawn or eventide?
As you follow your talents true.

Ivory keys beneath ivory fingers
Make love in sounds, in love
Keys ebony express synchronous
Earthly concerts rise above.

Will your gifts, God given, gifted
Give back as you are twice blest
Will you inspire man to be more humane?
By songs sung of your swollen breast.

Will your pursuits pursue heavenly
Tunes toward celestial chorus
As you pursue more perfection

You can answer this quest for us.

Will your harmonious traces sound?
As mistress of musical order
An aria or visionary theme
Whisper words composer's recorder.

Pursue each elusive chording
Strung on sweet staccato keys
Music, great influence mastered
In Time melody's vortices.

Play, Gretchen, music of angels
Represent Drama's fear, great grief
Perform harmony as tears release
Entertain lyrical relief.

Thank God in melodious communion
Command, applause music's source
Testimonials laud His holy name
Your birthrights gift resource.

Music wanders into Life's corners
Where dwells down trodden man
Delight in dulcets you can bring
Symphonies since Time began.

Song celebration outlives sermons
Softens feelings so tender
Let your trill thrill crowds many
Those in solitude would remember.

My friend, use talents wisely
Let Today be the today you choose
Gone is yesterday nevermore to return
Tomorrow waits you to compose.

Waste not precious moments
In trivia not your design
Aspire to inspire, determine to play
Titillating music crystalline.

One day you'll be called up yonder
To eternity's shore in view
God says "Well done faithful servant
My celestial choir waits for you.

With angels to praise forever
On trumpet, harp and lyre

With gifts I gave you on earth
Gifts more in mansions here.

Sing, Gretchen, sing in glory
Play hands again, play on keys
Eternal in song where you belong
Immortal, God given, now these."

From Dolly Me... a poem to Thee

Here I am, you in ME
In fact, that is my name
ME, being a composite
Of us the same.

I welcome courage
When life pursuits go wrong
Missing battles unsought
Discretion pleads along.

I meet headlong
Encounters ever many
Unafraid, steadfast
Fears I have? Not any!

I care for compassion
On those discriminate
My paths associate
Weak or souls unfortunate.

I am known as noble
Distinguished of a kind
Intelligent in my world
Curious in my mind.

I esteem honesty
Truth sends salute
Respect me venerate
ME, as first recruit.

I toast true talent
Music different stages
Organ, piano, or voice
Join in noted pages.

Gifted tones stir within
ME, to catch a chant
MElodious to my ear
A Mi note variant.

Strains of true friendship
Chorus serenade
Refrains bright as my red dress
Special for us made.

Rhythm ditty's frolic sounds
Beat soft on my heart
Small in size, but thumping
Love ME, your sweetheart.

You can share your feelings
With ME when you chance
Day, night, or afternoon
Quiet in conversance.

So, I am things you are
Known or secret things
Dreams of possibilities
Visions, sweet scatterings.

I play Bach and Chopin
Mozart, Brahms in style
As ivory and ebony keys scale
Symphonies awhile.

Though I may never see
Massive cathedrals tall
I hear organs pipes still play
Distinct differences fall.

Services for church choirs
At times, seasoned choice
Angels strum heavens hymns
When we sing in voice.

Place my message safely
In my heart shaped store
Designed for reflection
Read of ME more.

In friendships we do savor
Comrade gentleness
Unique, designed together
Bringing happiness.

Where I sit, we do contain
All we do possess

Set 1 of 4 of the dolls from "Personolly Yours" Available at ImeldaDickinson.com

Keep ME close, as friends are
At each new address.

Personolly, our birthdays
Record day April four, be
Sealed as our beginning
Come on with ME.

Let's sing some more
Pleasant harmonious music be
Together MElodious
Songs we sing you and ME.

Dear Miss Imelda and Bill...

I received "ME" my bundle of joy on Monday. She is adorable. She will be treated with lots of TLC, thank you so much. I will treasure her forever. The poem was touching and brought tears to my eyes. One day I will frame all the poems you write for me. I still take care of my mother who is ailing fast. Thank you again for "ME." God love you both! Love Gretchen"

Later...One Thursday evening Gretchen placed me in her book bag taking me to her church to practice music for Easter festivities. She took me out of the book bag and seated me on a bench near a stained glass window with a little boy and his father in a carpenter shop sawing wood and curls of wood had fallen to the floor. Gretchen practiced so long she forgot me on the bench and so I stayed in the church all night. The little boy found many wood curls and we fashioned them around my hair that was not blonde like the wood curls, but it was fun. I could still hear echoes of the music Gretchen played on the organ with harmonized songs on a piano and violin. Then next day, being Sunday, Gretchen came early, put me back in her book bag and kept me close to the pedals of the organ where she would not forget me again. My blonde wood curls were left behind. I could not find them again anywhere. I guess the little boy wanted to keep them in his carpenter shop.

Months later, and with many new challenges, Miss Imelda decided to stop by to visit Gretchen and ME in her visit to northern Wisconsin. Gretchen's mother died and she had to dispose of her mother's possessions and much of her own to move to a smaller place. I was placed in a garage with a sign FOR SALE near my feet; she said she had to abandon most of her items. Miss Imelda asked Gretchen who purchased ME and she did not know. Miss Imelda found out about the time she put her advertisement in the newspaper and listed an ad in the paper trying to locate ME.. No response. Miss Imelda left Gretchen; trying to understand her reasoning in putting her doll gifted in a garage sale. She left me no phone for contact, since her calls must be limited, with no long distance, but took her address and vowed to send her notes of encouragement.

Miss Imelda received a phone call from a daughter who thinks she may have purchased a doll with a red dress at a garage sale when she visited northern Wisconsin several months ago. She made an appointment to visit the lady whose name was Debbie. She bought it for her father Gary who was very depressed after her mother Sarah who died five years ago. Her daughter, Sarah, age four, named after her mother, visits her father, but he was grumpy to her and did not want to visit much.

Miss Imelda arrived at Debbie's modest home in the country and Debbie drove her to her father's home deep in the forest to see the doll bought at the garage sale. Gary came to the door and told Debbie he did not want to see me or let me see "that goofy doll you brought over the other day." However, Miss Imelda could see in the short distance the doll on the fireplace mantle looked like the doll ME. She thanked Gary for his time and she and Debbie left. Miss Imelda was elated where hearts beat in happiness when a treasure is found after being lost. Miss Imelda took Debbie's phone number and said she would keep in touch. Debbie named ME a different name for her Father's doll she visited at Gary's house. Her name was Hope for encouragement.

HOPE

Sarah excited to see Grandpa Gary
Comes in his house from her Mom's car
"Oh Grandpa, I have such great news
Your doll's new outfit I got at a bazaar."

He says "She doesn't need a change of clothes
She sits on the mantle. Says not a word"
"But Grandpa you'll see, she talks to me"
Gary says under his breath cussword.

He walks away from Sarah, but not too far
Sarah's visits gave him hope inside
He just didn't feel good for such a long time
Misses wife Sarah long ago died.

He watched Sarah wide-eyed unafraid
She took off his doll's red dress
His once wife Sarah's favorite shade
Exposed red heart on chest impress.

Her underwear stylish homemade
Sarah lifts garment old memory to convey
Looks like dress Sarah had when they met
He went to Sarah, took dress away.

He watches Sarah's tears on face wet
"Call your mother, don't forget
Take that dress with you, small apron too
Put doll on the mantle, or better yet.

Take her and her clothes home with you"
Debbie comes to get Sarah still crying
Tells Gary, "You are mean, but I love you so
I hurt so too when Mother was dying.

You are blessed with a little girl who knows
How to love you so innocently
Sees a Grandpa who loved her at first
As a baby, then age one, two and three."

When the world says, "Give up," Hope whispers,
"Try it one more time."
~Author Unknown

Sarah left doll on boot bench by front door
Hugged her tight, whispers in her ear
"Keep smiling for Grandpa, don't ever stop
Make all that you hope for appear."

Grandpa alone ready to retire
Walks by bench where Doll Hope lay
Undressed yet, little red heart so clear
Turns out light, Doll nothing to say.

Little Sarah visits not this week
Her knock on door Grandpa missed
Her wee arms around his thick neck
Pleased by her small lips kissed.

He looks at doll Hope, fully dressed
With apron tucks her waist around
How can this be, Little Sarah absentee?
Puts doll back on mantle spellbound.

A knock on front door once more
Gary opens, little Sarah beams pride
"I have a new outfit for Hope Grandpa
Come and see it inside!"

In box are blue jeans with red checkered shirt
A cap like his, he wears in the field
Tiny box of sandwiches, coffee urn carried
Like once Sarah delivers four wheeled.

"I'll watch you dress the doll, Sarah
Did you dress her when you left last time?"
Sarah replies, again wide her eyes
"Didn't you change her at bedtime?

Sarah dresses Hope's a new outfit
Child conversation tenderly
Tells her new chores to please Grandpa
Meets him in cornfield at three.

Then Sarah and Hope play in a kitchen
Sarah imagines is really there
Grandpa wonders, did he change doll dress?
Before going to bed up the stair?

Sees Sarah and Hope drink green tea
With wife's miniature dish set
A delight to watch them have fun
Pretend to eat Grandma's croquette.

Grandpa sits in his chair by fireplace
Near Sarah and Hope closer today
Thanks Sarah for coming to visit
Can she come soon another day?

"Grandpa you smiled at me right now
I did not forget smiles once known
When I was smaller than I am now
See, Grandpa how I have grown?"

Debbie comes to fetch Sarah for dinner
Brings some for Grandpa to eat too
Debbie's secret sews outfits like Mom's
Noticed Hope has blue jeans new.

Good memories Dad can't miss out on
Sarah's hug for Grandpa; hold Hope the doll
Places doll in Grandpa's right arm
"See you, Grandpa, next house call."

Sarah's sweetness in the air, her charm
Seems to be in doll Hope he carried
Back to the mantle more carefully
Like a miniature Sarah he married.

Talks soft, "Hope, the name you have
Glad you came to live with me
Help me to be happy once more?
To Debbie and Sarah kind be."

Next week a knock on the door
Opens wide as Sarah runs a skip
"Grandpa you won't believe it
We three will sail on a ship!

Hope's outfit for summer's sail
When you and Grandma rent a boat
See sights on shores of Apostle Islands
On Lake Superior remote."

Hope's Capri's white match sweater
Yellow top, tiny buttons green
Anklets green too, hat yellow
What a dear wife to love seen.

Hope in style for husband fellow
Grandpa made sounds of boats on the sea
Sarah giggles delight dressing his doll
Make-believe lunch made for three.

"Don't forget, Grandpa, your telescope!"
Grandpa reminds seatbelts to wear
Safety in water really a must
Sarah covers Hope's sportswear.

Sarah sense's Grandpa's wanderlust
They set sail along carved caves
Sarah believes stories as they splash
Grandpa says "fierce waters, wind waves."

Why, he caught Hope's hat in a flash
Their lunch hot dogs, beans, tea
Tastes good when far out to sea
Sarah more smiles, a lot to sight see.

Fun today, Sarah, Grandpa and me
Twilight's sunset coming in more
Holds Sarah's hand on right side
Grandpa guides sail boat to sea shore.

Door opens as Debbie comes for Sarah
Gladness wells in her heart deep
Knows her little girl and Grandpa's doll
Become a keepsake to keep.

Grandpa Gary is left, holds Hope's hand
His little Sarah leaves for today
Will his beloved wife gone understand?
He is much happier this way?

He decides to build a clothes closet
For little Sarah's new surprises
Will make little drawers for storing
Doll clothes she organizes.

At nightfall dreams of his Sarah
His wife is clearer to see
Since Sarah plays with his Doll Hope

His grief, long sadness breaks free.

How does Sarah know her outfits?
Resemble wife's Sarah's so well
Does Hope really talk with little Sarah?
Describe perfect to tell?

Grandpa Gary's sleep peaceful
Like when wife Sarah was here
Night passes, its early morning
At front door is little Sarah dear.

"Grandpa we'll go dancing tonight
Hope's dress is pink as can be
Her slippers satin, also pink
"You must teach dancing to me.

I want to know how to fox trot
Do you find a fox first to dance?
Is two step fun Grandpa, a lot?"
Hope smiles more at first glance.

"Teach me to waltz, twirl around
Let's dress Hope in her ball gown
Pretty full slip fluffed all out
Such frill you never found.

We're all set for a ball for a doll!"
Hope's pink gown full flowing
Ruffles of satin pink lace trim
Her neck bare; pearls glowing.

Gary put records on phonograph
His Sarah's first choice to play
"Blue Skirt Waltz and Tea for Two"
Move chairs for more room today.

Grandpa tucks Hope in his neck collar
Her dress flows out the front
Her pink slippers poke his chest
Buttons shirt so fall she won't.

"Sarah, its one, two, three steps for waltzing"
With little Sarah's feet on his shoes
Shoestring ties to guide them right
Each dance step recalls, amuse.

Just like cutting the rug with wife Sarah
Then a spin, a whirl, be sure hang on

Then a two step, just one and two"
Little Sarah his shoes she stands on.

Doll Hope remembers once music
Gladdened her heart to its core
Hopefully happy once more again
On Grandpa Gary, Sarah on dance floor.

Back home Mother Debbie busy
Sewing new garment for a doll
Bought at garage sale for her Dad
Encouraged by little Sarah small.

Hope hears music in her red heart
Next to Grandpa's chest at a dance
Happy to be playing together three
Gives hope to Grandpa, a chance.

So, be patient if someone grumpy
Does not like you, or care at all
Keep hoping as Doll Hope did
Encouraged by little Sarah's call.

Life often harsh, dreams delay
When grief of loss you can't cope
Absence causes pain unbearable
Until along comes new Hope.

CHAPTER 20. HOLLY CAROL

"Our hearts grow tender with childhood memories and love of kindred,
and we are better throughout the year for having, in spirit,
become a child again at Christmas-time."
A quote from — Laura Ingalls Wilder

Dearest Marianne:

It would be natural to burst into song as your dolly...Holly Carol...gifted to you on your Christmas birthday. My being visual and vocal as well, when you least suspect my activities I may dance on staffs and notes of music with my little piano. I may interrupt your daily duties, since my noel's will be in tune with the Spirit of Christmas every day of the year! Since our birthdays are on December 25, the day set aside to remember a First Christmas, we certainly have a lot to sing about! How did I know about the first Christmas? Miss Imelda visits her friend DJ and places me outside on a small wooden reindeer before she enters DJ's home. Read on...

HOLLY-CAROL

I am an owl named "Hoot" to telecommute
I live in evergreen trees near here
This kind lady feeds me seeds and corn
I live near these statues dear.

"Mary, this is Holly Carol, glass like you
Telling the world this season's dear
Child of yours, Infant son so new
Brings happiness and cheer."

Joseph, man of wisdom, takes care
Protecting them from harm
While shepherds watch flocks at night
Keeps safe on field's farm.

Bright star of creation told too
Those who search for truth
Of Jesus born, foretold in past
Grows famous from His youth.

Mary's dress homespun made
Blanket for her Son threadbare
"It's warm enough" she says
"It's her only blanket spare."

I would have given her my dress
My hat careful made too.
"No" she says, "she has enough
It was a pleasure meeting you."

Chickadee birds a dee-dee-ing
Blue jays bold come to see
How can a reindeer so small
Carry one as big as me!

A crimson colored cardinal
Perched to sing a tune
Red contrast view in evergreens
Bold finches join, commune.

Singing in light snowfall
Sparse fall crystal white
Song-throated melodies
Bird songs pure delight.

Beside crib a sheep watching
Babe born rests in manger bed

Silent nights shout glad tidings
Some humans don't listen instead.

Swift comes rush of wings
Beside cradle where they stand
Heaven's herald angels sing
"Oh come little children", and

"Little town of Bethlehem" go
To birthday of a Baby King
"Joy to the World" this "Silent Night"
Celestial angels sing.

How will man accept this gift?
Graced from heaven above
Sweet Mary sings her Babe to sleep
Cradled in arms of love.

I am going to leave stable low
Joseph and Mary, sweet maid
Hush! Lay still, Babe your birthday
On all earth your story's told.

All nature, birds of air rhythm keep
Wind, fields, skies, trees overheard
Angels sang to Baby King asleep
I listen close to every word.

Eve's twilight once gentle falling
In heaven above earth He did come
Go tell it on a mountain calling
Jesus is born, the Holy One.

"Hoot" startled by opened house door
Flies for tree perch, not a word
I am lifted, placed back in cold car
So grateful for what I had heard.

I heard Miss Imelda laugh with her friend DJ while they talked on the porch. She comes to me, takes me off the wooden reindeer, DJ then kisses me and says her goodbye with happy Holiday greetings. I felt welcome there, yet I cannot wait to come and live with you!

We leave DJ's home, a snowstorm has begun, Miss Imelda re-routes direction of the car to her friend Jane's house in town where we are greeted warmly and invited to stay the night. I am placed in a quaint parlor. Miss Imelda's footsteps toward me are soft and protective, as she comes to place me comfortable for the night. She re-arranges me facing a small scale piano, places my hands on small ivory and black keys. She takes my wide brimmed hat to rest on the piano top and sat a miniature bear against the holly pin fastening. She says his name is Teddy. I winked I was pleased to meet him. She did not turn off the Christmas lights on a mid-sized tree in the corner of the room. There were ball-gowned, dressed dolls in fine array in an elaborate showcase. She steps back and smiles at all of us. Night shadows crowd around each corner with wonder and charm flickering everywhere.

I am spellbound in this little world of enchantment, yet it does not quell my anticipation to have you find me under your Christmas tree! I feel overwhelmed with the melody "It's beginning to look a lot like Christmas" because it will be to me real life very soon. ...Holly Carol

Very fashionable HOLLY-CAROL

There are dolls all shapes and sizes
Stand by antique buggies of wicker paint
Some have toys of their own miniature
My imagination awakens to acquaint.

I met twin paired Dennison paper dolls
Smiles sweet on polished faces
Four numbers 1890 printed on hemlines
So fragile they appear in places.

Designed arms and legs move
Modest dressed, bright bloomers, lace bits
Satin edgings on slippers grooved
Their dresses create class outfits.

Draws attention from a larger doll
Carved 21 inches of moving wood
Smooth neck, shoulders, fingertips tapered
I would like to touch her if I could.

Standing near book of portraits
Of dolls from far off place
"Germany" she read, in Europe
Whispers from her wooden face.

"People, all continents been making
Wooden dolls hundreds of years
Most in Orient, but my heritage was
In Germany, cottage industry peers."

I see faint name of doll, Gretta
Scribbled on sole of her shoe
Feeling unimportant, overwhelmed
As glass myself, what next to do?

A Dutch doll told news of beginnings

In Flanders were babies, peggitys,
Penny Woodens, Betty's woodentops
Timbertoes line doll committees!

Queen Anne dolls, painted heads
Not like my own, not mine!
Singles proud of genealogy
Historic in their own time.

Eyes expressive, bangs curl, swirled
Her mouth closed as petals tight
Herself marbled and pearled
Her dress rustled moves slight.

Shoulders smooth textured flawless
Aristocratic in finest clothes
Radiant in holiday festive light
I'm excited, want not to impose!

My glass eyes drift room's other dolls
Stare at me, holiday finery, compare
To period-styled dress I knew not much
Doll histories of then and there.

I lean toward someone for comfort
Curious as I, doll porcelain faced
Bisque doll seats in wicker doll buggy
Covered blanket many colors laced.

Tassel colored pink caught my eye
Sleeves, collar matches hat, fur muff
Face natural like Miss Imelda's. Oh my!
Gretta said name Hope on her cuff.

Design in Spode factory in England
Made first Parisian parts fine China clay
Together fire a high temperature band
Make multi-marbled look all day.

Silky, delicate figurine finishes
I had to stare intent to look
My imagination never diminishes!
More wonders to write in a book.

Her smile genuine forthright
High-browed appearance-faced look
Exciting experiences tonight
Treasuring each wonder it took.

I told her my name Holly Carol
Gift to daughter Marianne to hold
I bring songs to people far and near
Of Baby born in a stable cold.

This excited dolls around me
I sit by piano on piano bench
Used by once doll broken past repair
Discarded now in throw away trench.

I feel bad this short story told me
Suggest we all special songs sing
Melodies from their countries
As history's melodious bring.

Folk doll of many nations in agreement
Area places I had never heard
Want me to play and sing
Attentive to every word.

My fingers warmed in room air
Christmas tree trims above piano keys
My first audition chosen tonight
What an audience to please!

I hear Miss Imelda has festive music
On tape recorder with friend Jane
I began to memorize holiday tunes
Listen careful to each refrain!

My music sounds like Christmas
More night falls in this room
Large snowflakes outside covering
Unshaded panes a pine perfume.

I see cotton-ball snowman seated
Sled made of flat sticks bright red
Mini-train chugs on makeshift tracks
Almost breaks gold ornaments ahead.

Train stops at Street Nonsense
Ceramic double-faced clown circles 'round
Wood- carved Pinocchio's carrot-shape nose
My curiosity here easy found.

Transport ornaments of coaches, airplanes
Trolley cars, tugboats glide ahead
Doll in wicker buggy humming strains
All climb stumbling over spread.

Wrapped holiday presents under
Christmas tree piled, curious wrapping
I prepare my dolly audition
Human guests unnoticed are napping.

Fun to last us through the night
Dolls move, lifelike motions do
I sing softly clear in night light
"It'll be a blue Christmas without you."

I ask them if they knew about Christmas
Halfway through song doll faces sad
All year in bookcase just posing
Move their heads "No" never had.

I explained greatest Gift of all
Was knowing Jesus in their heart
I point to miniature Christmas scene on shelf
Universal figures this Season's part.

I tell them in my careful design
Miss Imelda gave little red heart
To wear, reminds me others to care
Family and friends set apart.

Red hearts filled with cheer daily
I invite all, imagine hearts of their own
Like mine to see clearly in view
They can love each other as shown.

Share with other dolls too
I play "Unto Us a Child is born"
Tell of Mary, Joseph and Infant Son
Human history as timeworn.

I learn more news one by one
Inspires my performance well
Little Drummer's finger fast on his drum
His chords "Sleigh Bells" "Silver Bells."

Encourages doll buggies form parade
Fine lines in rows well done
Small dolls around table and chair
How excited is everyone!

Scramble for tea cup filled with felt mice
Scurry for forms of safe place
I caution them always be nice

Step softly, not to fast race.

Apple juice spills from a pitcher
Douses their matte fur
Delightful taste sample each other
A disorganized, yet festive stir!

Our group continues festivity
My fingers on piano happy play
More melodies for holidays!
Select sounds like a Christmas day!

If I should play a song for Him
What song choice is best?
My imaginings always child-like
I'll sing a Happy Birthday request.

In child-like wonder, wondering
I peered by small manger glass
Watched infant, arms outstretched
To me porcelain doll lass.

Young mother and father kneeling
Smile in fixed greeting
Images of recent memories
Reflective worth repeating.

Historic of first Christmas
Celebrated many years ago
Birthday of treasured Infant
A story whole world should know.

As Angels celestial caroling
Shepherds heard on a hill
Herald Jesus' new birth
Bible prophesies did fulfill.

Songs singing sermons
Preach on that Holy Night
Heaven rested on planet Earth
As brilliant star shines bright.

Occasion for a holly-day
Poetic songs I will play
Of Him music's recollections
Heaven born Baby's birthday.

"Silent Night" melody next to play
Let's all sing voices combine thrill

Songs for a Savior to bring
To world peace and goodwill.

If I were there, I'd nestle
By His stable manger bed
To sing a song from a doll
Once as doll-child visited.

My song of thankfulness
Making me rags and glass
Paint and cloth, forming me
As in world wonders I pass.

Bring measures of happiness
As all dolls gifted to bring
Stories lighting each world
Individual's new songs sing.

Piano keys play on doll piano placed
Manger scene glows near lit space
Russian dolls once egg shells become
On display enameled in place.

We fill night songs chosen well
More snowflakes flake window panes
Frost already frosted on glass swell
Forms pattern of musical notes strains.

Lace curtains lace gray shadows
Reflects looking panes of glass
Dolls that move more quickly
Gracefully nod to each other's pass.

Each unique their heritage
Life sized anticipated delight
Form fine line for doll parade
Eyes wide open this night!

Christmas tree ornaments practice
Sway colorfully to and fro's
Separate spots glide magically
Figures festive their moving goes.

Dancing dolls extravagant
In taffeta stiff and fine lace
Ribbons glow satin, fluffy soft dress
Ballroom curtsies graceful place.

Smoothing hair already smooth

Certainly not commonplace
My continued piano audition
Our parade perfect in space!

Celebration first for me to view
Of a Christmas long ago
To celebrate, me and you!
Now all these miniatures know!

In wonder, wonder as a child
Song singing sermons of worth
As on that Holy Night mild
Heaven rested on Planet Earth.

Heralds first birthday of Jesus
In Christ child's aura bright
Occasion for a Holly-day
Again, celebrate holy night.

"Come all ye Faithful" we sing
"Hark, the Herald, Angels" song
A "First Noel" these dolly's bring
"Three Kings" gifts brought along.

To "A little town of Bethlehem's" King.
While shepherds watched "Silent night"
"Joy to the world" a manger far away
Surely no silence this night!

Snowflakes fake shimmer pale gowns
On dolls so fashion dressed
More songs sing as night shadows bring
Song celebrations blessed.

A birthday party now in full swing
Little hearts symbolized in us
Dolls in mutual merriment
Fake hearts filled spill love plus.

What a party we have raised!
Together in Jane's room here
Inheritance royally praised
We're good news everywhere.

I thought this very evening
We'd never again be together
When we could have such a party
All miniatures in snowy weather.

Lights flicker slowly as night falls
Shadows lengthen, grow dim
Sounds shorten from all of us
I'll play just one more hymn.

Dawn peeks through curtain laced
Snowstorm clouds nowhere seen
Teddy bear fallen asleep
In clusters of my new hat green.

Tree ornaments quick trace position
At tree branch ends in place
Glass door showcase on doll faces beam
To re-enter night's magic in lace.

A birthday night party happy kept
Friends new in this room made
While humans soundly slept
All dolly's happy on parade.

At dawn I'll leave miniature piano
My doll mind will never forget
These things I am telling you
Good friends from small dolls met.

Will you and your family help me?
Keep Christmas spirit to bless?
Miss Imelda sleeps; I read your letters
Send to her cabin's address.

Of Kurt, children Korry, Bonny too
Me, Holly Carol, your doll face
Very happy birthday wish to you
As our lives daily interlace.

I dream dreams with your dreams
I'll see animals at your home face to face
When grass turns green from snow fallen
We'll see Spring Wonder's in place.

Should stars in heavens like snowflakes fall
If a butterfly darts in field where
Sweet sounds of love from a parlor call
A musical melody's from dolly songs there.

Bees buzz about budded wells
Lightning bugs flicker only their ways
Under moonlit sky, creation tells
Full motions of Nature's praise.

Green leaves enamel from hot sun
Flowers fragrance meadows spread
Song birds warble tunes one by one
Listen in trees branches overhead.

Summers fade, autumn seasons new
Precedes snow blanket on forest floor
Diamond shaped stars form in skies
I'll wish a Christmas party once more.

Night creatures chirrup, hum and whine
Eve's or daytime praises become soft
I'll be busy while you sleep my family
Find creatures in books in your loft.

Your children's smiles invite me to spend
Some time with them as moonbeams
Light our pathways to dream and lend
View singular Baby manger scenes.

Grandmother's gift not so long ago
In my poem in closing tells
How much love I'll have to show
Happiness a holiday wells.

I'll dream again of dolls dancing
To my piano music while candles glow
A Christmas party one stormy night
In a magic parlor long ago.

Then our birthday this Christmas my gift
Miss Imelda says will be grand
Will be small piano Once a Time played
Christmas tunes with my wee hand.

Birthdays will come, birthdays will be
Year's memory sweet recall
Of Mother who gave birth to you
Gifts you later, Holly Carol, a doll.

CHAPTER 21. IMELDA

> "It has long been an axiom of mine that the little things
> are infinitely the most important."
> A quote from Arthur Conan Doyle

Dearest Bonny:

When you were very small you saw your Mother's porcelain doll, Holly-Carol, I gifted her for her birthday Christmas day. You were certain, in spite of your very young age, that I should give you a porcelain doll also, and you promised you would take such good care of her so she would never break. My friend Art Nelson made a little closet for the many clothes I made for you to change for her comings and goings as you enjoyed your new gift. You chose to call her Imelda, after me, your grandmother. May you have many years of enjoyment with her and your dreams you share together. Thank you for being so careful with your Mom's fragile doll, now you have one of your own. Love, Grandmother Imelda...

IMELDA

My mistress Bonny, little girl
Years favored three and one
Has a baby brother also
As a girl the only one.

She asks for a porcelain doll
To play with, to dream, to surmise
Life in general for one so small
Savors each day a new surprise.

Such people, little as she is
Want to hold my glass pearl hands
Or kiss my lips like a rosebud
Make-believe in my wonderlands.

I come packaged outfits many
Like a dress for a shopping spree
Collecting packages well spent
Choices made best by me.

To church I'm dressed elegant
Go see God of things created
Was far away, I could not see Him
"He is real," little Bonny stated.

I have bathing suit to swim in
Bonny says I can't in water go
I just must look lovely to look at
Onlookers can say to me 'hello.'

She likes to talk in play room
To other toys she knows well
None have clothes needed like us
Going places for fun to tell.

My horse riding outfit unique
Her pony we ride trots slow

We travel in lands far away
She knows just where to go.

Bonny holds close her promise
Careful, I could break visits to and fro
Change for travel to friend's house
Not one has doll like me though.

Bonny lets friends touch my hands
Only if careful their promise be
As girls they laugh, talk long hours
I sit still, listen carefully.

When night falls from gray shadows
I slip down shelf carefully
Visit toys in nursery. Bonny sleeps
All toys greet me happily.

"I'm play nurse Bonny," I announce
Care-giving I'll learn, necessary
Make illness go, treatments to know
Doctor visits with my notes vary.

Tell cures for toys ailing
All this for humans it is said
To practice imagination, muses
By make-believes in my head.

I observe toys in the nursery
Neat on shelves self-controlled
Bears, clown, and dolly of rags
Different than I am, I'm told.

We visit, talk as twilight lags
Of children's stories so bold
I believe, make-believe I am caring
For animals sick maybe cold.

I cheer them to laughing
As best nurse attends their way
Their unseen hearts near breaking
Some toys break easy they say.

My little red heart, small as it is
Will take their hurting away
I'll patch torn eye of "Rabbit"
Hanging lower than yesterday.

I'll sew seams of "Polar Bear"

Torn from forest trail ways
Help calm her babies' mischief
Bright-eyed with bushy tail days.

I watch stunts of painted "Clown"
Laughs at his Self mostly all day
Toys smile, makes him feel good
His 'happy' in nursery to stay.

I comb yarn hair of "Dolly"
Fold carefully new nightgown
Button her dress unbuttoned
She might venture downtown.

I wipe "Patch Dog's" tears away
He cries since Mom is gone
I let him lick my porcelain face
His tears dry over my face on.

I'll counsel "Scat" her prowling
Scaring "Smouse" in a shoe
So small, but safe to hide in
"Shame, Scat, shame on you!"

I'll listen to 'D-know's' stories
Not knowing of this or that
Unsure himself what to believe in
Make-believe not where he's at.

We tell of rooms of rooms
Filled up of interested toys
Shared by children in Bonny's house
Friends growing girls and boys.

Classes held by teachers wise
Come too to visit all of us
Down or around the bend
Traveling on gold school bus.

Dawn beckons nurse duties
Playroom nursery I attend
Back to Bonny's place on shelf
Nurse books more views to mend.

Book small tucks under my arm
Treatment as nurse seem endless
Old toy's need mends day by day
Make-believes renew toys friendless.

By day proper in care my sitting
Perfect Model shelved at side glance
I ponder twilight wanderings
Maybe I'll teach toys to dance.

I write poems never written to see
Describe professional in pen when
By night, again, in Toy Nursery
I'm play Nurse, Bonny, R.N.

Bonny dreams she marries grown up
Asks Grandmother to make me a gown
White, lovely for me a new bride
With veil for my head as a crown.

We tell all toys in the playroom
Guess who will she marry, to ponder?
What kind of man will be worthy?
Of my mistress Bonny, I wonder!

My wedding dress posted by mailman
Bonny enters playroom, runs to me
Opens box from Grandmother dear
Lifts up my dress white as can be.

Skirt flared, bodice so modest
A shear veil more beautiful to see
Crown of white pearls, flute flowers
I'll be beautiful, I'll be.

Fine white lace seen all around
Bold beauty of dress embraces
My red rose bouquet hands found
Red satin ribs color contrast graces.

A gown to dream of, to marry one
Lifetime partner to adorn love's way
Always his bride always inside
Each moment share what we may.

A husband adores his new bride
Each day always a new day
White gown lasts forever
As marriage forever will stay.

Promises not forgotten ever
Blessed by words heaven's conveys
Little doll Imelda good listener
Ears listen what Bonny's words says.

She talks a lot; I pay attention
What new notion dream today
Bonny's ideas voice wedded wishes
Her thoughts many varied say.

"To marry an Accountant maybe
Like her Dad who manages money
As husband comes home faithfully
She greets him as wife, his honey.

Overwhelmed by so great numbers
Happy years together they see
As his bride number One always
As safe as she could ever be.

Maybe I'll marry a Teacher
Like my Mom who knows all things
Guide children's right pathways
Choice best for their life brings.

Learning of wide world places
Oh so far away each nation
Know people so unlike us
Discover new language translation.

In wide universe locate stars
View planets each new name
Constellations, solar form Bars
Research origin they came.

Seek seas of creatures unknown
Some large, some small, unique
Coral reef beauty unequalled
Oceans vast, rare life will seek.

Maybe I'll marry a Doctor
Heals humans, help them feel better
Studies so hard, studies so long
For his name beside MD letter.

Compassionate, guiding patients
Choose alternatives wise
Never to harm bodies, ever
Soothe inner body cries.

Maybe marry Painter famous
Draws pictures imagined to seem
Appear real, become to viewer

Exactly like once in a dream.

Or Artist, like my brother Korry
Makes graphics to suit every book
Gifted he was from tender age
His drawing pleasant to look.

Maybe I'll marry a musician
Compose songs just for me
Happy, not sad words ever writing
Of his choice once bride to be.

Bonny's dreams stop by doorbell
Her friends chose to visit today
She tells them of me her dolly
Gift from Grandma on her birthday.

Mother says we can't visit long
Trip plans to Grandmother soon
Bring doll Imelda with us, be careful
We meet photographer at noon.

Invitations by friends with dollies too
Public meetings main part of trip
We see Doll Karina, remember when?
Mother made her legs from the hip?

To become famous ballerina
Meet teacher, young Meredith to tell
Of her school class to learn first steps
Beginners memorize dance well.

Watch each master exact movement
Motions graced at a glance
Demonstrations nightly, faithfully
Team for forest ballerina's dance.

You'll see new friend Mandy
Holds Karina by local mill stream
You carry Imelda for photographs
For writer photographer team.

Printed story display on front page
"Of woman is just a doll in family's eyes"
Book "Personolly Yours" a rage
Volumes for family, a friend exemplifies.

Create charm, mirth, gladness
All make news, doll's different view

On human thoughts and emotions
Passed through minds of dolls new.

Miss Imelda hopes book delightful
By person select gift glass doll
Entertain all ages to breathe sigh
Restoring once Child in us all.

Outgrown by years passing by
Quickens minds to commandeer
Illusive minute flash to intensify
Images display frolics appear.

Delightfulness draws nearby
Curiosity close pursuit too
Lots to do on this trip you and I
Enjoy fun as family to do.

Preparations ready, trip route clear
Minnesota north, Wisconsin too
Family spaces, family faces
Visits happy reunions elated do.

Bonny falls asleep on long journey
Holds tight my new wedding dress
Always careful of my safety
Her promised promise express.

Kind care for veiled headdress
"Maybe", she dreams, "I will marry
A Scottish dancer performing wide
Entertains people his talents vary.

Creates music inspired by my side
I'll pinch pleats in his skirt
Firm touch by my loving hands
Hug him close tight on his shirt.

Maybe I'll marry a student
When studied to be a nurse
Share my care giving qualities?
Inspired by caring Creator erst.

Maybe I'll marry a poet
Writing free or rhyming lines
Loved by humans alive or long gone
Inspirations sound designs.

Whomever I marry I'll dress

In white gown brilliant to see
Adorned bride for my husband
Chosen, loving only me.

Hours pass we arrive at cabin
Of sister, awaits our coming
Prepared to go to town meeting
Town gossip stories humming.

First friend, little girl Mandy
Joins at lake graced with swan
Pose pictures with Bonny and me
Karina, her new legs sewed on!

We meet photographer promptly
Take notes for story on front page
About us as dolly's to be famous
Delightful to know at any age.

Karina's legs look perfect
Slim forms for ballet dance
I tell her my new wedding dress
Is designed for a dream trance.

We watch swans swim graceful
Close where we pose pretty
Not know they too are beautiful
To look at so close in this city.

At noon too we meet members
Of Monday Club wanting to see
Dolls brought to dinner by Miss Imelda
Deena, Dolly, CC, includes me.

A short poem of the event is written
By Miss Imelda tells the story
Of gifts of wee dolls as gifted
Bring happiness, often even glory.

Exposed to humans who us seek
To confide dreams grown inside
Concealed long, deeply they speak
Their minds reopen seek wide.

Legends, lore, myths, early, whilom
Express, soft caress, antique
Extinct, archaic experience
Child renewed on time each week.

Past, primeval, quondam, historic
Poets' free verse pantomime
Revive once Child within them
Venerate yesteryear yore's climb.

Timeworn, relics, once upon
Ancient armchair dates expressions
Dated ancestor once famous
Thoughts delightful impressions.

Encouragement to crowd contagious
Inspire thoughts to wander to wonder
Enjoy moment's fleet, stop to meet
Day hours or nightly slumber.

We leave club to Miss Imelda's gallery
Sewed dolls with dress to match
A new real bride's dress exactly
Viewed by brides for grooms catch.

Her dress yards filmy lace fabric
Brocade stems uniform laced
Bodice ruffled, ruffled again
Perfect sewn, perfectly placed.

Sleeves puff to wrists modest
Neckline kisses doll's chin
Veil crowns with pearls circled
White floral design, gloss satin.

Frame doll's face beautiful
Match real bride's happy face
Doll hands clasp careful viewing
Pink flowers single bouquet.

Highlight contrast bright white
Carry's flower girl wedded day
Bride adorned for her husband
With them her dolly will stay.

Dressed once her wedding dress
Couples vow consent decree
Doll's importance never varies
Select imaged view cast to see.

Reminder of wedding once
Display today by us three
We return to Julie's log cabin
Field flowers grace glen we see.

Bonny takes me in field flowers
Miss Imelda more pictures today
Prized day remember family hours
What news we made to convey.

Goodbye, my sister Karina doll
I recall diverse dolls we knew
Shipped far away, but still today
Remember fond renew review.

Someday, Karina, confides me
I'll learn to dance so well
Miss Imelda will invite dolls to visit
Her at cabin, their stories to tell.

Her invite by way of messages
By phone, letter, email or birds
At each recent doll's address
New stories, sequels, new words.

I'll wear my new wedding dress
I'll be only bride debonair
Bring stories to toys in nursery
Dolls from towns here and there.

Dreams live, stud a moon skyway
Join, events reminisce aglow
Karina will be so excited
Stories she doesn't even know.

Share, care, dare dreams to tell
At field forest once beginnings
Exclusive story each tells well
Finale of doll news they're bringing.

Become stars in clear night sky
Karina promised ballet dance
Legs perfect form gracefully by
Meredith rehearses taught stance.

Poised movement perfect closes
Karina's dream true in her dance
Gesture active as ballerina poses
Her dream fulfilled at last glance.

I return to spot on Bonny's shelf
Share dreams she has day by day
Watch her grow, I wear my wedding dress

Will meet her husband some way.

Reality became real today
Believe, always believe after all
Possibilities dwell some way.
To Imelda, Bonny's glass doll.

CHAPTER 22. MARGARET

"Music gives a soul to the Universe, wings to the mind,
flight to the imagination, and life to everything."
A quote from Plato

Dearest Brother Ed:

Never, in my wildest dreams, and I have many of them, did I ever make believe I would be a gift to a man! Miss Imelda tells me you are a very loving man, very understanding and most aristocratic, and yet very child-like in your attentions to family. And, so am I. This is where dolls belong...in childhood, in memories.

I am the memory of someone who loved truth, your Mother Margaret. The name means "Pearl" and that we are, a precious stone, sometimes solitaire, as she was in her life. A jewel, sanded by the grains of time, perfected into the gem she was in the eyes of everyone who knew her. She was an ornament of brilliance among the lives she affected. A flower, picked from the many gardens she grew, so too her house plants in as many places she could nook! She loved music, and she instilled in her children the love of music. She played eight different instruments, by ear, not knowing how to read notes. Her friends were the ivory and ebony keys on the upright piano she spent many hours on, as her children surrounded her singing. She developed that in you, Ed, and with your accordion she created in you the rainbow of musical colors, now confined as memories. You and your accordion became a band to love,
In the orchestra you developed.

My presence brings colors of earth that Margaret grew flowers and foods well. My flowered skirt will remind you of the blends of fabric flounced in your Mom's dress. Music. Margaret loved to play other instruments to express guitar chords of "The Blind Child" which was her favorite, or "Smoldering Embers" which was another favorite. She loved to collect rocks, some supplied by you; interesting her favorite Gospel hymn was "Rock of Ages. She walked faithfully in the swift footsteps of prayer on golden fetters of love with an occasional glimpse of glory along the way. She wrapped those she loved in the mantles of love. I like surprises, but I will spill the beans, Miss Imelda's got a doll sized guitar coming with me and I will play songs of yesteryear, so fresh still, in your memory. Future times will be with you, in Mother Margaret's fond memories. It is such an honor to represent her to you on this festive gift occasion, Father's Day. I bring you the ecstasy of loving and being loved....Margaret

MARGARET

For the sake of keeping
Tokens of remembrance
I am memento of our Mother
Gracious in significance!

To sing songs of days gone by
When once her presence there
Brought joy to girl and boy
Her music filled the air!

Titles of songs list below
Little stories create
Music loved by Margaret
By Doll Margaret your new mate.

'SOME SUNDAY MORNING'
'IT'S A MOST UNUSUAL DAY'
'LET THE REST OF THE WORLD GO BY'
'MEMORIES' come your way!

'SOMEBODY ELSE IS TAKING MY PLACE'
'BEAUTIFUL, BEAUTIFUL BROWN EYES'
'OH, YOU BEAUTIFUL DOLL'
As such, I am your surprise!

'I CRIED FOR YOU' 'ON BLUEBERRY HILL'
'JEANNIE WITH THE LIGHT BROWN HAIR
'DRIFTING AND DRFEAMING'
Over 'BLUE HAWAII' there.

Drifting as I am dreaming
'WHERE THE RIVER SHANNON FLOWS'
'I ONLY WANT A BUDDY' or just 'SMILES'
Kiss 'SWEET ADELINE' or 'MEXICALI ROSE'

'IT'S A SIN TO TELL A LIE' 'PAPER DOLL'
'IN THE EVENING BY THE MOONLIGHT'
'ROLL ALONG PRAIRIE MOON' up tall
Pretty Margaret In spotlight!

'WHEN THE MOONLIGHT SHINES ALONG THE WABASH'
I'm on ship, 'ANCHORS AWEIGH'
I won't be 'HOME FOR THE HOLIDAYS'
No 'WHITE CHRISTMAS FOR ME' I say.

Maybe, 'NOW IS THE HOUR'
'THERE'LL BE SOME CHANGES MADE'
'THE MORE WE GET TOGETHER'

Songs of 'MAGGIE' pervade!

'TUMBLING TUMBLERWEEDS'
Roll under 'BLUE SKIES'
Drifting along to make a song
Melodies I memorize!

'I'M ALWAYS CHASING RAINBOWS'
'ON MOCKING BIRD HILL'
Among 'YESTERDAY'S ROSES'
'DOWN BY THE STREAM' and 'OLD MILL.'

'YOU TELL ME YOUR DREAMS'
'BY THE LIGHT OF THE SILVERY MOON'
'ON MOONLIGHT BAY'
Let's all sing this tune!

'YOU ARE MY SUNSHINE'
'ON THE SUNNY SIDE OF THE STREET'
'I GET THE BLUES WHEN IT RAINS'
'PRETTY BABY, AIN'T SHE SWEET.'

'HAVE I TOLD YOU LATELY THAT I LOVE YOU'
To 'PUT YOUR ARMS AROUND ME'
'JUST BECAUSE', 'I'M A GYPSY GIRL'
'HAVE YOU EVER BEEN LONELY.'

'DRINK TO ME ONLY WITH THINE EYES'
'IN MY MERRY OLDSMOBILE'
'WHEN YOU WERE A TULIP'
'SPANISH EYES' are real!

'DON'T FENCE ME IN', 'LITTLE BITTY BABY'
'HAIL, THE GANGS ALL HERE'
'TIPPY, TIPPY TIN,' 'GOODNIGHT IRENE'
'BEER BARREL POLKA, have a beer!

'IRISH EYES ARE SMILING'
Sing 'THE WHIFFENPOOF SONG'
As the 'BELLS OF SAINT MARY'S'
Ring 'OVER THE RAINBOW' long.

'IN THE GOOD OLD SUMMERTIME
'LISTEN TO THE MOCKING BIRD'
'WHERE THERE'S A LONG, LONG TRAIL AWINDING'
There a 'RED WING' is heard!

'I'M LOOKING OVER A FOUR LEAF CLOVER'
By the 'SHABBY OLD CABBY'S' stops

'AS THE BAND PLAYED ON,' 'DARK
TOWN STRUTTER'S BALL' hops!

Such a 'SENTIMENTAL JOURNEY'
Whispers 'FOR ME AND MY GAL'
As 'RED SAILS IN THE SUNSET'
'IN THE GLOAMING' musicale.

'MOUNTAIN MUSIC' singing
Veil soft 'HARBOR LIGHTS'
Deep in 'THE RED RIVER VALLEY'
'BLUE MOON,' ' SIDE BY SIDE' sights.

'YOU'RE THE ONLY STAR IN MY BLUE HEAVEN'
There's a 'GOLD MINE IN THE SKY'
Coming from 'DADDY'S LITTLE GIRL'
'MARGIE', your 'BABY BYE.'

Take me 'HOME SWEET HOME'
As you're 'PEG OF MY HEART'
'YOU'LL NEVER WALK ALONE' 'BABY FACE'
'LET ME CALL YOU SWEETHEART.'

By 'MOONLIGHT AND ROSES'
'I'VE TOLD EVERY LITTTLE STAR'
'THERE'S A LONG, LONG TRAIL AWINDING'
'HOW WONDERFUL YOU ARE.'

'PACK UP YOUR TROUBLES'
'IN YOUR OWN KIT BAG'
With your 'LITTLE BROWN JUG'
Play 'WOODPECKER SONG' rag.

'SILVER THREADS AMONG THE GOLD'
'WHEN I GROW TO OLD TO DREAM'
'THE ROCK OF AGES', 'WHISPERING HOPE'
'SILVER BELLS' redeem!

The 'BLUE MOON TURNS TO GOLD'
'TILL WE MEET AGAIN' means
'SHOW ME THE WAY TO GO HOME'
Where 'LAST ROSE OF SUMMER' dreams.

'LET THE REST OF THE WORLD GO BY'
On 'THIS LAND IS YOUR LAND'
'ALEXANDER'S RAGTIME BAND'
Play last 'AULD LANG SYNE,' and

'GOODNIGHT LADIES,' hold my hand

All sing the songs of yesteryear
Mother Margaret did understand
Beyond her years, now silent here.

'IF YOU WERE THE ONLY GIRL IN THE WORLD'
'MEET ME TONIGHT IN DREAMLAND'
Not 'DARLING NELLIE GRAY'
'I WANT A GIRL' 'LOVE'S SWEET SONG,' and

I'd want to be the memory
Of Mother pearled, loved
Just a fantasy away!
Mother Margaret dreamed of.

Play a tune, or strum a chord
Dance on music's keys
In your home, bring her aplomb
Heirloom, Me, please!

'WJHAT A DAY THAT WILL BE'
'IN THE STILL OF THE NIGHT'
When I am 'IN THE MOOD'
After gray twilight!

Of course Eddie was a waltz King
'UNCHAINED MELODY' for
'CLEMENTINE' 'TONIGHT' sing
'ONCE IN A LIFETIME' encore.

'SOMEBODY ELSE'S MAN"
'MEET ME IN ST LOUIE, LEWIS'
'THE LAST WALTZ' if you can
'VIA CON DIOS' 'CHARADE' bliss.

'COULD I HAVE THIS DANCE'
'WHEN EVER FOREVER COMES'
'MISSOURI WALTZ' our chance
'MOON RIVER' 'BY THE WALTZ' hums.

'WALTZ OF THE FLOWERS' for hearts free
One more request tonight
'THE WALTZ YOU SAVED FOR ME'
Last waltz played tonight.

Mother's Spirit by 'THE RUGGED CROSS'
Her 'PEACE IN THE VALLEY' well earned
Shared songs as these to please
Lessons all of us learned.

I'll sing a little song
Jig, like her, maybe dance
Connect music like then
Remember when by chance?

I want to be the memory
Of dear loving Mother
She played these songs
Could never be another!

Join in chorale throng
Remember when by chance
Together you two played together
Melody's happenstance!

Mother conducted orchestrate
Ten piece live band diverse
"Texas Panhandle Orchestra"
Cowboy and Cowgirl" rehearse.

"Swing Music, Southern Styled"
Billie and Bonnie twin yodelers styled
Also together on electric guitar
Drummer Joe, blind since a child.

On violin, Roy is tireless on
Blown horn to jazz sounds go
Fingered keys another accordion
Clown comedian "Happy" to know.

Sister Adeline plays the piano, is
Called "Sweetheart of the West"
Sings solos or in the group
Eddie's orchestra musical conquest.

Each booking Eddie's holiday
Banjo music to dance some
Encouraged, uplifted, steady
Years of practice at home.

Dad Mel and Marge manage tickets
Often Mom says "Let's play Eddie"
Funds salaries, lodging, expenses
Pop Band gigs are steady.

Cooperation in self-confidences
Reservations for halls in states
Midwest, Wisconsin or Minnesota
Eddie's band success gyrates.

Two years melodies ring out
Eddie's accordion strums steady
NEWS World War II is announced
Players disband, some enlist ready.

This music to remember
As select songs were played
Orchestrator E.J. Dickinson
Music man faithfully stayed.

With love of music influenced
Mother modeled in his mind
His band "Darvey's Lumberjacks"
Real Zips, a different kind.

'FOR A GOOD TIME WE PLAY'
Their motto "Old Time Anytime"
Long hours practice night and day
Instructs instruments ragtime.

Banjo and drums harmonize
By handpicked music players
Firm, serious, no compromise
Diverse music in layers.

U.S. Navy calls him for duty
Boot camp rigid over coastwise
Board's ship to Pacific Theater
Opportunity maximized wise.

Iwo Jima campaign assigned order
Often ship was hospital to rest
Given order to Treasure Island's flagship
Midst crew, officers atomic test.

Navy duration is hardship long
His wife and children distressed
Honorable Discharge released
His music no more suppressed.

Starts band in blink of an eye
Eddie and his band play on
Peel out many a tune
At eventide until dawn.

Warm winds wake and whisper
Sweet songs to remember Ed
Music shared when he visits

Family at Minnesota Homestead.

Taught direct by musical Mother
Response unequalled in loving son
Doll Margaret will love no other
Orchestrator E.J. Dickinson.

Ed tutors me on my own guitar
My dreams so vivid to me
Hopping notes pulse rhythm's bar
Pages confirm my jamboree.

Practice over, it's getting late
Ed's gone to bed already
Dreams so real they speak
Mom says again "Let's play Eddie."

"Hi, Imelda and Doctor Bill... You might label this letter "take 26" as I have racked my brain in an effort to properly thank you for the most precious gift 'the doll.' The most remarkable thing of it all, it is your creation, what a work of art, and further, your dissertation is priceless. I have read it a dozen times and enjoy it more each time. To me, Mother was real special, in your words a "pearl." Our sister, Mardelle, told me your dolls are gifts to each sister and brother. I am overjoyed you included me in the gift offering. God love you for it. Your Pearl Girl doll of memories is extraordinary because she brought memories back to me. I can still hear Mother say "Let's play Eddie." She was most happy with her music. She had so many talents. Again, many thanks for the memories of a sometime forgotten past. What a lovely Father's Day gift!

Me and my family's thank you for this lovely doll, and you can be sure she has found a home with us. She has a special stand made for her in the living room. We are having the letter made up on a special wooden frame and it will be placed beside her.

Hi Imelda, Doctor Bill and Others... A note in your Christmas card in fond hope it finds you in the Christmas spirit and above all you are all well. You probably noticed the pictures, so will go over them first. "Margaret," the doll is sitting in a hand-made, doll chair made by my wife's great grandfather and is over 100 years old! The seat is leather thongs and also original. We would love to be included in receiving your Doll Book "PERSONOLLY YOURS" when published. I also saved your newspaper issue clipping on the dolls. Keep up the good work.

You mentioned in your letter you would like pictures of our H.O. train set up we had in the California house. I list them and talk about them by numbers, as follows:

Name of Valley is "Hoursville"; hours for the many hours it took to construct (one year). Ours of the name to imply it denotes the family re-entries. To the extreme right is a natural gas tank and storage unit to be a part of Dad's gas work. To the left is the farm with its barn, silos, cows and ranch buildings, you can see crops, house and plow and disk. To the left many buildings: gas station, boarding home, horse and wagons with people in it. The little station has people on the Platform, plus more on the station.

This is my wife's pet project. She made all the trees and garden, plus landscaping. The backdrop is a scene, but she brought it into the creek. We simulated it through the property; naturally, I put a bridge over the stream. A close up of school and area, plus church and graveyard, plus setting area by church. These buildings are all hand-made to half-inch scale. A mining scene in the distant backdrop. Above school is Brother Frank on a horse with his Western cow. He is coming home; won't Mother be thrilled! Ha-ha. Just show more detail, such as, horse-drawn wagon, Model A Ford truck. Note landscaping around buildings. The little building with green on it by the truck is Ray Davis Real Estate where I was employed. Ha-ha. Note back of the little section cart back at the station. It worked!

Well, it was great fun! Doll Margaret is up all hours of the night in "Hoursville" and just makes it to her rocker in time for my breakfast!

A SEEK WELL...Margaret
PS. That means: Passes suddenly...Brother Ed

A sudden illness took Brother Ed
He soared to eternity.
Doll Margaret given to daughter Roxie
Her guitar holds carefully..

Sharon and Roxie loved their father
Distanced many miles, until recently
Nurtured him his days with them.
Diligent their care lovingly.

At peace now Ed, in timeless
A golden accordion gift awaits you
In Heaven's orchestral ensemble
Songs you remember and new.

Human hands made new from clay
Echo world unseen, none other.
Play anew with celestials on high
Tutored again by Margaret Mother!

Harmonious voice of creation
Earthly music can't justify.
Concerts, themes and chants
A new band you occupy!

An eternity to compose music
Heaven scores perfect share
Wind whispers new melodies
Wondrously spectacular!

What songs will you desire Ed?
What tunes exalt as you climb?
Your golden accordion new to play
"Once Many a Time"

Family joins hands at your Memorial
A light flickers, glowing ember.
Flames fire legacy of your music
Warm your songs to remember.

Mother Margaret approaches you
Her beauty more than ever ready
Strums her golden guitar strings
"Come, let's play, Eddie."

CHAPTER 23. MARGARET / MARGARET

Dear Sharon:
Miss Imelda has finished making my dress for you. She takes pictures of me with my dress of aqua trim and pale light green fabric with a red rose at the waist of my full paneled skirt. I represent to you your two grandmothers you loved very much both named Margaret. When I come to live with you I hope I will see again my friend Margaret who was gifted to your father Ed. Now we will be family...all. of us...Love Margaret-Margaret

MARGARET-MARGARET

My father's Mother Margaret
Invites my sister Roxanne and me
Visits monthly to her house, better yet
We learn tasks sharing family.

I learned to make real butter
Sweet fresh cream from Grandpa's cows
I crank butter, cranking more
As separation of buttermilk allows

Globs of fat solid butter surfaces
Milk is stored for pancakes planned
Grandmother Margaret shows me recipe
Of pancake batter made by her hand.

One month both of us came to visit
We helped make bread from scratch
Kneading and pulling dough all directions
No eight grain will ever match.

We make our initials on top of each loaf

To take home to show our prize
To our Grandmother Margaret on Mom's side
Light to carry baked at high-rise.

Once Grandmother gave me a needle
Said, "Sharon, learn to sew buttons on"
Thread was as fine as could be
I practice, try again to catch on.

Carefully I hold this needle to sew
Any mistake sharp sticks my fingers deep
Steady, sure, attention so keen
My button sewed perfect to keep.

In summers we go to family garden
Organic grown vegetables many
Green beans, peas and tomatoes
Potatoes, squash, herbs if any.

I learn different leaf patterns
Newborn plants or random weeds
Grandmother's supervision kind and gentle
"Follow new pattern of seeds."

One month Grandmother Margaret has books
Points to me words I never knew
She says she writes her own musings
For local newspaper to read, me and you.

Sometimes we visit and listen
Many musical instruments she can play
Toe tapping fiddle, guitar picking, or piano
Mouth organ, banjo played yesterday.

As a doll Margaret I remind you
Of a Grandmother Margaret's love
Treasured in tender young years
Talents for future time use of.

Grandmother Margaret on Mom's side
Worked in local bakery hours many
Making apple strudel for regular customers
None better in our town, not any.

Muffins, sweet breads, rolls all sizes
Popovers another specialty
Introduced at home first at her table
With our Mom and Dad as family.

Hours early, comes home late so tired
Goes to bed to rest for next day
Roxy and Sharon rub her feet gently
Relief to her, to them child's play.

Strokes massage heels and toes
Muscles tight, tissue tender
Such kindness from two grandchildren
For Grandmother Margaret to remember.

She told us she dreams at night
Of little angels rubbing her feet
We look surprised but not really
It was us massaging discreet.

She was kind to us, never scolding
Always encouraging us to learn ways
To be good to each other hands holding
In love growing on life's pathways.

As your Doll Margaret-Margaret
I sit and muse past dreams
Of grand Grandmothers ministering
Each from separate bloodstreams.

Grandchildren blessed to each of them
Favorites not singled out from another
Children were flowers in their life's gardens
Margaret's as Grandmothers.

May my presence bring to you flowered
Petals loved by all of you once
Fragrance never leaving your remembrance
Ever increasing bunch by bunch.

May your dreams linger now years passed
As grown as grandmother's you became
Taught perfection by Grandmother Margaret
Margaret-Margaret by name.

When moonbeams light my bookcase
Dance on walls close straight and tall
I'll get up, my skirt flared
Dance dreams, Margaret-Margaret your Doll.

CHAPTER 24. DOLLY

"To see a doll of yourself is very weird
and very neat at the same time."

A quote from Thuy Thang

DOLLY

Joyously one August morn
A "Dolly" came to be
To Mother and father born
We're proud for all to see.

Daddy nicknamed her "Dolly"
Dressed her in clothes Mom made
Taught her to sing his songs
Would curl her hair, or braid.

She charmed those all around her
From toddler beyond preschool
Became her Daddy's treasure
And Mother's finest jewel.

She, Daddy and little sister
Would laugh at cartoons
On their new television
Funday Sunday afternoons.

Daddy went to heaven when
Dolly age six and a half
She helped raise her sister small
Together relearned to laugh.

She grew strong in loyalty and trust
Advanced in honor too
Fought for rights to her a must
In things she sought to do.

She loved birds and flowers
Made all green things grow
Liked to cook and sew a seam
Or be a friend to know.

Now she lives her life, her own
Dear God we love her so
Full grown "Dolly" from the past
Jeweled treasure years ago.

Dearest Julie:
Today is our birthday! What is more, I am being delivered to you at Superior, Wisconsin where you are attending the University there, which means both you and me are superior

also. You will know when I arrive. I am being delivered by your Mother, Miss Imelda, just like you were when you were born. I feel very stylish in my strawberry bag, smothered in strawberries with my glass face peeking through the large holed handle. When you dress me, perhaps it may be like when you would have dressed your dolly a long time ago....maybe not so long ago. Often time seems to stands still

While I was waiting for your birthday at Miss Imelda's log cabin, your son came to visit and helped her split wood for the winter heating season. I could see him as I looked out a large stained glass window. His cat, Snowshoe, a Maine coon cat, would watch him raise the ax and then split the wood with one swing. Snowshoe just scampered up his old log dog house to get a better view. He is very devoted to Bradley. Later, I saw them both come toward the house. Snowshoe jumped up on the couch right next to me. I could see why he was called Snowshoe. He had six toes on each paw. Having four paws that is a lot of toes, isn't it? I don't know if I have toes or not, being the lady that I am, I keep my shoes on.

Later, I saw Snowshoe sucking on an old folded quilt with red ties on it to keep from falling apart. It seemed strange that a 15 pound cat would be sucking on red quilt ties. The background of the quilt had boy-like scarecrows over it and the ties kept the scarecrows hat on. If this funny man was to scare crows away it was very successful since I could not find one crow. I heard Miss Imelda ask Bradley when Snowshoe would grow up out of this childish habit of nursing this old blanket. He said he was grown up. It was just that he had some pleasant memories from kitty days worth remembering. This pleased me that Snowshoe liked memories. It seemed to me to be very sensible to recall such as fine a thing as that since it has been said cats have nine lives and that is many kitty hoods not to get confused about. Bradley told Miss Imelda Snowshoe was abandoned by a nervous mother cat and left to die in their garage. When he was brought into the house, and slept with him, Snowshoe sort of adopted his old scarecrow blanket. It makes me feel I will be liked very much in your house. Miss Imelda has some real snowshoes hanging on her log walls in the cabin. They help her walk in deep snow when she walks the 150 feet to the mailbox I'll bet Snowshoe can follow close behind her, don't you?

Snowshoe just woke up. He still looks sleepy. Bradley pets his thick gray and white wolf-like fur and neck ruff and he makes the strangest sound. Like a motor. It makes Snowshoe happy and he rolls over on his back and is so happy he falls on the floor. I never do that. My happiness is more lady-like and quiet. The only other sound Snowshoe makes is a funny Me-Ow, Me-Ow. This seems to get Bradley to give him a bowl of food shaped like stars. I see his needle-like teeth break the star points. I am glad I will like Snowshoe and he will be my friend and not chew on me.

I think one time I must have knelt with you in a strawberry patch because I have strawberries all over me, even my straw hat! When you think hard enough you will remember big strawberries at the age of two. Miss Imelda said you fed the robin with the red breast at your Grandmother's house. So you see strawberries have been in the family for a long time. Whoops! Snowshoe just licked my face. Do you know why? Bradley dipped his finger in his saucer of milk and put some on my face, and since Snowshoe likes milk, he licked my face. I think this is the way we were introduced the safest. Do friends just plop themselves at your feet and fall asleep? Well, Snowshoe did. It is the first time my glass feet were so warm. It is nice to be family. I hear that motoring sound of Snowshoe again. It sounded like purrrrrr.

I am bursting with love for you and your family. There our hearts go again, spilling over. It is nice when a heart runs over with happiness isn't it. That's how dreams start. Sometimes, they come true. Let's start some. I love you, your friend and Dolly... Dolly

DOLLY'S DOLLY

As an infant August born
In spaces long past gone
Mom and Dad chose you to be
Wonderful to look upon.

As a child then full family
Your Daddy now at rest
Once pet named you Dolly
Very priceless to suggest.

My dress white, scalloped hem
Contrast red lace prim
Match tiny, red strawberries
Growing on wide brim.

Match my berry wee heart
Express love of many kinds
Your birthday set apart
My cast is porcelain fine.

Unique my sanctuary
Hearts like yours and mine
Easy to be merry
Lift heavy burdens sign.

Felt by man and beast
Soothe deep hurts unseen
Great or small not least
Stretch needs unmet mean.

Carry helpfulness
In mission's basket purse
Silent their successes
Pictures painting picture.

Sometimes so much alone
Mirrors such a large heart
Attractive as your own
Memories Time Once Part.

When Daddy loved you so
Short span of your life past six

He left Life's portico
Memory whisper's to self child.

A Daddy's Dolly choice
When you look at me each day
Imagine Daddy's voice
His old songs of Nature's way.

Creatures grown by God
Plants that knew burdens too
Streams were barefoot trod
Bread baked his strong hands do.

Dried raisins pushed in place
Cookies cut baked so round
Please his approving face
Social visits plenty found.

He would press your dress
Red ruffles ruffled all around
Tell all you're his Princess
Light laughter inside sound.

You'll see his grin so jolly
Plays with you, his time applied
Best to his best Dolly
What do you do with loss inside?

Your life had just begun
That bond has been broken
Grown to love someone
Buried deep within a token.

A Child you wrapped with care
Protected Daddy's pleasant sake
Both had to share
Cherish me your keepsake.

Of Father's meted care
Deep imprint you agree
Take it with you anywhere
His legacy, his empathy.

His nature fair and square
Rich soil for Wisdom's plant
In gardens on your path
Etched as true confidante.

Tokens tender aftermath

Graced both you and he
Of times misunderstood
Your spirits free you see.

Ideas frequent opposite
Mass multitudes pursue
You remain in name steadfast
For love is what you do.

If Dolly's named are special
Mention in this our poem
Then I must tell of my dolls
Come with me to your home.

Native twins you see they are
Beaded basket held by me
Companions for me as you dream
Sleep is dreams facsimile.

Slumber spurs your body
Deep wants wake in soul
I watch your imagination
Curious on patrol.

Stirs creative powers
Inside womankind
Peerless patterns just for you
Etched deep in your mind.

Stored sweet remembrance
Tokens to appreciate
We become heiresses
For life to communicate.

Memories grow younger as
Age older appears
On your birthday, you and me
Become odd souvenirs.

One day your Daddy will
Wait at pearl gates golden
Shout for joy again to see
His Dolly again for holdin'.

P.S. That means Past Sanctity

I was visiting my daughter Julie speaking affectionately about my Mother who passed away many years ago. I had photographs of her in my home at many stages in her life, missing her very much a lot. Recently, relatives comment how my hair is her silver white color and I resemble her, which is a true sincere compliment. This makes me miss her even more. Not long after my visit with Julie, she came to visit me with a small package. I had no occasion to receive a gift; she said it was not a gift. It was a memory I would enjoy. I opened the package and in it was a plain white dinnerware cup with six stones in it. Julie said, "When she was three years old she and Grandmother would walk in the driveway at the homestead where we lived and we picked up these stones. Grandmother said I should carry the cup carefully and save them. I did." Julie gave me the cup and stones holding six small stones; one quartz, four agates, and one carnelian. The memory of her so young and my Mother so thoughtful made me feel warm inside. I hold these six stones often because both my Mother Margaret and daughter Julie touched them a very long time ago.

> The Monday Club invites us to come
> To luncheon meeting to view
> Dolls dressed for display in their fine way
> A show off rendezvous!
>
> Miss Imelda holds me Dolly
> Holly Carol next to me in contrast
> CC, Dina Brigitta, Deirdre and Bessie
> Karina and bride doll in newscast

CHAPTER 25. JULIE

> "A friend is one that knows you as you are, understands where you have been, accepts what you have become, and still, gently allows you to grow."
> A quote from William Shakespeare

Dearest Janet:

The harvest moon smiles on August birthdays. Deep blue azure sky, cotton clouds drift aimlessly across the night sky. Tall dark trees shadow woodland forest leaves that cast images across my silken emerald green dress with pantaloons to match. Streaks of tiny dark green embossed fabric shimmers vertical lines down my dress designed by Miss Imelda. She has spent long hours on careful stitches to make my costume special; weaving threads, as friendships weave through the passages of time. Complete soon as an image of endearment between two female friends. I became familiar with images, especially the many varieties here in the forest. I will take them with me.

Did it not seem like yesterday when you two first met? It was the first time Miss Imelda enrolled in a six week secretarial correspondence course held in Boston where you were also enrolled and appointed as her mentor for her studies. She still uses Gregg shorthand in her notes. Later, when Miss Imelda's hands were clenched in fear and desperation at the foundling home in New York, you Janet, came to visit her often at a time when she was lonely, feeling abandoned as an unwed mother, you became so meaningful in her life. She was grateful that you were close enough to visit her often being so far from her family.

While she designed my clothes she would hum the sound of a train whistle. Her thoughts drift to another train whistle sound when she traveled on the night train to Chicago, IL and then on to the New York Foundling Hospital. Whistles shriek in the night with its familiar wail. Like her own crying inside, lonely like she was steeped in dark sounds of solitude. Life's hardships bring suffering, but can be overcome by a friend.

These same tracks brought you to her country home in Minnesota for a celebration...a birthday for a new, little newborn girl, cementing forever a lasting friendship with her mother. Then you held my namesake baby Julie, a child not much longer than me a doll. Miss Imelda has delightful memories of your visit to see her and little Julie. A precious baby for her, not to replace one lost, but to mend her heart, after her first one went away to live with someone else. Soon I will come to live with you, dear Janet, longest friendship Imelda knows. As I wait for my new clothes to be finished, I see the moon from her huge windows. A large slice of moon suspended in the sky, is perfect in contour, as it admires its silver reflection mirrored in her big pond on the south of 40 acres. Mirrors...that seem to express a friendship like yours I do think! Over long distances stretch lonely train tracks from MN to NY, but somehow your soul's beamed love, bright enough to find each other in the darkness of sadness...and then create a silver mirrored friendship, never forgotten through the years.

As dolls, we penetrate imaginations of all these things. Heartaches turned into happiness. Dolls depend on dreams, your dreams; day and night kinds of dreams, you can feel them in our presence. Miss Imelda says I will travel the same route as she and you. It is also the same route little Julie traveled to see you when she was grown up. Years passed quickly since Julie was an infant and you held her as Godmother. Now she has grown to womanhood with four generations living in her family and you have been there since day one! Miss Imelda and Julie were so thrilled when you chose to call me Julie. I am complete now for my journey across the span that has connected you three all these years! Memories shared and new memories to be made, I will tuck them into my little red heart. My poem is safe in the folds of my silken trousers and will express our love of jeweled friends,.Love... Julie

"Among Life's precious jewels, genuine and rare,
the one that we call friendship has worth beyond compare."
Author Unknown

JULIE

Doll dreams dare to drift
On fetters gold of love
Threaded finely woven as
Friends are woven of.

First, two young women
From promises broken meet
Light pursuing shadows
Bonding bittersweet.

Once a class you mentored
Her secretarial grades

At correspondence seminar
With supervising aides.

Friendship kindled quickly
Post letters continue
Practicing Gregg shorthand
Scrolls learn you two.

When she moves to New York
Closer friends became
You meet her again in person
Your supportive visits claim.

As love stood by her open door
Darkness lingers lengthy then
Male relation fades forever more
Your steady visits over again.

Bind you two and kept
Secrets silent, comforting
Tears inside wringing wept
Comrades true supporting.

Long years past threescore
Stately as pillar tall steady
Though miles shore to shore
Your love shared ever ready.

Memory portion generously
Relive girlhood dreams
Write letters love contained
Shared might-have-beens.

Not faultless but priceless
As often friendships are
Comforted companionships
Affects spectacular!

So, dolls like me animate
Rouse dream's command
Invite thoughts, though apart
Sure to understand.

Another August moon child
Same Mother again to take
Dreams a little magic
Born girl my namesake.

She grows with friendship

Always known as pure
Seals ties of fellowship
Three pals unite for sure.

Julie, titled is my name
In character esteems
Favored importance
Identifies our dreams.

Loyal, kind, fair she grew
Honest, some friends do
Extraordinaire exclaims
Rapport finds you two.

As ornament ring circling
Precious stones to wear
Emerald clad, jewel-like
Choice friends, so rare.

She lives in green forest
Tree Leaves emerald green
Shine enameled waving
Spring breezes gentle seen.

Or emerald oceanic sea
She dips feet cautiously
Living in Alaska carefree
Wades with Son Bradley.

A designer of fine jewelry
For jewels such as she
Her creations unique
Gemmed vision a reality.

Pearl, queen of gems
Round, creamy white
Form inside oyster shell
She threads, knots right.

Gems made for queens
Client's wealth no matter
Pearled by all means
Round balls small or fatter.

At night she sees moon
Round, in sky pearled
Suspended, balanced
In her wooded world.

Gems also beautify
She treasures ruby's flame
Like red wine blazes bright
Sips slow flow aflame.

A dinner date tonight
Of red hearts in love
Ruby red an ember
Transparent in white glove.

Shines brilliant crimson
Reminder moments sweet
Friendship has begun
Rubies blaze complete.

Treated by heat carefully
Fractures heal or conceal
Julie restores perfectly
Brilliancy you can feel.

Turquoise attracts many things
Money, success, love
Sacred to Native Americans
Guard ancestor grave above.

Spirit enlightened powers
Inner peace Native's claim
Julie gets jewelry orders
Honors gem turquoise name.

Peridot her August gemstone
Description of gem unclear
Only stone come in one color
Yellow green to brown sheer.

Or sapphire gems favor
Blue like lakes clear
Deepened sky blue color
Azure to revere.

Julie designs diamonds
Ear or finger ring
Wink like lover's stars
Love's engagements bring.

She likes amethyst
Purple royal royalty
Regal gem for them
Sovereign appointee.

Gem zircon unrelated
To diamonds may not know
Heat treatments change
Stay colorless to show.

Onyx intrigues her
Dark black a night sky
Many reasons favored
Secrets, don't know why?

If other worlds wanted
Rainbows sparkling
Fireworks, lightening
She makes opal ring.

Jewels such as these
Adorn us all unique
Gems become reality
New or antique.

Quality, as friends in time
Family gems extend
Compute qualities
Choice is Julie friend.

I announce my being
Silent still my pose
Thoughts bring past days
Tenderness glows.

Forever, three of us
Positions placed our own
Across miles, each one smiles
Separate not alone.

Then it seems a butterfly
Glass like me did call
Transmits wings me to you
My dreams not dreams at all.

Make room for Miss Imelda
Images for me a doll
Wrapped in fond esteem
A friend's memorial.

Overcome, electrified
Mesmerized in view
Usual scene in our dream

Julie, jeweled, me and you.

"The most precious jewels are not made of stone, but of flesh."
A quote from Robert Ludlum.

Dear Miss Imelda:
My dolly Julie arrived at such an opportune time; our beautiful Husky dog, Bandit got killed last week. I was so devastated; she was such a companion to all of us. I was so devastated, miss her terribly, and will be getting another dog soon, I can't be without a dog. So carefully I unwrapped my package of my Doll Julie. She is so beautiful, just like Julie, and my favorite color! It was so much fun to dress her, as I did little Julie when I was her Godmother. My children admire her as well, even my sons. My daughter Lori placed "Julie" on a shelf of honor so we can see her every day. I can't thank you enough. Her poem is Julie all over, a precious gem. What a memorial of our friendship after all these precious years not losing touch. Thank you ever so much. Just looking at her I thank you every day! Always, Janet

CHAPTER 26. GENIE

"A parent's love is whole no matter how many times divided."
A quote from Robert Breault

Dearest Carol Jean:

My brother Eugene, your Father, was my most favored. His thoughtfulness knew no bounds. When he met someone, no matter what position a person was walking in this life, he was always helpful and had a word of encouragement or praise, deserved or otherwise. When he joined the Army in World War II, I wrote to him and sent him pictures of you, his little girl, to share with his comrades. When he married, and later was asked to leave the home, his thoughts were always of you, his little girl. He did not believe in divorce, and though he separated from his wife, his favorite child was the one he helped raise, you, Carol Jean. After you left home I lost contact with you, after many attempts to locate you. I gifted to you, your doll named "Genie," because of your tender early childhood years you had a doll, with a pillow to sit on, (an intended storage place for your father's pictures and letters to you) long before I ever gifted other dolls to my family many years later. Your new doll is in remembrance of those memories.

GENIE

My Mistress you, Carol Jean
Years favor six plus four
Is sad, misses her Dad
He left out the back door.

Aunt Imelda is worried for her
Visits her after Dad is gone
Says he joined U.S Army for war
After boot training, he'll move on.

A snapshot is given to a daughter

Who loves her Dad so much
If only she could visit him once
To feel his gentle touch.

She hides his picture in small pillow
Under doll comfortable steady
Guards pictures or letters from Dad
Secretly stored when ready.

She kisses doll morning and night
Her parents separated now
She misses his hugs goodnight
If only with him she could go.

Her mother tells Auntie not welcome
Says stay away or make visits short
Wants no contact with Dad's family
Or to police she makes a report.

Aunt Imelda whispers to Carol Jean
"Dolly Genie will comfort her so
Take her with you to back yard swing
As forward and backward you go.

Look for tin can by willow tree trunk
In it will be letters from Dad
Hide his notes with his picture
In Genie's pillow, best safe you had."

So it was, no matter the season
Letters from Dad would be there
Printed words she herself could read
Pictures he drew or a prayer.

Folded flat, always, carefully
Stores in my pillow case, Genie Doll
Same spot by willow weeping
Her print letters closed for him small.

Her Auntie remained faithful
With secret by willow swing there
Going backward and going forward
See! Closed tin can? I declare!

Love notes for a daughter to bring
Exchange news from her dear Dad
Thanks willow tree, backyard swing
Plan works perfect, ironclad.

She was so proud of her Daddy
Got his photo...he won an award
A Purple Heart for bravery
She blessed his letters of reward.

"Courage is like love, it must have hope for nourishment."
A quote from Napoleon Bonaparte

Months went by then no letters
Then note from Auntie which read
Your Daddy, Carol Jean, is injured
In hospital, a lot of bloodshed.

His head all over bruised badly
His memory retains less and less
Now, you nearly age twelve, my dear
Check by tree or swing if any progress.

Carol holds tight to me Doll Genie
Whatever to do so full of stress
Yet I, Genie, good at distracting
Will dream away this distress.

Let's do works, help others I shared
Like be a nurse to wounded in war
Help those in need, ease pain
Volunteer duties to look for.

Nurse other's wounds over again
As you get older together we learn
You have known emotional pain
Understand disorders concern.

I watch Carol Jean sleeping
Some worries, some happy, at ease
Wanderings, wonderings, whispers
Will her hurt hearts heal too please?

I go back to Carol Jean's bedroom
With old letters in my pillow to tend
Dad's letters safe, folded with care
Auntie delivered what Dad would send.

She does not notice my worried fussing
As I move myself from my doll pillow
Gather together letters from Dad
Delivered in tin can by weeping willow.

They fall to the floor, but discerning

Carol sees at once their number
Quickly gets up and retrieves them
To console before she could slumber.

She reads all again, even his poem
Her long pause to reflect over, then
Kisses them tenderly and careful again
Stores safe in my pillow. Amen!

Retrieved by old willow tree swing
Reseats me poised on my small pillow case
Our secret foolproof as anything
Proof she's in Dad's heart special place.

No matter where he is today
Vows somehow when she's older
She'll embrace him, his strong shoulder
Finds him, be his nurse someway.

So she studies medical dictionary
Words about as long as her arm
Books of nursing all on her desk
Smaller one tucked underarm.

Learns treatments for success
No word from Auntie, long time past
No progress from her Soldier Dad
Her family and his are outcast.

Aunt Imelda passes house often
Child's age now close to eighteen
Carol Jean is never available
No tin can or willow tree intervene..

Carol Jean, a woman at seventeen
Marries good man early in her years
He is kind, thoughtful like her lost Dad
He soothes her when fall old tears.

She left home with only one thing
Letters written by her dear Dad
Delivered in can, near old willow swing
Taken from pillow case doll had.

Toy care at night I will promote
Old toys need love, private care
Make-believes choke up in my throat
Fond memories of Carol Jean where?

One day my little heart quickens
A voice I hear steps far away
Its Carol Jean home visiting
House quiet, family gone today.

She slips a scroll of paper
In my empty pillow nearby
Where I sit high on the shelf
Then kisses my cheek goodbye.

What message... does she want me?
To know, will I feel bad?
Is she happy, does she miss me?
Where is now her Soldier Dad?

My little hand fits in paper scroll
Neatly wound, unrolls on my dress
Read it now... it makes me memories
I have much less loneliness.

"Ás an infant Babe so wee
My Daddy always carried me
Becoming his lap favorite to be
Outside my very own family.

Wasn't I small upon your lap?
Newborn, feminine in wrap
Did my small fingers overlap?
Around yours after my nap.

Growing to toddler stage in glee
Pals we became, you and me
My Dad always my nominee
Promised favored guarantee.

Did I charm your heart to win?
Captivate you as your heroine
Nestled warm beneath your chin
Protected, secured, deep within.

School bells rang across the sky
Beckon books new thoughts apply
Yet, still dear Dad let's classify
I miss your lap to occupy.

Now, my age already eight
Past years you cause to accommodate
My growing from small in weight
Our precious years I appreciate.

Feeling warmth your love I feel
Spills over me, you can't conceal
Naturally, Daddy you're so genteel
My admiration for you still real.

Busy am I these tender years
With friends, family, with peers
Your place no one interferes
In my heart, have no fears.

Did my brown hair, long and fine
Smell good to you, so small you held
As toddler self you adored so
Until from me your presence withheld.

I miss you so when you had to go
I'm too tall now to sit on your lap
Yet my vivid memories are so fond
I wish I knew where you were at.

I've searched hospitals to unwrap
Your injury war torn, wound mishap
So return, Dad, to home once we had
Best memories with you only Dad.

Willow tree gone, as back yard swing
My doll Genie, faithful, sweet thing
Sits on her shelf so daintily
Many dear memories, her and me.

As a doll collection is visited today
My gift, my poem stories convey
Tenderness shared that we both portray
This lonely hallowed Father's Day.

Gifts given to absent Dads are
From me to you in particular
Representing love so far away
But feeling much sadness similar.

My heart quickens for you to know
I love you Daddy wherever I go
This poem for you in rolled page
Relive remembrance's upstage.

Genie's pinafore is where poems at
Now, what do you think of that
Her love lasted from once tree willow

Letters from Dad in my pillow.
!
In verse of treasured things
Words remain on angel wings too
Past every season into springs'
Keep precious old times new.

Dad's choice remembering
Love for daughter from Dad will do
As childhood dreams were teeny
A Dad dearly loved through "Genie."

Our messages wrapped neatly kept
Carefully in doll "Genie's" pillow
Safe hidden notes, care swept
In tin can by trunk of weeping willow."
...
Then, to my surprise, Carol Jean returns
She carries me tight like long ago
Pillow poem safe-stored in her hand
Out of this house, "Happy" I know.

"She missed me" she said, "You've a lot to do
My new daughter and son need you
So, don't misunderstand items so teeny
Some important as me "Doll Genie"

Dear Miss Imelda:

I am so sorry for not writing you sooner. It just means I can't think and write at the same time! I have received the new doll, also named Genie, and I just love her. She sits next to my little doll you gave me years ago as a child and they have become great friends.

I have great news, after my Dad got out of the hospital I located him with the help of my dear husband Ed, and we brought him home from the Veteran's hospital and he stayed with us. I have always been proud of my father, even as a child and so proud of him with his service to our United States.

My father was wounded in action during his role in the military and has bouts of post traumatic stress syndrome and permanent injuries to his body. It is a privilege to minister to his needs as a daughter. His gallantry in the military went beyond what was expected of him because that is the way he was. We enjoyed him with us, and my children loved him very dearly, which you will rightly know. I am pleased to share all this with you since you were so diligent to keep him in my tender life as a child.

GENIE, TOO

Last preparations made ready

My frock, green willow leaves
Bordered by lace edgings
Eye-lit in ribbon weaves.

My white pinafore spotless
Topped by bonnet to match
Inside basket net, fine flowers
Hides my poem's dispatch.

My notes just a few fold to see
Memories from Dad gone away
Left by Auntie by willow tree
Diligently looking every day.

My name Genie, from Eugene
Comfort for a Dad to remind
So strong, honest, dependable
So loving always so kind.

Original comfort doll to my Mistress
Shares memories choice as favor
When she kept love for a father alive
Stored in pillow she had Auntie gave her.

Notes, simple letters, and pictures he drew
Of planes, books and Air Force duty
Words she can read supply her need
Feels love for Dad to daughter beauty.

Together they are years later
Bonded in love never broken
Continue love with her new family
Two dollies, one new, one old token.

Qualities shared so gallant, steadfast
Faithful in separations alone
Blessed with more family unions
His children, grand children well known.

Military dangers haunt thoughts many
His courage calm the unknown fears
His Carol Jean again close by
She wipes away war-torn tears.

What dreams will dolls dwell on?
Surrounded by tokens of care
Bask in tenderness continuous
Dwell on why, what, when, where?

We ride moonbeams flashing
Hide thoughts we gather happy
Sprinkle generous images
Smile when they land snappy.

We stored dreams almost forgotten
Tucked them in one small pillow
Preserving love's memories
Notes left under weeping willow.

CHAPTER 27. LIZ / MELDIE

"To reminisce with my old friends, a chance to share some
memories, and play our songs again."
A quote by Ricky Nelson

Dearest Liz:

It is not often Miss Imelda gifts two dollies, you are an exception. Your friendship goes a long way back to when you and Meldie were teenagers meeting in a private girl's school. You were there from an orphanage after your Mother Elizabeth died and Meldie was there to catch up on her studies after dropping out of high school. You would visit Meldie's parents, Melvin and Margaret after Meldie left school. Meldie's brother Gene was appointed by her Mother Margaret to take you dancing at the Coliseum Pavilion. Mother's condition was only Gene could bring you two home and no one else.

Your friendship still continues after many years past, and rightly so, as. Meldie met her husband, your brother Robert, since you both were roommates after high school. Robert is father of her two girls Julie and Marianne. He unfortunately died at a very early age after they were married. It is when you were dancing at the Coliseum is where our stories begin and end. Loving to come home with you...Meldie and Liz.

Liz and Meldie

Dancing great exercise, fun too
Music choice diversified
Friends make arrangements often
Transportation others provide.

Friend Liz meets Meldie at her home
Permission from school permitted
Brother Gene will go to Coliseum dancing
Mom and Dad agree if supervision admitted.

Girls promise to come home with brother
Can other girls and boys dance?
Escort home is Gene, no other

Agreement with parents in advance.

Liz and Meldie dress in flared garments
Liz, white blouse, red sweater, blue skirt
Has appliqué of white poodle on leash
Sure to attract attention to flirt.

Dark suede shoes bought brand new
Black hair long locks in suspension
Tall, slim, agile and trim
Guaranteed dance partner attention.

Meldie, feminine likes laces
Her dress pale yellow, fabric flimsy
Full fashioned, lots of skirt room
Small waist, neckline shape silky.

Her shoes, white polished sandals
To keep step, no matter quick pace
Hair blonde-styled page boy
Make-up creams in right place.

Reflects, maybe she'll see Willie
Gene's friend of many years
He dances waltzes so graceful
Enough girl partner volunteers.

Gene dressed in smart coat and tie
Always gentleman no less
Likes dancing with many ladies
His manners delicate finesse.

A brother to be proud of always
Escort beyond reproach ever
"Handsome too" Liz says politely
"Comfortable to be with whenever."

Gene drives to Coliseum Pavilion
Dance hall near forest location
Live bands play modern music
Or old time request celebration.

Hand stamp identifies admission
Liz and Meldie leave Gene on his own
Find booth near visible bandstand
For men onlookers to be known.

Aware they are lovely to look at
Can refuse dance if they please

Or, accept dance suitor politely
Both agree fun to tease.

Liz likes polka steps lively
"Beer Barrel Polka" begins fast
Already partnered on dance floor
Three times go by Meldie passed.

Meldie sits, watches; refused suitors
This oomph papa not her style
Prefers romance a waltzing dance
Waves to Liz and her partner tactile.

Next dance active schottische
Liz's partner keen on his pace
Return to floor energetic as ever
Laugh in dance embrace.

Meldie sees Gene across dance floor
Ceiling mirror reflects him having fun
Glances on occasion, looks for Sis or Liz
Aware of agreement to parents done.

Meldie sees him dance next fox trot
Waves his finger shaped OK
Perfect in his step one two, one two
A brother rates five-star to stay.

No one like him, perhaps just a few
Enlists in Air Force next year
Who will Meldie or Liz dancing take?
To Coliseum Pavilion here.

Thoughts pass, wants no headache
Jitterbug orchestra changes
Most everyone strides to dance floor
"In the Mood" tempo exchanges.

Distinct style gyrate we glance for
Band players more music continue
Two more tunes as crowd goes wild
Jigging rhythmically bodies renew.

Movements uniquely self-styled
Embellished exercise to enjoy
Dancers quick change positions
Views girl and girl, girl and boy.

Band intermission commences

Brother Gene brings Willie to meet Liz
Family friend he never met before
Willie so impressed, Gee Whiz!

Will ask her to dance once or more
Meldie affectionately smiles at Willie
Beams back, then pulls Gene aside
Away near back door direction wily.

Meldie sees Gene shake head denied
Meldie wonders what's that for?
Willie strides to dance floor, girls to know
Bunny hop next on dance floor.

Line circles around snake forms go
Liz and Meldie close together, then
Not far behind Willie and Lenore
Willie's sister, hugs closer again.

Fancy she is older than he more
Attractive, adored by other males
Saves Willie dances to go for
Bunny hop stops, pairs return places.

Band plays Skater's waltz, Meldie's request
Hopes partner to be can waltz then
In time, Meldie's partner Willie
Elated chose her to waltz again.

At former dances Willie requests
Waltzes for Meldie if attends when
She's glad, ballroom dancing best
Smooth, follows his 123 lead then.

Effortless dancer guaranteed
Strong shoulder easy headrest
Four times circle dance floor
Willie her waist firm holds best.

Her cheek near his devotedly
Whispers soft request privately
Confides Meldie has secret to tell
Wants to share if she'll agree.

Gave details to Gene very well
He needs Gene's consent chancing
Describe in advance secret to be
Meldie stays quiet smooth dancing.

Willie presses lips to cheek devoted
Skater's waltz seems never to end
Kissed her again no more words said he
Brings her to booth, "thank you my friend."

Perplexed; unsure secret of Willie
Meldie beckons Gene to come her see
Waves "soon," she waits ill at ease
With Lenore fox trot to finish, agree.

Great friends each other to please
Gene comes to Meldie breathless goes
She asks him about Willie's plea
Says Willie can wait his secret he knows.

Undecided to take Liz and Sis Meldie
Meldie sees Willie in distance glances
Watches again while they chat
Liz partnered "Minnesota polka" dances.

Willie comes to Meldie, says Gene
Cautious, his secret Gene perceives
Willie holds Meldie's hands like no other
Tells her his dream unfulfilled, weaves.

Late nights he goes to deep forest
At wolf den new three pups are
Teaches wolves stand on back legs
For certain this dream bizarre!

Brings recorder, waltzes he plays
Pups learn fast, change partners too
Alpha male and female gone hunting
He needs partners, wants Liz and you.

Asks Meldie convince Gene you can go
Deep forest past Sauk River beyond
Lives wild animals few humans know
Meldie encouraged to Willie, will respond.

Talk to Gene, Meldie, he'll listen to you
Meldie excited to Gene goes
Before he finds lovely partner to hold
She pleads, Willie can be trusted, he knows.

We'll be gone two hours, only two
Return back promptly in time
Please give permission to Willie too
His request unique in a dreamtime.

Drives to forest short-lived event
His car parked close to wolf den
His timing pups alone evident
Perfect no parent dangers then.

Gene agrees, you talk to Willie
Strict rules in permission to leave
Gene fears dangers come to them
Strict responsibility rules preconceived.

Agrees, cautious Meldie looks for Willie
Sees him talk to girls not far from her
Beckons him over, come quickly
Departure to forest confers.

Willie comes to her, elated, gets topcoat
In breast pocket car keys in place
Checks hip pocket for recorder
Perfectly stored in its space.

Hugs Meldie walks to entrance
She stops Liz, polka again dancing
Doesn't tell her plan, takes her arm
Says their leaving "Willie's romancing.

Just joking, Liz, come with us"
Knows Liz well, loves animals, soul mates
"We'll explain details in car, discuss more
Outside Willie's car starts, waits.

Comfortable, runs smoothly no noise
They drive toward deep forest detail
Meldie tells Liz trip Willie in forest enjoys
Liz excited, says, "She knows trail.

As teen with brother Pete wolf pups play
He knew when alpha female and male
Were gone, hunt food far away
We play ball, wrestle pups small scale.

Bark, whine or howl at full moon
Scuffle near den in tall grass
Pete knew when to leave soon
Before pup parents find trespass."

Soon dark drive to deep forest
Meadow clearing's ahead appear
Willie stops car quietly together

Get out, takes our hands near.

Holds his recorder, starts to play
"Vienna Woods Tales" louder song
Two wolf pups come running
Female small pup slower along.

Together he shows Liz and Meldie
He takes each one by their paw
Introduces them to new partners
Friends human no young pups saw.

Willie takes first pup Hunter
Places right paw on his shoulder
Liz goes toward wolf, pup Elder
Unreserved, very much bolder.

Ready on two legs straight stance
Willie turns recorder up higher
Melody next "Blue Danube" dances
Wee Pup wolf whimper require.

Meldie takes Wee Wolf's right paw
Pup follows just perfectly
Looks, feet follow, his back saw
With Willie's wolf partners three.

Moon shadows dance with us
Willie, Liz, Meldie, pups happy sway
"Blue Danube," soon waltzing gone
Skater's waltz next melodies play.

Willie changes partners again
Pup wolf steps perfect to amaze
Partners waltz, still moon overhead
Wolf pups howl with polonaise.

To them dancing sheer delight
Willie stops, change partners to take
"Tennessee Waltz" plays clearer tonight
Waltz with wolf pups and Willie make.

New partners just right, Meldie and Liz
Look so happy, Willie waltzes best
What fun experience this is!
Human and animal fun conquest.

Dancing in dense field forest soon ends
Full moon shines high on scene

Willie's wrist watch alarm noise sends
Must leave soon, promised to Gene.

Willie gives pups each other to dance
Wee pup for recorder buttons press
Hunter and Elder together waltz prance
All growl, howl at moon access.

Willie, Meldie and Liz leave quiet
Deep dense forest to Coliseum return
Happy for wolf dancing in moonlight
Dancing with wolf pups, taking turn.

Back to Coliseum dance floor
At entrance stands Brother Gene
Waits patient, then smiles so wide
Sees his companions safely seen.

Friend's promise sure guarantee
All agreed to forest secret keep
Just Willie, Gene, Liz and Meldie
Individual new dream to sleep.

Waltzing with Willie waltzing wolves
Animal's wild with humans free
His dream fulfilled completely
Wolf partners Liz and Meldie.

Inside band plays "The Last Waltz"
Willie takes Meldie's hand graciously
Liz response, Gene offers his hand
"Dance? last dance, Liz with me."

Willie holds Meldie closer now
Kisses her cheek again tenderly
Meldie brushes his cheek with a kiss
"Thanks Willie wolf waltzes carefree."

Willie asks Meldie if he can take her home
Her response, "next time, ask my Mother
Tonight promised to my parents
Liz and I go home with my brother."

Back in forest Alpha male and female
Find their pups acting strange
On just two legs hold each other up
Wee one in grass, buttons exchange.

Music fills dense forest around pups

Unsure they should break up meeting
Pups seem to have so much fun
"They're young yet" whines female, repeating.

Alpha male growls pups overdone
Howls "what are pups learning?
While we hunt to keep them alive
Human danger to forest returning."

Research on wolf observations
By Kelly Overton, actress American be
Comments thoughts graciously and
Shared quote below for you to see.

"Working with real wolves has been exhilarating; they're so amazing
these beautiful, brilliant animals and they're great to work with."
A Quote from Kelly Overton

Back in dense forest, when wee pup
Presses recorder for music to start
Her brothers on two legs waltzing up
Pause song ends, then music restart.

Hold each small space apart
Waltz song sounds not as loud
When human partners danced there
Waltz on two legs in forest lair proud.

Alpha male growls; "humans last August
Pass large building. Come out of car
Couples walk to door in and out
I run fast this confusion far.

Same noise pups jump about
Holding each other with two feet
Must change den to deeper forest"
Alpha female barks, "Stop, let's eat."

Food from hunting, morsels ready
They bark, pups run to them fast
Hungry dancing on back feet steady
Wolf family together; human outcast.

Wolves function like human family
Concerned with pups so young
Intuitive, intelligent, have endurance
False harassment by humans among.

Some wolves list endangered

Species, concern may be true or not
Remember wolf parents, like humans
Next time as hunter you shot.

Now dolls Liz and Meldie stand on
Baldwin fun machine plays music varied
To each other, old friends from the past
Liz plays tunes, taught notes she carried.

Reminisce one night in dense forest
Willie waltzing with wolves three
Partners Liz and Meldie help dancing
Waltzing with Hunter, Elder, and Wee.

CHAPTER 28. KEEPIN

"Ask not what your country can do for you...
ask what you can do for your country."
A quote from President John F. Kennedy

Dear Richard and Irene:
Miss Imelda, your sister, brought me from a distant land to dress me up just for you in colors and shapes reminiscent of our country. I'm here to remind people of their wonderful heritage! I read about your country, now mine, in her copies of The Constitution of the United States, the Declaration of Independence and the Gettysburg address! Far beyond my most patriotic dreams, I realize my part of such a wonderful country.

Oh dear...I've got to go! But, I'll be back. We are going to a parade! A 4th of July parade and I am going to be in it! My '76 emblem skirt peaks over a flounce of red satin taffeta over Navy blue lace. Fleecy cloud-lace white trims my matching red cap holding a Liberty bell and a small American flag. It is the 4th of July 1987; 200 years ago our country was born!

Miss Imelda's friend Emil and his Welsh ponies Lahta and Dolly arrive at the cabin door. I see, from Miss Imelda's arm, their manes are decorated with red, white and blue sateen paper ribbons. Their tails are braided with blue and red, white ribbons; silver bells hang from their ears twinkling happy songs on their head! Little flags are taped to their harnesses. Banners wave softly in the summer air from the red, white and blue painted wooden, U-shaped wagon they will pull. There is only room for two humans. In my small, ribbon banner box fits a small red cushion with blue and white streams dangling from the base. Emil looks proud in his dark blue suit, white shirt and red necktie. Miss Imelda fashionably wears her white dress with Navy blue sash, and the reddest, wide-brimmed hat I ever saw! We're on our way!

The sun is hot with warm, soft breezes. Wild flowers wave to us as we pass clovers twisting to see and be seen, ox-eyed daisies winking to and fro; Indian paint brushes brush black-eyed Susan's moving around each as summer gazes. Queen Anne's lace smoothes her stately view showing we too are royalty, especially for this patriotic day. In the distance, I can see the parade entry canvas tent set up for us. We form in line. We park next to an old wicker doll buggy with several dolls seated. I am especially attracted to the black, cloth-faced doll, her name scrolled Casilda on her sleeve. She has red and green ribbon, braided between strands of hair. Beneath her face is coarse bees wax. Bits of wild grass seeps through a small rip in her seams. She is so unique. It is plain to see she never saw a factory as I did. Miss Imelda and Emil stroll over to the lemonade stand. Casilda told me her name as she whispered to me, "Once a little girl, Tazja by name, shabbily dressed as I am, took me with her to the village shops. She was proud of my peasantry. "Casilda's black eyes seemed to get bigger as she told me she used to watch her little mistress sleep and waken in the dawn hours night after night and dawn after dawn. She slept with her on her very own flour sack pillow. The bright flowers on Casilda's dress showed signs of fading of blossoms grass leaves. Casilda, continued, "One day my mistress and I were riding with her father in the old buckboard wagon. She did not know it but she drops me. I fell on the dusty, hot ground. For months it seems, who knows what time is, I lay there in the hot sun and dry dirt. Then one day, an American cowboy stopped to check his horse's blanket for wrinkles. I could see the horse hoof prints so near to me. I was found that day, and the cowboy took me home to his wife. She is very kind to me, but my dreams are of the village squares, Tazja and me, and the stories she told me shared with no one else." I assured Casilda she must be grateful for being here today. I asked her to be happy and think happy thoughts. It was a day to celebrate. It was a day to have a parade!

We can hear the local High School band drum out the march "Under the Double Eagle" as we see a pair of bald eagles fly high in the sky above Norway pines. When they played "Stars and Stripes Forever" I see the stars and stripes in my dress and felt so proud to be an American. I had to be so careful not to tap my glass feet to the "Cotton March" because I did not want them to break, but otherwise the FUN we had I shall never forget!

Miss Imelda and Emil returned to the wagon. We moved closer in line for the doll parade and special events, when I saw a doll dressed as Betsy Ross might have been dressed. She had a flag with less stars then the one in my hat. I must ask Miss Imelda why. Parades! Such reason to be excited!

The parade has begun! We move slowly. Dolly and Lahti pranced in unison. Emil was so proud. Miss Imelda waved to the children along the sidewalk as we passed by and she tosses red, white and blue wrapped hard candy to them. My ribbons and banners wave to people as we pass by. My poem will share with you what is deep in my heart. It is stored in the pockets under my skirt. I needed my hands for waving!

I could hear people talk as we drove by. I overheard a farmer's wife tell her friend she remembered when she could buy 'BUY BONDS' buttons, and when the military troops were entertained by USO centers overseas. I heard a grandmother tell her grandson when her neighbor, a Gold Star mother, had a decal in her window because she lost her son in a war…"in defense of freedom, "she said. I could see doll buggies with dolls of all shapes and sizes decorated with red, white and blue streamers and flags. I saw a bearded husband and his wife holding up their fingers in the shape of a "V". They said Winston Churchill coined this phrase "V"for Victory" while playing Beethoven's 5th symphony.

I hear Moms and Dads tell each other about ships, buses and planes bringing boys home after fighting abroad. I saw a middle aged lady dressed in overalls with the name "ROSIE THE RIVETER" across her chest shirt. She told her boy friend she worked in a defense plant riveting machines for military troops. I heard her boy friend tell her about the terrible Nola Gray Hiroshima and Nagasaki nuclear testing. He mentioned General Doolittle's Tokyo raid. Bits and pieces of patriotism and history, as we move slowly down a brick road celebrating a parade of patriots. Women talked of Equal Rights started in the 1940's still in their beginnings. Families. Like yours I am going to be in. I recall Miss Imelda told her sister over the phone she was calling my name "Keepin" because all the children you and your wife had were named with the Letter "K". Thirteen of them and both of you are still together. Gains and losses…like our country. Solid family. Carin' to be keepin', like me.

Dolly and Lahta clip-clop down the brick road around the bend back toward the Town Hall. I love America. Small town, U.S.A. The parade turns the last corner before the gathering stops for refreshments and the prize judging booths. It's been a grand view for me. Clowns fire cannons filled with red, white and blue popcorn and confetti, showering the crowds. Bright firecrackers and fireworks thunder out of nowhere as showers of silver and gold shimmer the sky. Behind me an engraved calliope plays "America the Beautiful" as a real monkey 'monkey's around the winder. His owner calls him "Sparkle." We pass the Judges booth; those appointed taking notes.

Two corn silk dolls attract me from across the wagon. I read about them in my night time snoops through Miss Imelda's books. They are made from a place called the Ozarks. They have neither pins nor glue to hold the husks in place. Instead, narrow strips of husks are tied where needed. Colors from native fruits and berries brighten their clothes. Dried corn silk, very much like that see in the cornfields by the parade, make up their hair. I could see notes on them. "Pedlers" they are called. They seem more like people than dolls. Originally, Pedlars dolls were owned by English women of the leisure class. They kept them under glass domes or on fancy mantle pieces only for admiration. They date back to 1750 and 1850 in their country. They were fitted to represent traveling merchants, many of them "Notion Nannies," perhaps because there are so many small notions in their baskets or trays. The 10 inch doll is dressed in a red cape, black silk bonnet on top of a lace cap. Her basket is filled with merchandise of laces, ribbons, buttons, piece goods, kitchen utensils, toys, jewelry, miniature dolls, and all in correct small scale! So much to learn, and what fun to collect all these trifles! Her 12 inch doll mate dates back to 1800 or earlier. She comes as a gift from Loudonville, New York. Far away visiting now in Wisconsin, I would say! Her locks are of real hair. She wears a sheer lace cap cut under her black taffeta bonnet, hooded cloak of red wool with a pink chintz petticoat. Her owner bumps the carriage and I can see her money pocket which holds a small white handkerchief. She is rearranged back to her stately position, so very proper to be sure. So citified!

Best of all you will never believe it! The crowd is cheering! Emil guessed it! We won First Prize! So, when you receive me in your home soon, you will have a celebrity! Dolly and Lahta nod their heads in approval, snorting acceptance as banners are placed around their necks and the wagon post where Miss Imelda and I sit. Emil smiles and says, "They do it every time, those darlings of mine!" Miss Imelda smiles prettily in her patriot's costume. It's time to go back to the cabin," she says. Miss Imelda lives in a town called Lincoln, named after one of our great President's you know. So, you see, already I am not just an ordinary doll!

KEEPIN

"As Inheritrix to affix on July 4, 1776
I'm here to relate by each United State
Independent installation
Freedom's configuration
Declared demonstration
Paraphrased proclamation!

"Preserve it," is my cry! By
'WE THE PEOPLE' fortify
America! Ratify!
'WE, THE PEOPLE OF STATES UNITED,
IN ORDER TO FORM
A MORE PERFECT UNION"
I'm here to inform!

"TO ESTABLISH, INSURE JUSTICE
HOME TRANQUILITY
PROVIDE FOR THE COMMON DEFENSE"
Take care, changeability
"PROMOTE THE GENERAL WELFARE
LIBERTY'S BLESSING SECURE
TO OURSELVES AND OUR POSTERITY"
Penned poem a tablature!

"DO ORDAIN AND ESTABLISH
FOR THE UNITED STATES OF AMERICA
THIS CONSTITUTION"
Document emancipates!

Articles and amendments
In their original form
Persist for preservin'
Against political storm
Ratifications noble
Known as "Bill of Rights"
By men of integrity
God-fearing foresights
Hold on to this heritage
Soon past 200 years
Independent, self-government
Fought by sweat and tears
Continue choice alternatives.
Changes only best
Emancipations, a privilege
AMERICA is best!

Precede protection of great worth
Great men sought to stand
Principles of God for man
Protecting our homeland.
Be constant, be steadfast
Preserve our country's shore
Fly our flag of Glory
Wave her evermore!
Shield out interlopers of
Covert masks unseen
Tearing strength once secure
Promote the Libertine!

Brace loyal countrymen
Shackle traitors all
Defend our Constitution
'Against corruption political
Be wary of the wayward
Promises emptied soon
Campaigned in deception
Liberty's impugn.

I'll hold your hand, America!
High amongst my dreams
Of open space, by God's grace
In all of our extremes!
Remain in our instructions
Practiced faithfulness.
Remember "WE THE PEOPLE"
In Gettysburg's address!
Humans of our nation
Living souls in masses
Populate, settling in
Our relatives all classes.

Community in members.
'WE THE PEOPLE' are
Voters, residents, a state
Of ancestors similar
Keepin' laws unsmitten
I'm keepin' faith in People
By Articles and Sections
Shout from every steeple!
Declaring independence
Selection by elections.
Remember, 'WE, THE PEOPLE'
Are we, you, they, and me
Secured by revolutions
Bond with those free

Years from years to celebrate
Patriots still free
Caused because of Freedom
Love her.... Liberty!

Do we now hold Nature's laws?
Past 200 years?
As Nature's God entitled them?
As decent pioneers
Are all men created, equal?
As Creator God endowed
With certain unalienable rights
Liberty and Life allowed?

Pursuits pursuing happiness
If when threats ensue
Rights of People to abolish it
For new government too
Laying a foundation
Of principles effect
Of safety and happenings
Powers likely correct
Not to change for causes
Light or transitory
Such governments overthrow!
Secure Old Glory's Glory!

Tyranny absolute avoid
By submitted facts ordain
For the good of public, People
May Independence reign!
Is bondage creeping in too?
Our Country's importance
Officials neglect attendance
Peoples accommodate absentee?
Are legislative bodies
Secret in record
Are elections made devious?
Invading Rights reward?

From without convulsing waters
In invasion by exchanger
Encourage migration?
Of even stranger
Does filter of aliens
Obstruct this Declaration?

American's! Keep listening
To pulses of your Nation!

Has Justice Administration
To judiciary power
Been absent in law and it's enforce?
Integrity's devour?
Are offices made for Officers?
For People's known harass?
Eating out their substance?
Swarmed official class?
Are salaries payment
Equal for work done?
Or payment held for higher-ups?
Exploit corporate shun!
Are armies standing hostile?
When in times of peace?
Are Legislature's consenting
Lives lost in false release?

Are you subjected contrary?
To Our Constitution
Unacknowledged by Our Laws
Stand for this Resolution!
Pretended legislation
Mocks by false pretense
Giving assent where is none
Legislation on defense!
Mock trials from punishment
Committed on People, We
Inhabitants of these States
Listen carefully!

Are worldly traders trading?
Their world on our own
Imposing without consent
Economic groan
Are Americans transported?
Beyond seas in offence
Pretense of unjust crimes
Without recompense
Are laws kept invaluable?
By lawyers in the court
Altering our Government
These statements do support!

Smuggled seas plunder
Our coasts ravaged too
Burning America, our towns
Destroying People, who
Many feel works of death
Tyranny, desolation

Parallels of barbarous days
Unworthy of civil Nation
Fellow citizens captive
Bearing arms against a brother
Executions of brethren
Bondage knows no other!
Domestic insurrection
Excites destruction
Undistinguished ages old
Sexes or condition
These petitions bear repeating
A tyrant is defined
To be unfit for People to rule
Oust from our Mankind!

By immigration circumstance
So settled in these States
Appeal as common kindred
Honest delegates
We, therefore, representatives
Of America's United States
Publish and do declare
As free confederates!

Support this Declaration
To form reliance on
Protection by Divine Providence
Forefathers signed thereon
Pledging to each other
Lives and fortunes said
Agreed in sacred honor
As Independence read

Have you read lives in history?
How much do you care?
For Today, For Tomorrow
Beware, People, beware!

Large books I saw dreaming dreams
Silent while you repose
Books large in tales
Past, present, History knows!
Noble casts of character
Actions done by Man
Decisions, sometimes overlooked
Known of God, the Artisan
Justice Judges unwise to cause
Miss-shaping God's early laws
Defenders defend charlatan's charade

As God, in His tower
Watch idiots on parade.

Integrity itself
Departs circumstance
Injustice injects favored consequence!
Greed grips both pulpit and press
Acts known by The Viewer
Don't acquiesce!
Politicians promise pledged potency
Prolific processions, much apathy
Rampant religious, ramblings pursue
As the Tower Onlooker
Observes, Me and You!
Dedicated dogmas unerring, correct
Sacra-religiously true to its sect
Will you march with multitudes promenade?
Or look to the Tower
Weaving fools on parade!

More books of History I read in dreams
Man's kindnesses flow from moonbeams
Man's gentleness serves Man in his wake
Gives to man with nothing back to take
Mix dream dust of this which makes
Mankind, His Maker 'keepin' keepsakes.

Welled in depths of human minds
Is Balance chained or freed
Declaring independence
Declaring Lust or Greed.
Search, probe deepest thoughts
Veiled in fractured places
Touch gently broken, shattered dreams
Freedom erases.

Help Americans see themselves
Outmatched by selfish chide
Find fragments blessed in each guest
Brought to you alongside.

In mirrored prism, careful search
In Wisdom's cautious sift
Aim beyond Terror's fears
Meet Liberty a gift!

Unique are they, behind beyond
Perception suggests reminder
Across our path, America

Walks Beauty and the Binder!

Keep keepin' declarations
Constitutions and Addresses
I ask you, as THE PEOPLE
Keepin fond expresses!

Now, I, too, an American
Patriotic, as a Doll
Claim rights to dream dreaming
As Constitutional!

Preambles, words on paper
Ornaments of democracy
Preserved in our Nations Capitol
In Washington's, D.C.

These poems, more than three
Are for THE PEOPLE, WE!
Are for safekeepin'
Carin' to be, "Keepin."

Months go by. Miss Imelda gets no response from Brother Richard or his wife Irene. Another month goes by and she hears from her favorite daughter Kristen her mother Irene is in a nursing home and wants little possessions and her father Richard is at home with a registered nurse caring for him. Kristen says their doll is on a glass enclosed in the dining room. I thanked her for letting me know. She says she will get the doll when her parents pass away. I am pleased.

A Seek Well on Keepin

P.S. That means Patriotic Safety

Kristen calls me to let Miss Imelda know her Mother died three months ago and her father two weeks ago. Miss Imelda was in Florida at the time and unable to attend funerals of either one. Kristen has doll Keepin and will take good care of her until her sister comes back from her military assignment in Iran where she serves as a first Lieutenant. She will then give it to her sister Kolleen who has requested it from her. Kristen does not have the poem that came with Keepin. I promised I would get one to her. Her sister is very military minded and very devoted to the U.S. She will be stationed in Washington DC. Again I thanked her for taking such good care and responsibility of the doll Keepin.

CHAPTER 29. TAI

"Where we love is home, home that our feet may leave, but not our hearts."
A quote from Oliver Wendell Holmes

Dear Connie and Doctor Charles:

"Hi, I am Tai, your dolly, like the word 'tie' used in America, like people tie together and become friends. I am so excited that someday I will come home to Taiwan where you and your husband live. On a time once I lived where you do, I am an Asian doll you see. Now, after long journeys from there to here and now back here again, I will be returning home two ways, back to my beginnings and a new home beginning with you both!

Miss Imelda, my mistress, has moved my body over and under making my clothes with your favorite colors. I even have a red heart, which makes me know how I feel when I am lonesome for Taiwan. It also teaches me how to be kind, thoughtful and I smile like I used too but not like it was when I lived in Taiwan. I remember the birds and ducks from there, but here I have a loon friend that lives in Miss Imelda's big pond. He is all alone like me without family, so we have become fast friends, I call him "Tiles" because is feathers have a checkerboard pattern on his back. His feathers were soft and his eyes are red, so they can see better under water searching for food. It is interesting seeing new things. I grew to love this family very much in just a short time; even now I love them more, because they will return me to my home, as well as give me to you.

I know Miss Imelda will send me to you soon because she has a large box with hundreds of white plastic peanuts to wrap me and little bags of many collectables I have since I came to America, but, she says, first she will enter a country fair contest for sewing! My dress and hat are all finished and guess what! I am the entry at the FAIR! Loon Tiles will cometh me in a basket, so excited, wish me luck. It's time to go! When it is over, you will hear of me on my way to you....Tai.

Dear Miss Imelda:

It is a great pleasure to receive your letter and that you are making a doll especially for me. My favorite colors are golden yellow and purple violet. After reading the newspaper clipping of your doll project, I am deeply moved by your enthusiasm in designing clothes and writing poetry about gifted dolls to your family and friends. I believe that from your work in expressing life experiences of human beings you will be achieving the ultimate goal of presenting truth, goodness and beauty of human nature to the world. We have many doll factories around the island mostly for commercial purposes; some private hand-made dolls just for pleasure. .. Connie and Charles

TAI

Once upon a country far, so far away in miles
In my travels I lost my in and outer smiles
Arriving in America was too much for me to bear
Miss Taiwan, my beginnings, my emotion past repair.

Since, I heard factory sounds, sewing stitches small
Costumes of flowered prints; we dolls so functional
Destined to gift privately, perhaps close to home
Is my wish, anguish increased, my trip far roam.

Now, stuffed in a basked small, imprisoned in a house
My companion crippled doll, one white mouse
Karina's legs broken, feet gone too I see
Smiles wide on her face sees were once smiles like me.

Dusk press windows tall, she promises sheer delight
Night approaches in glittered gown of twilight
My first day seems hopeful to chase my gloom
Since my design should incline euphoria to presume.

First glance makes me wonder, I do this very well
How does Karina get to where dreams cast a spell?
Says, "On roof high 'Soars' eagle carrier friend
Takes me to 'The Meadow" where begins Pretend.

He'll take you too; he will, his wings swift and strong
Forget your sorrows, Tai. "I felt then I was wrong
Snowshoe, fluff-haired cat, crept to our basket close
Holds Karina gentle on her neck, I'll trust him I suppose.

Returns for me wearing only little red heart
Gloom returns, I'm going to fall apart!
Up on roof we went into vast sky space unknown
Karina and I see night stars twinkle, blink clear shown.

Like skies I knew in Taiwan seemed to follow here
My eyes fill misty; I think I see Taiwan clear
Stars clear across night sky, some I know well
Back in Taiwan other dolls stories tell.

Karina whispers softly; thinks she knows a plan
Miss Imelda's husband Bill, will, he can
Talk to friend Charlie in Taiwan or Connie, his wife
May want to gift her to them to share their life?

Tai caught smile Karina gives to her, like one she lost
Together dreams float multiply, even glossed
'Soars' swoops down, to inquire Karina to go
To 'The Meadow' her new friend Tai can know.

Peace, comfort, brought to Karina even though
She's footicapped, unhurried repair her future shows
Needs time to learn steps as ballerina devisee
Without legs or feet to dance, how can this be?

Karina asks 'Soars' to come back, perhaps a week
Touched him lovingly, gratefully, on his beak
Greetings to his mate, new family this spring
For stopping by "The Meadow" remembering.

Snowshoe returns to roof after night prowling
Hunted, snooped, watched coyotes howling
Back to loft in wicker basket, Karina rests again
Smiles at new friend Tai, smiles now and then.

COME TO THE FAIR!

Oh "Tiles" my down-covered friend
To the Fair, my mistress US will send
To Bayfield County Fair we'll go
At exhibitioner craft show.

Your walnut Basket lined in straw
Purple ribbon tie, handles bow claw
Protects you from cold wind's snow
Your feathers checkered, smooth glow.

Oh Tiles stay close to me promise sure
We're celebrity, cultural art amateur!
I heard Miss Imelda say on telephone
Takes us there departs, we are alone!

People called visitors visit us on display
This Fair Day will be a holiday, hooray!
Is my dress shining gold today?
Like sun shimmers summer's day?

My star-like eyes gleam like lunar rays?
Is my lace, my ribbons worthy of praise?
Violet flowers, are they crisp too?
"Tiles" we'll have a hullabaloo!

Will my hair stay combed down?
I'm so excited, we might see a clown!
Other birds will be there, "Tiles" you'll see
Miss Imelda said, read form of Fair entry.

I'll take you where farm animals are
In barns, in pens, reserved particular
At cages, at cases, perchance perhaps
We see flags flap or balloons collapse!

The night before Fair came to be
Tai smoothes "Tiles" feathers tenderly
Next eve, about a quarter of eight
Tai, glass doll, 'n "Tiles pass Fair gate.

Held carefully carried to main hall

Doll lady holds pet loon at festival
Sign in Exhibit Lot 38, Class C
Department 18 "Arts of Culture" see!

Tai clasps wee basket quiet "Tiles" sits
Calm, unafraid, casual admits
Their seated, place on a shelf high
What a view to watch people pass by.

Tai sat with crafts different in smiles
Not one did she favor as her pet "Tiles"
At midday next day people walk by
Admired delightful "Tiles" and Tai.

Their faces smile, their eyes admired
Fine stitch of her dress, poem inspired
Photos of her mistress, stories some read
As carnival music strums in her head.

All day she sat, till darkness of night
Fair gates close, lights still bright
Tai took "Tiles' in basket bow strong
Slips down tables of streamers long.

"To barns" she whispers to Tiles to see
"Feathered folk or others, stay close to me."
Big doors were open wide and then
Tai and "Tiles" enter animal's pen.

"Pinks" pig snorted at such a wee lass
Let her by safe her piglets to pass
"Gerda" Guernsey cow just stared
Uncommitted she was, not even cared.

Her baby, named "Carmel" her calf
Looked like her, sized only half
Sheep wear black faces and feet baaaaa'd
Delighted to see new visitors, even glad.

Proud of thick wool, invite Tai to sit
On curly soft backs so exquisite
Warm comfort they were, gentle, mild
To strangers like her, both of them smiled.

Tai slides on their backs, onto the ground
To pick up Tiles as he was found
Off to pens past horses, tower tall
Except one shorter near small.

"Jolt" a colt, comical, starts to prance
Stall too small for his lively dance
Legs become still to mother did think
To suck her milk warm to drink.

Off to wire cages, individual
Birds all kinds inquisitorial
"Tiles" excitedly looked at a goose
White and gray feathers, two of them loose!

Tiles cooed his noise, as only he could
Flew out his basket on orange feet stood
"Opal" goose bent next to his size
Honks softly to "Tiles" to advise.

"You live in wilderness, not tame as me
Careful who you step on, will you agree?"
Off "Tiles" goes, Tai close beside
View "Lofty" peacock bursting with pride.

Eeeeeeeeeeeeee screams proud so high.
Notes in barnyard off walls did fly
His feathers shine moonlight's silver sheen
Circles like eyes each one a see-in.

Neck so long, graceful to view
"Come on up little fella, I invite you"
So "Tiles" did fly as high as he dared
Saw feathers no others compared.

"Lofty" does scream "I'm royalty, kingly bird
In palaces my ancestors live, I've heard
At Fairs, ribbons best go to me
Already I collected all three!"

"Come Tiles" Tai interrupts, "let's go see
Other friends before dawn, don't you agree?"
"Kwakken" yellow duck, downy and soft
Hid 'neath his mother, eying so oft.

Curious about bird's checkered coat
"Tiles" was beautiful, and his throat
Black like satin, shiny and smooth
Gentle noise he made, "Kwakken" mused.

"If he would stay with me at the Fair
Pals we'd be in water pool where
We swim a foot stroke, dive and dip
Fancy web strokes, maybe a flip."

Shyness kept "Kwakken" close underneath
Mother's feathers ruffled beneath
Tai did venture to cages of wire
Fluffed rabbits slept long in retire.

Wiggling noses, why I can't guess
Surely should be for her to impress
Ears taper long, some of them up
Flopped, lopped in their water cup.

They pass chickens all sizes cute colors
Some laid green eggs, some would be mothers
Good evening "Pluck" Tai said to hen
Clucking show chickens born in spring when.

Carefully she tenders feedings new
At night under her wings chicks peek-a-boo
Oh "Tiles" look there by the wall
Is a red rooster cocky and tall.

Crows to tell us dawn will soon be
Creep up night sky, enough of this spree!"
Quick back to shelf as Exhibits sit
Visiting over this night to permit.

Next day judging of displays in place
Rolled ribbons, all sizes, gold lettered, amaze!
Tai, tired from visits all night before
Notices "Tiles" sleep on his straw floor.

Everywhere people strolled by
Oooooing and Ahhhhhing past Tiles and Tai
Pinned in middle of their place she saw
Satin bowed ribbon, she stared at in awe.

"FIRST PLACE" said words in gold
Shining, for all people to behold!
Proud as a peacock, Tai knew now
Visitors pass by, slightly she'd bow!

People were people different from her
Yet chose them special, exhibit amateur!
She notices children, all shapes, all sizes
Admire, wave gestures, smiles, surprises.

Hears in distance, Kandu and Company
Magic show showing facts facsimile
Such magic to Tai, wasn't magic at all

Believing and dreaming is fantasy's call.

By nightfall "Tiles" to Tai's surprise
Stops at award ribbon, to try on for size
Red satin, felt like feathers to him
Happiness fills him up to the brim.

"We're First Prize, what words!" says "Tiles"
His beak moves best kind of bird smiles
Slip they go down streamers untorn
To carnival of wheels places heaven born.

Tai climbs on Ferris wheel benches wide
Looks up and over and under, outside
"Tiles" flew on button marked ON, what is that?
Up Tai went toward stars, think of that!

Around and around seats seemed to sway
Tai thought she saw home, when up and away
Seats stop sudden high before her eyes
Was Taipei, Taiwan, bright colors, a surprise!

National Theater, ornate Palace Museum
Theaters, Halls and the Coliseum!
War hero shrines, Lungshan temples of old
Gardens and streams, coast sunset in gold.

Lighthouses, seascapes, lush valley and hills
Coastal harbor, monastery, miniature thrills
Leofoo Safari Park, wildlife zoo sure
Window of China, tiny replica architecture.

In all Taiwan, Taipei her favorite place
Its parades, skyscrapers, ocean space
Becomes lonely, thoughts again blue
Do you too if homesick as she too?

Down in the distance, close near the ground
Sees a bright object, heard not a sound
Sudden Ferris wheel starts before her in smiles
Stands happy small clown holding her Tiles.

"Thank you," Tai said, "what a wonderful ride
I'm glad I took it, except when I cried
I saw Taiwan, where I was made
Among other dollies held on parade."

Clown still smiling, wiggling his toes
Asks Tai to take him wherever she goes

Tiles found him in rubbish can to discard
Lost all his laughter this poor reward.

Told "Tiles" attends class special for clowns
Learns to laugh, lost all his frowns
Beaming funny to everyone to see
Paints his face happy always to be.

His owners were pals but start a fight
Threw him in dumpster that very night
Tiles said "Please, think of a way
To keep us together, not just today."

"I'll dream on it, "Tiles" right it sure seams
Riding on Ferris wheel I saw beams!
'Beams' that's a name you will be
Someway three of us will be family."

Beams gifted her tiny bouquet
Blue forget-me-nots hoping someway
This friendship of three would stay
Convinced Tai would find a way.

Together they walk fairgrounds till dawn
Plan to hide "Beams" with care right on
Safe to return home after the Fair
"Tiles" wins points to rows of prizes where.

Unknown of danger to winner's surprises
Beams is placed in award row, all sizes
Sheltered under tiny discarded umbrella
Covers all smiles of purpled fella.

Saturday's fairgrounds everywhere
Action alive, auctions here and there
Races new, reviews, ceremony
Rockets and revue, no time to be lonely.

Performance plenty, what a four days
Cotton candy, popcorn, shows to amaze!
Today horse show, entertainment galore
Bayfield County Fair couldn't have done more.

Late, last night Tai's mistress did come
To the Fair with her devoted grandson
Bradley starts "Special Event" shooting game
Restarts shot each time wins same.

Causes red balls in square bottles to fall

Wins small purple clown at this carnival
Beams he places on exhibit shelf high
Seated next to Dolly named Tai.

Circled, Beams scatter balloons red and blue
Green and yellow beams of all hue
Play on his umbrella; it seemed the sky
Shone all around beams shining on high.

All announce Beams. Oh, My!
Happiness fills inside Tiles and Tai
"What an award, a gift, what a gem!
"Beams," royal gladness, purple paradigm!"

Dreaming and hoping never will pass
Believing beyond dreams of doll lass
Tai's mistress came to take her away
Along with Tiles, what a holiday!

In hat yellow-gold Beams wore flower
Like her hat bold as family wrote "our"
In his hand, pink and small
Holds a red heart, sensational!

Colored balloon hearts wave to and fro
As merry threesome leave Fair to go
Beams climbs down streamers. holds umbrella
So striking of all is smiles on this fella.

Pasted on his face side to side
Happiness spelled out and inside
Three famed exhibits winning rewards
Bayfield Fair fun with family awards.

Fireworks close Fair events display
Blaze heaven's rapid chain the way
Star shaped and sizes climax Fair event
Out Fair gate Miss Imelda went.

Fun at a Fair can last forever
If you believe past Never, whenever
Ties can bind us, no matter, it seems
Together like Tai, Tiles and Beams.

Dearest Connie and Charlie:

I am sending by special postal mail your Doll Tai, along with her friend Tiles and their clown friend Beams. Since Tiles is a live loon, he is protected by an open carrier with Tai close behind with Beams so they are together on their trip to Taiwan. The colors you requested are as vivid as I could make them. Please note the photograph of awards Tai and Tiles won at the Bayfield County Fair and the "Special Events Banner" for Beams, because it is authentic! Be sure to let me know if they arrive safely. Tai won't be homesick anymore and Beams is always laughing so that helps her too. A delightful threesome you will enjoy. My darling husband Bill read the poem and laughed at the antics they get into.

It has been exhilarating spending time with you in the brochures you sent. Thanks for them. Tai enjoyed them too. We have students here at the college I work at from China, Philippines, Japan, Europe, etc. I will go to Canada on a volunteer health project so I will be out of the country for six months. I have a six month leave of absence from my Library employment. I hope to hear from you before I leave in January. My beloved husband Bill will be working on his AIDS book and will meet me in Montreal just before graduation of our class participants and we will drive home together. Bill is a Canadian and American citizen. He speaks so fondly of you and Charlie and is looking forward to Charlie's visit in March. Love you...Always   Miss Imelda

Dearest Imelda and Bill:
Thank you so much for Tai, Tiles and Beams. They arrived all together by special "live packaging mail." Thank you for giving Tai the clothes with my favorite colors. I just love her and Charlie does too. My sons will enjoy her beauty and all the hard work you did to craft her. We will try and keep Tiles as long as we can, but we have to submit him to the LEOFOO Park wildlife Pet Corner, because he is wildlife and also very unusual since we do not have loons here. I will bring Tai and Beams to visit him often at the Pet Center. Beams will have to continue to be Tai's support. Again, many, thanks.

Charlie is looking forward to his visit with Doctor Bill in March. Both of you will enjoy Canada when you visit there.   Love always Connie and Charlie and Tai, Tiles and Beams.

CHAPTER 30. STAR

> "Cast your dreams as high as the highest star."
> An Anonymous quote

Dearest Andy and Edna:

STAR, ME, is born! What a destiny! My luck and good fortune is to belong to both of you. As a doll, I am a prized possession to celebrate with your 45 years of marriage, anniversary. Andy, your sister, Miss Imelda, designed my sapphire-colored dress with folds of a billowy skirt and a blue star tucked into my waist. I remember looking at it hanging on the brass hook with its lace bodice covering the satiny blue, so much like the dark sky that shows so bright from her tall windows.

What a view! It seemed a vast space above me. Silently, swooping towards me I immediately saw my friend 'Long Ear' the night owl. First, it was hard to tell he was even there since he blends so well with the bark of the trees. Long Ear's feathers are soft and he has more feathers on his feet down to the digits of his claws. His beak seems lost in more feathers fanning as if to give him a masked look. Because of his keen vision he is very obliging to me, showing me various focal points of the star positions, explaining their names. We spent the whole night looking at them and talking about them. His eyes do not move independently but his very mobile neck makes up for it. What a celestial welcome this night is to me. I want to share it with you both, on this anniversary day, with a corsage of white roses flecked with silver glitter... like the stars look to me. Dawn begins her sunlight spangle brushings across the eastern horizon. This night is enough to last my dreamtimes, when I come to live with you both. I hear the stars still telling me their star stories. What fine memories!....Star

'STAR'S' STUDDED SKY

Sapphire stars on years forty,
Plus five in lives for choice two
Threads weave platinum white
On Andy and Edna so true.

Years joined where star's floating
Reflect light on special lives dear
Years darkened too by shadows
Tempests of life destined here.

Ancients named stars long ago;
Greeks, Romans, Babylonian people
Honor them in universal dark sky
Singled its own stellar steeple.

'AURIGA', legendary king of Athens, Greece,
Choice chariot he did invent
Do dreams come to you?
Together your lives well spent?

'BOOTES,' The Herdsman, has two dogs
Chase GREAT and LITTLE BEAR
Around sky while 'THE GREAT DOG',
Companion of Orion, hunter where

Is seen the brightest and star
Easily recognized in winter sky
Artemis, Greek goddess of the hunt
Knowledge not fully known why.

They cling to the earth, cautiously
Delay dawn of each year's spring,
Singularly picture animals
Like stars or another thing.

Constellations move around skies
Tell changes of each season
Sailors; follow stars guiding their boats
All for their own reason.

Creature 'THE SEA GOAT' travels sea or land
Head of a goat, tail of a fish
'ZEUS, KING OF GODS,' disguises himself
'THE SWAN' Knows legendary wish.

See wide spread wings of 'CYGNUS'
View so choice is its worth
Monsters or villains roam constellation sky
As roam on our planet earth.

Like stars your lacings silvered, knit
Together, in 45-year marriage vow
Can you find 'THE NORTH STAR' in tail?
Of 'LITTLE DIPPER' seen even now?

'THE SCALES' justice represents
'VIRGO/CERES' harvest goddess serene
'PEGASUS', winged horse 'PERSEUS' rides to save.
'ANDROMEDA,' from monster of seas mean.

Greek hero of many brave deeds, along with
'HERCULES', warrior, same degree
Many stars, so many constellations
All for you and all for me!

There is a cat, 'LYNX' constellation
Hard to find in vast universe
Only eyes as keen can view
The 'LYNX' Cat sees in reverse!

Andy loved animals in life as well
The stars knowledge best
Brightly shining like my star for you
View nightly together at rest.

Heroes of the sky intrigue me
I share them with you two
Bright, nestled, glittering
In sky colors cobalt blue.

'AQUILA, THE EAGLE', companion
Jupiter, Roman God king, or
'LEO' fiercest lion of the world is
Choked by 'HERCULES' warrior.

Strongest, bravest man on earth
Kills monsters many, not few
'CANCER', crab, 'DRACO' dragon
'HYDRA', more heads than two.

'PISCES', the fish, represents 'VENUS'
Roman goddess of beauty and love
Has son 'CUPID', escapes monster
Turns into fish, leaves above.

Jumps in river and discovers
AQUARIUS, WATER CARRIER', grouped star
Viewed as man in these great heavens
Pouring water from a jar.

Look for 'BULL, TAURUS
Known as a Greek myth
Zeus disguised as a snow white bull
Wins Princess' heart with.

Jealousy 'CALLISTO' turns into bear
'URSA MAJOR,' 'THE BIG DIPPER', best known
'LITTLE BEAR' son 'URSA MINOR'. Star groups
'POLARIS' ' NORTH STAR' grown.

The 'ARCHER,' 'SAGITTARIUS'
Half man, half horse, giant scorpion aims bow
Creature known as centaur,
You may want to surely know.

Fascination with stars, both in or out
Andy and Edna where your travels go
View them together many more years
Learn about their beauty to know.

'THE INDIAN' spies near 'THE WOLF,'
'LITTLE FOX' stalks 'THE HARE'
The 'GIRAFFE,' 'CHAINED LADY' and
'THE HARP' tied to the 'MAST there.

'SHIP ARGO' or 'THE DOLPHINS,'
'THE CRANE,' 'NOAH'S DOVE' will last
All stellar, for your anniversary entertain
In marveled universe vast.

As your lives continue adding
More years' memories remain!
Let all stars shooting and shining

Fortune upon your estate reign.

A toast of the town, a sky-liner
A lamp your lives decorates
To have and to hold on forward
For better or worse, as mates.

Commitments behind and ahead
As your love illuminates astral chords
Dazzle, ever glowing outspread
Results in love's sparkling rewards.

True love continues growing
Star-like, twinkling as I no warning
Glittered views knowing
Beyond each night before morning.

Viewing stars you always find me
Grateful to be at your anniversary
On this holiday let all see
A sapphire star, sparkling merry.

Your linings continue connected
Part of Heaven's designing
Bonded promises, pledged happiness
Unity beyond these years signing.

Bind even tomorrow's tears
Your lives glisten to glowing
Your love sterling rewards years
On this anniversary jewel knowing.

Be blessed by universal Lightness
I'm sky-dyed, it is certain
All heaven's vaults brightness
As great deal of dreams curtain.

How wonderful to me it is
To be Anniversary news
Another kind of memory
When lovers said "I do's.

Celebrate all of these years,
Vows former not to undo
My mind's planetary mansion
Celestial mechanics play too.

Star-studded in on any sky
Star sapphires my bouquet!

Wrap them in a banner
Spread silver glitter display.

Twinkling, winking their light
Individually crowned.
Around hearts woven as one
Lovely years together found.

Come with me you two whose love
Many years love does not miss
Our journey beyond time while
We select stars to kiss, to kiss.

So, me, as star delegate
Suggests endearment long lasting
Your glass doll star impersonate
Is star studded everlasting.

My wee necklace fits around
My neck is shaped like a star
Reminds us to look beyond
A universe so far, so far.

Miss Imelda speaks as cathedral's Guest
Of a sovereign God of power, the best
Instructs me of things a doll never knew
Let me share her thoughts with you two.

In majesty of creation writes each choice word
I'm packed in box to you, overheard.
She speaks to crowds, listen carefully
Her poem below attentive heard.

Man's instruments in space probe creation
Wisdom for even a dolly like me
Pictures, probes, new discoveries
Confirm universal God's majesty.

Miss Imelda is asked to speak at a church gathering
She chose her poem on God's "Majesty".

MAJESTY

God in His Spirit spoke majestic dictation
Universal sovereign power creation
Wondrous works, light chambers grandiose dance
Stretched out heaven's limitless expanse.

God's sun 860,000 miles diameter glowing globe

Gas ball sphere clothed in bright golden robe
Ten billion years fuel supply for us planned
Planets and moon revolve around sun scanned.

Made to survive 5 billion years, cools by solar wind
Sun balances other heavenly bodies disciplined
Explosive of more billion hydrogen bombs power
Enormous sun spots large as Mother Earth can devour.

Planets named circle-spaced sun motion's raced glory
God in the beginning tells creation's story
No small wonder pagans worship Sun god gleaming
On pathways through ages brilliance streaming.

To remember journeys to Genesis of Creation
In the beginning God's word formed foundation
Night skies brilliant of stars known, not yet found
In heavenly places or from planet Earth's ground.

In Majesty, God, you ride solar wind's wings
All creation, its own song to you sings
Stars to Creator God of universe chorus wonders
Lightning bolts discipline joint praised thunders.

Who shall ascend to divine holy hills of spherical channels?
Who forms each timed pulse, pathways in sky's panels?
Who can fathom God's majesty of stellar rays?
Who can set planets to speed spin sideways?

Who can shout loudest as God bolts noisy thunder?
Who moves mountain peaks, volcano's lava asunder?
Who can look upon luminous lightning's face?
Who has 20,000 chariots in celestial holy space?

Who imposes landforms, awesome canyon crater waste?
Who shall stand in God's holy place?
God, who is everywhere on heaven's pathways ride
Can shake and drop meteorites at His dimension wide.

His strength spoken in planet's cloud's face
Staid in His majestic celestial heavenly place
Where is God's knowledge, where is His reservoir?
He sets cloud heights or opens numbered heaven's door.

Where is His sanctuary hid in His chosen high dwelling?
Who counsels Almighty God heavenly secrets telling?
Who in heaven can be compared to Lord God ever more?
Heaven and Earth is yours, works close, open to explore.

Thou hast set barrister borders edges on Earth
Designed shapes of each star, each meteor birth
Thou hast prepared daylight and nightfall for time
Thou wondrous works declare constant upward climb.

Thou prepared light, blazing blinding massive sun
Bursts of pulsars, ruptured rays of radium
Wide windows of heaven, God opens and shuts
Pathways of Paradise He kindles, He neatly cuts.

Possessor of heavens, God, majestic Most High
Celestial masterpieces yours in Alpha Centauri
Countless tapestry in Saturn, Uranus, Pluto, Neptune
Clusters of constellations of zodiac signs strewn.

Who multiplies stars in night skies, gives dew moist morning?
Who moves ocean depths for dangerous warning?
Gates of heaven stretch forth at God's beckoning hand
Frontiers vast in size, wonders each aura you command.

Portray panoramic stars multitude, twinkling in view
Milky Way 200 billion starred colors of beauty you strew
9,000 miles a minute of arms reach out to you grand
Glistening, shimmering, iridescent, lighting each strand.

One side of heavens to other side light beaming walls
Respond to God's creation, obedient to His calls
Heaven invites Earth to witness constellations complex spread
Precious things of heaven, studied plan from Godhead.

Listen to Him, God of Creation, He made you to hear
Sounds of His Majesty, glittering sights as they appear
Who should go up delve secretes from heaven for us?
Who but His Creation's appointed glorious.

Glance curiously toward glimmering heavens to see?
Why is God mindful of man, you and me?
Of erring mortal humans degenerate refugee
God looks down from heaven his children to see.

His heavenly view on women, children and men
If there were any that did understand, did seek Him, when?
Yet, Man flatters himself with his prideful eyes
Words of deceit, mischief in mind he will devise.

His iniquity is found hateful in thoughts or if he speaks
His will selfish Self in itself dwells week after weeks
Wounds stink of corruption because of foolishness
His desire to know God finds no need to profess.

Man, be more afraid of how unafraid you are!
Long ago, a Messiah as born, announced a shining star
Divine Creation from heaven God gives us His only Son
Who was sent to this earth as promise for man's evil to overcome.

Will you cry out to heaven created Being Woman and Man?
Will you know your days meted on earth, count if you can?
Will you know God bears you up lest your foot stumble far?
Will you know God set his love on mankind spectacular?

God of the Bible, out of a whirlwind to Bible servant Job said
Questions him, God spoke clearly, it is written, it is read
Where were you when I laid Earth's foundation?
Where are your supernovas, sky islands in flotation?

Where were you when its measurements were set in line?
Where were you when bases set or foundations laid fine?
Who closed sea's tomb with walled doors for returning?
Who made garments for clouds, dark, thick and churning?

Who made proud vast seas high waves to stop?
Who made Dawn waken bird song, their melody eavesdrop?
Who commanded each morning to know summits place?
Who entered curled springs or shimmered seas face?

Who walked in watery deep recess catastrophe?
Who measures light years, measures nebulae mystery?
Tell God if you can know all of this!
Tell God of his creations metamorphosis!

Who has entered steep storehouses of snow?
Tell God time reserved for distress you don't know
Who has seen dwelling place of iced stones hail?
Who knows days of war or battle to prevail?

Who knows paths Light has divided its way?
Who knows East winds scattered on tree tops to play?
Who retains channel vaults for floods when they come?
Who knows father of rain, soft or wild burdensome?

Who knows from what womb came frozen cold ice?
Who knows frost of heaven, its birth need suffice?
Who knows deep prison in cavern oceans vast?
Who splits plummeting stars bold brilliance blast?

Can you bind brilliant chains of Pleiades Star?
Can you loose cords of Orion's expanse light years far?
Can you lead all constellations in its season?

Can you guide Bear Satellite for any reason?

Can you lift up your voice to crowded clouds high?
As waters flow in abundance, rain pours down gray sky?
Can you send lightening that they may say?
Here we are powerful to crack, split skyway?

Can you count clouds as they form drops for rain?
Can you tip jars of water from heavens domain?
When the dust hardens into masses, clods together thick
Can you bring rain torrents softened by God's arithmetic?

Do you know heaven's sketched ordinances made?
Do you know how to fix them on Earth's crested shade?
I will ask you, says God, will you instruct me?
Who will you contend with, mankind? God Almighty?

Will you annul My judgments when they arrive?
Will your voice thunder as mine? Will you survive?
Can you clothe yourself with honor, with majesty?
Who is he that will stand against Me God, or disagree?

Who has given to God to ask him to repay?
Who can guide you in the Truth, Life and the Way?
Who calms wild whirling winds of the sea?
Who makes chambers of sky, south wind breezes balm be?

Who makes wondrous works in vast sky without number?
Who brings stars in night sky to shine while you slumber?
Who will question Creator God, "What are you doing now?
Who will discover depths of knowledge on God's brow?

Who can disclose pathways God's feet have trod?
Who can reach heights of His heavens, this Father God?
Who can measure depths of heaven, or length earth's measure?
Who can find His storehouses He piles as blest treasure?

Who has ascended into heaven, or who has descended?
Who has gathered winds in His fists or Him defended?
Who has bound descending waters glimmered garment cascade?
Who has established ends of Earth Creation made?

What is His name, and what is His Son's name?
If you know, go to the books written of Creations claim!
Who discloses broad seas tempest or calms oceans blue?
Who weaves Heaven's tapestry of rainbow colors hue?

Who can promise assurances like God? Who speaks to Planet Earth?
Who fights battles so great, who knows armies before birth?

What is Man, that God should be even mindful of him?
What is man whose likeness to God has become dim?

Made, creation made, in God's own image is Man made
Made, lower than the angels in heaven's places cascade
Made for his pleasure to know Him in particular
Made, each unique, like stars, planets dissimilar.

Made to know His Universe, tremendous in power
Made to sing songs in midnight or day hour
Made to enjoy beautiful things God created in His days
Made to have abundance, made to give Him praise.

Made to follow commandments God's finger's wrote down
Made to view celestial heavens He created starred gown
Made to love each other like lovers of self
Made to search their hearts; no other gods on a shelf.

Made to give to others in helpless need
Made to guide and teach truth to children of their seed
Made to remember laws commanded, written to guide
Made to follow Him, He gave shelter in Him hide.

Made to feed hungry, homeless or soul lost
Made to do good works no matter great cost
Made to glorify name of God only One
Made to become man like man to become one.

Made to be a bit lower than angels, what stance!
Made to be honorable, holy, perfected at a glance
Made, fearfully and wonderfully, made body and soul
Made with a spirit to desire balance, to be whole.

Made to be a triumph by God's creative hand
Made to discover heavenly designs majesty grand
Made to be protected, to have hiding place
Made to be desirous to know God, His face.

Made to sing songs of deliverance when spent
Made to ask for forgiveness, free to repent
Made to speak of God...but does mouth not open here
Made to have ears to listen... but deafens his ear.

Made to see a thing of God... looks but sees not
Made to follow God... but His way forgot
Made to smell creation... by choice does not smell
Made to look to heaven... but selects his own hell.

Made as mankind, from dust of the earth

Made poor and needy for God from his birth
If I, mankind, ascend to heaven, God you art there
If I, mankind, make my bed in hell chosen to prepare.

If I, mankind, what kind of man will not out of depths cry
If I, mankind, does not know where to go when I die
If I, mankind, does not lift up to heaven my eyes
If I, mankind, will not admit my treacherous lies.

If, I mankind, does not seek God's face
If I mankind, will not recover, will know disgrace
If, I mankind, die in my sin for which I choose
If I mankind, does not forgive, then I will lose.

If, I mankind, does not search heavenly purposes here
If I mankind, will not repent my salvation insecure
Father we have sinned against heaven where you are
Father we need to love more Your Son, Morning Star.

Need to reflect beauty of your character on heavenly display
In universal selected dwelling reflect your love night or day
Where your promises we will see heaven open in view
Where if we follow your directions, will meet you too.

God, we ask for your forgiveness of sin we have done
God, help us examine ourselves wrong done every one
God, dear God, how could you even care for us here?
God, our hope is blessed when you again reappear.

Fill us with your Holy Spirit, to tell others of Your Grace
How you came to teach us wisdom, to behold your face
How to model and pattern our lives like yours in all we do
How to praise your works, God, your Holy Spirit too.

What is man that you are mindful of his being?
What is man that you are mindful of his not seeing?
Your unconditional love for mankind, we understand not
Showered forgiveness on us, if we confess our sad lot.

Will we claim you our Creator in heaven today?
As our way of life, in all that you say
Then I shall not die, but then I shall live
I shall know the God of heaven, all He will give.

I shall know His testimony, His statutes penned in stone
I shall live in peace upon earth, I shall not be alone
I shall lift Ten Commandments seek precepts of old
I shall gather treasures of heaven's shimmered streets of gold.

I shall know Creator God of heavens vast expanse
I shall know tiny stars viewed by naked eye's glance
I shall study song of Psalms written by David, the King
I shall know God who made Pleiades, Orion, and Bear Sing.

I shall know chambers of south made for you and me
I shall know great things unfathomable in my humanness to see
I shall know I have sinned against heaven you made
I shall join ranks witnessing for your Jesus a crusade.

I shall know and watch for heaven's signs you foretold
I shall know one day our coming promise in Bible old
I shall know when I die God calls me from grave deep
I shall know my soul will be immortal in heaven to keep.

I shall know trumpet sounds when He calls me from rest
I shall know I loved Him most above all earth's best
I shall know my loved ones, those witnessed about Him
I shall know them saved as I am from Satan's dread sin.

I shall know God can do all things, as I doubt not His will
I shall know His purpose is not thwarted but to fulfill
As mankind, I declare that which I do not understand
I declare things too wonderful, I didn't know His command.

I declare all things in heaven and on earth God's possession
I declare Creation too wonderful, I plead my confession
Wisdom must be known by man, to know her well
Wisdom's book is written in the Bible books tell.

Wisdom is precious, more than rubies, or gold fine
Wisdom founded the earth, established heaven's stars line
Wisdom preserves them, love her, grace her ornaments many
Wisdom blesses you with years, stand atop high places any.

Wisdom was the Lord from the beginning too today
Wisdom prepared the heavens, God created their way
Wisdom set a compass upon depths of ocean's face
Wisdom established clouds, set earths foundation in place.

Wisdom rests in the heart where instructions not refused
Wisdom protects us from evil one's thoughts confused
Wisdom is God's glory it is His to conceal mute matter
Wisdom walks on the heavens where Milky Way's scatter.

Wisdom is breath of all mankind understanding life long
Wisdom is if we tear down cannot be rebuilt as it was strong
Wisdom imprisons where there is no open release
Wisdom restrains waters, they dry up, they cease.

Wisdom makes counselors walk barefoot or makes
Fools of judges, discernment of elders away takes
Wisdom brings darkness deep back into the light
Wisdom makes clean out of unclean sin's blight.

Mankind expires and where is he then?
He lies down, does not rise from the grave or know when?
Prayers are said for their souls knowing not wisdom no more
Until God comes with a shout to open death's door.

So God in His wonder was mindful of man
So God in His wonder prepared Salvations plan
In the beginning to the end of heaven's as we know
We look to God Our Creator where our life should go.

To our God, Our Refuge, Our Strength, Our tower
In time of trouble, God is to us all heavenly power
Beside Him there is no God, no other
Be you a child, father, sister or brother.

He will create new heavens, new earth, as He pleases
There will be no more sorrow, no more dread diseases
His powers of the air, of planned planets, set celestial stars
Speak of His glory, Neptune, Saturn, Jupiter, Venus or Mars.

Majesty, to search out, to seek wonders misunderstood
Mankind, in God's image, before Majesty bow as we should
To the God of Created Universe, His glory to impart
Mankind…. lift holy hands claim God, how great thou art.

We leave together for journey to you
Celebrate a wedding anniversary too
Majestic as well as you scan God's skies
Read His word, or hear Mankind's cries.

Keep me on display for all to see
How important I've become, gift to be
I know skies now better than ever
I dream more but forget never.

Me, as Star delegate
Suggests endearment long lasting
Your glass doll Star impersonate
Is Star studded everlasting.

My wee necklace fits around
My neck shaped like a Star
Reminds us to look beyond

God's universe so far, so far, so far.

CHAPTER 31. ROSE

*"Those who love deeply never grow old,
they may die of old age, but they die young."
A quote from Benjamin Franklin*

Dear DJ:

You and Miss Imelda have been friends a long time. Because of this, and also because your friendship with Rose at the nursing home is so unique Miss Imelda decided to make you a doll to remind you of Rose. She calls me Rose. We both agree Rose was a very elegant person. Miss Imelda used to visit the nursing home, and you having worked there as a nurse's aide Miss Imelda recalls she suggested you make contact with Rose because she was alone so much and rarely had a visitor. Later, one of my favorite snapshots was me in front of a portrait you drew of you and Rose together. Certainly you looked like you both belonged as family.

In just a small, but special way, Miss Imelda tries to express your unusual story of friendship between you and Rose in my poem to you. I hope you tell me soon why it was so unusual, I love secrets so much. Anyway I will be brought to your house very soon.

ROSE

Dorothy a nurse's aide, works in nursing home
Some residents too old to live alone
She tends to needs assigned, each different
Feeds, bathes, helps on the phone.

Comforts where she can relieve suffering
Dorothy gives of herself graciously
Her attention best, ever showing
Friendliness expressed sincerely.

Miss Imelda visits residents on occasion
Tells Dorothy a fine lady she notes alone
Takes care of herself quietly
Family lives far away from this home.

She greets others most pleasantly
Head nurse said Rose is her name,
Has daughter lives very far away
Suggests Miss Imelda come again.

"I'll tell someone to visit her today"
Immediately thinks of Dorothy
She asks her if soon will visit Rose

Gracious in her caring way.

Rose lives quietly at nursing home
May be glad to have someone care
Always keeps to herself alone
A visit would be nice to share.

Dorothy's tasks for day over
Plans to introduce herself to Rose
Casually, a friendly social visit
Walks to her room, Dorothy goes.

"I am Dorothy, I work here daily
I notice you read where you sit
Thought you might like a visitor
To share ideas, if you permit."

Rose greets Dorothy politely
Says, "My family live far away
Visit once a year, thank you, my dear
Sit here, if you please, do stay."

Dorothy says lives near in apartment
Sometimes works nights, often days
Rose asked again her first name
Saw "Dorothy" her name tag gazed.

Rose hopes she will remember
This person who visits her today
Heartwarming, such open kindness
Dorothy took loneliness away.

Rose asks her to visit again
If time permits her any day
Dorothy takes hand to thank her
For invitation, more visits her way.

Inside feels desire to minister
To another person in need
Is going through unwanted divorce
Separated union disagreed.

Each day their visits longer
Rose asks, "Take me to church, please"
Dorothy's glad, same church belong
Introduces Rose to priest, same diocese.

They worship God in thanksgiving
Bringing two people chosen by chance

Emptiness gone, good spirits remain
Rose waits for Dorothy's visit in advance.

She asks Dorothy her middle name
Jean was her prompt reply. Why?
Rose gives her a nickname DJ
Accepted prompt is her reply.

Off duty DJ goes to her room
Reads Rose poetry she enjoys so much
Helps her put on her make-up
Styles white hair brushed to touch.

DJ takes home clothes to wash them
Irons each one carefully
Rose, cared for elegant, so stylish
Values DJ's favor done willingly.

Offers DJ fund compensation
DJ declines, agree to each other
Her gift of service is done in love
Graciously given as if for my mother.

Home DJ calls mother out of state
Tells her devotion to Rose has become
Her Mother approves mutual need
Enjoy friendship DJ one-on-one.

Her sister, also there, writes verse
"A rose is just a rose that I might give to you
I may be off for a far off land
But I'll place a rose in your hand." I do

Doris, her sister approves too, a friend
Is valuable no matter the gender
Age differences existed no matter
Friendship valued great in splendor.

DJ relieved, sees Rose more often
To church services regular goes
Scenic drives all local seasons
Admiration for each other grows.

Rose writes in DJ's Bible wishes
If DJ her daughter would be
One day DJ read Rose's notes
DJ's heart softens, does agree.

One day go to church services

To priest, to ask him to bless
Friendship as Mother and Daughter
Before Blessed Mary statue confess.

Union sincere forever to grace
Friendship found, needs were great
Spiritual blessing granted in place
Happy and joy these two make.

DJ takes Rose shopping, new clothes
Easter, Christmas, and Mother's Day,
Delight making colors mix and match
Visits become their holiday.

DJ sings songs at nursing home
Rose joins group proud of DJ
Songs spiritual or sing a-longs
Resident requests right away.

Rose's daughter calls often
Visits her only once a year
Rose speaks of DJ tenderly
Is happier in nursing home here.

Often DJ brings Rose a rose
Sometimes yellow, often red
Places in small vase lovingly
Notes "I love you" near her bed.

One day DJ came not to visit
Unlike her, Rose seemed to fret,
Days go by, Rose knows not why
Her daughter DJ no visits yet.

A day DJ drives home from son's visit
From city miles from home ahead
A deer hits her car head-on three times
Car rolls over; hood fell on DJ's head.

Her ear cut off, eyes damaged too
Critical condition hospital report
Bruised scalp, injury to body not few
DJ helpless, pain to body contort.

Wants to die says, "God, take me today"
Daughter Cindy to nursing home goes
Gets permission to take out a friend
Of her mother; her dear friend Rose.

To Mom in hospital room tend
Encourage her Mom in odious pain
Find reasons for Mom to live
For family, for friend Rose again.

Rose visits room where her DJ lay
Bandages all over her head
Bends closer, her tears fall softly
On DJ's face, awakens in hospital bed.

Her face moist, wipes Rose's wet tears
Fallen on her bruised face
Sees Cindy and Rose friend-mother
Tries lifting head off pillowcase.

Rose says,"DJ we need you
Residents at home miss you too
My days empty of your visit
From my new daughter DJ, you.

DJ's suffering salved by visits
Of daughter Cindy and a Mom
Taking time to encourage her
Life, though difficult goes on.

DJ tries to please them again
For children, for her dear Rose
Prayers lift her desire to remain
Life's blossom bruised, not closed.

Soon DJ gets better, yet slowly
Hair, once auburn, now white
Teases Rose they are more the same
Two heads white, beautiful sight.

Weeks long, DJ visits nursing home
Resume duties to Rose once made
Friendship renewed even stronger
DJ can't work though as nurse's aide.

Dj recovers, still in her apartment
Rose telephones just four rings,
Then visits her in an afternoon
Reminisce past joyful things.

Artistic and talented Dj
Draws portrait of Rose and she
Together both white-haired
Smiling, happy as can be.

Next to portrait stands a dolly
Named Rose, for memory's store,
Picture paints words unsaid
A friendship both of them wore.

Doll a gift from Miss Imelda
Recognizes friendship treasure
Expresses also her fellowship
Both of them equal in measure.

Rose happy DJ's health better
Go to church together again
One day nursing home gets letter
Shocking news surfaces when.

Rose's family posts legal decree
Bans DJ's visit to their mother Rose
At once, no exception to be
DJ devastated, no visits there goes.

Rose, knows DJ's apartment location
Walks to her apartment door
Disagrees with legal citation
DJ tells her not to come anymore.

Rose older forgets court order
Calls DJ on telephone four times
Love for DJ renews toward her
Rose visits less but sometimes.

DJ notices Rose's health fading
Goes to home Head Nurse to say
Asks Rose be medically examined
May have new illness to convey.

Doctor examines her health over
Finds Rose has cancerous tumor
Heartaches, treatments begin difficult
Rose weakens with age, tired, no rumor.

DJ suffers silently some more
Delicate, fragile poor lamb, Rose fades
Can't walk near to DJ's apartment
Space empty behind her door shades.

One day DJ's priest goes to her apartment
Tells her to get in his car soon
Dj's complies, asks where will they go

He says to nursing home Rose's room.

DJ walks inside sees her Mother Rose
So ill, does not speak while she stays
DJ tells her "I love you Mom, always will,
Forever all the rest of my days."

DJ remains in room with the priest
Caresses soft Mother Rose's face
Holds her hands close to her lips
Her wet tears fill ailing space.

Gets up to leave her rosebud
Tells her always she loves her so
DJ leaves, walks toward priest
Rose says "I know you do, I love you,
I'll save a place at the Lord's Table
In heaven" words said, Rose is able.

Closes her eyes as she's speaking
Rests again, so tired is she
DJ and priest leave the room
DJ and Rose's last visit grantee.

DJ back to her apartment
Thanks priest very very much
To be able to see Mother Rose
Hold her hands, her face to touch.

DJ ponders these past eight years
Of friendship's treasure near end
Rose will leave, pass away
Leave behind memory to spend.

Hours reflecting Mothers memories
Grown out each different need
Pure, simple, generously given
DJ gives Rose to heaven indeed.

DJ hears her telephone ringing
Four times, could this be Rose?
Lifts up receiver, no response
Same time Rose to heaven goes!

She said goodbye with four rings
Left friendship's beauty behind
Rarely on earth's in this life brings
Perfect peace for two in one's mind.

DJ visited by state ombudsman
Inspects nursing home, Rose's record
Confirm DJ's love to Rose did not warrant
Cancelled visits. Her visits righteous accord.

Her attention to Rose honorable
In fact, example for others to see
Nursing home residents miss visitors
That includes you, also includes me.

So let it be, all who read this
Poem written in a story by a doll
Love those confined to rest homes
Never forget visits regular at all

Bring gifts, sing songs, read poetry
Take drives in Nature's display
Enjoy all season's splendor
Show love is the only way.

As a doll named Rose standing
Near two people who found each other
Blossomed true as chosen friendship
Blessed as daughter and mother.

CHAPTER 32. RUTH

"If I had a flower for every time I thought of you
I could walk through my garden forever."
A quote by Alfred Tennyson

My dearest friend Erica:

Hello new Mama! I am your doll Ruth. You have no idea what I have gone through waiting to be sent to you far away in Texas from Wisconsin. First of all I am glad Miss Imelda found me in a garage sale, having been cast off from a family who did not think I was good enough since they had a collection of expensive and famous dolls. When Miss Imelda brought me to her house she took all my clothes off and put me in a basket with my head down and my feet in the air! I was put in another room but only this time I was not upside down. There are many stuffed animals here. They are for sale, but the sale is not yet, so I can meet them all. There are tigers, bears, cats, parrots, dogs, more bears, leopards, horses, more cats and a very large lion named Leo. Miss Imelda says you like animals so while I am here I will get to know them all. I do not mind not having any clothes on because they don't have any on either. We talk all night when Miss Imelda is not here.

As you know my story is about Ruth, named in the Bible. She worked in the grain fields, whose owner was a man called Boaz. He is very kind and respected. Naomi, her mother-in-law says they are related. She took Ruth in when her husband died, even though she was not her religious faith. She wanted to go where she goes and she is going to join family.

My dress is a pale ocean blue with little flowers on it. Ruth likes the fields she gleans for food. I also have a bag for my seeds and grain brought home for Naomi. My rake is placed beside my pink apron where I keep it when I am not using it. My hair is long and braided to keep from the hot sun. My bonnet matches my dress. I will be wrapped in lots of paper to send to you so I must visit with my animal friends so I can remember each and every one.

I can still hear Miss Imelda sewing. She tells her daughter she is making a new wedding dress for a very special bride. It is beautiful she says and the veil has pearls on it plus a pearl necklace with lots of lace. I wonder who that dress is for? She says there are a dozen pink roses for a bouquet the bride holds walking toward her husband to be. I wish it was mine because pink matches my apron that I wear in the fields.

Today, Miss Imelda moved me over, placed me in my box to you, and put another box next to me. It has lovely blossoms on it to remind you of the cherry blossoms in Virginia when you lived there and met her. Maybe you will have use for the lovely box.

We will have lovely times looking at each other. I hope your cats will like me. I hope your son Tristan will like me also. I will stay in your family forever like we are supposed to do. I know we will love each other like you and Miss Imelda love each other. Truly your people will be my people and wherever you go I will go. ...Love Ruth

"Every flower is a soul blossoming in nature."
A quote from, Gerard de Nerval

RUTH

I am a doll to remind you of someone
Named Ruth living long ago
Lost her husband so her mother in law
Invites her to stay with her, so

When she leaves to go to family
She follows, religion not same meaning
Naomi accepts her graciously
Ruth works in farm fields gleaning.

Grains for family foods to store
Muffins/rolls of grain use wheat
Oats for cereal to prepare
Rye use bread loaves to eat.

Barley for different soup
Grains so healthy each group
Without them cannot easily live
Glean fields from farmer to give.

"Just living is not enough...one must have sunshine,
freedom, and a little flower."
A Quote from Hans Christian Anderson

Ruth looks beside grain fields
Sees flowers lovely to see
Knows some describe character
'Healing, happy life is peony.'

She likes 'lily-of-the-valley'
Grows thick on widened trail
Means 'sweetness, beauty gaiety'
Traits of friend Erica full scale.

Further in fields are 'petunias'
'Your presence soothes me' it said
Quality of friend Miss Imelda
'Forget-me-not's' hide at rock bed.

'True love forever' they meant
Keep alive memory's ember
In this poem lovingly sent
'Faithful memories, remember.'

Ruth looks closely finding flora
Admires all back to home frequent
'Honeysuckles' grow closer to Naomi's
'Sweetness, happiness' is sent.

'Heather' grows on curved hillsides
'Admiration or solitude' assert same
'Iris' blossoms in short distance
'Warmth of affection' they name.

'Wisdom or inspiration'
Erica's nature she has everyday
'Gardenias' recalled from Virginia
Perfume pleasantly sprays.

Mention of 'joy' continues
Miss Imelda and Erica meet
At Wellness Center everyday
Mention of 'joy' so complete.

'Daisies' grow in meadows
'Loyalty, innocence' decree
Fond flora of both of them
'Together affection' they see.

'Sunflowers' tower in sunshine
Follow beams faithfully
'Devotion' they pen surmise
Commitment loyal decree.

'Zinnias' tall at Wellness Center
Short stay weeks Erica spent
'Remembrances' they utter
Both friends loyalty lent.

'Bluebells' back to fields grow
'Delicacy, humility' express
Traits both friends mention
Avail generous access.

'Baby Breath' minute petals
Hide near 'amaryllis' seed
Assert 'drama, poetry, pride'
Friends together agreed.

'Carnations' grow at far border
'Pure love of woman,' remark
Colors varied to be chosen
Special occasions a trademark.

Gifts 'chrysanthemum' bouquet
Voice 'cheerfulness' to her friend
Promise friendship straightway
Companionship will never end.

"I always like walking in the rain, so no one sees me crying."
A quote from Charlie Chaplin

Clouds form in high heavens
Raindrops small begin to fall
On flowers of their friendship
Drops commence a downfall.

Find Erica's location living
Kisses her window pane
Slip down smooth window glass
Long chain waves soft rain.

Flower leaves green enamel
Raindrops paint them so
Erica regards rain affectionately
Miss Imelda tells her "hello."

Once told her "forget umbrella

Walk, sing in rain's outpour
Feel moist wetness to cleanse
Make clean sad thoughts explore."

Your lives known tragedies
Hearts injured, broken intense
Read my poem times you need it
Salving inner self's cures immense.

Each flower, no matter location
Covers bruise healing perfume
Fragrant aromas all become
Love theme from Imelda's chat room.

"You dwell in her heart friend, Erica
Loved as a "flower in the rain"
Decide which select flower
Choose beauty on memory lane.

Single petal shape different
Treasure pressed to your breast
Where fruit of seed develops
Occasioned perfect as best.

Select 'lotus' for lost husbands
'Mystery and truth' its assume
Value individual happenings
Flowers elusive grow full bloom.

Enjoyed as a youth together
When love of man loved is gone
Look at me your Dolly Ruth
All four seasons is weather upon.

'Jonquils' ease deep pain
'Desire for affection returned'
Certain for flowers in the rain
Moist fragrance wrapped earned.

Each petal blossom a Guest
Kissed many wet raindrops
Today's flower for friend's request
Easily found in flower shops.

Though distances separates us
Love knows not distance or space
Miss Imelda looks at a flower
Mirrors her friend Erica's face.

So I am where you go, my friend
In my Spirit I am always there
Beside you if you need me
Dedicated trustworthy anywhere.

Flowers are words to express
Character traits explain plain
Loving each other always
Erica, a "Flower in the rain."

Look at me your porcelain doll
Language written of truth
Florets express 'happiness'
Friendship's award gift Doll Ruth.

"A good name in man and woman is the immediate jewel of their soul."
A quote from William Shakespeare

Naomi's knows her relative Boaz is
Owner exceedingly wealth great
Who sees Ruth in his fields gleaning
Comes home, more stories relate.

In grain fields Boaz regular patrols
Speaks to his young women and men
If troubled often consoles
Encourages, instructs, he guides them.

Boaz notices Ruth working his fields
Approach to her assertively claim
Says "Glean where my young women glean
I insist their protection no shame."

"I command men not to rebuke them
Provide water their thirst, treating"
Ruth bends knees implores him
"I bow humble at your feet entreating.

Why favor me, I am a foreigner?
Why notice me your favors to think
Include water when I am so thirsty
Refreshed abundantly to drink?"

Boaz admits he knows her history
Journey with Naomi kindly chosen well
Yet away from birth relatives leaving
Family separated by travel, Naomi to dwell.

Ruth thanks him again, then returns

To tell Naomi Boaz's fond favor
He assures her, her Lord's wings refuge
Can glean his field safely, a lifesaver.

Women and young men work on the farm
Throughout fields Boaz releases
Ruth gleans with women also young
Protected, her grain supply increases.

Doesn't know Boaz tells male gleaners
Purposely let fall grain bundles more
In field where Naomi's gleaner Ruth
Instructs, let her have more to store.

Ruth resumes glean fields of Boaz
Until barley harvest was over
Goes home to Naomi food abundant
Is next year's supply left over.

Sssh, Naomi tells Ruth, she has a plan
"Go to threshing floor where men are
Do not let men know this program
Your safe, Boaz, is your benefactor."

"Conceal yourself with your shawl
Find Boaz's night bed place selection
When men done drinking and eating
He'll notice, listen to his direction."

Ruth goes as instructed by Naomi
Follows course explained very well
Lays at Boaz's feet where he lies
Uncovers his feet, what will he tell?"

He sees her, asks her who she is
"Ruth, I glean in your fields," she replies.
Boaz tells her take shawl, hold it, fills
Six ephahs of barley measured in size.

Directs her to return home to Naomi
Obediently departs, instructed in truth
Her gifts generous of barely carried
From Boaz's threshing floor booth.

Boaz decides next, goes to town elders
Learns history land of inheritance
Buys land of Naomi and Ruth's relatives
Gets witnesses recorded in advance.

Announces to elders Ruth he will claim
For his bride, certain God's holy order
Their marriage arrangements soon became
Happy news, must now prepare her.

Land purchase sustains Naomi's old age
Naomi praises foreigner friend Ruth
Better than any daughter or son
Lives life's way totally in truth.

Ruth accepts Boaz's offer to marry
Overwhelmed by good fortune event
Kindly donates her clothes for gleaners
Thanks Naomi her counsel and consent.

Naomi buys textiles lovely express
White gossamer fabric soft graces
Ruth's body ornate, sews wedding dress
Naomi beams watches couple's faces.

Beautiful bride of Boaz prominent
Poverty poor by circumstance
Viewed by one who saw qualities
Values for wife, finds union romance.

Ruth devoted, generous, giving
Benevolent, faithful by his side
A foreigner now part of society
Has proper name, no reason to hide.

Naomi's benefactor, Boaz's bride
Her poverty engulfed by happiness
Her vow to go where Naomi goes
Her people Ruth's people no less.

Providential circumstance love blossoms
Continues toward husband vow he knows
Wife and mother any reproach devoid
Boaz arranged preparations new clothes.

Ruth grateful, happy overjoyed
She bears him sons, Bible revelations
Conceived in marriage quote bizarre
Prophecies made in future generations.

Children of Boaz and Ruth are now
Heirs earlier before David the King
Each heir important in Scripture
Names recorded in each offspring.

> A bride flower complete blossom
> God's blessing again and again
> In graced garden loving each other
> Bride Ruth Boaz's "flower to reign."

> Second gift with Ruth in box ornate
> Design similar wearing it in truth
> Wedding gown sewed by Miss Imelda
> Gift by Erica's doll, rain flower, Ruth.

CHAPTER 33. BUTTERFLY

> "Man's love is of his life a thing apart,
> 'tis woman's whole existence."
> A quote from the opera Madame Butterfly

My dear Elfreida:

It is as if butterflies carried you next door, where we live not too far apart, to have Miss Imelda hand deliver your Dolly Butterfly's box. I have butterflies all over my dress! Then I find out you are leaving your "War Bride" husband because he treats you so intolerably, and you will join your daughter, Sylvia in California. I am delivered promptly, before you have to leave. It is no small wonder you chose to have a Dolly telling the story of Madame Butterfly's opera since you enjoy different opera stories. I am sorry your experience in America has not been pleasant, I am glad at least your husband allowed Miss Imelda to see you, but no one else. So you have raised your precious daughter, Sylvia alone with him as your keeper, not as a husband should be

Your dear friend and neighbor Miss Imelda took such a long time to make me perfect for you. I have a mask with hearts and tears painted on a lovely porcelain face. It is very important to me to wear when sad, like you, as it is difficult for us to show how we feel. All the time I was waiting for my gown to be completed, I was reading about operas. Your dreams can come true; Miss Imelda says if you wish hard and long enough. I am good at that! Friendships last and last, as yours has with Miss Imelda and her children, so close to you as a neighbor, when you were brought to this country from a faraway place Germany. Her daughters Marianne and Julie remember you and child Sylvia well.

While I was waiting for holidays to be over I have been reading Miss Imelda's poetry to her husband Bill. Someday she wants her poems titled"The Meadow" to be opera. One night I imagined myself in this wonder- filled place called a meadow to find out from my friend Doll Karina that such a place exists. It is in the hearts and mind of those who believe in meadows no matter where they are or what their life will bring.

I know you will like me. I know I will love you. Miss Imelda does. She says I will give you lots of joy, now that you will be with your daughter Sylvia, and her husband and children. She says I will hear about the whole story of Madame Butterfly when you receive me as your very own. This is another story, like that one, about a boy named "Trouble" and his butterfly! Love Butterfly...

BUTTERFLY

Pinkerton, Lt. in United States Navy
Is charmed by a house quaint and small
A dwelling for him and Japanese bride
For short time in Japan does recall.

Lovely to behold, so attentive
Sings songs in far meadow so clear
Her love for him forsakes family
He loves America, not here.

Butterfly, her name delightful
Considerate, devoted is she
Caring, pleasant for her husband
Someday soon returns to the sea.

He promises to return in the springtime
When robins sing building new nest
He will bring her to his America
Gifts small American flag as interest.

Three years pass Madam Butterfly
Takes her son, almost age three
Gives him a doll dressed like her
Sleeps with them tenderly.

He plays with small American flag
Many stars in left corner he can see
Rows of ribbons red and white
Waves flag with fingers wee.

Lives in small Japanese home
With Mother Butterfly, servant Suzuki
Does not know his Father far away
Left for his American country.

One day people come to their house
Butterfly holds him in other room
Bandages his eyes with long fabric
Games they play in this costume.

She puts his doll in one hand
Other hand holds American flag
"Hide, you seek" her command

Eyes blind-folded play tag.

He must find Mother Butterfly
Struggling he twists, turns in spite
Cries, then in her arms calms him
It's dark in his head, like night.

Someone comes in room quickly
Takes him in daylight with strong hand
Away from Mother's warm embrace
(So small, Trouble doesn't understand).

Bandages taken off his head, his face
Man brings him to garden near by
Joins a lady stranger he never met
Never holds again Mother Butterfly.

Lady smiles to little boy bewildered
Says his little flag he can bring
Soon when they board a big ship
Sailing to America this spring.

He holds his doll from his mother
Talks little English yet to say
Wants to remain near his mother
Knows not what "sailing" means today.

He sits still, this kind lady sits too
Polite as he was taught to be
Asks if his dolly can sing?
Shakes head up and down to agree.

Out of his home walks a man
Clothes white like clouds in blue sky
Stands tall next to kind lady
To man with strong hands says "Goodbye."

Trouble is placed in middle of lady
Man in white clothes other side
Walk to wide sea waits a big ship
Sailing soon taking long boat ride.

This tragedy can't end, it is too much
For a Dolly, for me to contend
I need porcelain face mask to touch
Miss Imelda in wisdom did send.

I can't be sad, cry wet tears spent
Such pain for me to go through

I'll wear it in front of smiling face
Learn pain bad dreams never knew.

Will I know myself as Doll Butterfly?
Her loneliness feelings to share
Hearts on glass face mask bleeding
Emotion I felt not anywhere.

I will experience tragedy a moment
So back on my dress mask can go
I need to follow little boy with a doll
Gift of Japanese Mother did know.

Tender years she cared for him
Loved his American father so
In an instant his life is changing
Walks to harbor, ship waits to go.

Aboard vessel they sail a long time
To American country arrives
Little boy with only toys two
Goes to home in car man drives.

I don't know dreams as nightmares
How will Pinkerton and his wife mend?
A little child's love for his Mother
Shared by servant Suzuki her friend.

Few years in two rooms filled in love
Mother naïve, innocent and pure
Was she like a real butterfly?
Beauties brief visit to earth sure?

A faithful wife against all odds
Japanese war bride her crime?
Misses husband, has his child alone
Devotion continues lonely in time.

Now little boy the stranger
In family taken to country new
His father, American wife; his home
He doesn't know what to do.

His name named "Trouble"
Name a kind of word spell
Of grief, trials, heartache
No one understands feelings well.

Except small flag and dolly did take

I'll dream supernatural appealing
Of people in opera scene
As God beckons Butterfly's healing.

Takes her life in desperation
Dies in arms of husband once known
Gives to him their small son
Cared for, now age three grown.

Will she be angel in heaven?
Fly vast universe everywhere
Her joy for little child boy
Permanent, always will be there.

See her husband Pinkerton?
With strange woman, his wife
Unconditional love given to "Trouble"
Now as American boy's life.

Can she fly above America?
See lands she may have known
Fly to her homeland Japan?
Her families loved since grown.

Outdoors season of spring new
New birds, red robins have come
Busy building bird nests new
His Mother talked of these some.

Strange lady he met in garden
Near home he knew in Japan
Touched gentle his hands like his Mother
Her first name Marianne.

His father he knows as Lieutenant
To big room called a parlor came
Together tell him his first name will
Change no other American name.

A Japanese name called "Cio San"
In honor of his Japanese Mother
Is proud of new name, only one
In America there will be no other.

His last name is told Pinkerton
Cio San happy thoughts then
Tells Doll he names Butterfly
Holds small flag from her a token.

New places mother said to imply
New birds, robins in springtime
Build strong nests for new family
He found in America meantime.

Marianne takes him to garden
Beside large window in their home
Shows new growth of seeds planted
Weeks ago, for him seeds sown.

Says, "Flowers attract butterflies
Here is 'cornflower' called by name
Repeat after me slowly if you can"
Watches her lips, he repeats same.

"Very clearly said, Cio San, each word
"Next, 'Cosmos, Zinnia, phlox"
'Butterfly weed, ox-eye daisies' in box"
Listens intent each name heard.

He glances up for a moment
Sees man dressed in white
Salutes to them in the garden
Waves back to him to invite.

Presence with them in the garden
Tells them of "common milkweed
Weed not a flower, but lovely
Planted for him, comes back indeed.

Thistles, nettle, wild roses
Transplanted by him last year
In back of garden they grow
Apple, cherry trees also south near.

Marianne helps name repeats to know
Says, "Stems grow budding flowers
A surprise waits for you here when
Spring rainfall will bring showers."

Three of them return to home then
Listen to phonics, practice repeating
Summer sun fades, raindrops falling
Spring seasons wait summer's greeting.

Cio San visits garden every day
Repeats each flower he learns
Flowers he knows now by name
Full blossoms, new beauty returns.

Hummingbirds fly to drink nectar
Butterflies like flowers fly air blown
Orange sulphurs, Tiger swallowtail
Brown satyrs, Coral Hairstreak shown.

Bronze Coppers, colorful Angle wings
He'll ask Marianne their name
Lovely, so varied wee things
Spring Azure, known Monarchs came.

Orange, black bold stripes
Milkweed visits for butterflies
So diverse, different types
Patterns differ in size.

Cio San sits in lawn chair content
Holds doll, his American flag small
Watch birds and butterflies frequent
Misses Mother most at nightfall.

Robins, hummingbirds, butterflies flying
Visitors of air currents, stormy air
Drink flower nectars in resident
Fly fast in their garden there.

He dozed a moment, then a Monarch
Rests on his cheek like fingertips
Wings span golden black fan his face
Monarch moves quick to his lips.

Drinks fruit juice in creased space
Back to his eyelashes skips
Butterfly walks on his eyelashes
Down nose over his cheek dips.

Inside Boy Cio- San wonders
Do Monarch butterflies speak?
Monarch flies to American flag
Up, down stars walks mystique.

Flits to sit on his doll's dress
Feels fabric, flowers gets on
Back to his cheek wings flutter
His memories of Mother cast on.

Once like his mother's eyelash
Flutters, tickles his baby skin
His mind a memory back flash

If Mother was this butterfly thin?

Migrated to America to see
Little son where he was living
In house window watch his family
Caring for her son their love giving?

Monarch moves to his lips again
Finds juice taste had before
Fans, unfolds wings as eyelash blinks
Then soars skyward once more.

Inside Cio San was singing
Song heard in Japan a long ago's
Monarch flies back rests on his face
It's his Mother Butterfly he knows.

Sings louder, then softly, then whispers
Monarch rests on his face again
Cio San's song ends now
Opens small hand wide when.

Monarch flies briefly to his brow
Fans wings aflutter like an eyelash
Tickles his face like once long ago
Flies in air, sun sets, gone in a flash.

"Beauty is not in the face; beauty is a light in the heart
A quote from Kahil Kabran

In your life you may see a flower
Beautiful to view at a glance
Flies smooth as you get closer
It's Butterfly in her garden dance.

Graces air with wind wings
Stops by high tree, robins nesting
Happy in New Year, each spring
Birds new mates, family investing.

Her beauty, none other, unequalled
Nourished by flowers passes by
Sweet nectar of life sustaining, is
Memorialized Madame Butterfly.

Each spring as two robins nesting
Look closely in garden if you can
Monarch returns, kisses her son
Renamed for her, Cio San.

Dear Miss Imelda:

I have received my Doll Butterfly and she is loved immensely by my three grandchildren and their mother and even my daughter's husband. Her shoes are so delightful, have never seen a dolly's shoes so lovely. I chuckled when you indicated her dress was made out of an under slip of yours! It certainly is admired more as a dress for her. I chose to call her Butterfly because I was a war bride, though not Japanese. I was terrified when brought here while waiting for my war husband to bring me to Wisconsin. Then, I was secluded from others with only him and raising my daughter. I was so gifted meeting you in the mobile home court and being allowed to visit with you and your children Julie and Marianne. I don't know how he agreed to my seeing you, but he felt you were safe for me to be friends with.

When my daughter married and moved to California, they asked me to join them, I was overjoyed. I am a member of several social clubs here and a clerk at our local J. C. Penny's Department store. I also volunteer at the USO club. Thank you for not letting my husband aware of where I am or where my daughter is. It is a book I would like closed since I am so much happier now. I have my U.S. Citizenship papers now and proud to be an American. My grandchildren, all three are in school now. They have helped me speak better without a Germanic accent. Thanks again for Butterfly. We will cherish her always. I agree with you we will not contact each other anymore since I like being anonymous with Midwest contacts.   God bless you so much and thanks again for my doll Butterfly. I do not have your poem, but I know the opera well, and go to several operas here locally. When it is complete please send to me at the J. C. Penny Department store, marked "Personal." I will let the secretary know it will be arriving in a few weeks...Love Elfreida.

CHAPTER 34. MARY BETH

> "Southerners love a good tale. They are born reciters,
> great memory retainers, diary keepers,
> letter exchangers, great talkers."
> A quote from Eudora Welty

—

Dear Miss Imelda:

I finally arrived in the "cotton-picking" state of Georgia. It sure has been a long journey for me. At last I am loved and cared for by my Southern Gal Miss Zola. My story in my poem below is a long one but true...Mary Beth

MARY BETH

I'm told it began year 1957
Miss Imelda from the north and
Miss Zola south, next door neighbors

In central Minnesota town land.

Both have two small children
Miss Imelda girls, Julie and Marianne
They become one big family
Zo and Burt, a boy Greg, girl Diane.

Miss Imelda and her girls going through
Death losing husband and father
Miss Zo very unhappy too
Lived in South, state of Georgia, rather.

She is lonely, family roots far away
Northern state husband married
Dreads coming winter's day
Bond like blood sisters carried.

Comfort each, friendship flourishes
Unite, attach, destined to remain
Each need instantly nourishes
Balance, no longer a drain.

They sew dresses together
Prepare summer picnic lunches
Throw a towel on green lawn
Picnic with four kids in bunches.

. Miss Imelda fond of little boy Greg
Having lost their own son at birth
They remain friends a long time
Pledge friendship always on earth.

Miss Zola with husband Burt decide
To move south, put house up for sale
House sold sooner than expected
Miss Imelda invites a folktale.

All families move in, connected
Until short time left preparing
Moving possessions to keep
Family and friends sharing.

Family leaves her for south journey
Zola happy Midwest to lose touch
Hug close best friend Miss Imelda
Family left behind loves much.

Letters, phone calls, more correspondence
Keep loveliness open good as gold

Miss Imelda gets different employment
Close to Minnesota winters cold.

During next 25 years or so
Letters exchange, new address, new places
Keep alive friendship's glow
Their children grow older faces.

In the meantime I was "born"
Miss Imelda told Miss Zola she'd make
Her a doll and wanted to know
Her favorite colors, doll name take.

We are going to Florida to live
Takes me with so I won't be cold
A state closer to Zola, I'm excited
Maybe her too to behold!

Need a dress for my naked body
A Southern Belle dress so swell
New hair, new hat so pleasing"
To me Miss Imelda says "Farewell."

"I sure was glad to be going south
Tired of my naked butt freezing"
Mind forgot about Northland cold
At Miss Zola's sunshine pleasing.

Later she packs rest of possessions
Moves to Florida sun controlled
Brought will all fabric she promised
Though me boxed up getting old.

Their correspondence still lingers
Two years I'm packed naked still
Miss Imelda busy as work planner
Programs don't include me to fill.

I don't relate to Wellness Banner
Forgotten doll in a dark box I'll be
How will I meet my Miss Zola?
As Southern Belle promise to me.

I didn't even have warm coat
Repeatedly forgotten over again
Traveling to another town remote
Miss Zola wonders always when?

Miss Imelda's promises Dolly will come

Zo never doubts friend many years
Will soon send her, dressed all done
She'll arrive, lost time disappears.

Wellness Center in Florida completed
Transfer back to Wisconsin agreed
By contract Miss Imelda drives back
Going through Georgia indeed!

Two friends on telephone held maps
Her travel Northward she'll take
Where Burt and Zo lived long ago
When first a friendship did take.

Miss Imelda's Florida job transfers
Back to Wisconsin near family
I'm packed new in box with books
What is heavy stored on top of me?

Without clothes yet past years
Small red hearts on dolls I recall
I wish I had water to make tears
Can't remember dreams at all.

Old dress I came in discarded
Do friends lose track of time?
Some doll dreams disregarded
Certainly they include mine.

Twenty years between friends meet
In Georgia, thrilled together to see
I'm still in a box as both did forget
Busy in friendship so happy be.

I hoped my Miss Zola to meet
Alone in gray car in driveway
Packed stuff on me, on the seat
No one my thoughts to convey.

Still naked, alone with my fabric
No new hair or hat decorated
Eyes open nothing in dark view
I think friendship under rated.

Out of Zola's house I hear her
Hug Miss Imelda fond goodbye
No concern for me so obscure
Packed in box wondering why.

To Wisconsin Miss Imelda drove
Cold winds began closer we came
To log cabin where I once was
Undressed still naked, no name.

One day in cabin the sun shines
Thru long glass window it gleams
I'm taken out of car months ago
Wait some more it seems.

In morning in evening I would stare
At Miss Imelda so very busy, stressed
I remain on stand without underwear
Same as before still undressed.

She finally says, as I shocked collapse
"It's time my friend, Zo's waiting will end
For you Dolly get dressed to go south"
Past worries begin to mend.

I could shout for joy, but forgot how
She places red heart on my left chest
Instantly, I forgive her my long wait
Thread needle through, lacy cloth best.

Sew quickly together interlink
Peach flowered fabric like peaches hover
Blossom flowers cherry petals pink
My new Southern hat flowers cover.

My mind quick my dreams return
My blonde curls cascade on my sleeve
Fall smooth down my back each turn
Lace borders my dress cleaves.

In mirror A Southern Belle I see
Miss Imelda calls Miss Zola on phone
Says, "Mary Beth" I guess, "That's me!"
Again, am packed in a box alone.

With paper and packing on my face
This time only happy thoughts linger
"I was used to this my thoughts race"
My story typed neatly one finger.

My cotton ball in my pocket space
Dressed perfect for permanent home
I smile wide under stuffing's place
I travelled these same miles alone.

When packed so naked, so alone
This journey ends for my summerhouse
Moving south to my new home
I arrive at Miss Zola's house.

My box she won't open, too excited!
Sets me on a table, flat I can feel
Waits for someone to open, I'm slighted!
Who will open the package seal?

My new red heart is thinking
"Will I live in box my life whole?
Who will let me out, take me out
Miss Zola I need you to console.

I am now in your southern country
Land warm, my new red heart warm
Don't be afraid to see my beauty
I'm just perfect, no need for alarm."

By chance the first one to come over
Is son Greg, now a grown up man
Miss Zola asks him, "Open box, to tell her
She's too excited, please if you can.

Tell me what my dolly looks like
She may have love letters to read"
Greg's strong hands lift me out
"He's so handsome I think indeed."

Miss Zola sits in next room on a chair
Greg brings me to her, happy tears mist
Flow softly down her cheek on my sleeve
On red heart Miss Imelda kissed.

In fond friendship they telephone
Both agree I am well dressed
A Southern Belle from Yankee
"I am more beautiful than she guessed."

Long friendship through a doll display
Plans to be near two friends' lifetime
Or beyond where doll dreams stay
Miss Imelda and Miss Zola still mine.

Children Diane and Greg come in
They see Miss Zola, me Mary Beth
Name by Zola by her call-in

We're family no matter weather.

In states far away other seasons
This story is told by Miss Zola, yet
Don't doubt friendships' reasons
Lifetime friends since two met.

Never knew many years end
Twenty three years those years
White, graying hair aged friend
Fellowship in spite of my tears.

Beauty is in eyes of beholder
Miss Zola thinks of us all three
Carefully gives me tender care
Has other dolls but none like me.
$
So lovely none can compare
We display in china closet again
"Cabbage Patch" are dolls their name
When they learn to talk, we'll visit then.

I'll tell them from where I came
Miss Zola writes letter, to north get it
A "Cotton Picking Gal" now my game
That's why cotton pocket is full of it!

One cotton ball enough for me
My dress design garment sewed well
Adorned by request of Miss Zola
Only name for her Southern Belle.

Miss Imelda called her lately
Zola says for over ten years
She visits elderly in nursing homes
No visitor ever, lonely, tears.

Now that she has Mary Beth
They go together to see again
Men and women just love her
Bring back memories "of once when."

Sometimes they want to touch her
Or hold her little glass hand
Some add one more cotton ball
In her dress pocket to expand.

Miss Zola brings them tidbits
Box of chocolates, peanuts or fruit

> Most of all want to see her doll
> Mary Beth, her Southern Belle cute.
> Dear Miss Imelda:
>
> A card comes from postman
> Amanda Bradley, her poem wrote
> Miss Zola sends in appreciation
> Of gift of beautiful doll, so devote.
>
> "Some people seem to specialize
> In doing thoughtful deeds
> Before you ask, they understand
> Your problems and your needs."
>
> "They help because they want to
> They find joy in being kind
> And making others happy
> Is the first thing on their minds?
>
> They make this world a better place
> By practicing the art
> Of reaching out to others
> And by giving...from the heart.
>
> It is good to know
> Warm, considerate people
> Who try to help others?
> In all they say and do.
>
> People whose lives
> Show the meaning of kindness
> It's good to know
> Special people like you."
>
> End..Amanda Bradley's card.

Miss Zola signs the card...Mary Beth is just beautiful and I will enjoy her. The poem in this card explains what I can't do as well. She was well worth the wait. Diane and Kristen like her also. I love you, your friend Zola

CHAPTER 35. NICOLE

> "To express nostalgia for a childhood we no longer share is to deny
> the actual significance of humanity of children."
> A quote from Perry Nodelman, Ph.D.

Dearest Gerri:

Well, here I am! Colors just like you wanted! I hope you like me moving in! All of us! My dress has little hearts, lots of them to show Miss Imelda's love for a friend of such long standing as you are. My skirt is little, tiny checks. Do you know why? I have to check up on my two friends, Billie and Clarisse. Since you and your childhood friend Nicole were such good friends, and my name is Nicole, I thought you would let me bring my two friends, like old times it used to be with you and Nicole. As you can see they have a basket of things already to play with, tennis rackets, a baby bottle, a can of pop for them to share, and the little white kitty belongs to someone on the block, but they are not sure who! The clothes pin is included in case it may come in handy someday.

It is like it was with you and Nicole when you were children as special childhood friends. My pocket in my pinafore is for my poem. It was so crowded in the box labeled "sleeping bag." I like you already. I know even though Miss Imelda had a hard time to let us go, I will see her again, since she visits you from time to time. I hope you will like me as much as she does. Love, Nicole, Billie and Clarisse

NICOLE

Child-like we are when children
Creative, innocent
Enthused about all we do
Learning development!

See me, a doll, with my two dolls
As children Once Long Ago
Between ages three, almost four
Two girl friends to know!

Nicole knocks upon your door
Doorknob closed, almost too high
To reach to find her little pal
Inside welcoming "hi."

Giggling, you join hands in hands
Tight to clasp, to hold
Other selves with all your might!
Playmates two times told.

Eager to visit everyday
Excited to be friends!
Sharing dolls, toys, little thoughts
Among our Never Ends!

HOB, hobby horse runs fast
Across fake hills and glen
Sometimes we fall, often sprawl
Get up mount again!

Pet Mexican Chi-wa-wa
Barks to join the fun

We dress him in sweater and cap
Cast-offs from anyone.

We lunch midday a special way
On dishes small and quaint
Tea cakes cute, so minute
Frost flowers colored paint.

"Please pass chocolate milk
With marshmallows, when through
Do keep your napkins close
Being polite is what we do.

Careful, eat your soup today!
I spilled it all, almost"
Eat jelly and peanut butter
Spread thick on dark toast.

Children's toys few, our own
We make fun our way
Imagine playthings come alive
From a catalog on display!

Dolls parade around the room
From lands we do not know!
Climb aboard boxed long train
Whistle stopped to say "Hello."

An ark, home for animals
Paired in seven's and two
We walk entry plank to live
As friends, like me and you!

We sail seas in silver boats
Drive pink motor cars
Ride three-wheeled tricycles
Guided on crystal stars!

Dress in gowns, satin lace
Hems trail smooth on wood floor
Down stone stairs of castles high
In lands Not No More!

We hear our Mother's chattering
(As grown-up Mother's do)
Of how wonderful we were
When babies brand new!

Babies! Not us! You see

Already past age three
We talk, walk, eat, we're sweet
Aren't we, Me and You!

Three years plus Nicole played
With Gerri Golden Times
Shining in their childhood
Many pantomimes.

One day, Nicole came not again
To knock on Gerri's door
Her parents move far away
Children parted heart sore.

Too small to exchange addresses
Too small to write were they
Parents driven apart in time
Childhood memories ran away.

Permanently. Undying
Beyond past years did pass
Children, unforgotten friends
View Life's lost looking glass.

Page closed in friendship's span
Never real again
Older years relive, of times
Youth meets Age when.

Were once close ties
We children do discover
Last from best beginnings
Ending cannot cover.

My dolls, Billie and Clarisse
Age three, I would guess
I tuck beneath my fluted skirt
Bring back happiness!

Animate, pleasant, laughing,
Delight in make-believes
Glimmer from Once Wee Past
Remembering weaves.

Frolic with their roustabouts
Childlike discoveries
Capture imaginations
Curiosity guarantees!

Reflect childish fancies
Genuine, sincere, at most
Out tumbling toddlers
Elated friendly Ghosts!

When you close eyes in sleep
Summon recalling's
Somewhere Nicole recollects
Unchanged, wonderings!

Now, as doll gifted
New years, friendships made
These adult years and years
Regain Past Promenade!

Parade beyond heart and mind
Deep in bottomless soul
Time you see me your gift
Childlike as Nicole.

CHAPTER 36. SHARIN CARIN

"For myself I am an optimist it does not seem to be much use being anything else."
A quote from Sir Winston Churchill

Dear Donna and John:

Here I am after five months of waiting to come to you, but I have been busy. Miss Imelda opened a special package marked "Mill Ends" and I wondered who Mill was, to find out there is dress fabric in the box for an outfit dress she is making for me. I watch her as she places a little red heart on my chest.

There are angels and hearts all over my fabric so I will have a heart inside of me and outside of me! I never had a slip and pantaloons before. She said the heart and angel patterns on my dress will remind me all the time how I should be, good hearted and in love with everyone and anyone if they are kind to me or not. My briefcase is also ready. I have my Bible excerpts of important passages to know and my small Precious Promises book. Before she decided to change my dress she gave me Scriptures to read and stories about love and caring for people. I have done so well in my training she has included my M.S. in Natural health and Vegetarian Nutrition certificates. I will be in Doctor John's office, listening to his patient conversations on the phone.

"How will I ever listen on the phone?" I asked. "You'll see," she said, her daughter Julie came over one day and had a phone headset all ready for me. She said I look like a Counselor, now, must have been Miss Imelda's dream for that to happen!

Miss Imelda says I will be with human angels when I go to Florida because even if she works alone in her office up here in Wisconsin, there are many men and women who work for you in Florida and each is doing their special job.

I hope you will love me. Miss Imelda says she is sure you will. I love you already. She is sensitive that way. Love... Sharin N. Carin

"Just because you're not sick doesn't mean you're healthy"
A quote from Author Unknown

SHARIN N. CARIN

Doctor John and Nurse Donna bring
Me to John's office up steep stair
Placed on a shelf near his telephone
Perfect place to be there.

His assistant Tanny's office next door
Introduction pleasantly made
What a nice person to be with
Home school Doctor John does persuade.

Her study of alternative remedies
To be smart like Doctor John
A privilege to make his acquaintance
Intuitive, resourceful to call on.

I can ask Tanny questions if in doubt
All employees help each member
Trained well in this ministry about
Pay health claims January to December.

There are guidelines Miss Imelda
Incorporates manual with a team
Revising, implementing, in charge of
Fulfilling Doctor John's dream.

Miss Imelda came here starting
Wellness Department with Doctor John
Guide counselor's referral remembers
For policy procedures to add-on.

Supply to member guides placard
Following changes to be made
Counselors follow up at intervals
Progress reports at intervals grade.

Months go by me as Sharin Doll, listen
Know why callers Christian Ministry fuse

Programs in place continue to improve
Health improvements good news.

Arrangements made by Miss Imelda
If member needs extensive support
Sends to Wellness Center sessions
Involves staff Doctor's endorsed report.

Health counselors continue follow up
Sometime directives full year
Excellent program well planned back up
Advantages of lifestyle changes clear.

Attend other Centers health news
Practice, follow series presented
Habits change as they choose
Individual members self-contented.

I am not here for health counseling
I represent a fixed intent greeting
For those seen in this business space
An Agent potential in meeting.

Health counselors on phone, or in person
Educated to encourage members made
If following natural ways of life
Can heal from within as first-grade.

I am told we must be enlightened
We must breathe pure outside air
Where negative ions fill us
With oxygen needed to share.

Humans breathe 47 pounds of air
Twenty four hours in and out
Waterfall ions high negatives there
Also sea water, shrubs trees about.

Grow many plants in your home
Take out carbon dioxide, oxygen give
Primary examples listed below
Where healthful leaves pure live.

Chrysanthemum, coconut palm
Or spider plants, weeping fig
Research gerbera family of daisies
Popular plants as flowers big.

Deep breathing part of all of these

Expand abdomen rather than chest
Complementary alternative treatment
Deep slow breaths inhale nose next.

Slowly, remember then count ten
Exhale very same way, slow then
Complete exhale carefully, count ten
Repeat deep breathing, abdomen again.

Five to ten times each time
Do again several times a day, same way
Bodies appreciate your lifetime
Do Deep breathing everyday!

Ions negative, positive balanced
Less oxygen breathing out and in
In bloodstream health a complaint
Disease breeds fill in may live in.

Large populated cities a restraint
Electromagnetic fields in any
Environment we need to ponder
Other atmospheres many.

Excessive use not so wise
Research, think carefully wonder
Especially symptoms of lethargy
If in your life appear out and under.

I also represent caring. Why?
My name Sharin Carin someone
Double group to stand up for
Kind, attentive, consideration.

Divide your possessions more
Perhaps portions nutriment
Donate whatever you can
Bake bread or cookies invent.

Visit a neighbor to divide
Your clothes, theirs threadbare
Offer transportation rides
Needs needed anywhere.

I wonder if angels on my dress
So many printed around
It's said heaven has lots of them
Sent to earth, visions abound.

At night when offices are quiet
Books shelved like me stand on
They'll open wide for me to view
Information for my talkathon.

For dolls who stand indefinitely
Same stand, one of the same
No children to dream dreams with
Only their beauty to claim.

Grown-ups stored away visions
Possibilities out windows blew
Fear crept in bringing guilt
This grieves me right on through.

Happy thoughts I encourage
Positive thinking first class
Prompted by a caring, sharing
Porcelain doll made of glass.

Dear Miss Imelda:
What a special wonderful surprise! You are so special to have created this precious gift of love.

Sharin seems very happy but she wanted me to write and let you know that you sent her to a family that thinks she is "super special." She enjoys hearing all Big John's phone messages and is happily watching everyone who comes in and out of the office. Now she can pray for the many needs she hears discussed lately for all members we have around the world. We love and appreciate you...
Donna and John

CHAPTER 37. GINGER

"Let food be thy medicine and medicine thy food."
A Quote by Hippocrates

HAPPY SURPRISE!

Dear Doctors Hans and Lily Diehl:

When Miss Imelda called you Doctor Diehl, she asked you if you liked ginger cookies, and you said, "Yes, they are snappy!" She told you then she was sending you a surprise, but you could not open the box unless Doctor Lily was with you. A special gift doll to both of you in appreciation for all you taught her in the years you have known each other and worked together. Also, the special people she has met and still keeps in touch with; Valerie in Canada, Dr John and Donna in Florida, Dr. Yew Por and Julie Ng in Idaho, Doctor John and Virginia In Mississippi,, Doctor Alicia and Art in Michigan and Tanny in Florida.

Enclosed is news clipping my mistress, Miss Imelda, wanted to send along with me. It says many wonderful things about you, so I think I know you already. She tells others about working with you during your health seminars, special suppers, and multi-faceted presentations about the eight natural laws of health from the wellness Center Weimar, NEWSTART, located in northern California. We will concentrate on the first one, "Nutrition." I have pleasant emotion, mixed with happiness, that I will represent this important facet of health. There is much love sent to you both through me. I hope waiting for me has been worth it.

As always, the dolls Miss Imelda designs are dressed from the inside up so that now you can notice the special shiny red heart that means so much to you in your lectures. My red heart means so a lot to me too since I never had one before. Please, be sure to brush my hair. Traveling can be so difficult for dolls stuffed in a box! Please place me on the support stand enclosed. I use it during daytime hours, and especially when I am in crowds. When I am alone, well that is a different matter! I need no support in my nighttime wanderings!

For my doll times, I plan on getting to know every fruit, vegetable and seed for nourishment there is in America! So, be sure to leave your books around the house, and, as Ginger, I am touchable.
I look forward to meeting your wife Doctor Lily. She teaches piano to clients from all ages. Please place me on one of her pianos so I can observe her classical music instructions. Music and nutrition should work very well together. Doctor Lily, Miss Imelda confirms, has a beautiful high soprano voice and sings at graduations of Dr. Diehl's health seminars. What a privilege to be part of this household. I am handpicked "Ginger."

While Miss Imelda was employed at the Christian Care Ministry she studies for her Master's of Science degree in Natural Health. She graduated with Honors; part of her Essay explains succinctly my endeavors; it is entitled "A Touch of Ginger," that's me!

A TOUCH OF GINGER

What a deal, Dr.Diehl let me tell you how I feel
Lifestyles for you, practical, wise
For me, fancy notions crystallize
Fancies fanciful clearly in my brown eyes.

I'm a touch of ginger, russet, spicy
Autumn colors ripened yield
Used in cooking, herbs or medicine
Gift of earth's garden or field.

Said to restore, nurture, strengthen
Reaper's gathering harvest crop
I'm love gift to you Drs. Lily and Hans
Listen to my story. Do eavesdrop!

On my dress wee tan leaves scatter
Like your message "To Your Health" should

Wise instruction for people that matter study
Life's lifestyles misunderstood.

My sun yellow pantaloons beam beams
Of vim, body vigor, sharp mind
My shiny red heart's robust glow
Model fall season's increase find.

Admire my salmon tint pinafore
Satin ribbons, pastel blush fall
Spill over tiny ornamentations
Fine fettles fashion exceptional.

Streaming sashes account for Sabbaths
When harvest crowds for more space
Why, all things I represent sent you as a gift
Remedies for a healthy look face.

Preserved in my basket is plenty
Books copied, your tapes or cassette
Bible full of Wisdom, a rare flower
Paint brushes crimson-fired yet.

In my imagination I suppose them
Little dabbers for all good things.
You write in your books, talk on your tapes
Help heal humans in encouraging!

I see grains spread seeds profusely
Fruits distinct to tastes
Vegetables stout shapes, all sizes
Healthy pasta and tomato pastes.

For health, need be nutritionally vital
Aid healing for man to keep well
Why, my basket, though wee, sincerely
Have remarkable teachings to tell!

Laden with leaves golden to view
Flowers spread as blaze sunset
This seasons' produce rendezvous
Such gathering you never met.

All fruits and vegetables pictured
On your album unannounced, animate
Politely introduce each mini-self
Delightful display on each dinner plate.

Fruits and vegetables do clamor

Colorfully exhibit their worth
Out of dark soil fall's harvest
Blossoms produce of Mother Earth.

Red or green apples fall on my lap
Crisp, shiny, fresh brand new
Pears 'n peaches perfectly ripe
Pert, pretty, polite peek-a-boo.

Oranges, grapefruit 'n lemons
Roll down aisles of fence-carrot sticks
Lettuces, beets, stem parsley too
Parade shaped sizes intermix.

Celery crisp with leafy greens
Bush beans, snap peas, live endive
Beet tops boast veggie proteins
Harvest for humans to survive.

Onions 'n garlic will overpower
Potatoes, plump round me filed
Add yam flavor enhancing
Such activity is driving me wild!

I kiss honeydew's moist skin,
Watermelons oblong, mangos round
Bump me into near meadow
Where blackberries ripe abound.

Strawberries hide under lace leaves
Dew dropped covered, plump to see
Raspberry cups offer me juice
As red as my shiny heart wee.

June berries burst on blueberries
Boysenberries, juicy to touch
Flavor's taste after their own kind
Grapes bunch full so much.

They become raisins in sunlight
Then banana skins skin unpeel
Odd fuzzy kiwi, green inside
Divine artistry is quite the deal!

Beside me coconuts sunning
In a tree top too tall for me
Whipped corn tassels wave worn
Harvest winds whisper giddingly!

Squash scrambles my viewing
Cucumbers grow pickles on ground
Tomatoes, red, round ready to split
Such harvest unequally found.

I'm carried by autumn winds up lift
Dropped in leaves I fall and crunch
Near fields of golden wheat heads
Make multi-breads for your lunch!

Rains aplenty with different sizes
For cranberry-date-cookies, oodles
All cereals! Eight grain surprises
Pasta ribbons, veggie swirl noodles.

Millet nutritious delicious
Geometric rice waffles, pearl rice cake
Cornmeal muffins, date breads plenty oodles
What masterpieces humans can bake!

Tumble them all to harvest bins
Eaten daily long health will supply
Foremost vital bodies evermore
Continue vision; then wave me "Goodbye!"

Wondrous windows of food marvelous
Plentiful, like autumns leaf season
Carpeting ground before winter's wind
I'm grateful to be part of health's reason!

Thanks God for Earth so wondrous
Food sizes or shapes so unique
For mankind to feast, none the least
Build bodies for wellness physique!

Though we are human's mystique
He provides for mans appetite well
Creator loving feeds His creations
Our appreciation surely can tell.

Harvests from our Creator so special.
So teach nutrition NEWS as lifestyle
Your "Lifeline" letters autumn leaves
Are about harvest's rich food pile.

Enjoy me, Ginger as a gift, Drs. Diehl
Do remind all that's vital to health
Market books "Dynamic Living"
"To Your Health," wellness wealth.

Perhaps, when you least expect it
(Since dolls' eat in public infrequent)
You'll find tiny fresh fruits tasted
No, never a sugar condiment!

I see veggies crisp and snappy
Gathered secret in shadows of night
My savor of flavor from humans
Anticipates small dolly a delight!

I've got spunk, my essence is dashing
Pungent vibrancy to get up and go
Should honor health library's space
Ginger belongs in your health studio!

Hope you like my appearance frilly
Privileged I like to be there,
With you Dr Diehl, and Dr. Lily
Your children too, say silent prayer.

Is this, though tiny my measure
Leaves laden on autumn's dress
Fall on your health message spread
Help give humans robust happiness.

Enjoy me, your doll, created with love
That appreciates your expert direction,
Grateful, I'm gifted "Ginger" to inspire
With respectful and admired affection.

My dear Miss Imelda:

We followed your instructions to be together when we opened your gift of the Doll "Ginger." We were child-like and enjoyed immensely her letter and all her "attachments." What a delight explaining all we do together. Thank you very much. She is placed on one of my teaching pianos so my many students (60 of them a year!) What a perfect and delightful way to explain the health messages. Thank you so much for "Ginger's" dress design. Most appropriate for "her teachings." Thank you for including Hans' book publications. We enjoy working with you during the scheduled seminars.

Again, thanks so much for a touch of "Ginger." Love, Drs. Hans and Lily

CHAPTER 38. CRYSTAL

"A word is not a crystal, transparent and unchanged;
it is the skin of a living thought and

may vary greatly in color and content
according to the circumstances
and time in which it is used."
A quote by Oliver Wendell Holmes, Jr.

My Dearest Valerie:

Miss Imelda says you two have been friends a long time, meeting first in Cornwall, Ontario Canada during one of Doctor Diehl's health seminars. At that time, Miss Imelda drove across Canada en route to Cornwall in the middle of winter and alone! She was in the midst of a snowstorm, worsening on the main highway, dangerous enough to turn off and stay in a motel overnight. Next day it was sunny, and she arrived in Cornwall just in time to meet Dr. Diehl's staff. You first!

Remember when she showed you a doll she brought with from Wisconsin to Canada? Her intention was it to be for a special person she hadn't even met yet? You thought it was you, but she told you "No" it was for someone she did not know who it would be! Later, on a weekend when the staff was visiting the area, she found a lady who was a volunteer at the Holocaust Center in Montreal. Her name was Renata. She promised you she would make a doll and you would get it next seminar. She did, and that is me, Crystal. I am designed with your own color choices and your human likeness! Miss Imelda recalls during the rain storms on your other jobs together raindrops were like little crystals. That is what my name is. You wanted all your names included, as listed below in her poem to you, so she wrote you a separate one. They are all beautiful, so am I, Crystal. Happy Birthday. I came to you on our second Dr. Diehl seminar in Kalamazoo living in Doctor Alicia's home. I kept you company all the way back to Canada! Both of you bonded so close, you called Miss Imelda "Mom." We'll be close together too, you and me.

CRYSTAL

Doubt not, my quaint companion
Imagine, muse or reflect
Stories told, meek or bold
My doll visions recollect!

My green bag holds choice treasures
For stories to be penned
Add more trinkets to describe as
You tell stories to never end.

Words written cry, lament or sob
Laugh, just frolic or scold
Poetic verse lectures converse
Delightful for young or old.

Pen or prose, my goodness knows
Sounds feel; smells, see and taste
Outfit a disguise, then realize

Inspired words experience traced.

Sounds sung awaken vocabulary
Words wink, often words tell
Marvel fancied report in a moan
Costumed flavor comments well.

Measure sounds, try tunes or bark
Snap, whine, howl or wail
Capture thought, write as you ought
Wave your marvelous tale.

As two friends and a doll, dreams mingle
Summon stories sharing our life
Delightful ditty's suppose, meditate
Or pray in tempests of strife.

Shadows of books line wide wall
Ballads authored most alone
Rest your sweet head on my porcelain brow
Within stories thrive yet unknown.

Slip through my dream catcher's web
Escape, unmasked solitude in time
Hide in envelopes sealed for the post
Perhaps publish CVVN paradigm
HAPPY BIRTHDAY!

Dearest Valerie Violet:

Here we are in Kalamazoo Michigan working together with Dr Diehl again. We are so blessed. Miss Imelda met you at the border in Canada and we drove in your fancy pick-up. She did not want to give you me, Crystal, until we got to Dr. Alicia's house since I can be a lovely distraction. While you two were scheduled for rooms together, I was as busy as you were. I dream of so many shapes of water frozen like me, crystal. Thank you for sending Miss Imelda pictures of me when you returned to Canada. I am lovely and I am pleased you liked the quilt she made just for us. I watched her make it; it matches my green dress! Enjoy her always; Miss Imelda's poem from me is below. Love, Crystal

CRYSTAL

My smooth shiny bag glistens
Your favorite color green
Inside filled with happy things
Basket of violet flowers seen.

Bouquet mention of first name

Valerie Violet, petals remind you
Once name as Grandmother same
Bible verses give comfort too.

Favored page 43, John 14: sixteen
"I am the way, truth and life"
Example to live lives pristine
Times of joy, times of strife.

Miss Imelda's signature card includes
Though generations apart, legacy
Attempt claims my identity doll Crystal
You have much to learn from me.

Meet in country Canada first as employee
During health seminars pre-arranged
Work together with efficiency plus
Dr. Diehl, Master in health degree.

Work side by side with people registered
Lectures many, support slides analyzing
Eight natural laws of health teaching
Each law Dr Diehl symbolizing.

You, registered nurse, Dr. Diehl available
For counsel, blood work, ever reaching
Miss Imelda supervises clerical details
Registrations, attendance, outreaching.

Banking funds, graduations, book sales
Friendship grew close between you two
Memento of your union so choice
I am your doll made only for you.

To tell your story, be your voice
Green dress lace apron with flowers
Crystal-shaped heart necklace rests
On my neck glistens like showers.

Like you and Miss Imelda work together
No matter specific employ reason
Dedicated to Dr.Diehl's messages
Springtime or late fall season.

Affecting total body wellness
I dwell on long hours you two spent
Needed here or other someplace
Together busy, efficient 100 percent.

Promote, aid Dr. Diehl's lectures
Walk brisk to and fro with briefcases
Crystal goblets arranged at dinners
His receptions, concerts, display places.

Colorful, arranged certain spaces
Crystal, a high quality of glass
Solid substance, mineral, clear rays
Glass filled with water, first-class.

Clear fluid crystal dream-like phases
A substance storing memory
Picture thoughts, many a word
Feelings I feel in dream story.

Of love, Thank You's I heard
Of your Dad, missed so, his demise
Image of gratitude, respect, love
You're Mom, great Aunties prized.

Photos of laughter, joy, kinds of
A husband beloved you've chosen
As couple wed, Dale and you
"Happy" forms in crystal water frozen.

Marital enjoyments for you two
Water, beautiful, iced in place
Shows pictures lovely to view
Its own images, it's formed face.

Photographic records not new
Water shapes seas, lakes and rivers
Waterfalls from streams high
Water steams, in my doll dreams.

Portraits to tell stories whereby
Sees you and Dale drink from a glass
Water unfrozen liquid clear
Memorizes attitudes first-class.

As I sit proper on my bed quilt
While you are gone or asleep
My memory listens to a water glass
Stories my mind wants to keep.

A glass vessel like one outdoors
Left on bench last fall in patio
Cold winter froze thoughts inside
For me to ask or to know.

When water crystal observed
Water as ice mirrors thoughts
Attitudes record how others feel
Many sizes, all different, lots.

Grateful love by you and Dale
Frozen crystal styles make
Shapes vary if sad or lonely
Lonely shapes shatter or break.

I reflect at home your address
Season of winter I observe snow
Frozen atmosphere to earth falling
As sculptured snowflakes to know.

Their memories softly calling
Mankind's emotions, hope or sadness
Photo images frozen plain to see
As beauty, gorgeous, or gladness.

Can't decipher unformed tragedy
Memories too grave to be seen
Mixed lines no pattern to follow
Water forgets mould between.

You play choice classical music
Soft, rhythmic, mellow, calm tunes
Of Bach, Tchaikovsky, Mozart
Patterns favor smooth opportune.

Snowflakes sort patterns of fine art
Happy to know them, you and me
Iced crystal water observes, I do too
Investigate theory, you'll see.

Water in human skin bodies
Have memories we must agree
Speak to them in your daydreams
Talk wellness, tiny cells heal, you see.

Salve suffering, relief or mild aches
Mend, resolve pain center wells
Recall by water's memory makes
Crystal thoughts of virtue it tells.

Captures prism said, devout prayer
Genre happy, ease, contentment
Joy changes figures disfigured there

Caused no forgiveness or resentment.

Anger, cruel hate, deep despair
Discerned photo deforms, absent
Water misunderstands these photos
Snapshots unclear misrepresent.

Water we drink, bathe, fell from skies
Photos lovely or surely bizarre
Teardrops fallen, once unhappy
Trace tragedy deep inside char.

Wants to cleanse, to wash away
Plan of ugliness too hard interpret
Actions to annoy, notions to destroy
Negative thinking finds a fret.

My blithe, blissful, buoyant smile
Content to please, come to enjoy
See me, I smile all the while
Consider never ever annoy.

Dolls assemble pleasant pictures
Cheery types make us glad
A merry show to grow and grow
Best water in body we ever had.

Water flows to vital organs
Responds to happy photos well
Renews energy from pictures made
Of water's memories to tell.

Drink at least eight glasses a day
Dr. Diehl's lecture clearly taught
Cleanse, moisturize stress away
Plus other health topics a lot.

Even more studies everyday
Water clear, crystal important
Muscles need over 50 percent
Tissues fluid, prevent bone implant.

Aches or pains with water prevent
Ingest pure water everyday
Moistens skin on top or within
Enjoy when warm rainy day.

Join children splash puddles in
Water retains fish vast area sea

Animals in cold Arctic far away
Live in snow and ice crystals free.

Shower or bathe in pure water
Cleanse all impurities away
Wash your hands often daily
Scrub unwanted germ decay.

Hot/cold foot baths soothe aches
3 minutes hot, 3 seconds cold timing
For twenty minutes, end in cold
Well worth taking the time in.

Refresh bones, this water treatment
Hydrotherapy not new, very old
Familiar treatment worldwide
Home remedy too controlled.

Choose pure water for drinking
Adult body water 70 per cent
Don't dehydrate. My dreams thinking
Aged percent lower, no argument.

Healthy, once created to be
You need water, water needs you
As Crystal my dreams continue
Of water beverages, wonders new.

Keep thoughts human enlightened
Caution minds what to do to think
Recall body water photographic
Takes pictures each time you drink.

Conceive thoughts, its memory
Deep down depths of your soul
A mind a body's design to heal
Completes total wellness whole.

Dear Mom and Dad, Girl and Boy
Without water you cannot survive
Drink a toast to water and enjoy
It's great to be humans alive!

I'm glad you chose a chosen Mom
As Doll gifted, enchanted things
Fascinated, pleasing to everyone
Transparent happy-ness brings.

I will delight your home spaces

Where I, Crystal, designed to fill
Where I dwell with you and yours
New family for me to thrill.

In glee my pleasures fancied
Opaque moon hours so late
Untroubled, I rant or rave
Discover tales new to create.

As luck would have its favor
Crystal, titled by you, my name
My enthusiasm you will savor
For all who visit to exclaim.

Convenient in nick of time
High quality Crystal my name
In seconds a dream I muster
Catch thoughts of Mom who came.

A chosen daughter acclaim
Relationship mutual so tender
Together permanently profess
Happy-ness's in its splendor.

Though separated by address
Intimacy whispers to say
Communicate lives often
Rhapsodize time well spent today.

Smile in relief sure belief
Crystal, happy, you're like me
Frozen friendship like water solid
Beautiful bond permanently.

Artistry lasts indefinitely, as
Your doll Crystal, my Mom's choice
Is you Valerie Violet beloved
Listen to my crystal voice.

Dearest Mom Imelda:

The moment I held Crystal in my arms for the first time I fell in love with her. She was carrying a basket of violets, my middle name; how very touching because my middle name is Violet named after my Grandmother. Tucked inside the violets is a miniature precious little, white Bible, selections from every book. The print size is easy to read. It also holds your signature card explaining your heritage.

Crystal is wearing a handmade green dress. Green is my favorite color! She has light reddish hair and green eyes, just like me! I loved her pantaloons and lace socks. A delicate lace apron matches the wrist cuffs and ribbon with a pearl at the base of her throat. Flowers in her apron and in her hair makes you want to touch her gently. Around her neck is a crystal shaped heart necklace that reflects her dress and shimmers in the light. Crystal was hand made by you, my beloved friend Imelda. If ever I ever had a "kindred spirit" it is you, Imelda. I thank God for my remembrance of you. We worked, laughed, played, ate, cooked, taught and did all we could to help Dr.Diehl's CHIP (Coronary Health Improvement Program) seminars. Crystal sits on top of the quilt you made for me, Imelda, just for me. A fitting place of honor for her. Thank you, Imelda for your loving creations.

I am glad you write that you don't have to "grow up." I hold you close to my heart, Imelda. I thank God for every remembrance of you. I love you dearly. Valerie Violet

CHAPTER 39. JANKA

> "You gain strength, courage, and confidence by every experience
> in which you really stop to look fear in the face.
> You are able to say to yourself, 'I lived through this horror.
> I can take the next thing that comes along."
> A quote from Eleanor Roosevelt

The Holocaust Memorial Center Museum
5151 Cote Cite Catherine Road
Montreal, Quebec H3W IM6

Dear Sir:

I had the fortune to visit your center a weekend ago. At that time I was privileged to visit with one of your volunteers, however, I did not take the liberty to ask her name. She sits in the corner next to names listed of people who did not survive the Holocaust. She is middle aged, dark hair and medium build. She volunteers only on Saturday afternoons. Please give her my name and address while visiting here in Canada; I have a gift for her. My name is Miss Imelda and this is my phone number.

Dear Miss Imelda:

I have received your letter sent to the Holocaust Center in Montreal. I would be happy to visit with you. My name is Renata. I look forward to meeting you.

Later...   I kept my appointment and was received by a charming middle aged woman. I explained how I came to be in Canada. I told her "how I made a porcelain doll that I wanted to gift to a special person. I did not know who it was, but I felt the Spirit within me would tell me who she was. It certainly was you!"

Renata explained she survived being placed in a Holocaust concentration camp through the influence of her Nanny named Janka. She would like to accept the doll and call her Janka. I agreed. I watched her dress Janka near a portrait of her mother Natalia. The photograph was lost for many years but recovered in Renata's lifetime. I left her in good spirits and asked her to enjoy her gift and its memories.

JANKA

What words can I add to this story?
Why was I inspired to make a doll?
Bring to a health seminar miles away
To gift a person I knew not at all.

Occasions evident others wanted
This mystery I kept in a box when
I tour the Holocaust Center
A woman stranger I saw then.

My inquiry of a Volunteer noticed
In the Center quiet in place
Miss Imelda impressed by presence
Kind expression on her face.

Strangers agree for a meeting
Explanations of me is a gift explain
My dress I'll wear proudly
New Guest will give me a name.

Small doll was received warmly
As once treasured a doll lost
Lives after all in this doll
To survivor of Jewish Holocaust.

Happiness found Renata
She dresses a doll like her own
Recalls as young girl abandoned
Her doll once loved then known.

Dreams return if you let them
Pleasantly inside and out cover
Shroud in aura around a doll
Gift resembles her once doll another.

Memories made dreams recover
Of a Nanny protective and dear
Loved, cherished Janka, servant
Visits by stranger now here.

As a doll I know not her hardship
Or terror she had to survive
Or loneliness so deep to bear

Or struggles remaining alive.

I know of love and kindness
Of loyalty to family or friends
Integrity beyond in care-giving
Nanny Janka generously lends.

Renata's love to Janka remains
As she sees daily me, her doll
Soothes again tender reflections
As stranger visits Canada's Montreal.

Dreams surface beyond boundaries
Of continents far and wide
Bringing joy to enjoy by me
Doll Janka at Renata's side.

CHAPTER 40. GRACE

"Grace is not just enough; it is more than enough."
A quote from John Paul Warren

Dearest Alicia:

It is many weeks now since you talked to Miss Imelda about receiving a dolly...me...and your choice to call my name "Grace." Since then she has been busy making me a dress. In the meantime, when the night is young I hear music and can dance in my new special shoes that make my toes wiggle. I do not have any socks, but maybe I won't need them. If my feet get sore from dancing all night I will just dance in my bare feet. All this time I was waiting to belong to someone, I did not have any shoes. Miss Imelda has a dolly who had a pair of shoes and she gave me her shoes to wear because she is being saved for someone special when they grow up; and she does not need them now. Miss Imelda sewed a red heart on me so I can practice make-believe while I wait to live with you. My dress has butterflies on the skirt, because they are her signature in all she sews. My petticoat is supposed to show out of my dress to be extra stylish...makes me blush, so please do not tuck it in!

Miss Imelda makes lap quilts for nursing home residents, newborns and disabled veterans. So she made me a lap quilt too since you have patient's with children who bring their toys, bears or whatever is dear to them. I can place them on my small blocked quilt for safety as well when I do what I can do to make them feel better. The squares on my quilt are small, like me, with lots of different colors and shapes or images so children can imagine with me what is special to them. My lap quilt also has words that I will always try to be "love, patient, kind, hopeful, caring and endearing. I guess that is why you called me "Grace" because I am trying to develop all these things.

I hope you are excited about my laboratory coat that is special cloth that has pictures of all the instruments; stethoscopes, thermometers, crutches, smiling band aids, first aid cases, red hearts and wheelchairs. I can use all in my helping with children and toys. I will be able to use them all since my reference books are with me to read about in between appointments. The pictures are just my size, Doctor Alicia, and will become real as soon as I need them. Please notice my name on the lab coat Grace Ful, N.D. because that is what I will be to your patient's children and their treasures. Miss Imelda says eventually I will be in a book called "Personolly Yours" and I will be remembered with dollies sent away with love. Love like you have when she lived with years ago during Dr Diehl's health programs in the town of Kalamazoo very close to where you live.

If I have forgotten anything, Miss Imelda will remember it in my poem to you. I will miss her, but she says with my new heart I will experience emotions humans do and I must always have happy thoughts about everything and everybody. She says you and your husband Art and your grandchildren will help me to be a good example. For now, thank you for letting me come and live with all of you and your family with six grandchildren! Fun! I know I will learn many things to feel better and also be a good example to be graceful. Always...Grace

GRACE

I arrived at Doctor Alicia and Art's home
Her hands unpack my big box,
A quilt for my lap first, then love message
My lab coat, my blue dress frock.

She smiles happily, already loving me
She tells me her grandchildren six,
Will visit on weekends to see me
I might have an illness to fix!

She looks at my library book bag
Interest in books as I am, she is
In helping humans feel better,
I'm happy to be sent here, Gee Whiz!

I see a mantle place and warm fire
"Goochie", big cat nearby sleeps
White spot on belly, otherwise black fur
Slowly tiptoe, else quick cat leaps!

Rufus seems raccoon but is a cat
Plays with a red ball, chases on wood floor,
Not much interest in me a doll
Leaves house when open is the door.

I am placed on ledge curved window
Outside pine trees snow garments wore,
See play pens for children placed neatly
Until visits on weekends come indoor.

I must be patient see child's faces
Wait till they hold my small hand,
We'll look into each other's eyes
View each secret dream land.

Let's see, Liam age six already
Likes Spiderman's antics diverse,
Will explain Spiderman web wonders
Or how quickly evil he'll disperse.

Cartoon character he acts out in play
Spider maneuvers learned while he grows
As a scientist, with skills may help me
He fights crime, so I suppose he knows.

Senses future of evil outcomes to be
When enemy hides, where enemy goes
He is clever, quick, slyly waits
Cunning like spider always knows.

Moves in a flash and changes gaits
Best time to act in air flow
What a hero is this Spiderman
Model of respect for Liam to know.

Quick action unequalled to view
I'll enjoy him too I expect,
Liam and I doll brand new
Buddies we'll be, never to neglect.

I see dear Isabella's photo
Heard said it's frogs she's fond
Their eyes so big round to see with
Hop in and out of marsh pond.

Males croak songs their own style
Message understood not even by me
Lure other frogs to talk night or day
Find friends easy by voice selectee.

A tree frog, leopard, bullfrog or horned
Some not all green, some yellow
Frogs black, red or orange
Different colors a frog fellow.

May become pets too I see
Hop on your shoulder or head
Leap on your bed carefree
But I'll watch frogs eat instead.

Often my eyes or mind wanders
Look for objects vision catching
A wee tree frog so very small
Sits on the outer deck watching.

He jumps through door open wide
An interesting site down long hall
Frog jumps into green plant display
I strain my eyes to see it at all.

Leaps on bamboo plant pot inside
Blinks, sees me as he winks
Looks around for more plants to hide
Jumping games all the while he thinks.

At nightfall I got my wee wheelchair
Invite tree frog I named "Less,"
To show ornaments in house so many
Offer to sit on my new coat-dress.

"Less" saw fat fly on glass window
Jumps off my chair in a flash,
Ate fly in less than a minute
As I blink my pretty eyelash.

I wheel him to plants in full blossom
Philodendron perfect hideaway
"Less" sips drops of pooled water
On plant leaf watered today.

Doctor Alicia, garden keeper does see
"Less" lounge on part of leaf display,
Scoops "Less" up so very gentle
Places outdoors on maples to stay.

Isabella knows frogs she likes best
We may find tiny tree frog again
Or entertain new frog as our guest,
She can design a tiny frog playpen.

Hope we find "Less," as he's the best
Plan days I play with Isabella, when
About frog activities I'll learn more
Make notes with my fountain pen.

Searching outside on our knees
We'll look for another tree frog like "Less"
We'll find him in yard on some trees

She may find him as I did fond impress.

Grandchild Leo likes toy trucks
All shapes, all sizes, color or skill
He's two years old, neat like me
After play parks trucks careful still.

Sometimes he carries new gravel
Levels the neighbor's long driveway
Or hauls wood logs for the fireplace,
Planning ahead for winter's cachet.

He has truck with extendable arms
To cut dangled tree limbs on power lines,
Protects human homes from danger
What marvelous machinery designs!

I like his Semi-truck with trailer attached
Made heavy to haul most anything
Like toys big and small packed safely
Takes me with them and we sing.

Leo looks out for more trucks to see
Like the mail truck on wide highway
One brought me here to family
This home wonderful where I stay.

I told Leo "packed boxes not noisy"
Except one wrapped stored music box,
When bumps on highway were too high
Music rang rhythm with road knocks.

On my way to State of Michigan
Hear Kalamazoo town called when
I know I'll be with Doctor Alicia
Never be shipped ever again!

Joy ride wave to truck drivers passing
Cargo pictured on truck outer wall
Photos of items often truck carries
Some trucks no photos at all.

Other trucks carry machinery
To dig roads long and wide,
Short trucks belong to family
Transport house things inside.

Shop toy store now so inside we go
Leo shows me robots display

For children to create or just see
Project directions teach the way.

Leo gives Jack rights to hold me
As he looks for new types of trucks
Jack holds me so I can clearly see
A robot already made like a bus.

He whispers he'll make one for me
From parts he'll buy, Grace you'll see,
Our robot scientifically designed
Jack shares toy shelf with me!

Jack creates Robots special inner
Workings against aliens of space
Our robot will be the winner
I work hard to keep up the pace.

Helping at night when Jack can't sleep
Forgets mornings to wash his face,
He'll tell jokes instead of secrets to keep
Distracting friends with questions erase.

I whisper to Jack in his small ear
If on space journey he hurts his knee,
He may need my chair with a wheel
My treatment heals first degree.

So show our robot stars from below
In vast sky above, amaze all living
For humans, even robots to see
That star wink from Creation giving.

Spacecrafts meant to go out and explore
Jack's robot will control a space ship
So into Universe he can travel more
Planning ruminations makes Jack skip!

His face beams as stars in the night
Quick mind to earth returns slow
What a child, my dream's delight
To more planets again we'll go.

Back home, James, age four now
Likes tractors, so busy is their need
Digs earth straight furrows to plow
Prepare land to grow big from small seed.

Grow fine foods here and now

Make tracks as tractors crossway
Some grow seed corn for selling
Or pull wagons heavy with hay.

Staked right for animals to eat
When winter snow blankets show
Green grass dried stored in barns
Tractors large plow heavy snow.

Piled high even higher each time
Weighted cover from winter storms
Strong blades pile piled snow drifts
As highway snow danger forms.

Tractors clean road pathway right
Protects people driving safely there
Carefully all day or dark night
Alone or with family's to care.

One weekend all children gather
"Let's make a snowman" says Grace
Liam knew how to make snowball
James shapes snowball for face.

Isabella forms snow belly for size
Leo puts on a wide brimmed hat
Belongs to Dad from hall closet
Did children ask him for that?

Grace took coal from outside grill
Used last summer now a need
Isabella pokes face long carrot nose
James two dimples of sunflower seed.

Liam finds melon rinds cast away
Makes smile wide... happy snowman
Jack finds peach pits recycled today
Make buttons five straight as he can.

Pokes in snowman's snow chest
Two snow arms hold mismatched mittens
One high one lower than the rest
Isabella finds scarf, colors so many.

Wraps snowman's neck to say
Such artistry, comments the postman,
Children deserve high five today
Grand children all built snowman.

No sign of bright sun in the skies
When this family is asleep, my muse's
A companion for him I'll devise
Cats to look like Goochie and Rufus.

One weekend child Grace came to visit
Age seven and a half, almost eight
Draws best with markers magic
For her pictures I hardly can wait.

I'll tell her my name is Grace too
We are polite, respectful, we adorn
We're kind, gracious to people
We comfort easy sad or careworn.

We apologize if we are wrong
Forgiveness so graceful, like us
Ever so courteous, we are strong
Speak easy topics delicate to discuss.

I saw her draw people pictures
One of Melissa her Aunt who
Shares son's Jack and Liam
Play together fun things to do.

A portrait of Melissa, so like her
Sketches John's face magically
Draws fine her mother Carrie
Eyes bright shine lovingly.

Outlines clear father Wade
Such wonderful this family
Grace makes markers magic
She draws figures specifically.

To my immediate surprise
Grace draws portrait of me!
Beside my open porcelain eyes
Lips smiling, sketch a must-see!

I sit still quiet as can be
Such fun to be sketched, exciting
Hair jet black frames my face
Cascades long on my back inviting.

Happy I am to be in this place
In front door husband Art enters
Home from school all day teaching
Eleven and twelfth grades mentors.

Prepare pupils for college reaching
Or life in world of employment too,
Blest I am in this family to belong
Individuals have talents not few.

Should you come here to visit?
Enjoy grandchild's happy face
Accept new person in family
Alicia's Doll me she named "Grace!

Dear Imelda:

Thank you so much for Grace. She is so beautiful. I have admired each button and special touch you lovingly placed. Winter has fully arrived and covers us with a beautiful snow blanket. Grace will enjoy cats and a warm fire until our grand babies visit on the weekends. We have six of them, four boys and two girls. They are Liam, Jack, Grace, Isabella, James and Leo. They are all under age eight and we so look forward to their visits.

You are so special and I send love to you for Valentine's Day. Art and I will be celebrating our 32nd anniversary on Valentine's Day. Again, my heartfelt thanks for mailing my Doll Grace to me. Love...Alicia.

CHAPTER 41. DORA / ISAAC

"A smile starts on the lips, a grin spreads to the eyes,
and a chuckle comes from the belly,
but a good laugh bursts from the soul, overflows,
and bubbles all around."
A quote from Carolyn Birmingham

Dear Dr Ng and Julie:

Dr Ng, I am so pleased you have accepted my application to come to the Christian Care Ministry as part of or Wellness Team, along with your wife Julie. Together as a unit it is my purpose to put an effective program for our members in making healthy lifestyle changes.

As I indicated to you Julie when we met, I have started a doll project as a diversion from all the demands at work. You said you would be more than delighted to receive the gift as an Endorphins health team, Dora and Isaac. I will send them when complete. Love, Miss Imelda

Dear Miss Imelda:

As we unwrapped the care packages from the box of pleasant surprises you sent, Yew Por and I were simply lost for words. As we dressed and assembled Dora and Isaac, we were filled with admiration for the beautiful qualities and enormous talents that God has blessed you with. Only someone with your creativity, talents, love and patience can come up with such ideas for the adorable dolls with valuable messages, and the delicate and detailed trimmings. Thank you ever so much for that labor of love ingenuity, thoughtfulness and care.

Dora and Isaac brought me down memory lane to when I was about four years old. My mother took me to visit her friend who owned a doll shop! The variety of dolls in the store so fascinated me that I refused to leave when the visitation was over. You can probably imagine the scene that took place.

As a teacher in Thailand, my mother cannot afford to get me the dolls I so much wanted. Well, guess what? After 40 plus years you have just given me the very dolls I wanted since I was a child. The only difference is Isaac has a delightful childlike laugh, whereas the doll I wanted as a child cried when turned over. It probably is appropriate to say that is worth the wait!!!

Not only did you fulfill my childhood dream of having a doll, encouraged us to utilize the Endorphins and inspired us with the Christ-like attitudes we developed. You also gave Yew Por and me the opportunity to dress a girl. Now that our nest is empty, we have two more 'children.' Your timing seemed so perfect. We will definitely value them.

We will cherish Dora and Isaac, your encouragement, graciousness and kindness. You are very much appreciated. May God abundantly bless you as you have graciously blessed others. Gratefully yours, Yew Por and Julie Ng

DORA and ISAAC
The ENDORPHINS

Miss Imelda gives local seminars
"The Endorphins, the happy one
In Eight Natural laws of Health"
Planned well, fine spun, well done.

I like non-perishables of nobility
Nutritious in eight laws of health
Listed briefly as much as we can
Placed in human bodies as wealth.

Dora my name in middle of En...Phins
Last not least in verbose parade
N. Dora Phins my full name
Brother Isaac carefully made.

My P.D. doctorate degree
"Petticoat Down" Isaac describes
Laughter we like best of all laws
As wrinkles as a smile transcribes.

Widened for laughing giving
The "Endorphins" title smiles bring
Bursting into laughing for living
A "Merry Heart" song sings

A merry heart doeth good like a medicine
Like a medicine is a merry heart
But a broken spirit drieth the bones
A merry heart doeth good, doeth good
Like a medicine." Proverbs 17:22

Endorphins are so very good
Natural pain, stress fighter
Small proteins produced naturally
Non-additive, block pain biter.

E: enthusiastic, laughter
N: necessary, never ending
D: daily delightful
O: optimistic, overflowing
R: ready, real, relaxing
P: positive, participating
H: hearty, happy, healing
I: ideal, infectious
N: natural and spontaneous
S: social, sparkling sunny.

Moderates appetite, boost moods
Enhances immune system too
Relaxes sex hormones
Endorphins so good for you!

Persons produce different amounts
According to direct stimuli
Naturally they make you feel great
Endorphins for you and I!

Participants many, "Merry Heart"
Tall Doll dress fabric of many hearts
Ribbons, lace here and there
Children in painted smock theme parts.

Accompanied by guitar or piano
Some song words to sing
Understand lessons you to show
Instant smiles crowds bring.

"Merry's" friend "Bones" white skeleton

Wants little heart like "Merry's" too
Clothes print motif ghosts and skulls
Black fabric backgrounds strew.

Backdrops for demonstration's clue
Attractive help tell explanations
Social outlet for children young
Health, healthy foundations.
Instructions clear among

Children select for smocks, small singers.
Girls hold doll "Merry Heart's" hands
Boys bargain for "Bones'" bony fingers
Each role each understands.

A play we present today is mine to teach
Eight laws of health history
Children dress up for each.
Display health's story.

Six different smocks hand painted
Green foods, vegetables, nuts and seeds
More root vegetables, melons and fruits
Grains plentiful, breads, our needs.

Hand painted all wearing smiles
All children wear painted storyline
Come to the middle of the room and sing
"A merry heart...and I keep time!"
Music starts, everyone sings along
PROVERBS 17:22 happiness song
"A merry heart doeth good
like a medicine, like a medicine
Is a merry heart
but a broken spirit drieth the bones
A merry heart doeth good
Doeth good like a medicine"

Isaac and I find situations plenty
Living this way easy to survive
Smiles, whisper of laughing wide
Bring them with you as you arrive.

Sounds of children dreaming dreams
Daytime naps or night sleeping
Isaac smiles fast asleep it seems
Laughter a word for keeping.

Smiles created open heart's door

My dress fabric of smiles many
All shapes, sizes and spheres
Colors brilliant, shaded or shiny.

I'm a "feel good substance"
All human's body make their own
Thousands a day made to protect
Promote healthy full blown.

Natural narcotic-like essence
Central nervous system where
Aid against pressures of life
Be sure always to share.

Come with us, chuckles cheerful
We acquaint whimsical thoughts
We'll tickle your funny bone often
N.Dora Phins and Isaac...forget-me-nots.

I am in all foods natural
Gifted, pure, candid, real
Plain, normal your choice
Cooked but raw diet ideal.

Isaac eats orange "Orange" slice
Put between lips makes a smile
I notice right away, he likes to play
Chase away sad doom awhile.

Disabled cripple, Isaac can't walk
I help always ease his mind
Body, mind, keep up talk
Laugh together we remind.

Isaac tells me beasts weep
When they hurt they can't laugh
God smiles on them anyway
Look at long neck of giraffe.

Finds food on branches so high
What a view of morsels avail
Big Bear finds blackberry bushes
Isaac tells funny foods tale.

Timid Tomato peaks all around
His bed quilt, juicy salad space
Give all greens smiles abound
On Isaac's old "Krazy Kwilt" lace.

Mittens now laugh, used up north
On snowman now most melted
Warm sun warm beam bursts forth
Ann Apple and Andy Apple belted.

Everyone loves doll Merry Heart
Happy hearts on her dress display
Most boys really favor Bones
A skeleton can't eat any day.

Isaac asks is Blue Berry blue?
Colors nutritious I respond
Like Real Raspberry too red
Goose Gooseberry near a pond.

Sam Squash's smiles widen
Rounded, of vitamins full
Believe it, plenty grown seen
Yellow, green, orange; hands pull.

Cool Cucumber surfs in ocean
Liz Lettuce floats on Kid Kale
Patty Parsnip pretty in curls
Rick Romaine eaten by a whale.

Miss Imelda works in Florida near
Palm trees sigh at high noon
Wind air blows clear clouds
Should I reach up, grab pale moon?

In bubbling brook Miss Manatee
Swims gently close to our walk
Makes happy noises our meeting
Interested her way to talk.

Wisps of wind-blown clouds see
Wrapped in mantle of fresh air
Spoken on earth by waters of sea
Some humans live far places there.

Far away from sandy beach
Lightening thunder voices speak
Where my owners Julie and Dr Ng
Love us each day of the week.

We left area of seasons hot and cold
Northern snowflakes wet my face
Isaac crawls under his blanket
Laugh lines already in place.

Snow treasures glad glisten
As bright stars twinkle all
To Seminars we attend, listen
Now live where rainfalls fall.

Brought happy thoughts with us
Endorphins live in every town
Every ready to discuss health
Join us coming downtown.

Exercise walks with Miss Imelda
Be it a stroll, a jog or a dance
Six days a week you'll find her
Endorphins actively at a glance.

Lily Laughter petals singing
Underneath Mae Mouse hides
Clara Clover flowers bringing
Vivid rainbows light landslides.

I cover Isaac while he sleeps
Butterflies fly off his covering
Near vegetable pictures he keeps
String Celery close hovering.

Nuts, seeds, breads on display
Children have fun as they laugh
I acquaint fruit painted the way
Smocks laugh's like a photograph.

Kate Carrot pokes Pete Potato
Bob Broccoli bumps Gene Green bean
Scatter as Fun Onion weeping
Carl Cauliflower pompously seen.

Rich Rice mixed soup cuisine
Anna Banana, Kim Kiwi converse
In refrigerator for a breakfast
Ma Strawberry in honey immerse.

Green Grape greets Mimi Melon too
Smile while waiting till morning
Find more fruits you may like too
Wash them, pesticides warning!

Willy Water always so helpful
Best beverage creatures consume
So stay away from drinks harmful

Study vital in seminar classroom.

Sam Sunshine smiles in our room
Beams healthy later in the day
Sun gives us Vitamin D generous
Left over when clouds in the way.

Tomorrow we go to local zoo
Leisure entertainment choice for us
Tazja Tiger will be there
See her when we get off the bus.

Brother Isaac laughs at her then
To show her smiles best anywhere
We greet other creatures living there
Give smiles freely in zoo there.

Try to live no matter our condition
Me, N.Dora Phins with Isaac brother
I love The Endorphins so much
Love laughing best at each other.

I will miss their smiles many
We have lots of our own to bring
Hearts happy find fun stories any
Maybe we'll go with Doctor Ng.

To his office with dear wife Julie
People chat about this and that
Introduce us as "Yours truly"
As we sit on his "Welcome" mat.

Isaac has more stories on his quilt
Brings up laughter from inside
Caricatures surface any old time
Sure to make anyone smile wide.

When night falls wherever placed
Doors close, people now gone
We'll practice lectures to amuse
Plays with 'Laughter' first star on.

Isaac always riotous and witty
Show laughter, us as dolls
While I stand looking pretty
While doll Merry Heart calls.

When you see smiles around us
We'll be joyful, laughter we take

Energetic, spontaneous Endorphins
N.Dora Phins and Isaac make.

CHAPTER 42. COOKIE

"Nobody teaches the sun to rise, a fish to swim,
a bird to fly, a plant to grow, a child to cry
And nobody teaches me to remember you, I just do."
A quote Author unknown

Dearest Patti:

I am a 16 inch doll and I live on a shelf near Miss Imelda. I do not have any clothes and my hair is long, blonde and mangled. I see in a box next to me a picture of Miss Imelda who has a white bird on her shoulder and they look very happy. I do not know what happy is but I would like some. The picture is of the same real bird standing on a cage preening herself and am told she murmurs something like "I love you Cookie," whatever that means. I feel nothing inside my cloth body except being alone and useless. I see other dolls in another room, they never look at me, they are lovely and I am not.

One day, Miss Imelda, my designer, took me down and, next to my left arm she placed a red heart on me. All of a sudden I felt warm all over, just like she said I would. She told me, "Cookie, you are going to live with a beautiful lady who lives in Virginia, where I used to live with my cockatoo bird, also named "Cookie." I could see why my new dress she was making was white with hundreds of red hearts with a border of more red hearts. I was beginning to feel what "Happy" was and it was great!

Miss Imelda said you knew and loved bird Cookie too. My new dress fits so well and three-strand pearls are sewn in place around my neck, with pearls also on my ears. I have a bracelet of more pearls and my apron is tied around my waist. My shoes lace tightly around my new stockings and my hat is lovely. But, I cannot wear it yet, until my hair is washed and styled to fit. The next day my hair gets washed and I am put on a box near a warm woodstove for my hair to dry and be combed. I am not lonely anymore. My little red heart has a faint beat that is regular and feels good. I may be lonely for Miss Imelda, but she says you need me and I will love you lots, dear Patti. You and Miss Imelda have been friends a very long time and I want to be friends too. Miss Imelda says bird Cookie is very intelligent and she will tell our stories in the poem below. I can't wait to hear the story when I come to your home far away. Soon to love you, Cookie!

COOKIE

I am a yellow crest Cockatoo bird
From original egg brand new
My mother a human named Gigi
Raises more tropical birds too.

My bird mom was sold, left my egg
Gigi kept me in incubator warm
I'm ready to hatch now

My first contact her soft arm.

She feeds me from eyedropper
My down wet feathers she cleans
Holds me close to her face
A Mother best by all means.

When busy for safe keeping
She has dog Shoo-Shoo I met
Carries me in warm house on her back
Cocker Spaniel fur best yet.

I grow, eating good food
Gigi prepares every day
Shoo-Shoo plays on back porch
I sleep in front paws every day.

Gigi and Charles won't sell me
Companion to this family belong
Seasons pass, I grow full plumage
Tapered feathers white and long.

My wings white, broad, perfect
Beautiful as a cockatoo can be
Shoo-Shoo has toys to play with
Her playmate mostly is me.

We frolic daily new nonsense
Sometimes help her chase a ball
On porch floor, or over low fence
I fly now for her toy "recover all."

In sun fly high in mulberry tree
Shoo-Shoo barks command quickly
Come back to porch to her safely
Shoo-Shoo my sentry for Gigi.

I get lots of attention and food
Seeds served at meals every time
My tongue and beak open quick
Healthy nuts for Gigi anytime.

I preen my lovely feathers daily
Shoo-Shoo's coat too daily need
We remain pals together everyday
Hardly ever we disagreed.

Unless I fly in mulberry tree
I delight flight, a high soar

Obey in five minutes calling me
I could not love her more.

Gigi named me "Cookie"
Says to me "I love you Cookie"
So I learned to say it also
Understand it says I love me.

Spring passed into summer
I'm happy as a bird could be
Friends come over visiting
Admire Gigi's bird Cookie.

A winter day Shoo-Shoo is taken
To vet doctor; she's so sick
I'm put in cage till they return
I look for Shoo-Shoo's return quick.

She doesn't come to porch
Lays in box in room quiet to keep
Looks at my cage, blinks her eyes
Closes, unawake from sleep.

Gigi and Charles wrap her tight
Close box she used to lay in
I never saw my Shoo-Shoo
Not a day or night ever again.

For weeks I sit on cage perch
Locked inside is lonely me
Gigi can't give me her time
I can't fly mulberry tree.

Not on porch free anytime
I miss Shoo-Shoo everyday
Every hour she never returns
No one wants me to play.

In emptiness I pull my feathers
Off body's beauty no concerns
Miss dog I knew as a newborn
I suffer, never to me returns.

I shared my life with her as I grew
Inseparable companions we were
Bird Cookie and dog Shoo-Shoo
Friends to be forever for sure.

Gigi takes me to vet, fits a cape

I wear it as no choice any other
Gigi watches new feathers grow
Now so happy is Gigi, my mother.

Vet's cape now comes off me
New feathers sadly I pluck
I can't control my actions
Cape on me proven no luck.

Gentle visitor came to visit
Gigi explains to her my plight
Considers putting me to sleep
Will I see Shoo-Shoo tonight?

Visitor sees no need drastic
Never to consider as she knows
"A bird should not be punished
If she plucks off her clothes."

So Gigi's friend Will make plans
For my move to visitor's dwelling
A totally new environment
Deep love, new attention telling.

New place has clear windows
Birds come to shelf and feed
I see birds almost my own kin
Miss Imelda serves different seed.

A blackbird Imelda calls crow
Talks too if taught carefully
Miss Imelda lets everyone know
No bird as smart as her Cookie.

Weekends guests need outings
All go up to mountain high
I cling to Miss Imelda's shoulder
Forget that once I did fly.

At lunch she serves watermelon
Miss Imelda knows seeds I favor
I walk from guest to guest's table
For seeds of watermelon flavor.

I see tops of trees once I knew
On porch with Shoo-Shoo my friend
Will she not waken from sleep?
Missing her never will end.

Miss Imelda and I walk pathways
At this center, my new home
String on my leg she's close to me
Without wings I can still roam.

She has friend Patti visiting
Stroll and visit by mulberry tree
Not far away is her own home
I climb far as string lets me.

Eating fat juicy mulberries
Oops, Miss Imelda let's go of me
I climb higher and higher
She calls "Come down Cookie."

I don't come down, not ready
Mulberries good to eat
She knows I can't fly away
Higher I climb on claw feet.

Miss Imelda's visit is over
Has friend Patti climbs up high
To get me still eating berries
I think I'll climb to the sky.

Patti reaches out hands gentle
Her voice soft, soothing too
Brings me back to Miss Imelda
One last mulberry to chew.

Evening for prayer chapel
Miss Imelda takes me along
Maybe I will learn new words
She hopes perhaps a new song.

My down soft feathers thicker
Gigi comes to visit me
Delighted I am to see her
Bird Mother as chick baby wee.

Gigi and Charles are selling
All tropical birds not few
Going on mission field far away
Gifts me to Miss Imelda true.

Our lives pass quick monthly
She'll return to Wisconsin her home
Travel arrangements difficult
Because of my "bird syndrome."

Can't take a bus, I'm sickly
No entry to fly an airplane
Can't take bird with no feathers
No tickets allowed on a train.

Her friend Patti says we'll drive
A fine bird needs travel best
Boss Will's father makes a cage
Fits car back seat for a test.

So three of us together
Friends we are for trip too
Wisconsin far from Virginia
Two friends loving a cockatoo.

I will miss my local hometown
Packed for journey in Patti's car
Oft I perch on Patti's shoulder, or
Miss Imelda's steering wheel bar.

She drives; I see a bridge low ahead
I duck my head, we're gonna crash!
Somehow I lift my head, still looking
Miss Imelda drove thru, we didn't smash.

"Design of bridges," she says are high
"Roadway makes tall bridge spaces
You needn't bend your neck anymore
We are safe, Cookie, all our faces!"

Though I don't have long feathers
I travel well, high class a lot
I still squawk, I talk, I scream
Bark like Shoo-Shoo, I squat.

We arrive in another apartment
Patti stays with us awhile
Bids goodbye, hugs me tightly
Miss Imelda gives her a smile.

I break nuts with Miss Imelda
At breakfast she gives me fruit
Shares with me part of the nut
Grasp oatmeal bowl with claw foot.

One day we visit Friend Leslie
Loves birds, lives on an Isle
Miss Imelda sees her often

Birds come often, meanwhile.

I hear a turkey gobble noises
That racket easy to learn
Goose honks louder or louder
Chicken clucks twice my concern.

Ducks walk on water quacking
Sea gulls fly, cry over head
Canada geese may be foreigners
Strange noise honks ahead.

Cat meows my fluctuations
I choose to avoid sharp claws
Miss Imelda rescues me close to house
On outside porch hang Mackinaws.

I find big round buttons
All sewn neat in a row
One by one my beak clips them
Down on porch floor they go.

Leslie did not even notice
My plucked buttons on floor
Go back to bird yard, same birds
Need new ones to learn more.

We leave Lake Isle, Miss Imelda
Me too in my cage to carry
Across blue water long and deep
Long ride on Superior boat ferry.

Miss Imelda talks on phone as job
To clients in every single state
Encourages them choice counsel
Of water, rest, foods they ate.

About exercise, sunshine, attitudes
Often I crawl down perch stand
To her office, like to bite phone cords
She captures me, yells her demand.

"No phone wire!" Beak cuts quick!
Not enough toys for boring days
Strewn over floor here and there
Weekend's best back on roadways.

In a car trees fly like I used to
Sideways, don't know how to fly

Miss Imelda great companion
Plays records with sounds I try.

Visit family living new places
Unafraid now of wide bridges
Get admired by new people faces
Claws learn new chair ridges.

Last week Miss Imelda gets phone call
Job offer Wellness Center staff hire
In state much farther away
Will find home best for me, inquire.

Only person attentive loving birds
Must make choice for her Cookie best
Temporarily nice home to stay in
Who can be chosen in this contest?

Later, a phone call from Patti
Assures Miss Imelda that she will
Take Cookie home to Virginia
Miss Imelda's request sad only until…

Her new employment assignment
To Florida a franchise to start
No room for her bird Cookie
Patti her choice to care for apart.

So Patti, our friend, drives here
Again to Wisconsin comes for me soon
Miss Imelda makes her a glass dolly
Sews long, Patti comes next afternoon.

Her Dolly has hair like my wings
Yellow crested, her dress white
Over little red hearts painted
Long pigtails tied red ribbons tight.

Her basket boasts creatures
I learned voices of one more yesterday
Including three dogs and a cat
Know exactly which noise each say.

Chick, goose, quail, turkey, cluck
Seagulls above big lake that fly
Bird swims in water, a duck
I practice all noises, satisfy.

Miss Patti arrives, glad to see her

Such friends we three became
A cockatoo loved un-feathered
Cookie her favorite name.

Patti and Kiss Imelda laugh
Enjoy my antics varied
One day I'll learn to autograph
Famous for noises I carried.

Before they leave we visit Nancy
Imelda's friend has doll collection
Her story she told me absurd
Dolls serve tea at house in affection.

Take pictures Doll Cookie counted
Last number to seventy three
She forgot what number follows
I squawk, no matter to me.

Dolls admire her basket and dress
Long braids a new surprise
So doll Cookie attracts them
Think many look human, small size.

Uniquely dressed separate dolls
Important selection as she too
Stories will be written she says
She explains of me, a cockatoo.

"Smart I am like human child
So talented a bird can be
Spend time now doll Cookie
As I mimic birds unlike me.

All words Doll Cookie can say
But favorite for me to speak is
Three words from my birth mother
Gigi where Shoo-Shoo once lives.

"I love Cookie" she taught me early
It's the sound best I know
I take them all in my travels
Wherever without flying I go.

CHAPTER 43. TANJEURIE TRACY

"Unless and until we rest in God, we will never risk for God"

A quote from Mark Buchanan

Dearest Janet and Brother Will:

I am your Dolly gift finally completed. Please open the box together. Janet. Brother Will has chosen my name 'Tanjeurie Tracy' designed to mention Saturday, the Sabbath Day. My leather shoes are hand-made by Miss Imelda's daughter Julie just for you as adopted family. My basket is significant of the sun and moon fashioned after a Native American dream catcher, which I am excellent in catching dreams you will soon learn.

My poem rests in my basket next to my little Bible and Promise Book. Miss Imelda said she waited five years before she decided who would get the Dolly who represented the health message of REST. You, Will, introduced her to principles of Sabbath rest. I have spent many dreams with my friend Karina who sits in a basket and all she does is rest because she does not have any legs, having been broken in her transit here. She will ponder dreams of kinds of rest we have learned together. Enjoy me.
Tanjeurie Tracy

TANJEURIE TRACY

If dreams are good desires
A hope designed as illusion
My muse, my colorful imaginations
Reaches only one conclusion.

Such dream reality is mine given
To remind mankind of the first day
God rested from creation He made
Names Sabbath rest to convey.

I am made from porcelain and cloth
Rest difficult for me any day
I'm excited, illusory, projected by one
Who loves you and Janet wife to say.

Respectful designs my being to exist
Once on a time blessed in your employ
Introduced holiness of God's Sabbath
Rests from Even to Even enjoy.

In return Miss Imelda gives you me a dolly
My thoughts, her thoughts believed in
My name Tanjeurie Tracy
Chosen by husband Will, weaved in.

My color-coded dress sunset's splendor
Reminder of those who see me
To be grateful to God so tender

Who commands from golden glory?

Rainbow hues circle His throne
To remember keep holy day Holy
Remember creation His own
Love inspires Imelda to design me, dolly.

Gifts me to your wife, Brother Will
For your family and all your friends
To witness Sabbath-keeping's thrill
Your dream of "Young Disciple" lends.

Flourished now world wide
A God of creation by their side
Outreach, training, skills, choices
Recreation, fellowship, new voices.

Evangelistic crusades organized to minister
Guiding young people, lass or mister
Once stories made by young mother
Flourished by God's blessing, none other.

A ministry reaching out to young people
To fill God's church temple steeple
Dreams are for sharing dreams
Miss Imelda, your favorite people.

Beauty and happiness brought
Share dream, so lofty a thought
Clothed in fabric so lacy
Your gifted Doll, Tanjeurie Tracy.

In the beginning…….

Dawn's twilight breaks infant day
As sun annual motions direct way
Cross celestial equators to North
Beckons Spring's season "come forth!"

Zero point celestial's coordinate
Mystical meridians navigate
Ecliptic sphere intersects clocks
Spring awakens vernal equinox.

I flirt by lace curtains, my mind's eye apart
Sunbeam's golden, rainbow diamonds dart
I climb vast heavens on ladders of light
Paint, blaze my pen, quickly I write.

Music spheres strum rhythms salute
Prepare voices melodious tribute
Syncope scales announce rebirth under
Cold white shroud yawning wonder.

Moments lapse, intervene wide stance
As drops of rain on my window dance
Slide and chase each other to blend
Till mist to clouds earth again glance.

Caress soil, satin smooth sash
Wash spirals washings splash
Winter's white blanket bold disarray
Touches gently spring rain's sachet.

Clouds capture showers display
Tempests form fierce frantic display
Thunders cross celestial sky smash
Rainfall shimmers bolt lightning's flash.

My mind's window shuts with a start
Work day alarm clocks set me apart
Warm breezes dark from forest beyond
Springs, my footsteps seem to respond.

Ecliptic spheres intersect man's clocks
As spring awakens vernal equinox
Day over, twilight still fell on me
Cabin dwelling warm fire I see.

Climb in bed, dim night lamp make
Silver moon's filmy garment opaque
Spells of seclusion spray on me
Spring's song on our world I see.

Sense wondrous wondering trod
Recall...In the beginning...God

EVEN TO EVEN

At nightfall at day's end, at dusk
Twilight at sundown's sunset
Earth's heaven's ablaze, colorful display
An annulet not to forget.

God said, always the same
Yesterday, today or tomorrow
Remember days of my Sabbath
Your pleasure, your work makes me sorrow.

Rest, my people, begin at sun's set
My sunsets ablaze in dusk sky
Herald my time for you to rest
My holy Word does, will testify.

Obey, God said, then my blessings
Causes your ride earth's high places
Joy will be yours in my presence
God said this I guarantee trace.

Spend time with me in your worship
Gather together, be holy this day
Study my books of Nature
Talk to me my children, pray.

Blessed those who keep my command
Written by My hand numbers ten
Remember from evening to even
God's gift of the Sabbath to men.

Rejoice, adore universal Creator
Who made heavens and Planet earth
Remember His creative power
Making all things from their birth.

A lingering taste of once Eden
God's promise then, today given
Memorial of His creative power
One sunset to another hour driven.

Last rays of sun setting asleep
Remember rest Sabbath to keep
Reflect wonders of creation days all
Sabbath day hours will recall.

Even to even reflect worship rest
From heaven even to even blest
Remember Sabbath at end of week
God's commandment rest unique.

Admire my dress sunset colors
Blazed beauty exampled to blend
As I doll, weekly days recall
Tanjeurie Tracy's sunset end.

Karina poses with Tanjuerie Tracy at Eve
Says her Master Will and Janet she will love
Kindness and love spills over each day

A family to be proud of, no other above

We will all miss you so much when you go
With each sunset our memories will view
Colors of sunset's happiness you know
Personolly yours, ours too

Distance won't distance us though apart
Dreams travel in an instant may shine
Then rest wherever beats a heart
Then glow like your sunsets and mine.

CHAPTER 44. KARINA / MEREDITH

"Dance. Dance for the joy and breath of childhood.
Dance for all children, including that child who is still somewhere entombed
beneath the responsibility and skepticism of adulthood.
Embrace the moment before it escapes from our grasp.
Therefore, the only promise of childhood, of any childhood,
is that it will someday end. And in the end,
we must ask ourselves what we have given
our children to take its place. And is it enough?"
A quote from Richard Paul Evans

DEAR FAMILY

To all my Doll Friends,
I am sent to no one. When I arrived at Miss Imelda's cabin in the woods she opened my package and my legs and feet were broken. She took off my clothes and threw them away. She pasted a little red heart on my chest, kissed my cheek and said I would belong to her. Someday, she said you will be a ballerina. Right now you will have lots of time to dream about it and believe it. I sit in a box near a machine she sews doll dresses on next to her address book that has a picture of a ballerina on the cover. Oh to look like that is a dream!

My doll friend who lives here is Victoria and she belongs to Miss Imelda's husband Doctor Bill who is a scientist. He talks to her and loves her very much. Victoria told Doctor Bill I was 'footicapped.' Victoria has introduced me to her friend Emily. Emily is rather shy, not like Victoria, and she encouraged me to "Dwell in Possibilities" a phrase from Emily Dickinson, a poet lady she is dressed alike for and her poem is about Emily. I am encouraged with a possibility I will have legs and feet someday. Victoria also introduced me to "Joey" a rag doll that used to belong to Miss Imelda's Grandson Bradley. He likes to be among all the dolls as they come and go but he likes Bradley's cat "Snowshoe," a Maine coon cat, who is very busy with duties around the cabin. He knows all the spaces to escape from in the night when he wants to go out prowling or just watching the stars outside.

Miss Imelda is dressing dolls for each one of her five sisters and six brothers. Some of them have started getting new clothes; some look like I did with the same dress and shoes. Since I will be here a long time dreaming about legs and feet I will see many dolls come and go from here.

Mimi Lea will be sent away to a farm in the country. Rainer is already packed but room must be made for Mimi Lea who is not done yet. Johdia will be sent to a sister in a city. Honey Girl will be sent to Miss Imelda's sister she talks to on the telephone a lot. Joy sits in a box with two other dolls that will go with her to her sister Julianne far away on the west coast. Jennie is almost finished being packed in her box that has Rainer packed and ready to go, and they go to Minnesota next to me here in Wisconsin. Rainer said Hi to me before Miss Imelda covered her face.

It has been several months now and I am alone here with Victoria. She has a sweet little mouse that she calls Anony who goes with her to look in a small microscope Miss Imelda has in Doctor Bill's small bedroom. I hear them fussing about what they see and don't understand. Victoria says she will know soon because Doctor Bill and Miss Imelda will be moving in New York for awhile and he has his own laboratory there. Oh dear, I wonder if I will ever get legs and feet. They may forget about me entirely. What happened to my dwelling in possibility dreams I have been practicing for so long? I must look for them and practice again.

Today Miss Imelda's brother called and he wants his Dolly in one week because he wants to take her with on his ore boat when he leaves. Miss Imelda's daughter Molly's doll Frances Ann is helping Miss Imelda sew Hanna's dress.

I wish I could do something around here. Snowshoe meows there is lots I can do at night with him. He meows he will pick me up at midnight. The moon will be out white and full and he will show me interesting things to do. He meows I will be easy to carry since he doesn't have to worry about legs and feet getting broken. When the clock shows hands together is midnight appointments with Snowshoe. He comes just on time and we go through an opening in the loft roof where there is a trip door to the roof. Then he jumps down two roofs to a ladder that takes us down to a big pond. He puts me down near the evergreen tree and says he will see me later.

I am not afraid, I am not very big to even notice without legs and feet. A wee green tree frog jumps into my lap. It can't talk, just sits there and then jumps back toward the trunk of the tree. I see five white images swim across the pond; they come closer. Snowshoe shows up at the same time and introduces them to me as a family of geese named Jacob, Sarah, Leah, Rachel and Isaac. None of them were interested in what I was and swam away. Snowshoe asked me to look at the stars because Miss Imelda was making a doll called Star and we can talk together about the sky. He will be back later and put me down closer to the pond where I could see the stars better. The sky was so big and wide and the moon was like a large round plate with faint shadows on it. I will like these midnight outside visits with "Snowshoe." I looked at so many stars it was time for Snowshoe to come back. He picked me up as he meowed he would and back to the cabin loft we go.

In the morning Miss Imelda had her Brother Frank's doll Hanna is ready to be packaged. Miss Imelda had a ceramic lighthouse to go with her for a place to stay. Miss Imelda is so thoughtful. Her next doll Joey told me was Laura for a little girl named Kristen who could not see very well but could faintly see colors. At the same time she was writing stories in poetry. I will ask Snowshoe to bring me closer to her sewing machine so she does not forget who I am. Next to Laura I saw a guitar for the Margaret doll and an American flag for the Keepin doll for her brother and his wife. There are little boxes with doll names on them; hearts for Cara, computer for Bessie, a sad mask for Butterfly, an elf for Deirdre, a piano for Holly Carol, roses for Rose, a Lab coat with medical instruments on it for Grace, a loon for Tai, two small dollies for Nicole, strawberries for Dolly, and a white star for Star. The last little box was a round ball of cotton for Mary Beth next to tiny books for Rebekah. The next day Miss Imelda packaged all of her little boxes, along with what was left of me and we were going to New York where Doctor Bill and Miss Imelda will visit her daughter Molly and her family. Who will make me some legs and feet?

We arrived in an apartment next to Doctor Bill's small laboratory. Victoria and Anony wanted to stay there forever because Victoria was learning so much and spending so much time with Doctor Bill. Miss Imelda visited her daughter and family a lot during the day. I wasn't even unpacked and saw only a glimmer of light in a box full of little boxes I already knew what was in them. I missed Emily who was gone already and no new dolls to meet. I opened my dream for "Dwell in Possibilities" and I was beginning to have legs and feet. I dreamed I was having a party at the cabin with all the dolls came to visit and I was going to dance for them. That sure is a dream since I don't know what ballet dance is but Miss Imelda's' address book lady is very beautiful in one pose.

We stayed in New York for a long time and I continued to dreamy dreams without legs and feet. One day my box was picked up and Miss Imelda and Doctor Bill said they were returning to the cabin in the woods in Wisconsin. We arrived a week later. My box was opened and placed in the same place it was when I left before. Her daughter Julie called and said she had a present for her and she said she would be right over. When she arrived Julie showed her the most real ballerina doll I ever saw with legs and feet shaped like Miss Imelda's address book and I knew I was replaced and my dreams would never come true. I needed Doll Emily to talk to so quickly and at the same time Snowshoe came over and licked my face and puts his body over me and started purring. It was such a relaxing sound I did not want to worry about something I did not know for sure. Miss Julie left and Miss Imelda brought the ballerina doll over to me and introduced her to me, her name was Meredith. She was a famous ballerina, who fell and hurt her neck, but Miss Julie fixed it and she will teach me how to dance. What does that mean when I don't have any legs or feet?

The next day I heard Miss Imelda talk to her daughter Marianne who asked her to send me to her, she was going to make me new legs and feet since she is home schooling her children by making rag dolls in large numbers and needed a diversion of just one pair of legs. My little heart almost fell off my chest! As Miss Imelda was packing me carefully, I know she noticed I was smiling wider than ever before. My dream to "Dwell in Possibilities" is coming true. I asked her to call Loni to tell Emily. She said she would.

I arrived at Miss Marianne's in the same way I left Miss Imelda. All around me were legs the same size, arms pinned together faces hanging on a tall line close to the ceiling and bodies next to the faces. It is no small wonder why Marianne needed something different, like me! Her little daughter Bonny came out with a doll named Imelda dressed in a wedding dress. She winked at me, I was glad she remembered me since I am only half there. Next to her was Holly Carol who smiled wide at me. Marianne knew just how long legs should be with a taper at the foot and made me a body to hold the legs up. Little Bonny took some stuffing and a wooden stick and filled the spaces with what looked like was going to me! While Bonny stuffed me with cotton very full, Marianne was sewing the smallest ballerina slippers that would fit on my new feet. I could almost feel them already on the other half of my body. Wait till I show Snowshoe! The next day Marianne held me carefully as she sewed tiny stitches next to my body that welcomed the stitches happily. Little Bonny kissed me and then put my face next to Marianne's so that it was me kissing her! I never kissed before. Now I have a new dream to dream. I was packed very carefully to send back to Miss Imelda to make my dress. I did not give the rag dolls left behind any thoughts because I was so happy. I felt sure in my little red heart my life would be forever fulfilled, in my forever home with my creator, my Miss Imelda! Much love... Karina

KARINA

The box I am packed in has arrived
I can feel it placed on mail stand
I wait and then I am picked up again
Truck drives down driveway, and

Man knocks on cabin door, Miss Imelda
Opens, thanks graciously, then
She carries me in my box upstairs
I hear her open box carefully when

Lifts out paper and breathes s a sigh
"Katrina! How delightfully!
She hugs me so tight my knees bent
Sees new legs and feet on me!

Miss Imelda hugs me all over again
Goes down stairs by the phone
Calling Marianne to thank her
I'm next to Meredith alone!

Since I didn't have a dress on
My body is clear plainly seen
Meredith touches my legs and my feet
Whispers, "you have now your dream."

"It'll be easier dancing without a dress
"We'll start tonight dance steps
You are beautiful to me, Karina
What formed quadriceps!

Let's practice our first dance lesson
We must point toes front and back
A "tandem', a parse' raise arms and lift
Feet together, open and slack.

A "port de bra" does spin and shift
Part your arms graceful display
Feet together open and close
Called "escape – schappe.'

Practice again twenty times "K"
Then rest, begin again, today when
The magic world of dance enters
'Dwell in possibilities' again."

Karina's new legs and feet respond
Meredith watches close each step
Her new balls of feet rise – releve'
Now up and "jump – a sauté prep."

Meredith stands next to Karina
Shows her each step carefully
Together they dance in unison
Dance dreams positively.

Meredith's training learned
At "Storybook ballet" classes
"Dance into the fairy tale"
Live music for child masses.

"Magic world of dance" lessons
Her teacher Meredith Mast
Professional ballerina dancing
Houston Ballet's group vast.

Restored now for teaching
Tales of fast legs and feet
Steps Karina didn't know
Till ballet Doll Meredith meet.

Possibilities continue dwelling
Together practice dance devotedly
They can't wait till Miss Imelda sees
Her doll Karina "ballerina will be!"

Meredith rehearse more exercise
Karina must learn dance glissade
"Pas de chat, pas de bourree"
Karina learns first-grade!

Leaping, fluttering airy steps
Daytime see costumes in place
Miss Imelda's designs so lovely
Imitations of dancing grace.

Karina's gown pinch pleated silken
Soft aquamarine blush sash at waist
Colorful tiny butterflies plenty
Sewed skirt soft light green placed.

Meredith's colors purple with pink
Jewels, ribbons dot gathers sheer
Satin ribbons purple ballet shoes
What artist's we have here!

Karina and Meredith's viewing
Of costumes for them to wear
Relax for a moment, Karina's muse
Our celebration plans no compare!

Invitations will go out to each dolly
Miss Imelda will see to that
By phone, mail, email, in person
By eagle, owl, crow or bat.

I'll introduce them to my owl friends
Wolves, ducks, loons, bobcat, deer
Coon cat faithful Snowshoe
My bat friends, four geese here.

More practice dance steps repeated
Meredith so thorough so new
Karina's dreams ever repeated
Her ballet slippers know what to do.

Her eyes watch careful her teacher
Whose steps are perfect to view
Memorizes motions graceful
Meredith says, "Again, let's review."

Snowshoe arrives in the loft
Not much room for his napping here
Suggests they practice in the forest
He'll carry each one in the clear.

To a grassy meadow newly mowed
Snowshoe takes ballerina's to dance
Moonbeams sparkle on dew drops
Night creatures assemble by chance.

In the meadow dancing is easier
Graced glissade near Meredith teaching
Again "pas de chat, pas de bourree"

Perfection close reaching.

Karina repeats toes front and back
Raises arms and lift upward
Becomes a "tandem, a parse"
In unison with Meredith costarred.

Together they spin and shift
Parting arms graced display
Their feet together open then close
Karina recalls "escape – schappe."

"Practice again twenty times "K"
Then rest, begin, again, today when
The magic world of dance enters
'Dwell in possibilities' again."

Moonbeams shadow two dancers
Alive in creative splendor
Whirling bodies curling
Formation's pose surrender.

Snowshoe meows Dawn arriving
To the loft to return is best
Miss Imelda will soon awaken
Soon check list for future's guest.

Imelda in loft sees Meredith with Karina
Their shoes have stains green!
Her suspicions verified by their smiles
More impish than she has seen.

Miss Imelda fashions new shoes
For practice steps over and again
She stores pink and purple slippers
For doll reunion coming soon when

Karina's dream becomes reality
Now her days footi-capped are gone
Fine example of believing
'Dwell in possibilities' has won.

Weeks pass Miss Imelda sends invitations
To all dolls for reunion at cabin then
Karina and Meredith's dance performance
Late summer, full moon therein.

"Life is not measured by the breaths we take
But by the moments that take our breath away"

From the studio of Sandra Magsamen

Doll Bessie sees mail collected
Miss Dorothy writes stories less and less
Bessie views invitation to all doll friends
They must arrive in full dress.

At last a reporting assignment
Delegated to her Dorothy's doll
Miss Imelda will send driver early
Performance plan sensational.

Other dolls she'll report their arrival
How exciting this news will be
It'll be her best assignment
Miss Dorothy will be proud of me.

At dusk a YouPS truck
Parks at Dorothy's house door
Driver beckons me, Bessie to come
My computer in my arm to work for.

Driver stops for Dina Brigitta also
CC was visiting, Laura too came
Driver stops at Northland College library
Mary brought Doll Deirdre by name.

To the cabin in the wilderness we go
Sit on front seat properly
No boxes, just five dolls travelling
Full moon as bright as can be.

Driver stops at the meadow briefly
Carries us to nearest oak tree
We are first to arrive, how exciting
Will see dolls arrive quickly.

Sunbeams set multi-colored
Forms doll Tanjuerie Tracy plain
Smoothly she beamed in the meadow
Sunset journey brilliant to obtain.

Bessie sees Snowshoe carry Emily
She has arrived with Honey Girl and Annie
Johdia and Mimi Lea come shortly
Excitement rises so promptly.

A flock of Canada geese approaching
Deliver Crystal from province Ontario

With news from Renata once gifted Janka
Where is Janka? Bessie asks to know.

Renata planned flight to Europe
Brought Doll Janka to her family
A memorial for them to treasure
Doll gifted again graciously.

Brother Frank's ore boat arriving
Dispatched by crow flying then
Has brought Hanna, Ruth and Star
Bessie will ask him, how, where, when.

Miss Imelda meets Frank by the lake
Close to Ashland marina
Thanks him for his delivering
Doll friends for her Doll Karina.

Star tells Bessie she lives in Texas
With Pearl, Andy and Edna's child
Not sure how to plan her journey
Frank calls to join trip north; she smiled..

Ruth's mistress Erica near Dallas
Brought along, their meeting so new
Dolls traveling with Hanna's captain
Best voyage for them to do.

Bessie sees Liz and Meldie at distance
Brought by three wolf pups bold
Introduces Hunter, Elder and Wee wolf
Standing on two legs to behold.

Wee Wolf has a recorder to play
If their music stops too soon
They can dance waltzes, says proudly
May even howl at full moon.

Karina greets Bessie inquiring
If her notes all clearly taken
This reception beyond her expectations
Makes her delightfully shaken.

Miss Imelda says JC Penny wired
From Duluth to pick up Butterfly
Return promptly in 24 hours
Bradley lives near, he will stop by.

Miss Imelda's brother Lea's son Douglas

Recently wed a new bride
Brings her to Minnesota to meet family
With dolls Joy, Faith, Heaven beside.

Molly, Frances Anne, Irene, Victoria
He'll pick up in Oregon on the way
Also brings Mary Lea from his sister
Eight dolls include his bride today.

He'll meet his father's family
Introduce Bernie, new bride
With doll dreams becoming real
As dreams do deep inside.

Bessie sees in clouds a white bird
It is Cookie with full feathered wings
Carries Doll Cookie and Doll Mary Beth
Deep South Southern Belle brings.

Cookie lands perfect in the meadow
Karina applauds his grace
So beautiful, Cookie, full feathered
Strong with two dolls' happy face.

Miss Marianne drives down the roadway
Parks car by maple tree
In time for dolls Holly Carol and Imelda
Run to hug doll reporter Bessie.

Doll Imelda beams excitement
Her mistress Bonny now married
Her Doctor husband Sean loves her lots
Delights in stories Bonny carried.

Holly-Carol brought her piano
Miss Marianne thought just in case
She has practiced other music
Perhaps a waltz could take place.

An "Into The Blue Plane" flies lower
Perfect parachute Doll Genie lands
In welcoming arms of Karina
More Dollies' greeting hands.

Hoot the owl friend of DJ
Swoops down on crowd with Doll Rose
Unafraid she slips out his talons
Not a rip in her dress clothes.

Me/Hope rides waves of music
From her home to Miss Imelda's place
Oh Bessie, I have so much news for you.
New name, new clothes, new face.

Doll Bessie types out her stories
Computer slower than before
Then sees Miss Imelda placed electric cord
Hangs from poplar tree wore.

Sharin's box comes from Florida
Bessie and dolls unfasten then
Sharin crawls out, met a new friend
Tanny got her as a gift back when

Doctor John and Nurse Donna
Retired from Ministry last year
Gifts Tanny Doll Sharin for keeping
She returns to Miss Imelda dear.

Rebekah arrives by black raven
Who has learned many a new word
Distance they flew two hours
Will remember her stories he heard.

Wants to view this doll reunion
To tell his family or friends too
How humans and dolls dream together
Personolly Yours, too for you.

Keepin belongs to Lieutenant Kolleen
Important military roles play
Flies in Cessna Sky hawk to see Karina
Special assignment only today.

Tai leaves her beloved country
With Dr. and Connie for a week
Connie drives to Mason for Miss Imelda
Drops Tai by meadow moon unique.

Bessie hugs Tai so closely
So many stories to write down to tell
"Don't forget Bessie, I'm only visiting
I still love my own country so well."

South winds moving north slowly
Brings Nicole under eagle wingspan
Eager to leave busy city
In wilderness he originally began.

Relates to Nicole he will return her
To her place in Minnesota when
She sees her old friends as friends should
His vision perfect always been.

Dolly rides back of white Sally Swan
Her dress contrast strawberries
Glides graceful to meadow shore
Sally best of water ferries.

She carries boy doll Joey
Eager to meet all dolls again
Will some ask him to dance?
Watched Meredith and Karina often.

Cara lives nearby Miss Imelda's cabin
In wilderness's live Bob bobcat
Travel together often, being kind
To forest creatures where they're at.

Cara brings her little red hearts
Describing what love means
What an opportunity sharing Karina
This occasion living her dreams.

Friend Janet with Doll Julie driving
To Midwest; a long time it's been
Eager to see Miss Imelda and Julie grown
Friendships choice memories then.

Margaret and Margaret-Margaret Dolls
Overnight delivery just came
A guitar strums song "In the light
of the silvery moon" by name.

Bessie unwraps package
Both dolls perfect in shape
Margaret's guitar strums again
"Smiles," all of us make.

Rainer rides down the driveway
On back of white tailed deer
Her music box plays "Raindrops"
Dismounts, no rain rains here.

Deer makes himself home in the forest
Promises her to home return
Will learn new things in Wisconsin

Teach his own new skills to learn.

Hired helicopter flies over
Drops basket with Ginger and Grace
Returns for Dora and Brother Isaac, then
Flies away to another place.

"All here" muses Bessie
Checks her list, "Where is Jennie?
Has she come, got lost in the crowd?
So many dolls here, so many.

In an oak tree close to Bessie
Jennie doll sits as before
Once as a wren sang near Catherine
Insecure, loud commotion near her door.

In her purse stores sunbeams
Tonight too bright shown here tonight
She'll tell Jennie about moonbeams
Fulfills dreams for Karina like light.

Joey practices steps he watched when
Karina and Meredith's toe play
Dances they know now for all to see
Karina's performance in ballet.

Snowshoe, coon cat finds doll Joey
Doll Dolly thoughtful to bring here
While he was hunting far away
Relaxes, purrs in gay atmosphere.

"Swan Lake" music begins from Time Now
Dolls position themselves in green meadow
Make room for Meredith and Karina
First performance beneath moon glow.

I dance with Meredith who taught me
Steps to make with my ballerina feet
All dolls came, I know them by name
Dance with me, our meeting complete!

Stars twinkle, fireflies glowing
Frogs and crickets both sing
Imelda's invitations a reality
Forest fairies with dolls make a ring.

Ballet dolls dance steps perfect
Karina's a few different to view

Meredith keeps her in moonlight
Her dreams fulfilling come true.

Music changes to "Blue Danube"
Just what Doll Margaret did desire
Karina beckons all dolls to join in
Forest animals too admire.

Doll Margaret strums her guitar
Plays "You tell me your dreams"
"Put your arms around me" song
Dolls change partner often it seems

Doll Meldie takes friend Liz
Together like once before dance
Recall once danced with wolves
Almost instant without a glance.

In shadows of festivity watch
Grown wolves Hunter, Elder, Wee
Wolf pack relocate to North Wisconsin
To escape human's activity.

Now with wolf pups of their own
They teach them on two legs to dance
But the small humans dancing they see
Are much shorter to invite at a glance.

Wolf Hunter sees Dolly Emily
In her pocket pencil and pad seen
Overheard she was a famous poet
She will write a poem about this scene.

Hunter visions a dream he met her
He will ask her to dance on meadow green
Unafraid anymore moves closer to him
Famous Emily with infamous wolverine.

Wolves three hear parent's howling
Obedient, but reluctant must leave
Wolf Elder brings Wee wolf's recorder
For future dance make-believe.

Meredith strolls to Doll Joey
He appreciates her choice as a star
She knows ballet steps he observed
Dance together in green meadow so far.

Karina weaves around each dolly

Her dancing smooth so divine
Beckons Jennie in the oak tree
Celebrate memories yours and mine.

"Oh you beautiful doll" now playing
"Hail the gangs all here" next on guitar
"Put your arms round me" then
All dancers dance tunes popular.

All dolls converge again in meadow
To watch Karina and Meredith dance
Dew drops form diamonds on green grasses
Moonbeams fade from first glance.

Return transports begin arriving
Each doll knows them respectively
Karina and Meredith stand watching
Hugging each one reflectively.

Dances, visits, pre-dawn approaches
One by one in the meadow leave on
Each doll with appointed escort
Returning to homes gifted upon.

Dolls grateful for once again meeting
As last one leaves meadow lawn
Snowshoe brings me to single seating
New morning introduced new dawn.

Goes back for Meredith my teacher
We can't risk her ever to lose
Together returned to loft of cabin
Safe with green-tinted ballet shoes.

Miss Imelda in loft fakes sleeping
Her mind planned this invitation
She knew I'd love a ballet show
Reunion of dolls in formation.

In morning sees ballet slippers blemish
Slips gentle off our tapered feet
Will return them this afternoon
We wait on window seat.

I dream dreams now, a reality
Meredith and I talk all night
Can teach animals known in deep forest
Need only two legs upright!

They heard while dancing wolf howls
Not too far away it did appear
They will consult cat Snowshoe soon
Can teach dancing on two legs here.

Meredith laughs at this notion
A dream dispatch to Dora tonight!
Laughter to her an elation
Bessie can design a skywrite!

Isaac the gander growing nicely
Looks in the pond at his face
Tells his sisters he is handsome
Impossible ever to replace!

"How will he dance on water?"
"When it is frozen," Meredith replies
"Dora will love that, talks about water
Crystal memories shaped in size."

Brother Isaac must see his namesake
He'll really laugh to find
A Gander name same as his
One more laughter dreamlined.

Dolls muse nighttime hours
Candidates teaching to dance
Taking notes for future contacts
Must tell Miss Imelda in advance.

In morning Miss Imelda has Doll Bessie
With her computer clutched in her hands
Meredith's concern she didn't leave last night
With all the Doll's wonderlands.

Karina says Bessie needs support
Miss Imelda will know what to do
To make this reunion public
Personolly Yours, for us too.

Karina says, "in newspapers
Creative columns do exist
Miss Imelda submits news on occasion
To News Editor she will persist.

Her mother Margaret long ago
In Saint Cloud Times locally
Printed her "Musings from Marguerite"
Creative column for all to see."

"That's right, Karina, I saw on her desk
'Imelda's Images" notes so many"
She has recorded all of us
Missed not one doll, not any."

Karina hugs Meredith closely
Content as friends forever
Will doubt no more on news clips
Dwell in possibilities more ever.

Dance, dance, dance when you can
Believe dreams wait to come true
Thank a Creator creating everything
Plus Dolls Karina, Meredith and you.

June 13, 17

Dear Jeanne —

You are a gift to so many people. May you be appreciated always. See you repeatedly in my book —

Always,

Imelda Dickinson

Made in the USA
Lexington, KY
23 February 2017